A GOOD DAY TO KILL

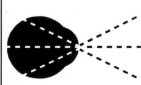 This Large Print Book carries the
Seal of Approval of N.A.V.H.

A BYRNES FAMILY RANCH NOVEL

A GOOD DAY TO KILL

DUSTY RICHARDS

THORNDIKE PRESS

A part of Gale, Cengage Learning

GALE
CENGAGE Learning·

Farmington Hills, Mich • San Francisco • New York • Waterville, Maine
Meriden, Conn • Mason, Ohio • Chicago

GALE
CENGAGE Learning·

LIBRARY OF CONGRESS CATALOGING-IN-PUBLICATION DATA

Richards, Dusty.
    A good day to kill / by Dusty Richards. — Large print edition.
        pages cm. — (A Byrnes family ranch novel) (Thorndike Press large print western)
    ISBN 978-1-4104-8001-9 (hardcover) — ISBN 1-4104-8001-1 (hardcover)
    1. Large type books. I. Title.
    PS3568.I31523G66 2015
    813'.54—dc23   2015007269

Published in 2015 by arrangement with Pinnacle Books, an imprint of Kensington Publishing Corp.

Printed in Mexico
1 2 3 4 5 6 7 19 18 17 16 15

A GOOD DAY TO KILL

CHAPTER 1

The strong smell of chloroform saturated Chet Byrnes's nostrils. He decided he must have been held hostage in some never-never land and was coming out with the worst hangover of his entire life. The medicinal smell surrounding him didn't help soothe his fear that he'd been shipped off to some foreign place, but he strained to regain reality. Both of his fists opened and closed, and he could feel his toes wiggle under the sheet. His feet were still there. He'd been in a dream world for a long time. Whenever he moved, his left shoulder felt on fire, and he could see that bandages covered that side of his body where he'd been shot.

"You alright, señor?"

"Jesus? Yeah, I'm a little dry. How about some water?"

The sight of the tan face of his *compadre* was a relief to him. Jesus Martinez, along with Cole Emerson, rode everywhere with him, to protect him from the enemies he made as a lawman.

"Certainly. I am so glad you are alive, *mi amigo.* Your wife is coming."

"She didn't need to come, especially in her condition. I'll be fine."

"No way we could talk her out of doing that." The pleasant-faced young man was one of his right arms in the border law enforcement unit he managed for the U.S. Marshal's office in Tucson. The twenty-year-old youth smiled in the dimly lit room and held a dipper of water toward him.

Half raised up, he sipped from the cool metal cup. After a satisfying couple of swallows, he thanked Jesus and laid back down, shocked at how little strength he had. "Where have I been?"

"In bed, here at the doctor's house, for several days. They gave you much medicine so you didn't hurt."

"You can stop that. I've been in a half-world and I wasn't really sure of anything."

"You better tell them about the medicine. They won't listen to me. And we all wanted you alive."

"Where are all the men now?"

"Roamer, Shawn, and Cole are down on the border checking on a stage robbery. Since you were alive, JD and Ortega Ninni went to check on the squatters and look at some of that ranch land. They took those squatter women more food, too."

"Good, they only have us to feed them. But we need to get them moved out of there."

"It would be a long drive by wagon to go down there and move all those women and small children. One wagon couldn't move them."

"But it must be done."

The young man made a pained face. "I can't believe their men just left them in such a hard place."

"Me, either. But you took them food and never did learn anything."

"I think they are Indians of some tribe from deep in Mexico. They don't speak border Spanish that well."

Chet agreed, already half-asleep. "No more pain medicine. . . ."

When he woke again, the lovely face of his wife, Marge, looked into his own. He started to raise up.

"Lay there, big man. I'm here. I sent Jesus off to get some sleep."

His own voice from inside his head sounded so dry. "How long have you been here?"

"Not long. Jenn came with me. She left

the two girls to run the café."

His wife was very big with their baby and seated in the chair next to his bed. But she looked fresh faced even after her long coach ride from Preskitt.

"Everyone in Preskitt said for you to get well." Jenn, a tall rawboned woman in her forties with thick blond braids wound on her head, smiled, then bent over and kissed his cheek. "You look good, buddy."

"I feel weak as a pup, but I'll whip that."

"My lord, Chet, this town is big, isn't it?" Jenn asked, and shook her head in amazement.

"Tombstone is still growing."

"We have a hotel room," Marge said. "So we'll be close to you if you need anything. I spoke to your doctor a while ago. He says you're healing well, but he doesn't want you moved or that wound jarred for a while."

He gazed at the copper ceiling tiles. That doctor would soon learn he had things to do that were better for him than to while away in bed on his back. "We'll see."

Then he reached over and squeezed her hand. "I'll be up and running in a few days."

He didn't like how she nodded so condescendingly at him. He knew her well enough to know she hadn't agreed with him. But he'd soon be stronger.

Marge and Jenn took turns sitting with him, and Jesus relieved them part of the time. Lucie, and his sister, Susie, wrote him long letters and they picked on him as well. *You are finally getting some rest. Mind your nurses.* The letters were cheerful from some great women. Lucie was his nephew Reg's wife. JD's brother had married a real cowgirl. After she became pregnant, they decided she should be housebound, but she could out rope any man and did.

Susie had been real close to him throughout their family's Texas feud that forced him to move them to Arizona. Her first husband was killed in a horse wreck and she married one of his foremen, Sarge Polanski, who operated the monthly ranch cattle drives to the Navajo Agencies over in New Mexico.

The women in his life, including his wife, were due to deliver in the next few months. His nephew, JD, called it an approaching baby diaper occasion.

With each day, he felt himself grow stronger and the pain in his shoulder from the bullet wound became less and less. He was soon walking around the doctor's house unassisted. Then he strolled around the block with Marge. He felt naked not wearing his Colt, but no one looked dangerous in the residential neighborhood. That first walk was long enough for him and he was glad to return to the house. When they came in sight of the house, he saw two jaded horses at the hitch rail, and that meant some of his men were there.

Seated on the porch waiting for him, JD and Roamer nodded and smiled at the sight of him.

"You two lost?" he asked, pausing before climbing the three steps up on the porch.

"Sort of," Roamer said with his hat in hand for Marge. "Good to see you, ma'am."

His twenty-year-old nephew, JD, added the same greeting.

"I'm warning you," she said. "He can't ride out with you today." She smiled and went on inside.

Jesus came out with a straight-back chair for him.

After taking a seat on it, Chet asked, "What's happening?"

"We've located another bunch of bandits hiding in the Mule Shoe Mountains, but there's a bit of a problem," Roamer said.

"What's that?"

"One of them is Old Man Clanton's nephew. His name is Israel."

"He isn't protected by law. Who else? Tell me about the rest of the gang."

"Mostly Mexican thugs and a few *gringos*.

They held up two stages we know about. Should we call in the Wells Fargo man?" Roamer asked.

Chet nodded. "That's Dodge. I bet he'd like to be in on it. They pay nice rewards."

"Damn right," JD said.

"We've stayed out of Old Man Clanton's way so far," said Roamer, the freckle-faced, reddish-haired, thirty-year-old deputy sheriff he'd borrowed to help his task force. "I wanted to be sure about this with you. I know the old man has lots of political pull up here."

"The old man stays in Mexico. But I figured since he supplies so much to the Army and Indian agencies we needed to keep our eye on him. But, yes. Clean them up."

Roamer looked around. "We better not go look for Dodge. It might make someone suspicious. We need to be very quiet. Wells Fargo pays good for any arrests involved. But we need to slip into the area under cover."

Chet agreed. "Right. This town is full of informers. Everyone alright?"

"Oh, yes, and we miss you," JD said. "Any word on that Diablo Ranch deal?"

Chet looked at his nephew and shook his head. "No, I'm going to write Russell, my lawyer in Tucson, a letter and find out."

Roamer was on his feet. "Well, with that resolved, we're going to move on this gang."

"Sorry I can't attend the church picnic."

They laughed.

"Is everyone's wife alright?"

Both men nodded.

"Tell the others I'm thinking of them."

"You look lots better than the last time I was here," JD said, and started off the porch.

"You know your mother-in-law is here?"

"Oh, we've talked already. She's a great lady. Bonnie's doing fine."

"Good. Keep your heads down."

The two men left and he stood up. The walk had drained his strength. He went inside to lie on his bed for a while.

"You alright?" Jesus asked, accompanying him.

"I'm fine. They want you to go with them?"

"I told them that I was here for you first."

"Can you meet them tonight?"

Jesus nodded. "Yes. They told me where to go."

"Good. I won't get into any trouble with those two women here. You'd feel better joining them to get those outlaws."

A relieved smile crossed his man's face.

"*Gracias,* I would like to be there. I can join them when they gather there."

"Do that."

"More trouble?" Marge asked, coming in the room.

"No, just everyday business in this game. Big secret. Tonight, Jesus is going with the team to get those outlaws. He needs to be there. They'll be stronger with him, and you two can watch after me."

Marge laughed. "I won't tell a soul. You be careful, Jesus."

"I won't leave until dark."

"Good. Jenn and I will load our guns then."

"And," Chet swung his legs off the bed and fit his feet into felt slippers, "next week, we're going to Preskitt. It's getting too damn hot down here."

"Just like Texas is in the summer," Marge teased.

"I sold that ranch, dear. No, I want to recover at home. Besides, the baby can be born up there. These men can handle this business for a few weeks. Then I'll relieve the three married men for them to take a week off."

"Maybe." She stood studying him as he started for the facility out back. "You aren't looking that tough to me."

15

He stopped in the doorway and turned. "I will be. Trust me."

"Alright. I hope you aren't going too fast."

"I'm not."

At sundown, before he left, Jesus came to see him. "See you in a day or so. I am ready to do some real work. Thanks for letting me go."

"God be with you, pard. Tell the men I'm thinking about all of them."

"I will."

Jesus left on horseback and Chet settled back in the rocker. Jenn and Marge joined him a bit after sunset, as the air cooled off.

"Will they get these men?" Jenn asked.

Rocking lightly, he nodded. "They're some of the greatest lawmen in the territory. They've rounded up more felons than any half-dozen county sheriff offices have in the same time. Of course, more bad guys drift this way as the law in Texas and New Mexico tightens the noose on them, so this is the place to go and try to commit crimes."

"What will Roamer do when this is over?"

"I hope someone puts him to work for them. Maybe I can talk to the Wells Fargo man, Dodge, about hiring him. Roamer doesn't really want to run a ranch or a business."

16

"What about him being chief deputy at home?"

"Sheriff Simms won't ever make him his chief deputy, because Roamer knows more about the job than Simms does."

Jenn agreed. "Plus Roamer doesn't like bookkeeping, and a chief deputy has to do all that for the sheriff."

"Well, good luck. Now tell us about this Rancho Diablo business," Marge said.

"That's what JD calls it."

"Why?"

"It's a pretty dry country. Lots of grass and maybe water can be developed on it."

Marge threw her hands up. "Another ranch that requires a lot of attention. All you need."

"We're doing respectable with our other places. If JD will put his shoulder in it, it'll be a helluva ranch."

"JD is the least stick-to-it person you have."

"He acts very serious about his marriage. And he's not dumb, a little too sarcastic, but he'll outgrow that. He knows what work is, although he's avoided it since he and Kay broke up. But since he got here, he's rode and worked damn hard on this job. Not a man out there that works with him would complain."

"What was that all about?" Jenn asked. "I never heard the whole story."

"Kay's husband was avoiding her and she wanted out of her marriage," Marge said. "Chet knew her. He danced with her and felt sorry for her. I felt the same. When her husband left, JD took up with her. She needed someone to run the ranch. He was working his backside off down there. Chet offered to help them get going. The place had problems — machinery was broke down — horses were, too. She had a fit. We heard she said they didn't need any help from anyone. JD left her after that and never said why."

Jenn nodded. "I knew when he left her."

"Neither of us knows the details. But he hasn't been JD since," Chet said.

"Maybe someday we'll learn the facts." Jenn acted satisfied and sat back to rock. "I think my daughter and him can make it together. I deeply hope so. Both of them can get stormy, but if they love each other that will pass like a thunderstorm — lots of noise and then it's over."

"Your Bonnie and our JD," Marge said, shaking her head. "Some matchup. But, I agree, that match will work if they want it to last."

"Well, big man," Jenn began. "Has it eaten

your guts out yet, not being up in those mountains with your men on this business tomorrow?"

He smiled. "You know it has. But, like I said, they're the best lawmen around. Before I shut my eyes tonight I'll pray for God to take care of them."

Later in the evening in his bed, he shut his eyes and prayed for them . . . *since I can't be there, Lord, take care of them . . . amen.*

CHAPTER 2

Seated on the front porch in the rocker in the early morning, Chet heard a horse snorting dirt coming down the street. An hour earlier, the sun had swung up over the Chiricahuas and there was still some coolness in the air. The mine hammer mills were rumbling the ground and the giant pumps roared in the distance. Sounds of shod horse hooves on the caliche street brought him to his feet, and he leaned on a white four-by-four porch post to observe. Roamer, aboard one of his good roan horses, came at a swinging walk in the lead. One by one, he counted them, and his men were all there with their Winchesters resting across their saddle horns, guarding their captives on horseback. Several belly-down corpses strapped across their saddles came behind, led by Shawn.

"They all here?" his wife asked, squeezing his good arm when she joined him.

"Every last one of them. Yes, they did good. Like I said, best damn lawmen in the territory."

"Well, bust your buttons then," she said, and laughed.

"Morning, ma'am," Roamer said, removing his hat for Marge and Jenn who'd joined them by then. "I'm sending a taxi out here for you. We want you at the courthouse when we turn the prisoners over to Behan."

"You ladies come with him, too."

He turned back to Chet. "Jesus said they were your new guards."

They laughed.

"I don't —" Chet started to protest.

"Yes, you do. Trust me, you don't need to walk down there. And this posse is your posse. You gathered us and have done a great job teaching us. You'll be there at the exchange. Israel Clanton is one of those dead. He chose that way himself. That may raise a stink, but he was involved in those two stage robberies and ranch raids."

"No problem for me. Send the taxi. Send a boy to tell the *Epithet* and get word to the Wells Fargo man as well. Dodge may be in one of the saloons by this hour. He likes to play poker. Between you and Cole, send Marshal Blevins in Tucson a telegram about this at once. We can all meet at the Cochise

21

County Jail by then."

"Now you're talking, boss man," Cole shouted.

A cheer from the rest of the men followed his words, and they and their prisoners rode on down the street.

Marge kissed him. "Did you see Jesus's face? You did well to send him with them. He's sure part of your Force."

"Oh, yes. Ladies, get ready. We're having a public gathering down there. Behan will be wearing his best suit accepting them. How many outlaws were there?"

"I counted four dead and the same alive," Jenn said.

"Those boys have earned four thousand dollars right there, plus the outlaws' horses, gear, and guns. There may be other rewards as well."

"Wow, they'll be well off when this is over," Marge said.

"It's counting up. Let me get some better clothes on."

"Yes, you need to do that. But don't you overdo things today."

"I won't."

"You heard him, Jenn — 'I won't'?"

"Hey, this will be fun. I have never been to one of these things before. Oh, Marge, he'll be fine," Jenn said to his worried wife.

"Keep telling her that. Keep telling her that," Chet said, going inside.

When the taxi man came by, both women had on new dresses and straw hats to shade their faces. Chet wore a brown suit coat, pressed pants, and his dusted off hat. He also wore his six-gun for the first time. Not that he figured he'd need it, but it felt better strapped on than without it.

When they reached the courthouse, a crowd had already gathered around his men and their captives. A funeral home hearse parked close by was, no doubt, there for the bodies. The Wells Fargo representative was a burly man in a tan suit — fortyish, and his name was Tom Dodge. At first, Chet couldn't recall his given name — but he did when he saw his face and was satisfied that the man would handle getting the rewards for his men.

No sign of Behan. Chet helped the women down and they moved to the boardwalk to stand aside. In irons, the four live gang members sat on their butts in the dirt. The dead ones rested on the ground in a row. A photographer was there taking photos of them. A puff of smoke and a flash and he would have a negative to print, a grim picture of the dead outlaws with their arms folded on their chest and their eyelids closed.

Chet wondered which one was Clanton's kin. The blond curly-headed one must be him; the others were Mexicans. He didn't know any of the men seated in the dust. Roamer brought him a paper with their names on it.

"That's who they are."

"Thanks. Is Behan coming?" Chet glanced around for him.

"They sent for him."

"Good." Chet felt put out that Sheriff Behan was late, but Dodge did join him and shook his hand.

"Great work. You're healing?"

"Yes, I'm doing fine. They brought in a large part of the outlaws operating around here."

"Yes. Your men have quite a stack of rewards coming."

"My men get that money. They're the ones taking the risks."

"Oh, yeah, I know, but I'd say you took a big one in the shoulder getting the last bunch." Dodge scowled at him as if still concerned about him.

"Part of the job. This is my wife, Marge, and our friend, Jenn Allen, from Preskitt."

He swept off his hat. "My pleasure, ladies.

24

I understand you two came down here to take care of him."

"He says he's about well," Marge said.

"Well, he does look better than when I first saw him last week."

About that time, the sheriff made a grand entry. "Well, ladies. What a bright glorious morning to be in Tombstone. Nice to have you here. And may I have your names?"

They introduced themselves and he turned to Chet. "What a lovely wife you have."

"Yes, I am blessed. But I need to get our business concluded so I can take her home. Here's a list of the outlaws my men apprehended in the Mule Shoe Mountains last night. They robbed two stages and made various raids on small ranches that my men will elaborate on for you."

"Is that dead boy Israel Clanton?"

"Yes, he was part of this gang and involved in the crimes that the gang committed. He could have surrendered last night. He didn't."

"Oh, such a waste. Has his mother been notified?"

"No. I guess she can read about it in the paper."

"His mother is Iris Clanton. She's a sister-in-law to the old man."

"Behan, these men are to be held not only on these charges, but others that will surface now that they have been captured by order of the federal court. I expect you to keep them here in your jail."

"Why, of course."

"Several men have walked out of this jail because a cell door was not locked. Be damn sure they're all locked in, and that's an order from a federal officer."

"Of course. My deputies will jail them. I need to go tell that poor boy's mother about her son's death. Excuse me?"

Behan left.

A deep voice cut the air. "You tell him something bad?"

Chet turned and shook hands with the Earp brother he liked so well. "How are you, Virgil?"

"Better than you are." He chuckled deep in his throat. "Glad you're recovering. I meant to drop by but got busy. I see your bunch has got another gang rounded up."

"They did well. Now if the sheriff can contain them."

"When I walked up, I heard you set him straight there. He will have to, after that."

"Is Iris Clanton pretty?"

Virgil shook his head. "But she does have some money."

"Behan sounded upset she had not been notified."

"Between you and me" — he dropped his voice to a whisper — "that might be worth a toss in the hay for him."

Chet agreed and thanked him. Virgil smiled, winked at him, and shook his hand to leave.

"Have a nice day, ladies." Earp tipped his hat to them.

Dodge was talking to the news reporter — good, that should suffice his part. They tossed the outlaws' bodies in the hearse like cordwood. He reckoned the county would pay the usual seven dollars and fifty cents for burying them in Boot Hill, but the Clanton boy, no doubt, would have a funeral. The funeral home would make some money on his services.

"Ready, ladies?"

"Yes, we are," Marge said. They held their hems out of the dust and headed for the taxi.

Still talking to the reporter, Dodge waved to him. "I'll be by later to talk to you, Byrnes."

"Me, too," Roamer said, and smiled.

He acknowledged both of them and climbed in the taxi for the ride back. Seated beside his wife, she asked, "Did that wear you out?"

"No. I'm fine."

"Tell me about this Dodge," Jenn said. "Is he married?"

"Not that I know about. They say he has a good-paying job."

She sat back, facing them, with her arms folded and a smug set on her lips. "I want to meet him."

"You have a deal, my friend."

"You know those two girls have husbands now. I don't have to slave in that café anymore to make work for them two if — well, if I had a good man to support me."

"It might work, Jenn," Marge said with a grin.

"Best thing is what Marshal Virgil Earp told me. The big man who came by to talk to me," said Chet.

"Yes, we figured he was law, too." Both women agreed with nods to each other.

"Virgil is a town marshal. Behan had a real problem with me that Israel Clanton's mother had not been notified of his death."

"We saw the hassle he gave you."

"Anyway, I asked Virgil about Behan being so anxious to notify Mrs. Clanton about her son's death. He said the information might be worth a toss in the hay with her."

The women shook their heads in disapproval and then laughed.

"Behan is a real peacock," Marge said, and Jenn agreed.

Chet had made some plans he intended to tell them about later. He wanted to go home, rest some at the ranch, and in two weeks go back to Tubac to let some of his married men run home for a week. That should work.

Back at the Doc's house, he sent word by messenger to Dodge to meet the three of them at Nellie Cashman's Restaurant for supper at six thirty. Jenn smiled, pleased, when he told her his plans. Marge agreed. Blevins's telegram came after the light lunch the women fixed.

CHET
GLAD YOU ARE BETTER. SOUNDS LIKE THE TASK FORCE IS REALLY GETTING LOTS DONE. I AM COMING ON THE STAGE TO TALK TO YOU ABOUT A FEW THINGS. NO REPLY NECESSARY.
                    THANKS. BLEVINS.

Later that afternoon, they took a taxi downtown to supper. Tombstone's boardwalks were loaded with prostitutes, drunks, filthy dust-coated miners, and muleskinners.

It was no place for his two ladies to tramp through to get to supper.

He told the taxi man to be back around eight thirty to take them home. The man agreed, and he told him he'd pay him then for both ways.

They had not heard from Dodge before they left the house, but, all dressed up, he met them in the lobby. He was very attentive to both women, and they were shown to their table. Chet had a notion the tall blond-headed Jenn had intrigued him some. This could be interesting.

The evening went fine and the two of them — Jenn and Dodge — were talking almost in private the last half of the meal. Dodge finally pulled himself away a little from her to tell them, "I plan to be in Preskitt in a week. I have some work to do up there."

"You must stay at our house," Marge said.

"The company pays all my expenses. I'll take a room at the hotel."

"Then you must come out to the ranch one evening and have supper with us. I can send my driver, and Jenn can tell you all about the countryside coming out there."

"What do you think of that?" Dodge asked Jenn.

"Sounds like I have already been appointed as your tour guide."

"Wonderful. I accept."

Chet had to admit, though Jenn was a rather buxom lady, she still had lots of appeal. The fire had been lit. Might work. He sure hoped so. Onward, he must go. It would sure be good to smell those pines up there again. And be home.

Marshal Blevins arrived in Tombstone the next day by stage. They met on the porch and spoke in low voices. "I know you knew that Clanton boy who was killed was the old man's nephew. And when we delivered them, Behan complained that we hadn't notified his mother."

Blevins nodded. "You know the old man has lots of political sway in the territory."

"I have no doubt. Are you telling me we have to step around him?"

"No."

"Good, 'cause I was about to tell you to stick this job in your ass. I haven't challenged him, because he was in Mexico. But I have some good information that the Skeleton Canyon murders and robbery were carried off by his men. If I had a worthy witness, I'd press it."

"I have to warn you, there will be some public complaints coming forth over these

31

arrests."

"Let them come. Those men we arrested were stage robbers and had raided several small ranchers to rape and rob folks."

"Easy, easy, Chet. I came to tell you what I expected."

"Words won't kill me."

"Good. I'm proud of your success. I'm certain it will blow over."

"Tell me, who is this that thinks our efforts weren't right?"

"Oh, I'd call them the idle rich in Tucson."

"Idle rich? Feed me a few names. I'll invite them along when we make some of our arrests."

"Oh, Iris Thompson is the lead one."

"What do they do?"

"Rich-blooded folks."

"I ought to bring one of these border killers to her house for supper."

"I wanted to warn you. You have the backing of all the men that met with you in Tucson. But there are some people suggesting we're using dictator-like tactics."

"It won't change my operation."

"You don't have to. You just need to keep rounding up these bandits down here. I don't believe what you and your men have done here could have been done better by anyone."

"Well, you wanted this region cleared of border bandits."

"Yes, and you're doing a great job, but we'll get some buckshot out of a few."

"My men won't stop pressing to get these outlaws."

He was still upset when Blevins left to go check on the prisoners. He'd told Chet he planned to remove all of them to Tucson. His faith in Behan and him keeping the cells locked was about the same as Chet's.

When the Tucson newspaper's latest edition reached him that afternoon, he saw what Blevins had warned him about:

Citizens are concerned that the federal law enforcement agency in southern Arizona is taking a dictator role in enforcing their own laws. A recent arrest of some area ranchers ended with four unprosecuted individuals being shot down ruthlessly by the Task Force. One was Israel Clanton, the son of a prominent Arizona ranch family. According to his parents, their son was a hard-working ranch manager. His body was delivered belly-down over a saddle, like a common outlaw, to the Cochise County Courthouse.

According to the representative of Wells Fargo Bank, these men had held up stagecoaches, and some turned state evidence to testify against the others. However, there is not a list of the names of the men who served in the posse. Are they real lawmen? How would anyone know? Their names are hidden. There is a petition being served to have a grand jury formed to learn all about them and discover any illegal methods they implemented in arresting all these untried individuals like they were common criminals.

He put the paper down with a snap.

"What's upset you so?" his wife asked, stepping out on the porch to join him.

"People who are questioning our efforts."

"How?" She frowned and picked up the paper to read.

Jenn joined them. "What's going on out here?"

"Read this." Marge shoved the newspaper at her.

"Well, ain't that sweet? A handful of men are out there doing what a half-dozen sheriffs can't start to do, and they complain."

"Let's go home tomorrow, and I can sulk up there," Chet said.

Jenn bent over his chair and squeezed his head with her arm. "I want to stop in

Tucson and tell that editor what I think of him for printing such trash."

He shook his head, amused.

"Is Jesus coming back?" Marge asked.

"Yes."

"The stage to Tucson leaves at ten," she said, and looked at him and Jenn.

He rose out of the chair. "Let's plan to be on it."

The two women nodded in unison.

It was set. They were going back home.

CHAPTER 3

One more long rocking stage ride ahead of him and his still sore shoulder.

In Tucson, Chet faced the gold lettering on the coach door, ARIZONA TERRITORY STAGE LINE. The lanky driver opened the door and helped his ladies into the coach. His drawling voice flirted with them and they came right back.

"Well, do you think we can get those ladies to Hayden's Mill?" he asked Chet when it was his turn to climb in the coach.

"We better."

He lowered his voice. "You ain't turned LDS on me, have yuh?"

"No. One of the ladies is a friend of ours."

The driver swiped his forehead like he was mopping sweat away. "You sure had me worried."

Chet climbed in, laughing about the driver's referral to Latter Day Saints.

"What's so funny?" Marge asked.

"He thought I'd changed religion on him and both of you were my wives."

Then they did laugh as the coach rocked out of Tucson. The trip was uneventful, and later they shifted to the Black Canyon Stage lines and headed across the Salt River at Hayden's Ferry. Marge had wired Monica when they'd arrive home and sent a request for Jimenez and another buckboard to take Jenn home.

It was dark and cool. His wife snuggled under his arm and he hugged her close as the rocking coach rolled northward. "You making it okay?"

"Oh, yes." She stretched her arms up. "I'm glad I went. I know you're worried about me and the baby, but I'd have been crazy at home."

"I worried you'd get too tired."

"I'm not some baby, am I, Jenn?"

"No, he knows that now, too." Jenn laughed. "I wonder how bad my business has fallen off with those two in charge?"

"Oh, I bet it went well. When is Dodge coming to Preskitt?" he asked.

"In a few weeks. I doubt anything happens between us. But I like him."

"I'm not so sure about that," Marge said. "I mean about nothing happening between you two."

"We'll see."

He agreed. His plans included sleeping for twenty-four hours in his own bed. His men in southern Arizona would have to tough it out a few weeks without him. He'd seen his land lawyer, Russell Craft, when they stopped off in Tucson. Russell was convinced Buster Weeks's so-called deed to the Diablo Ranch headquarters was an absolute fake document. He was to be in touch with him.

Late in the night, the turpentine aroma of pines finally reached his nose. It sure smelled damn good to be back home.

By that evening, his Camp Verde Ranch foreman, Tom and his wife, Millie; his sister Susie and Sarge; and Hampt and May and the kids were at the ranch house. A fine reunion that Monica had planned well for and no doubt spent all day fixing food to serve them.

Things at the get-together went smooth. Everyone was satisfied he was going to be fine and talked about their own ranch operations to him. Sarge felt the Navajo Agency people appreciated all their efforts to make the beef deliveries on time at the various locations.

"Getting six hundred head split up to five locations is not easy," Sarge said to him, "but I have some great hands. We can split up and do it. We even did it twice last winter, in the snow."

"Indeed, they did. Marge said that the government keeps redeeming that script they pay us for them, so we're on the move."

"Good," Sarge said. "That crew is busy building our house up on the Windmill. They have it framed and they work hard."

"I can't wait," Susie said, hanging on his arm. Those two were expecting, also.

The purchase of the ranch about a third of the way to the Navajo destination had been a big help in assembling those cattle and then driving them on from there. The income from the beef contract made his whole operation work, and would let them expand when he found the right places to do that.

Tom ran the big ranch down on the Verde River that Chet bought to replace their family's Texas operations. All he lacked there that evening was his nephew Reg and Reg's wife, Lucie. It was a long ways from their new ranch up on the Mogollon Rim, plus she was expecting, too. The long ride would have been too much for her.

Hampt and Tom continued to talk to him about their operations. Hampt had planted forty new acres of alfalfa with barley for a nurse crop.

The big guy talked about the seeding process like it was his baby. For a tough cowboy, he talked about the field like it was the child in his wife, May's, belly. "I've been watching it emerge, like hatching chickens coming out of the shell."

"Well, we're with you," Chet said, to be as serious as his man. "A good stand would sure be great."

Hampt agreed. "Tom plants things and they all come up. But me and the boys sure want this to work, too. The hay ground fencing is about done. Tom can start fencing down there. John and them boys at our blacksmith shop have become experts at making our own barbwire."

"They sure have," Tom said. "Hampt said he hasn't had a head of stock get in his hay field."

"It sure must work," Chet agreed.

His foreman, Tom, had bought twenty Hereford bulls at Hayden Ferry and they were going to be delivered in thirty days. They decided to ship them by freight wagons to Preskitt. He didn't want them gimpy on their feet when they got up there.

"Reg will sure need some bulls up on the Rim," he reminded the two of them.

Tom nodded. "They're tough to find and

expensive. We'd sure need to freight them up there, too. But I have feelers out all over."

"I don't want Reg to think he's our step-child." He looked at them with concern.

Both men nodded.

"I guess finding enough draft horses and bulls is my toughest job," Tom said with a small smile.

"We have the horses, right?"

"Not too many, but we're almost there. I wouldn't pass up buying a few more teams, if they were good."

"Is Rose bringing more from California?"

"He says when he gets enough together he'll be back." Rose was the dealer who brought them horses from California to Arizona. A dependable source, but even he had problems gathering enough to make a drive that long worthwhile.

Chet understood. In the years ahead, upgrading his cowherds would be an uphill fight. He might need to save some selected half-breed bulls to supplement his program until they could get more Herefords. His plan was to talk it over with all three of his ranch managers before he tried that.

They finally excused him and Marge to go to bed. He thanked them all and climbed the steps. It had been a long trip, and they fell asleep in each other's arms. In the

41

middle of the night, the cry of a baby woke him. He bolted upright in bed and tried to clear his mind.

"What's wrong?" Marge asked, waking up herself.

"Oh, I must have been dreaming. I kept hearing a baby crying."

"Not here yet." She laughed, amused. "Ours is still under cover."

He shook his head. "Good."

They went back to sleep.

A boy delivered a telegram the next day.

JESUS IS RETURNING TO PRESKITT TO BE WITH YOU. WE ALL VOTED FOR THIS TO BE SURE YOU HAD AT LEAST ONE OF US WITH YOU. ROAMER.

"What is it?" his wife asked.

"My men voted to send Jesus up here to be with me."

"We talked about that before we left. You told us and them that you'd be housebound for a while." She snickered. "Those men of yours didn't believe that, did they?"

"I guess not."

"Your men care about you. Having Jesus here will be a good thing."

"I suppose." He peered out a nearby window. "Looks like rain. That should make Momma Hampt happy."

"He's mothering that new alfalfa, isn't he?"

"He's set on it making a stand."

"I can't imagine, in the length of time we've been home, how no one has come by needing your help."

"I guess they don't know I'm home."

"Probably — that's saved you." She kissed the side of his face. "I wasn't egging them on, either."

Later on, his Preskitt Valley Ranch foreman, Raphael, stopped by for a visit. The Preskitt Valley Ranch was his wife's home place that her father recently signed over to them. Raphael was an older Mexican and his hands were all *vaqueros* and top men. Some were married, but he'd seen them in action when a hired gun tried to assassinate him at the house. They spread out from the ranch and treed the gang within twelve hours.

When he told Raphael that Tom had found five purebred Hereford bulls to replace some of the older ones, he was very pleased. The man was also proud to be the foreman on the home ranch and took his job seriously.

"I wish I'd been there when he shot you," Raphael said.

"It all happened so fast. I was shot and he was, too. He never got away."

"I just hated it when I heard."

"Just a small incident in my life. If I buy a ranch in southern Arizona, I may need you to move some women and children off of it. They were abandoned down there by their men. If we didn't feed them, they'd starve. Jesus thinks they're backwards Indians."

"That sounds bad."

"Sorry, but I don't have control of it yet," said Chet.

"You ever need me, you send word and I will be glad to come help you."

"I'll do that. I'll send you word how to find me."

"I am so glad you are getting over that wound. We all prayed for you. We are all one family here."

"Amen. Tell everyone I will be up and running in a short while."

"Don't rush it." Raphael rose and shook his hand. He replaced his wide-brimmed *sombrero* and adjusted the chin string. *"Vaya con Dios, mi amigo."*

When Chet walked him out on the porch, he studied the blue sky and moving clouds, grateful he'd come back to the mountains and the cooler environment. His brain had cleared more and more. There were things that happened from the shooting incident that he'd never recover from, but he didn't need them, either.

A boy brought him a telegram later on. It was from his lawyer in Tucson.

THERE WILL BE A GRAND JURY CALLED TO LOOK AT THE LAND CLAIMED BY BUSTER AND WHO IT MIGHT HAVE BEEN THAT FILED THE FICTITIOUS LAND PAPERS IN THE PIMA COUNTY BOOKS. WE CAN'T PROVE HE WAS THE PARTY INVOLVED UNLESS THE GRAND JURY FINDS SOMETHING. BUT I AM SURE THE JUDGE WILL ORDER HIM AND HIS OPERATION OFF YOUR RANCH. THIS WOULD EXPOSE HIM TO CIVIL ACTION THAT CAN BE TAKEN BY YOU. I WILL KEEP YOU INFORMED. RUSSELL CRAFT, ATTORNEY AT LAW

"What did you get?" Marge asked.

"My lawyer says they're forming a grand jury to find out who filed that original deed. It was a false one."

"He suspected they would do that, didn't he, when we were there?" she asked.

"Yes. Now authorities are trying to trace it."

"Did this Buster figure, since the landowner was in California, that he could get by with doing that?"

"I think so. But proving who did it will be much harder."

He kissed her and then looked down at her belly. "We any closer?"

"Hey, this in *numero* one for me. I'm ready for it to get here."

He hugged her, large belly and all.

"I have no idea how this will work. Aside from May, none of us has any experience at this. She's been delightful to explain things to me. I think I'll be the first to give birth and she has a midwife who can deliver it. Besides that, she will also be here to get me through the whole thing. Doc Norman said it looked positioned well to him. He said if there was any problems, he'd come out."

"I need to go see Tanner tomorrow. I'll have Raphael send two *vaqueros* along. Or should I wait till Jesus arrives?"

"Either way will work. You decide."

"I'll do that. Have you needed to dip into any of that government cattle money we've been getting to use for payroll?"

"Not yet. I told Susie and Tom that one day we'd need to transfer some of it to the real ranch account. So far, we haven't used any from the Navajo operation."

"What were they making money on? What's paying us?"

"The mill lumber haul has really been busy this year. Tom sold some cull cows down at Fort McDonald and they cashed that contract in thirty days. We did combine that with the ranch funds."

"Fine. Maybe I need him to collect up at Gallup."

She shook her head. "They were on a different pay cycle. I'll tell Raphael to have two men ride with you in the morning."

"Fine."

In a short while, they went to bed. He fell into an easy sleep, then woke up sharply. What was wrong? He slid his Colt out of the holster and it filled his fist. Then, barefooted, with the silver starlight shining through the window, he carefully walked across the smooth polished hardwood floors to check on what had awoken him. Sounded to him like someone running across the porch.

Then he heard more fast boot heels running across the porch for the east side.

"Alto, hombre." The command came from

one of his *vaqueros* outside.

Then gunshots, more gunshots, and a few horses ran off in the night.

"Saddle and ride. I want those *bastardos*," A guard's voice rang out.

"You alright, Chet?" Marge, wrapped in a housecoat, asked from the top of the stairs.

"Go back to bed. I'm fine. You, too, Monica. Our night guards stopped them."

"Good. Who were they?"

"I have no idea." He opened the front door for the concerned foreman.

"You all are fine?" his man asked.

"Yes, we are."

"I have sent three men to go get those *hombres* who were here. One of the night guards came; they woke me and said there were some riders here."

"Need me?"

"No, go back to sleep. By daylight, they will no longer breathe."

No trouble for him. He understood the man's Mexican justice. Ahead of him, he herded his women down the hallway.

"Who hired these men, do you think?" Marge asked.

"No idea, but I suspect some of the southern powers. We'll see." He guided her back inside their bedroom and they tried to sleep some more.

On his back, staring at the shadowy ceiling, he wondered who wanted his hide this time. Too many enemies, that was all he could think about as he laid uncomfortably on the sheet. He had to recover faster. He'd known that regaining his strength would be a slow process, but he didn't think it would be this endless.

Turned over on his side, he finally found some shut-eye, but it didn't answer his own question — about when he'd be completely himself again.

CHAPTER 4

He shaved and went down to breakfast. Monica had coffee made like she expected him. She busied herself at the dry sink, slicing bacon. "You real hungry?"

"No."

"I'll sure be glad when you get your appetite back."

"Maybe when the baby comes, we'll all be better."

"You worried about that?"

"I don't need to lose her."

"You won't lose her. Childbirth is natural, maybe some strain and pain, but women do it every day."

"I'll try to remember that."

"Men can't get involved. Can't do anything but wring their hands and fret, so get ready."

He laughed at her explanation. The coffee cup in both hands, his elbows on the table, he turned when someone came onto the back porch.

"Raphael," she said to settle him.

Sombrero in his hands, he came in the kitchen. "Señor, those men said an *hombre* named Larry Masters hired them. They were from Sonora and he paid them two-fifty to ride up here to kill you, and the rest he promised to pay them when they could prove you were dead." Then he solemnly shook his head. "They won't ride home."

"How much money did they have on them?"

"Close to two hundred."

"Split it among your men, sell their horses, guns, and saddles. Do it quietly."

"That is generous, señor."

"No, that is how I do my men."

"Do you know the man who hired them?"

"He's a man who manages a ranch that squatted on my new ranch down below."

"If you would like him shot . . ." Raphael dropped his hat lower in front of his body, waiting for his answer.

"Thanks, I would rather confront him myself."

"I savvy."

Chet thanked the man and walked him to the door. Then he shook his hand. "You and your men are a great part of my Force. I can always sleep when I'm away, because

51

you're prepared for any trouble."

A few days later, the *Miner* newspaper reported:

Three unknown men of Mexican origin were found earlier this week hung by the neck east of Prescott Valley. According to County Sheriff Simms, the lynching is under investigation and his office is holding an ongoing investigation of their murders. No notes were left on the scene, so whether these men had appropriated another's horses is unknown. If you have any information please give it to the sheriff's office personnel at the Yavapai County Courthouse.

Chet thumped on the page with his thumb. "If I had Masters's mailing address, I'd send it to him and tell him he's next."

"Maybe your lawyer could find it?" Marge asked.

Monica laughed. "I bet if Masters got it, he'd get over being constipated."

He agreed with both women.

Two nights after the incident, Jesus arrived. He sent a wire from Hayden Mills saying when he'd arrive, and Jimenez was there to meet him at the stage depot and brought him out to the ranch. Looking a little tired, but smiling from ear to ear, he joined them for breakfast the next morning.

"Good to see you, ladies. You, too, boss man. Jimenez told me they tried to kill you a few nights ago."

"They raided the place, but didn't get by Raphael's guards. His men ran them down, quizzed them, and then hung them, but that last part is secret. I won't tell my Force down there, but the outlaws said it was Buster's ranch manager, Masters, that hired them. I don't want JD or Roamer going over there and wringing his neck."

"You met that *hombre.* I never did. I was feeding the women that trip."

"They're still eating?"

"Oh, yes. But like you said, they need to go back to Mexico."

"The land claim is a false one. So we'll be getting that ranch."

"JD will be happy."

"Maybe. Lots to do down there at Diablo, as JD calls it."

"I know. How is everything up here?"

"Good. Hitch a buckboard. I'm going to town."

"The poor man just got here," Marge protested.

"No, señora. I am so glad to be back riding with him again, I will have no problem."

"Finish your breakfast."

Marge looked with a frown at her husband.

After they climbed the tall hill, and the horses went stiff legged down into the main business district and the courthouse, they found Preskitt bustling. Thumb Butte still stuck up in the west and he felt good to be back. The girls at the café hugged him. Jenn came out drying her hands to tell him Dodge had sent her a nice note to say he'd been delayed, and hoped he'd be able to visit them at a later date. Chet made a mental note to tell Marge. She'd be disappointed.

"What's the matter with the Tucson paper, writing that slanted story — Israel Clanton, a ranch manager, my backside?" Bonnie, JD's wife, looked upset. "He was worthless as everything back when the two of us were down there."

"Hey, they haven't got anything better to write is all I can say." He hugged her. "Blevins warned me the idle rich were mad we didn't let them in on it, and we have no plans to do that."

Cole's wife, Valerie, added, "That bunch're always trying to run things. Jenn said you got chewed out by Sheriff Behan for not informing his mother about his death."

Chet nodded at her. "You can tell who his friends are."

They all laughed. After a cup of coffee they went to his land agent Bo's real estate office.

Bo had a desk piled high in paper. "See what sobering me up has cost?"

"No rush, but the lawyer in Tucson says the land filing is phony. As soon as he gets that cleared, I want to buy that ranch."

"No problem. And I bought four home-steads that are patented land up near the Windmill. They have houses on them, but you know what they must be. All have water and one has alfalfa acreage. They ranged from five hundred to six hundred fifty dollars apiece. Two more pending deals."

"Buy them. Even when the cattle drives are over, we can ranch up there. I want maps for Sarge to go look at them. He and Susie will be excited."

"There are some places up by Reg, too, that I can buy."

"Buy them. Get me a list and maps. They'll tell me how good we did."

"Your people from Oak Creek Canyon, Leroy and Betty, brought me a flat of ripe strawberries yesterday — not a box, but a flat. Said they loved it up there and I was the reason you bought it. They're going to take some to Marge today."

"They're good people."

"He still can't get over you and Cole and Jesus rescuing him up there in Utah."

"Part of our business. You spent any more of our money?"

"That's it for now. But I can't resist homesteaders with clean deeds wanting to move on from places that are near one of yours."

"That's fine. Jesus and I need to see my banker next."

Bo looked him over hard. "I'm damn glad you're still alive."

Chet found Andrew Tanner busy and they took a seat. Someone went and whispered in his banker's ear and the tall man came to the door. "I'll be right with you. Good to see you."

"Don't worry. I'm fine."

Tanner nodded and went back to complete his business. Chet sat back down. "You understand banking?" he asked Jesus.

Jesus shook his head.

"How well can you read English?"

"Some."

"Marge can make you a scholar. I want

you to learn all you can about banking. You may have to read some kid's books before you get to the tougher ones. You'll have to practice numbers, night and day. But she can make you a banker."

"Do you think so?"

"They are going to need Hispanic bankers. Even down at Tubac, those brothers couldn't borrow money to buy cows. They would be great ranchers. But they'd need a Hispanic banker."

"I know what you mean. I will apply myself."

"Glad that's settled. After this meeting, let's go by the mercantile. Then we can go home after that."

"You getting tired?"

"I will be by then."

Jesus smiled. "I won't tell anyone."

"Good."

His visit with Tanner took a while. The cattle money account was bulging. The banker was pleased, but he thought Chet should invest some of it in stocks and bonds.

"I'd invest in some young rancher you thought would pay me back."

"There are some loan applications like that here."

"Find some. We can go over them, say, on Friday morning?"

Tanner agreed. "Yes, that would help me, as well as the community."

Chet and Jesus went by the store and he spoke to Ben Ivor and his pregnant wife, Kathrin, who was working at bookkeeping.

"I should of ordered a hundred mowing outfits," Ben said. "But, I'm learning. I've found several. They're shipping them, but the hay season will be half over before they get here."

"Sounds busy."

"How is your wife?" Kathrin asked Chet.

"Doing fine. I'd say, any day now."

"I bet she's ready."

"Oh, me, too."

"Glad to see you're back in one piece. I guess you're taking a long break from that work?"

"Not very long."

"Sounds like you."

The men shook hands, then Jesus drove him home.

"We can go see Tom tomorrow. Monica will have an early breakfast ready." Chet climbed down from the buckboard.

"Need anything else?"

"No, it was a good day."

"I'll be ready. Get some rest. I can tell you are getting stronger."

"I'm getting there. Thanks. We better take

the buckboard tomorrow."

Jesus nodded and drove toward the barn.

After Chet washed up on the back porch, his wife hugged him.

"Everything in Preskitt is fine."

He smiled at Monica. She was putting out lunch. He'd rather have gone to bed for a few hours than eat, but he couldn't. Her black coffee woke him some. But he didn't have much to say to either woman, and then excused himself, intending to sleep for a while.

"Did you get the mail?" Marge asked.

"No — forgot."

Marge shook her head. "Get some sleep. I can tell you're ready to do that."

He kissed her and waved at Monica. In a short while he was sound asleep on top of the bed quilt. When his wife came by and threw a blanket over him, he hardly stirred and went right back to sleep.

By late afternoon he was downstairs, but barely awake, when he received a wire. The young man who delivered it stood by, waiting for a reply.

THE FEDERAL TASK FORCE WAS AMBUSHED IN THE MINING DISTRICT SOUTHEAST OF PATAGONIA YESTERDAY. SEVERAL MEM-

BERS HAVE BEEN WOUNDED –
ROAMER – COLE – JD. THE REST
HAD MINOR WOUNDS. THEY ARE
AT THE FORT HUACHUCA ARMY
HOSPITAL. ALL SHOULD RE-
COVER. SEVERAL OUTLAWS WERE
KILLED. THEY TOOK SEVERAL OF
THEIR WOUNDED WITH THEM TO
MEXICO. ROAMER THINKS THEY
WERE WITH OLD MAN CLANTON.
SHAWN.

"What is it?" Marge asked.

"They attacked the Force. It sounds like up in the live oak country east of Patagonia. According to Shawn, several were wounded but all should recover."

"Shawn sent that?"

"He's a good man. He says our crew killed several of the ambushers. He thinks Old Man Clanton was responsible for the ambush."

"What now?"

"I need to go back down there and get things straight."

"I imagined you'd say that," she said, looking disappointed. "But you aren't a hundred percent yet."

"Marge, I have to get there. I'm sorry to leave you, but that Force is mine and those men are mine. I may have to raise a few more men. Clanton, if he's the one ambushed them, will pay."

"I've lost two men in my life. I don't want to lose you, Chet Byrnes. But I do understand that tiger inside you. I've seen you go to great lengths to solve crimes and bring criminals to justice. For God's sake, though, for the baby and me, please be careful."

He hugged her. "I will."

Jesus was there by then. Chet told them they were taking the night stage to Hayden Mills and then showed him the telegram. His man read it slowly.

"Do you need me to read it for you?" Marge asked.

"No, I can read it."

"Good. You two are off again."

"No idea how bad they are hurt, huh?"

"No idea, but in about forty-eight hours we'll be there."

"Yes, sir. I will be ready. Jimenez can carry us in there."

"Right."

Chet went upstairs and packed a war bag with Marge seated on the bed.

"I hate to leave you, but they need me."

She nodded. "Old Man Clanton's thrown down the gauntlet on you, hasn't he?"

"I told Blevins I left him alone because I

61

couldn't prove he did anything illegal in the states. That twenty-eight-year-old, Israel, shot in their raid, was running around pulling off robberies and raping women. That was his nephew. If I can prove he had one thing to do with this ambush, he better go to wearing his best suit."

"Just remember, lots of us depend on you."

"I know that, Marge. When it's settled, I'll be home. You and the baby take care. I'm counting on the two of you."

She shook her head. "Just watch where you step. I love you, big man. The ranches need you, too."

He nodded, closed the drawstring closure, and swung the bag on his shoulder. "I'll wire you when I find out how the men are doing. Tell Jenn and the girls they'll get a report, too."

"I just wish I could go along and help you."

"You have your plate full."

"Oh, yes."

That night, he slept most the way downhill off the mountain, rocking in the stage, facing the back. A few times, the bounce was rough enough to bring him awake. A glance out at the moonlit silver night and he closed his eyes. There were saguaros out there and the night had grown warmer. They'd spill out soon on the desert floor. He'd gotten off and emptied his bladder at Bumble Bee. The Tucson Stage was supposed to carry them on after they got to Hayden's Ferry. He and Jesus talked about getting some food from a street vendor and going right on. No one shared the coach that night, so they had no competition for the seats. No telling what was waiting for them down south.

The sun was up when they shifted their things to the new line. Jesus ran off to buy some food. The stage office man served him some coffee. "You and your bunch are serious customers."

"Get Jesus some coffee," he said, and put some silver on the counter.

"Put your money away. You and your men do more good for this territory than any men I know."

"Thanks."

Jesus handed him a tortilla-wrapped meal and took the coffee Chet handed him.

"Thanks for the coffee."

"That was him." Chet indicated the agent was the source.

"Oh, thank you."

"We're all grateful."

Chet laughed.

"You must feel better," Jesus said to him quietly.

"Tell me that tomorrow."

Jesus nodded. "Does your shoulder still hurt?"

"Not much. I know it's there. I get jarred on that side, I damn sure know it's there."

"Let's load up," the driver said, standing in the door. His lifted his hat and scratched his long, gray, unkempt hair.

They finished their coffee, thanked the agent, and, food wrap in hand, made their way out. A full-bodied woman clambered up and about overturned the coach to get inside. When the rig settled down, she'd taken the backseat and left the back-facing one for them. Last on, a skinny drummer in a striped suit and bowler hat saw he had a small portion of the rear seat and managed to sit in it by un-planting her until his butt was on the leather. She cleared her throat and sniffed her nose at him. He looked pretty sour at Chet, but that was his luck of the draw.

The day's heat was rising. Dust rode the wings of the hot breaths of air propelled off the greasewood desert, and the two teams of horses raced eastward for Bentsen under the whiney voice of the driver. No shotgun guard on top, so there must not be a thing valuable in the coach. After passing through the giant forest of saguaros, they rocked out into the chaparral country. With purple mountains on the left and right, rising like loaves of bread, the road headed east. Horse changes were precise and they rolled on to Bentsen. There they left the fat complaining woman, who was obviously going eastward.

With their things placed on the next coach in late afternoon, they climbed on. Chet felt pretty drained as the shadows began to lengthen on the settlements along the San Pedro River.

Jesus had bought them another wrapped meal and they ate it while rocking out for St. David, the next town on the route south. Later, they swept into Tombstone and then made the fifteen miles up to Huachuca City. It was near ten o'clock by the time they found rooms in the hotel and hired a taxi to take them to the fort hospital.

It was cooler up in the canyon. In the moonlight, Chet could make out tall cotton-woods and a row of officers' houses lined around a large parade field. The taxi man let them out at the hospital.

"Wait. We'll need to go back," he told the taxi man.

"Sure."

A guard stopped them.

"I'm Marshal Chet Byrnes. I wanted to check on some of my men here."

"Yes, sir. Talk to the officer in charge inside, sir."

"Thank you."

The screen door creaked when Chet pulled it back. There, seated on nail kegs, were Roamer with his head bandaged, JD with an arm in a sling, and Cole, all of them playing cards with the officer in charge.

"Hellfire, the boss caught us," Roamer said.

The whole bunch laughed, folded up their cards, and the officer had some chairs brought in for him and Jesus.

"A bunch of outlaws had begun raiding ranches down here," Roamer said. "I had all hands out questioning folks about what they knew. We were thinking they came out of Mexico. They were vicious and moving fast. They cut a small boy's ear off in one raid, for no reason but that they were simply damn mean. It pissed off every man in the outfit and that sumbitch is now dead. We made sure of that. They used this same route to go over the border several times. So we wanted to set up and ambush them, but it turned out like Skeleton Canyon did. They must have had us watched. We rode into a trap."

"All hell broke loose," JD said, shaking his bandaged head. "But they'd struck the wrong guys. We laid down some rifle fire and discovered that the only weapons most of them had were cap and ball pistols. We knew all about those guns from New Mexico. We spread out and they began to pull back. We were killing anyone who showed himself. Shawn was bringing us ammo from the packhorses. I'd look up and he'd be back with three boxes of cartridges and then be gone again for more. How he went back and forth unscathed, I'll never know. But he let us shoot and we kept them pinned down and killed any of them tried to move. There was so much gun smoke in that canyon — you couldn't breathe."

Cole went on, "After a couple of hours, their reserves arrived, but we were dug in and we shot several of them before they got most of the bodies out. They didn't want to fight us. They'd grab a corpse and run like hell."

"Why did they take the dead men?"

"We figured it was so we couldn't trace them to the old man's ranch."

"Are all of you recovering okay?"

"Hell, yes," Roamer said. "The three brothers were only scratched, so they went home. But let me tell you, if we ever get in another ambush, I want these guys with me. Chet, they never took a breath, had loaded rifles and were returning fire. We soon learned our raiders were mostly armed with old pistols. That was the difference. Those 44/40 Winchesters were great."

"Those three brothers fought like fierce tigers," Cole said. "They went around their west flank levering rifles and mowing them down. They had no fear."

Roamer agreed. "I wanted to shout at them to get down. They cleared out the west side of the canyon. Only got scratches. But the others were dug in on the east side and they weren't going to be drove out that easy. Then the damn reserves came and they were shooting up everything. Luckily, they had mostly cap and ball pistols, too. It was obvious they wanted the bodies, so we used them for bait. That worked till sundown, then we let them have the rest.

"Shawn fed us. And he sent a boy to the fort for medical help, and the Army got to us right after sundown."

"They're a great bunch of guys," the officer said about his crew.

"I think so, too."

The officer shook his head. "We wished we'd been down there to help them."

"I know about the rules. That's why we're here."

He nodded. "I can put you up in a guest-house."

"We rented a hotel room."

"Have your man go get your luggage. You two can sleep in nice beds tonight."

"I'll go get them," Jesus said.

"When you come back, my guard will show you where to go."

Chet gave Jesus some money for the taxi and he nodded thanks, then left to get their things.

The soldier at the door showed Chet to a fine two-story white house in a row of similar houses and told him Shawn was sleeping there.

Chet thanked him and rapped on the door.

"Coming."

"No need." Chet opened the door and entered to see a rumpled Shawn coming toward him. "Just didn't want to get shot. Jesus has gone back to town for our luggage. He'll be along. I just need a place to fall down and sleep."

"You doing alright, sir?" Shawn looked at him with concern.

"Fine, you've done a helluva job down here. I wanted to thank you. They said you kept them in ammo — a very important job."

"Damn." He swept back his hair from his face. "I thought they were eating it, sir."

"I also appreciate your sending me word."

"That was hard. Roamer said to tell you we were all alive. But it was tough."

"You did good. Thanks. Where is that bed?"

"Coolest place to sleep is on the second floor on the porch," Shawn said.

"It's cool enough for me to sleep here."

"Go in that bedroom."

"Don't forget Jesus is coming." In the dark room, he shed his boots and gun belt and fell across the nice mattress. He'd overdone it the last two days. Things could go slower now. In seconds, he was sound asleep.

Dawn tried to peer into the canyon that housed the fort. Chet could hear troops marching to mess. They were black buffalo soldiers and they sang out cadence songs that rang in the cool air. These were Black Jack Pershing's men and they were serious Indian fighters. He was getting his first taste of them.

"Should I wake Jesus?" Shawn asked, joining him.

"Let him sleep. Where do we get food?"

"Officers' mess hall. Food's better there

than in the troopers' tent."

They walked to the officers' mess, where a soldier saluted and opened the flap. They filled their trays, then a black soldier brought them hot coffee in mugs.

"Be anything else you's need? Make yourself at home."

"Thanks, soldier. We'll be fine."

"Yes, sah."

Fried eggs, German potatoes, biscuits and flour gravy, plus oatmeal if you needed more. He savored the coffee to wash out his dry mouth from sleeping so hard. Of all the forts he'd been to, this was the best located and best built.

"You must be Marshal Byrnes?" The captain, a man in his thirties, stood above him.

"Yes, I arrived last night. Have a seat."

"Captain Evans, Marshal. I'm assigned to help you and your men any way I can."

"Wonderful. They had a close call up in the canyons in that ambush."

"My Apache scouts said that was no fight. These cowboys killed them."

"I understand they turned the tables on them."

"That they did. Go ahead and eat. I understand you're healing from another raid."

"I'm about well."

"Your men are about healed, too. They're a well-organized law enforcement group. But you don't have to leave here."

"They need to go home to check with their wives. Have some breathing room. Then we can come back later, fresh and ready to start this war over again."

"I understand. Who cares for your ranches while you do this?"

"A set of top foremen who, like these men, are damn tough. They aren't tough like a bulldog, they work with their crew. But they're solid."

"Folks say you're building an empire."

"A family one."

"I was simply curious."

"No problem. I get asked all the time."

He wondered about Reg. Poor guy must think he'd gave up on him. He'd write him and Lucie a letter. Reflectively, he sipped on the still hot coffee and looked across the near empty mess hall tent.

Plans began to form in his mind. Take their horses to Ortega's, then load everyone on stagecoaches and take three weeks off. Get his new ranch plans rolling in Tucson, as well. Poor Marge was probably having their baby all alone.

He gathered his crew midmorning in the

mess hall. The men were all drinking coffee that Captain Evans ordered for them.

"What have you heard about the old man's crew?" he asked Evans.

"He's damn shorthanded. And he's been borrowing *vaqueros* from other ranchers to move his beef shipments. My informants say he lost as many as twelve men, or more, in his ambush of your men."

"Good," Roamer said. "I'd like twenty more."

"Damn right," JD said. "They started in shooting at us and it took us several minutes to realize they had no rifles. Their powder was real sorry and by then we had our Winchesters blazing."

Shawn took up the story. "I was running as fast as I could to get them ammo. Bullets whizzing all over. I couldn't help the brothers. They were taking the west mountain. I was never so shaken in my whole life, but I had no time to think about it. I recall taking more ammo to Roamer and he said, 'Kneel down.' Then he went on, saying, 'We've won. Find the others. Have them come down here, if they can make it.' Blood was coming down his face and he looked real woozy. When I asked what I could do for him, he said, 'Tie my silk kerchief around my head. That may stop the bleeding some.'

"JD came in with a bloody arm. Cole had four small wounds. The brothers were just scratched. I sent a boy to the fort for medical help. And, boy, they arrived quick and they were good. Then Roamer told me to telegram you that we were all alive."

"I figured they were trailing back to Mexico and I wanted them stopped," Roamer said. "We agreed when they went over the mountain we'd strike them. They never went over. Instead, they set up to ambush us."

"Any idea who led them?" Chet asked.

"Kurt Holder. He was the main man. Big man, stood six-foot-six. Standing on that ridge he made an easy target, shouting in German to Mexicans what he wanted done. He thought we only had pistols, too, I guess. But we shut him up in a snap of the trigger and spilled him on his ass. That shocked his men that our bullets could reach him. They kept shooting their old pistols, but we were counting bodies," JD said. "The brothers were tearing up the ones on the west side, and because they had rifles, they could even shoot at the ones on the east side."

"Then their reserves came from somewhere and they acted interested in getting the bodies off the field. That's an oak-juniper country and really tough to get around." Shawn shook his head. "They didn't bring rifles back, thank God."

"Do you think those reserves were supposed to be there at the start of the attack?" Chet asked.

"Probably, but we had the original ones cut down so bad, they would never have gained the edge again," Roamer said.

Captain Evans laughed. "I liked the tall target story. Him ordering in German to Mexicans what he wanted done."

Everyone laughed.

"You think that was how they cut down the Skeleton Canyon pack train?" Cole asked.

Chet nodded. "Yes, but they must have had some rifles there."

"What's next, boss man?"

"Take our horses to Ortega's. Get on a stagecoach for home. Take three weeks and see what we can do best after that. We should be healed by then."

"I'd vote for that," JD said.

The rest nodded.

"Evans, you have anything on Clayton's sons?" Chet asked.

"Mostly drunks. Small crimes, and they hold up stages on both sides of the border."

"Maybe we can round them up when we come back."

Evans agreed with a nod. "I bet you could get them cold-handed. I have a half-dozen Apache bucks that love to trail people. You need trackers, send me word."

Everyone nodded.

"I'll have them feed you some lunch and you can get on your way."

"You ready to pull out for Tubac?" Roamer asked Chet, sounding concerned about his strength.

"I'm fine. You have a horse for me to ride?"

"By damn, we can get one for you."

"Let's move out then. I want to thank you and the Army." Chet shook the Captain's hand.

"I wished they'd still been hanging around when my scouts found them."

"Yeah," JD said. "We'd have let them in on the action."

Evans assured them the Army would help in any way possible. In an hour, Chet on one of his roans, they all headed westward. It was a long day and after sundown when Ortega's wife, Maria, greeted them.

"Oh, I am so glad, Chet, you are alright. Is something wrong?"

"Oh, we're a little bunged up, but we're going to take a break. The men will go home and get rested. Where's Ortega?"

"They took some cattle to Tucson for a man. They did not know you were coming back so soon."

The brothers were not back in the morning. Maria said it would take them several days to drive the stock up there and sell them.

"No problem. We didn't know yesterday we were doing this, either. All will be fine. Can you feed my horses while we're gone?"

"I can do that. It is so good to see that you are alright," she said.

"And Ortega will need to take those deserted women some food this week."

"No problem. What are you going to do with them?"

"Take them back to Mexico. But I'm too damn busy right now."

Maria laughed and hugged him. "You are always too busy."

Cole found him a bedroll. They were unsure where his roll went after he'd been shot.

She offered to feed them, but instead they gnawed on some jerky before they turned in.

"Breakfast in the morning," she promised, and left them.

After breakfast, Shawn used the ranch buckboard to take them into Tubac. They found a mail wagon headed north, and Chet offered four dollars to the Mexican driver to transport him and Jesus to Tucson. Saddles, bedrolls, and war bags were transferred, and they headed north at a good trot.

"My name is Pablo," said the driver.

"I'm Chet and he's Jesus."

"You must have much business in Tucson?"

"Yes, we're U.S. Marshals."

"Oh, I see. You are the Force, huh?"

"Yes, we're part of it."

"God bless you, *hombres.* I will drive, feeling much safer on my route with you riding with me."

"Good. That's why we're here."

Late that evening, the two took a hotel room and then went out to eat. Jesus knew a nice Mexican food place with soft music and a dancer. He promised Chet great food. It was all of that, and afterward they went back in the breathless city night to their hotel.

"Sure be nice to be home," he said, pushing into the room.

"Oh, much better." Jesus laughed.

After a sidewalk breakfast from a vendor, they went by and saw Marshal Blevins. Chet knew he'd be there, since his boss was an early morning man. They had a nice conversation, and Blevins hoped they could return and finish their efforts.

"I plan to do that. We need some time to heal. I need to see about my wife and my ranches, then we'll be back."

Blevins shook his hand. "I'm counting on that. You've sure done your part here."

When they left his office, the day's heat had set in. At the law office, his secretary said Russell Craft would see them right away.

"Well, the head man of the federal force is here. Have a chair, Chet. Nice to see you, too, young man."

"Any news on our real estate problem?"

"I have spoken to the prosecutor and he acts like maybe he doesn't want to go forward with this case."

"That would be like me letting captured killers return to Mexico unscathed. Prosecuting criminals is his job."

"It might be good for you to tell the prosecutor what his job is."

"I can do that."

"What else?"

"Buster's man, Masters, hired killers to shoot me at my home. Promised them two-fifty more when they killed me."

"I'm sorry. You've done a tough job down

79

here. The prosecutor should be on your side."

"What is this prosecutor's name?" Chet asked his lawyer.

"Niles Proctor."

"I met with several businessmen and lawmen who wanted the law enforced when I came down here and set up my command. You think he was there?"

"I doubt it."

"As a U.S. Marshal, can I request his help on this crime?"

"You sure have that authority. And, at your request, a judge could call on him to answer why he's not working on it."

"I'll do that. I intend to buy that ranch and make it a working one."

"I'll remain on the case for you. It's a simple case of fraud."

They shook hands.

"You ever trout-fish?" Chet asked.

"Oh, yes."

"I have some rough cabins up on Oak Creek. Drop a line in and it's a cool, sweet place to hook fish."

"I'll be up to see you."

"Let me know when you're coming. Take a stage to Preskitt, and one of my men will show you up there."

"I will make plans to do that."

"I'm going over to see Proctor."

When they crossed to the federal court building, the day's heat was already building. They found Proctor in his office. When his secretary showed Chet into the office, he blinked and took his flat shoes off the desk. "Marshal?"

"Marshal Byrnes. I came to see you about this scandal over some false filings in the courthouse land office. I believe it was done to gain control of a large plot of land and was done by some prominent people."

"You have any proof?"

"A grand jury could pry it out of them. If you don't get rolling on this, I plan to speak to the Chief Justice about your neglecting your job."

"You . . . you . . . can't threaten me."

"I can, and I'll take the top off this building when I do. If you don't have this grand jury under way in ten days, I'll call in the judges and find out why."

"You can't do that."

"Your buddies, Weeks and Townsend, are in my sights. But there are others who were going to get rich by stealing that ranch. I say you know who they are."

"I won't be threatened."

"I'm not threatening you. I will press for this. Are you ready to get on with it?"

"Listen, you little Texas rich boy. Folks have trouble making a living here, and small deals ain't that important."

"If I shot your wife this afternoon and said she got in my way, would you defend me that I was only trying to make a living?"

"That's crazy."

"There's a ring here ruling things about business. Now if you want them on the front page, then you refuse to bring this bunch to the bar. I have more power than you think. Besides, I'm not some little rich Texas boy. I stand six feet tall. I'm an Arizona resident. I'm a livestock rancher and, also, a deputy U.S. Marshal. And if Old Man Clanton messes with me again, he'll be in Boot Hill with his nephew."

"You're a gawdamn fool!"

"I may be, and you may be in Utah next, if you don't get it done." Chet knew federal judges and prosecutors hated to be assigned to Utah worse than Arizona. He turned to leave. "I'm counting. Get your ass busy."

Outside the office in the hall, a smiling Jesus joined him. "You are mad. Did you do any good?"

"We'll know in a few weeks." He lowered his voice. "He's tied into this ring. They don't want to be investigated. I promised him they'd be next. He may have to decide what he wants."

Crossing the blazing-hot street, Chet looked over at his man. "Wouldn't it be nice to be back home?"

"Let us get stage tickets. Hell, I hate this place."

"Let's go."

"Yes."

They headed home at eight o'clock and even the moonlit desert north of Tucson felt cooler as they rocked northward. He soon slept.

CHAPTER 5

Hayden Ferry matched Tucson's heat, but he and Jesus arrived there late in the day. Due to repairs being done on the coach, the Black Canyon Stage hadn't left yet, so they bought seats. He wired Marge they were coming. Tired because of his still sore shoulder, he hoped he could rest at home.

Jesus woke him on the stage-line bench. "I have all our things aboard. JD and Cole came through here last night. They're all split up, like you asked."

Chet smiled at him. "Wonder why those newlyweds want to be the first ones home?"

They both laughed.

That night, the stage swept them out of the desert's heat into the mountains' coolness. He could smell the pines and felt better when he disembarked and shook Jimenez's hand.

"Good to have you back, señor."

"Jesus and I can say the same thing. No baby?"

"No baby yet, señor. We are all waiting."

He could imagine his wife was as well.

"I will get our things," Jesus said after him.

"Thanks, pard. Sleep in. We both need some rest."

Jesus waved that he heard him and in the starlight headed in the opposite direction. That boy was so damn dedicated to him, he wouldn't listen. Chet was grateful for such loyal help.

Marge hugged him in the dark on the back porch. "Sneaking in?"

"Yeah. How are you?"

"Full."

"I'm here to help for a few weeks, until my men are all rested."

"Can I say, I'm sure tired of being a mama in waiting? Oh, it's so nice to have you home — I won't complain any more, I promise."

"Hell, complain all you want. I won't tell anyone."

"Good. Is everyone alright?"

"No one is seriously hurt. They ran into a bad enough ambush, but the enemy didn't take them serious enough in the first place. They shot their way out."

"What now?"

"We rest. Get ourselves back together and beat them again."

"Your new ranch?"

"Oh, it will be ours shortly. That will be alright."

"How will you handle it?"

"Get me a foreman and go from there."

"Will JD stay there long enough to run it?"

"I think so, or I have a man better than Raphael to run it."

"Who is that?"

"Ortega Ninni."

"Oh, I'm keeping you awake. You hungry?"

"No, let's sleep."

They hurried upstairs; he undressed and the cool night air washed over his bare skin. Good to be back home and away from all that damn heat.

They slept past dawn. He started the boiler and took a shower, shaved, and dressed in the fresh clothes Marge laid out for him. Felt good, and he went down to join his wife and Monica.

"Strawberries and blackberries are from Oak Creek," his wife said, setting the two bowls on the table. "That Leroy is a genius at growing things. He's going to have peaches and apples this fall. Oh, and cherries are about ripe."

"You made it back in one piece," Monica said.

"I'm here."

She put a plate of food in front of him. "Eat. We have big things for you to do."

"What's that?"

"I don't know yet, but you won't sit there long before some damn fool will come by and need you."

They laughed.

"Is it hot down there?" she asked.

"Hotter than hell."

"I used to live down there," Monica said. "You were smart to buy ranches up here where it's cooler."

"I agree."

After breakfast, he found Jesus shoeing horses at the big barn. His man looked up and smiled. "They were behind on this job."

"Hitch a team and we'll run down and see Tom."

"I'll have them up and ready in a few minutes."

"Going to rain?" he asked Jesus.

"Better wear a long coat."

"I can do that."

They were soon on the road. Jesus had picked a fast team and lost no time heading to the top and then down the long mountain grade to the Verde Valley. They rolled into Chet's sister's front yard in a cloud of dust. When she rushed out to greet them, he hugged and kissed her, then held her off and smiled at her new size.

"How are you, Susie?"

"Big. You look good. I can fix lunch. Tie them up, Jesus, and come in."

"Yes, ma'am."

"How is the house at the Windmill Ranch coming along?" he asked.

"Slow. I should have ordered a three-room shack."

"No, you'll be proud of this one."

"Oh, heavens, yes, I will. But me being so big and so anxious is all hard on me."

He hugged her. "You'll make it."

"I think it's raining up on the mountain. Was that thunder?" she asked Jesus.

"Clouds were building when we left up there."

"Good, we can use it."

Tom dropped by to join them. The men sat at the table and enjoyed her rich coffee.

"My corn crop sure needs some moisture down on the Verde," said Tom.

"You have it where you can water it?"

"Yes, but rain beats irrigation on small grain."

"How is the new alfalfa?"

"Doing great, but I didn't spit on it like Hampt did."

"What is that?" Chet asked, amused.

"Man, he has babied it. But that cowboy is going to beat us. He has a wonderful set on his new land. I think he used more of the black dust on the seed than I did and it shows."

"Can you catch him?"

"I doubt it. I didn't take it serious enough. He did. I'll let him plant the new stands."

"You two may fight over this. I'm grateful we're going to have so many acres of good feed for our stock. We can push our Hereford bull calves to use them at two years of age."

"I've tried."

"Tom, I'm not complaining. We're all learning this ranching business out here, and we'll be a tougher team because of this."

"We're doing all of our own hay this year. We have all this ground down here in hay. Save for the cornfield, which, I think, can help us. Most of the alfalfa land you bought is doing good. We're refencing it with barbwire. The range has lots of grass and now that rain is drumming down, God is smiling at me." He indicated the sounds on the roof.

"Tom, I'm as proud of this place as I can

be. We still need to learn how to ranch better all the time."

"I can't believe we've got this far from the mess Ryan left us."

"Amen. Let's hold back some three-quarter blood bull calves that are well muscled and look more Hereford than longhorn. I think we can find a market for them. We aren't the only ones running around looking for bulls to improve their herds."

Tom agreed. "We could sell a few. It might help some folks get more from their cattle." He started to rise from the table but settled again when Chet waved him back.

"Tom, I'm not disappointed at anything you've done here. This is a helluva big job. But I can be gone and I never lift my head at night worrying about this ranch or its operation."

"I know, but Hampt beat me this time."

"No, you both won. Tell Millie hi. You getting any berries?"

"Wow, yes. We all are. Leroy is really good at that stuff. He's happier than a full pig in the sunshine. You hired another winner. I've eaten more strawberries this spring than any time in my entire life."

"Did you really think he could do that?" Susie asked Chet.

"I knew he was a farmer. He never before had all the good dirt and water he has up there."

"Those nephews of yours think it's heaven to go up there, catch fish, and eat fruit all day. Tell Tom about Rancho Diablo," Susie said.

"Massive place down there. Hot and dry, but lots of feed. Developing water will be the big push. Their land claim is fake. The judge will order them off. Before it's all over with, there may be some shots fired. It was Buster's man, Masters, who hired those killers to come to the house and kill me." He paused and shook his head. "I spoke to the prosecutor in Tucson about calling a grand jury investigation. I think it will step on some of the Tucson ring members. I threatened to call in the federal judges if he didn't move on it."

"How big is this new place?" Tom asked.

"Forty-eight thousand acres, plus the deeded places that Bo is buying around it. He has a half-dozen homesteads he's bought around Windmill, too. He's making Sarge a list. Most of those are completed homesteads that usually have good wells. And some more for Reg. We are expanding."

"Who will run the Diablo?" Susie asked.

"JD wants a chance. Two of the men helping my posse, the Ortega brothers, want to help him. They are *vaqueros* like Raphael's men. Tough as cactus ribs."

"How much longer will you be on the border?" Tom asked.

"I hope no longer than six months. Then Blevins can get himself a new head for the Force."

"Who would he get?"

"I imagine Roamer, if he'd take it."

"How will you ever come back here, settle down, and simply be boss?" Susie asked.

"That we would have to see about, sister dear."

Chet checked on John, the blacksmith, and the barbwire process. It was really going and John smiled when he saw him.

"Can't sell you any wire. You're the third man today dropped by to ask me."

He stuck out his bare hand and they shook.

"You're doing a helluva job," Chet said over the rattle of the twisting wire.

"I'd bet there's an engineer somewhere doing this full steam in a plant. But we're not doing bad. My crew has it down and I can't see us making it any faster."

"Don't worry, you're doing excellent."

"Thanks. Hampt says the cattle don't mess with it."

"That counts."

In the buckboard, Jesus swung it around and he studied the rim off in the north. He planned to go see Reg and Lucie in the next few days. He and Jesus stopped to shrug on their canvas coats — it was raining again. Thank God.

Their drive home was a wet one, but he wasn't mad for a moment of it. He and Jesus laughed and joked about it. Thunder rumbled and more wind swept them. A helluva great day to be in Arizona.

The big house was being pelted by more moisture and there were three buckboards with soaked teams, heads down, parked in the yard. Marge must be in labor.

He jumped off the seat and hit the sloppy ground on the run headed for the back door. In the back porch, he took off his soaked hat and coat, then his muddy boots, and looked up at Jenn's face.

"Anything wrong?"

She shook her head at him. "No. None of us wanted to miss the event."

"Is it close?"

"He should be here before the sun goes down."

"He?"

"That's my guess. You can go in the living room where they've set up Marge's bed.

Then go up and change clothes. Those look damp. How are things down there on the Verde?"

"Busy, like always."

Marge lay under a sheet on the bed in the living room, and he took her hand and squeezed it. Head bent over, he gave his flush-faced wife some words of encouragement. Her head nodded and she gave him a shining smile. That made him feel better and he started upstairs to change. This would be a long evening for both of them. *Lord help her.*

After changing, he slipped back downstairs and into the kitchen. Monica nodded at him.

"Any problems?"

"I don't think so. But the midwife told me she wanted the doctor here. I sent for him, and Jenn as well, since they've become such good friends after going to Tombstone to care for you. They're both here."

"You did well. Who else is here? There are three rigs out there."

"Kathrin Ivor. Didn't you see her?"

"Faces were blurring on me. Yes, I know Kathrin."

"She told Marge she owed you her life for bringing her out of Utah. She knows Marge is very important to you, and she wanted to do anything she could for her."

He picked up a fork and started on the roast beef, gravy, and mashed potatoes. "I wonder if this would be easier if I was ten years younger."

Monica laughed. "No."

He nodded and went on eating. This would be a long day for him, as well as for Marge.

Minutes rolled by like hours. He spoke twice to Kathrin and thanked her for coming. To pass the time, he went to the horse barn and talked to Jesus, Jimenez, and Raphael. They were little help.

Close to sundown, Jenn came for him at the barn.

"What is it?"

"You will know soon enough."

"Aw, come on."

"She'll show you the answer."

Marge was sitting up and looking tired. Hair in her face, she swept it back and with a huge smile held up a red-faced baby to him. "Here's our son, Chet."

"Yes . . ." He paused. "Thank you, Lord. Thank you, Marge. Thank all of you for helping her and me — what did you call him?"

"Adam Chester Byrnes."

"Well, Adam Chester, you've got lots

ahead of you around here." The baby in his arms yawned like it was all beyond him.

Marge nodded. "Does he suit you?"

"Fine. You're alright?"

"I'm doing fine."

"Good. He's a great boy."

So his son was there at last. Things at home should settle down. He rocked the baby in his arm. One more of his widespread family.

CHAPTER 6

Marge and the baby were fine, and Chet had Monica round up plenty of help. He intended to make a check of things on the Rim, so had Jesus load two packhorses. He planned to stop and see Betty and Leroy Sipes at the Oak Creek place, visit Tom at the sawmill, and then ride on to Reg's at the Mogollon Rim Ranch. Bo had bought him, sight unseen, ten homesteads near the big ranch on the Rim and he wanted to look them over, if he had the time. Word of his plans must have slipped out, because the morning they were ready to leave, Cole was there to go along as well.

After Chet kissed his wife and baby goodbye, the three set out for the lower place. Down on the Verde River Ranch, Susie met them on the front porch and laughed after hearing the news of his son's birth.

"Well you won this race, big man. How are they?"

"Fine, how are you?"

"Ready to get it over with. Come on inside. When they tell Sarge you're here, he'll come. I'll make some coffee."

"Can't stay long. We need to also see the Sipeses today."

Susie shook her head, amazed, and put the pot on the range. "That man is a wonder. He sends us food twice a week."

"Monica says he even brings her garden stuff."

"I don't know how he has time for anything."

"Betty is probably doing a big part of that."

"I bet you're right."

"Besides, he really wants to prove he's valuable to us."

"He sure is that."

"Well, the threesome is back," Sarge said, taking off his hat and coming in the doorway. "Papa, congrats. We understand your wife is doing good."

"She's fine. I'm headed up to see Leroy, and then Tom at the sawmill. We'll ride on to Reg's after that."

"The mill must be going full blast. We're making money dragging logs. He says he'll need at least two new teams before fall."

"Sarge, don't complain. Between him and

his crew, we aren't using any cattle sales money so far. His operation is carrying the ranches."

"We have hay and grain going his way in the next two days."

"How's Barbwire John?" he asked his man with Sarge.

"Making rolls. But, for us, there is no end, is there?"

"I don't think so."

"Herefords doing alright?"

"Great calf crop on the ground. The ranch is having a good calf year, too."

"And we should have some steers to sell off this place at long last."

"Oh, yes."

"Sarge's drives are working. Bo Evans has bought us several homesteads that join the Windmill ranch, too. That usually means there's water at these places, maybe some farm land."

"Do you have a description of where they are?" Susie asked. "I'd love to go find them."

"You can do that — after the baby is born."

She wrinkled her nose at him and began pouring coffee. "I won't be a housewife forever."

"We'll see," he teased her.

They rode on, and by evening were at Oak

Creek. Betty and Leroy hugged the three of them. Horses put up, Leroy showed them the cabins nearing completion and his acres of vegetables, fruit trees, and berry bushes. While they walked through his crops, Betty rushed off to cook supper for them.

"Anyone ever tell you that you have a green thumb?" Cole asked.

"No, it's the rich land I have to farm."

"Everyone that gets the fruit and vegetables appreciates them," Chet said.

"I don't miss a soul but Reg, who is too far away. Robert Brown at the mill gets his share, I feed the big ranch, send stuff for Sarge, and to your wife's place."

"You're doing great."

Leroy was beaming. "The great ones are you three. I'd of died up there had it not been for you men. No one else was coming for me. I can farm, but only because you went the long miles to save me."

Jesus rubbed his shirtsleeves. "Well, it was a long cold mile going after you."

"Too cold, but we sure don't regret it now," Chet said, and headed for the house.

The next morning, after a great breakfast, they rode up on the rim to the mill. Robert Brown and his smiling new bride, Agnes Jean, met them. He acted excited to see them and the four men had a great talk on the porch of his small house. Robert asked about his feed shipment, and Chet assured him it was coming and he settled down after that. He told them the mill operation was going full steam. He thought the future railroad track would run close to the mill, but Chet knew the end of the iron tracks were still back in Kansas. A long ways from the snow-capped peak of the San Francisco Mountains far north of them.

The next day, they reached the base of that mountain, where several had struck homesteads, rail-fenced some of it, then planted alfalfa in plots and kept large gardens. Too early for much development and no money or markets was what he saw. Only the railroad would ever bring this region out of its weak financial problems. As they rode along, they passed near where Susie's first husband died in a horse wreck. They camped on the high plains west of there that evening, then went on to the Mogollon Rim Ranch the next day.

Stock dogs barked at their approach. A very pregnant Lucie waved at them from the porch. Three men came running from the blacksmith shop in leather aprons and heavy gloves to greet them.

"How the hell are you, Chet?"

"Great. What are you guys making?"

"Oh, a gadget. How is that new man at your house?"

"Got lungs. He's all boy." Then he shook hands with Lefty and Haze, two cowboys he'd hired for Reg the summer before and they'd stayed with him.

"Weather didn't get too bad for you two?" Chet asked them.

"No, and Lucie's about the best cook we've ever found," Haze said. "Besides, me and Lefty don't have a place to go, so as long as he puts up with us, we're here."

"So is my cousin Willy," Lucie said. "He's gone to check on a heifer. Coffee boils slow up here. It will be ready in a little while. Who's next on the baby delivery?"

"May, I figure," Chet said.

Lucie nodded, looking thoughtful. "We've been reading in the letters about your border Force down there."

"We're taking a short break from that. I had to come see your wonderful house."

She about blushed, shook her head, and then smiled. "My crazy sisters call it a mansion. We're finding furniture for it and I love it."

Reg came by and squeezed her shoulders. "She's getting used to it anyway."

"How are all those mavericks doing?"

"Aw, we have the damnedest set of calves.

You'll have to see them. Of course, I need some Hereford bulls to breed them back to. But we have a calf crop and their mommas never missed a bite this past winter. We never got to plant any alfalfa. Guess I better get Hampt up here to do that, huh?"

"Tom said he beat him at it, and that's doing something. 'Course we think he prayed over it every day it was coming up."

"If that's what it takes, this crew can do the job," Reg said. "They all agreed. Now tell us about Rancho Diablo. JD wrote me some things."

"Big, hot, and dry. The squatters have three hundred mother cows on it, but they didn't make a dent in it."

"You getting it straightened out?" Reg asked.

"Law grinds slow, but I figure we're closer by the day. I have a good lawyer in Tucson. There are over forty-eight thousand deeded acres in the place. By the way, Bo bought about ten homesteads around here that were deeded to join this place."

"Where are they?" Lucie asked, pushing in to pour coffee.

"Jesus, the papers are in my saddlebags. If you'll go get them, we can go over them. Bo also has about that many he bought over by the Windmill Ranch. That usually means

103

there's a well and cabin. We'll have to see what they are."

"Back to Diablo," Reg said. "What needs to be done?"

"More water developed, like all these places. Headquarters built and get going. We do have some squatters dumped on us."

"What?" Lucie asked.

He told them about the women and children abandoned on the ranch. They shook their heads, and Willy arrived back from his heifer search to shake hands.

"She had a big bull calf," he said proudly. "Doing great. Sure good to meet you at last, sir."

Chet smiled at him. "Me, too."

Jesus arrived with the deed copies and descriptions.

"Lucie," Reg asked, "you recall the place we called Cornfield, for the old stalks there?" At her nod, he said, "Yes, well we own it now."

"There's squatters on this one," Haze said. "Reg, that's north of Hatter's Hill."

Reg nodded. "They look like a rag-tag army, too."

"Didn't you and him have words?" Lucie asked with a knowing grin.

"Yeah, he had a hide nailed on a shed that I recognized. Told him not to eat any more of our branded stock or I'd brand his backside. He'll be packed and gone tomorrow."

"What was his name?" she asked, refilling cups.

"Crowley, Jasper Crowley. Said he was buying the place."

"Maybe we need to be there at daybreak, like the Texas Rangers did?" Chet asked.

"Half-asleep, you ain't got half the wits to put up a fight," Cole agreed. "It damn sure worked down on the border for the Force."

"We can be there then," Reg said with a laugh. "Guys, we've got help this time."

"We've had a few others tried to set roots here," Lucie said. "They finally went on to California."

The next morning when they rode into the yard, dawn was a soft flannel glow over their shoulders. They came in from three sides with their rifles balanced on their horns. A rooster crowed at the set of dark buildings and pens.

Chet fired his gun in the air and the shot woke up hogs, dogs, and a cow. "Jasper Crowley, this is Chet Byrnes. Get up and get out here. Any show of a weapon and you're dead. Hear me?"

"Yeah, I hear, whoever you are." He struggled to get his last galluses up and sleepy-eyed, plus barefooted, stood on the porch and eyed the posse. "What are you boys up to?"

"This land is Byrnes's land. You're trespassing. I want you and yours out of here in twenty-four hours. If this place is burned or damaged, or the well soured, we will be on your trail and hang you. Keep moving at least west of Hackberry. We have no qualms about hanging you, either — remember that."

"I savvy. I'll be gone."

"For your life and safety, I suggest you do just as I've instructed. We're through here for the day, boys. Let's ride."

Reg booted his big horse in close. "I'm still learning, Uncle Chet. I'd never have guessed anyone would do that to a place — damage it."

"They will. Don't ever cut them any slack."

Reg looked back. "Where do you reckon he'll go?"

"West, and look for another empty den."

Chet and his crew found three more of the new places. All had dug wells with water in them and would make good windmill with tank sites. On the back of old calendars, Chet gave any finders notice that this was the property of the Quarter Circle Z

Ranch and to treat it as such. It was not for sale or squatting, and to see Reg Byrnes at the ranch headquarters for more information. He left that notice nailed up at each place, satisfied that Reg would have some more water sites before fall.

"Slap a windmill on them and build some water holding tanks below it and you will have some good watering places to spread your cattle out more," he told Reg.

"I'm sure impressed. Reckon Raphael can find us some tank builders to work this summer?"

"I bet he has some on the way up here now," Chet teased. "We can get some going. I'm certain John at the blacksmith shop can make the mills or assemble them. Robert Brown can get the timbers cut. We should be in the business. So far, you need four."

He turned to the young man behind them. "Willy, you cut across country and look-see if that Crowley is gone. Don't go close. If he's gone, fine, just head back for the ranch to meet us there for supper. If he ain't left, you just come on in. We'll settle with him in the morning."

"I savvy, sir." He left in a lope.

"That boy's a hand," Reg said. "He'll get it right."

"That's why I sent him. I saw that yesterday when he reported on the heifer."

Lucie had a big roast cooked for them and she was all ears to their reports and descriptions of the new places.

"Four windmills, so far. He says John can build them at the Verde Ranch and we'll haul them there and set them up. Then we'll get a crew of Mexican masons to build holding tanks."

"Wow, that will really help spread the cattle out, won't it?"

Chet agreed. "That damn Bo to the rescue, huh?"

"Oh, yeah. How's he doing since he lost his wife?"

"I think he's quieter. He misses her badly."

"He hasn't gone back to drinking, has he?"

"No, he's over that and damn busy working on his business."

"Good. You've turned so many lives around in the building of this ranch. I can hardly believe it. Like Hampt becoming the hay expert. I never believed he'd do that," said Lucie.

"Or how he got May to sing?"

"That, too. I love her voice. Or stiff-neck Sarge running off with Susie and making such a success of the outfit's cattle-selling business. You and Marge didn't shock me much after the three of us searched out this ranch. But you've sure been busy besides."

He hugged her. "You and Reg are part of it."

"Oh, heavens, yes. It's been fun, too."

Willy reported Crowley was gone before supper that evening. Two of the places they looked at later had doubtful wells, but eight were marked for windmills and tanks. Reg's cattle looked good, but he needed a dozen breeding-age British bulls.

Chet and his two men left for home the day after, seeing everything was going great. Lucie had plenty of help coming for the baby, and she kissed his cheek. "Pray for us."

"I can do that, Lucie."

"We'll be fine then."

He thought the same and swung on his horse. Reg had some local boys to hay for him that summer. So that was settled — he and Jesus, and Cole, were headed home again.

His wife would be grateful.

CHAPTER 7

Chet, Cole, and Jesus stopped over at the Verde Ranch. Susie fed the men' and put them up for the night. Sarge, as usual, was gone on a drive to Navajo Land and he wanted her close to help if and when she went into labor — so her plan to camp at the Windmill in a tent wasn't taken serious.

The next morning, Tom came by and Chet sent for John to talk windmills with them. John, his chief mechanic, arrived in the living room looking smiley faced.

"What do you fellows need now?"

"Windmills to pump some water. We have some homesteads we bought with already dug wells. Some are pretty strong. What do we need to put up windmills on them?" Chet asked John.

"We'd have to order the mechanical parts. Takes me too long to make them, and I don't have the milling machinery to do it. Then we'd have to get the lumber cut and buy some pipe, connectors, and faucets. When we had them set, then about all we'd need is water in the well and wind."

"Let's go to pricing everything. I'd like several set up this summer, especially up at Reg's. He needs the water to scatter his cattle to other grazing."

John nodded. "It may be too late for this year, but we can try to get some up. Sarge has two, I think. I sent two men up there to get them running this spring."

Susie poured coffee for them. "Last I heard, he said they were running good."

"That guy who sold you that place over there," John said. "He makes them."

Chet recalled Joseph McQuire and where he had moved outside of Preskitt. "I'll go see McQuire. You give Tom the lumber dimensions they need and he can get it ordered for six of them to start."

"First you make your own barbwire, now windmills. What comes next?" Susie asked, and laughed like in the old days when she was in on all of Chet's plans.

"A self-propelled hay stacker," Tom teased.

They all laughed. Chet thanked her and told everyone how he appreciated their efforts. "It's going great. Time the railroad gets here, we'll be ready for them to ship our cattle to market."

"Those tracks ain't left Kansas yet," Cole said, and shook his head. That was the truth of it.

They were back to the top place by mid-afternoon. Cole asked for his plans, to be certain it was alright for him to head for his bride in town. Chet excused him, and he and Jesus shared a grin. Marge came out on the back porch to meet him and kissed him.

"How is Adam?" Chet asked.

"Fine, he's a great baby. I don't have enough milk for him, but Raphael is getting a few milk goats to try on him. I didn't know goats give different kinds of milk from what they eat, but I'm learning. He and Monica say we can find the right nanny."

Monica had a sliced roast beef sandwich on sourdough fixed for him. He sat down, and while he ate he told them all about Reg and Lucie and the plans for the windmill setups on the homesteads he'd bought.

"More expansion," Marge said. "You need three of you. One to run the Force down south, one to help your neighbors get out of the hot grease they fall into, and a third one can oversee the ranches."

"We're holding our own."

She hugged his neck. "I know, but it gets

harder. You're going to try JD on that desert place he calls Diablo?"

"That's my plan."

"You know he is the least dependable one in this whole lot?"

"He's also tough as rawhide and it will take some men like that to run that ranch."

"Your problem, not mine."

"He's made a big turn riding with the Force. I'm betting he makes it."

"Ranches from hell to breakfast. Next windmills. You are a winner, my dear husband, but it will have to stop someday."

"When I am old and gray."

"Your dad wasn't this expansive, was he?"

"No, but my grandfather was. He brought all the family down from Arkansas to build that ranch before the Texas Revolution. Later, my dad lost his mind from searching for the twins and the other boy we lost to the Comanche. Some Texas Rangers brought him back home, but he was delirious. He never got over it. My mother's mind went, too, over their loss. As a teenager, I had to take charge and run the ranch."

"Oh, I know you enjoy this entire thing. I didn't expect a stay-at-home husband."

"Good," he said before taking another bite.

"Save some time for Adam and me."

"I will. I'm going to go see McQuire tomorrow and get this windmill deal going if I can."

"Isn't he kind of odd?" Marge asked.

"I thought so, but great inventors are sometimes like that."

They both laughed.

The next morning, he and Jesus found the tall man in his shop. McQuire waved at them and kept working on a wind vane, soldering on the blades.

"I'll be done here in a few minutes."

"Don't worry, we have all day."

"Good. I understand you're sure busy selling cattle to the Navajos."

"That's why I bought your ranch."

"I'm glad. My windmill business is going good here and getting better."

"What do you get for the hardware for a mill?"

"How many?"

"Six mills to start."

"If I can get the metal, fifty dollars apiece."

"I want six of them."

"I have material to build two. I'd need an advance to order more material. A hundred-dollar advance, say, for the six."

"Order the material. I'll get you the money."

114

"Sounds good. Who will assemble it?"

"I have a blacksmith at the Verde River Ranch. He's good."

"Have him come up here for a day and I can show him how to assemble it."

"I'll arrange that."

They left McQuire's place with Chet feeling the windmill operation might even work some that summer. He needed to keep finding ways to ranch better.

When he reached home, a telegram from his lawyer waited.

CHET
A GRAND JURY IS GOING TO INVESTIGATE THE LAND FRAUD. A NEW PROSECUTOR HAS BEEN APPOINTED TO HEAD THIS. I BELIEVE YOUR PRESSURE HELPED GET THIS GOING. I WILL KEEP YOU INFORMED.
RUSSELL

He sent word to his lawmen. They were going back to Tubac and try to wind up the Force's efforts. So as not to forewarn the elements that supported the border outlaws, they'd start back, two at a time, the next Sunday.

"What about the squatter women down

there?" Jesus asked.

"They need to be taken back to Nogales."

"Who'll do that?"

"I'll have to hire someone to do it."

Jesus nodded.

When he went back to that country, he had to resolve that issue. He also had to find Masters — his attempts to kill him needed answered. He didn't forget people who were out to do that. And he'd made it a part of his own plans to take care of them.

In a week, Chet and the crew were back at Tubac and the Morales Ranch. Horses shod and everything gone over that they'd need in pursuit of any outlaws, like packsaddles, cinches, breast straps, and holsters, as well as weapons cleaned and oiled. No detail was too small to overlook.

When he went by his office in Tucson to return to the job, Blevins handed him a thick stack of reported crimes that had happened during his break.

Later, at the camp meeting, Ortega told him about a man who would move the women and children squatters, and take them to a place he'd reserved for them near Nogales.

"How much will he charge?"

"He says three hundred dollars."

"Plenty big price. Would he treat them nice?"

"I think so."

"You and Jesus go down and rent them the place at Nogales for six months. After that, they'll be on their own. Get him lined up to move them. Two of you will need to go along, to be sure they're treated humanely."

"Jesus can be in charge of that team," Roamer said. "He knows them better than any of us."

"Send my brother Bronco help him," Ortega said. "He knows, too. While you were gone, he's been feeding them."

"Good, we'll have that settled." That issue was about to be over, but he wondered about Masters and his boss. That needed to be straightened out, and development of the new ranch started.

He and JD spent two hours by themselves that morning, talking about the big Diablo Ranch.

"I doubt we can run straight British beef on that place," Chet said.

"It'll take a part-longhorn cow to thrive on the Diablo," JD agreed.

"Cross cattle won't be a shame, but a straight British cow would be a mistake in the heat down here, and some dry years will sure test them."

"I'd wondered. Since we came down here, I've seen a lot of these Mexican cattle in the brush. We could do that — cull the sorry ones and build our own breed."

"Yes. Things we'll learn as we grow."

"Think we can find some artesian wells?" JD asked.

"I do. They show up all over. No reason for us not to find some, but they cost money to drill, too."

JD nodded. "Can I hire Ortega as my foreman?"

"I think he'd be a good choice. I don't want you two fighting. You and him will have to give and take on decisions."

"I think I understand; I've watched you all the time."

"Now, how much have you and your wife talked about living on the Diablo? It gets damn hot down there." He wanted to have a clear understanding with JD and his wife.

"I told her there was room to grow down there, and that I'd build her a nice home and we'd have a good life."

"You're convinced you two will make it down there?"

"Yes. We aren't kids. Face to face, we made rules and they include that neither of us is right. So far, we've seen other things we needed to include. I feel it's a forever arrangement."

"This ranch is a big investment for all of us. I think it'll be a good one, but it will take everyone's dedication to get it there."

"I remember when you asked if I could lay adobe bricks. And I can, if we need to."

"If you see a wreck coming — let me know."

"I won't walk away on you."

"Good. The squatters will soon not be our worry and we can figure out what Buster and his crew are up to."

"When will that be?"

"Soon. I expect a letter from Russell any day that we can move in."

"Will they sell us their cattle?"

"I don't know. We can learn that when it happens."

"I guess we will, huh? You won't regret putting me in charge."

"I don't expect to."

They shook hands.

A telegram from Blevins came after lunch.

CHET
A RANCHER SLOAN HIGGINS
SOUTH OF TOMBSTONE ROBBED
AND HIS WIFE BURNETT HAS
BEEN TAKEN HOSTAGE FOR

MORE MONEY. SEE WHAT YOU CAN DO. BLEVINS

Chet knew Higgins. He sent Roamer and Cole over there to check on it. They were to wire him if they needed help. He cautioned them not to fall into any traps. Holding the man's wife could be bait to coax them into one. No telling who was behind it, but they needed to be extra careful.

"If we see a trap, we'll back off and wait for backup," Roamer promised.

"I don't need you guys shot up."

"We'll be more careful," his man promised.

The three rode off the next morning. Chet met the contractor who was moving the women to Nogales. Pueblo Sanchez was a very thorough man and he took this move serious. He planned to take three wagons to deliver them to the place Chet had arranged for them at the border.

"It may take three days to get them down there."

"Speed is not important. Just move them smoothly."

"I can hardly believe you have fed them this long."

"They were desperate when we discovered them. I couldn't let them starve."

"Señor, I will be careful moving them."

"Good."

That settled, he sent Jesus to Nogales to rent the place. JD was appointed as Chet's guard for the day. Shawn was shoeing the last of the horses that needed it, and JD helped him. Chet worked on his expense book. Maria brought them lunch and stayed to talk. "How is your son?"

"Fine, when I left him."

"I bet she's glad he is here."

"Yes, her past experiences had her real worried. But it went very well."

"I'm glad it did. Tell her I want to meet her someday. I didn't meet her when she came to Tombstone to take care of you."

"You two would enjoy each other," Chet said.

"Good, I will look forward to meeting her."

"I'm sure, in time, she'll want to see the new ranch. I'll make it a point to introduce you to her then."

Maria smiled. "I never thought I would be glad there were outlaws down here. But if there had been no outlaws, we would never have met you and your family."

"Can't tell, some things are mysterious. But, yes, we did meet because of outlaws."

She leaned over the table and kissed his

forehead. *"Gracias, mi amigo."*

He almost laughed. Good woman.

Things were at last under way to ship those abandoned women and children to Nogales. When that was finished, he was ready to ride up and confront Masters about his plot to have him murdered. He'd turned that over in his mind a hundred times.

Cole came back and reported that the outlaws had gone to Mexico with the rancher's wife. Standing under the tent, he took a sip of coffee. "All the information we could get was they were staying around the village of Los Palmas."

"That's a little farther into Mexico than that saloon was down on the border," Chet reminded them.

"We hate for them to get away with this kidnapping," Cole said.

"I agree. Jesus is the man we need to go with us. He's gone to rent a place down at Nogales and then take the squatters down there."

"Ortega can do our Mexican business. They want you to meet them down there at El Conejo. I said I'd show you the way and we could case these bandits' place and see how to get her out."

"That woman's safety comes first. We

can't go blazing in there and get her hurt or killed."

"I figure we can handle that," said Cole.

"The *Federales* won't appreciate us acting like we're lawmen down there."

"Well, do I ride back and tell them we can't do it?"

"Cole, I can hang up this badge. We'll leave Juan in charge. JD, Shawn, you, and I will split up, then each take a packhorse and head south to arrive there separately to get less notice."

"Good." Cole drank some of his coffee. "This is lots better than the piss I've been drinking."

"That's why Mexicans drink red wine," Chet teased him.

"What's happening?" JD asked as he joined them.

"We're packing two horses and splitting up to meet down in Mexico and see if we can get that rancher's wife away from those bandits. You can ride with me."

"I better go tell Shawn. What about Jesus?"

"He's renting a place at Nogales for the squatters."

"I know that. Is Bronc coming back today? He would be good to take, too. Jose can watch the ranch and our things."

Marie came on the run, having discovered Cole had ridden in.

Chet leaned back on the bench and asked her, "Is Bronc coming home today?"

"*Si.* He will be home."

"Good, he can go with us. We're going to Mexico. The outlaws that have the rancher's wife are down there. Ortega and Roamer are spotting them. We're going to split up and join up with them down there."

"My brother-in-law Juan and I can handle this place," Maria said.

"Good. Jesus is in Nogales. When he gets back, tell him to move those squatters, but for him to be careful. I don't know how long we'll be down there."

"*Si,* I can do that."

"You ladies be careful. We have made enemies over our arrests and curbing the lawlessness."

Marie reassured him. "We will be fine."

"Good, just so nothing goes wrong. We'll pack for tomorrow."

She went back to her *casa,* and everyone else went to work. He wrote Marge a long letter and set it out for someone to take to Tubac and post when they went for food and mail.

Mexico could prove to be a challenge, but the two brothers knew how to get around down there. When they found the rancher's wife, this had to be another lightning raid and a quick escape. He had no idea of the strength of the bandits, either, but maybe by the time they reached the area his men would have information about the gang and their whereabouts.

They left before dawn, and as afternoon slipped away they faded into Mexico. The border wasn't guarded except at the road points like Nogales and the other places where they collected fees for import or export of goods. The trail they took paralleled the Santa Cruz River, and they split up at the border. Chet and Cole went one way, Bronc, JD, and Shawn went another, to meet up later near the kidnappers' location.

They avoided towns and camped in the desert at night. Cole talked some about his wife, Valerie.

"I'm sure happy I married her. She's a great gal. You know, I worried a lot about whether she'd put up with my job and me. And she's real careful what she spends, for some day we want a ranch of our own. These rewards we've been earning may help buy it one day."

"They could," Chet said. "When I met her in Tombstone and sent her to Preskitt, I knew she was alright."

"Yes, she talks about that a lot. How she served you stew, and you didn't know her, but went out on a limb to help anyway. That really impressed her."

"There are right and wrong ways in this world. You do them right, they usually end up good."

"You've picked some good ones. Your place in Texas would never have been this big, would it?"

"In a lot of ways, I chose the right thing to do. I had money to expand there, too. But with the circumstances I was under, I couldn't risk doing it."

"You saw some things here no one else saw. Buying a ranch being run by a crooked, tough foreman?" Cole shook his head as if in disbelief.

"Yes, it was. But I saw it as a large ranch astraddle a river in Arizona. It had to be a bargain."

"I know the rest of that story. According to Hampt, it was a tough one to take."

"I look back and think it was only a page in my life. The worse page was when I started home and the stage robbers killed my nephew, Heck. I guess those kind of things drove me to become a lawman and to try to end the outlaw reign in this country. Someone had to care."

"That was before you married Marge. Your wife helped you through that time?" Cole reined his horse up and looked at all the tall tube parts of the Mexican cousin to the saguaros standing six feet tall. "We take the right-hand trail here."

Chet nodded. "Yes, and I had an intended woman in Texas, but she couldn't leave there because of her parents' health. But, Marge, bless her soul, got me through it and understood my problems. And she waited, too, with no promise of anything. For all she knew, I could have come back with a wife."

"I laughed about how she went around and paid all your bills. She was set on having you."

"At first, it made me mad. But the poor girl had a case on me, and with all her money and schooling she picked me." He turned in the saddle and checked their back trail as they rose higher on the side of a small range of mountains. No rising dust, no sign of anyone on their back trail, so he turned back and shook the saddle horn. It was good to have the roan gelding under him — a great mountain horse.

"Then you married her." He coaxed Chet into telling more of his past, parts that hap-

127

pened before Cole joined the outfit.

"Bo found this tract of land for sale on top the rim and I wanted to go see it. So, since Marge was willing to traipse around with me, I planned to ask her to go. My sister, Susie, told me Marge was unmarried and had been to a finishing school, and that she wouldn't go."

Cole was laughing by then. "She would have gone?"

"Hell, yes. She said she would, but my conscience bothered me. The stigma of folks finding out she went, regardless of how proper we were, would have been bad. So I asked her to marry me. We got married, and Sarge's cook, Victor, went along and we found Reg's wife, Lucie, who was our guide."

Cole shook his head. "You fell into a pile of shit and came out like a rose." He went on laughing. "I only met Lucie a time or two, but she's a swell person."

"Neatest lady I ever met. And she can out rope the two of us. That smile never fades and she laughs a lot. Just what Reg needed."

They caught up with a wood train, so Cole reined up. Several burros loaded with bundled sticks on their backs filled the entire trail through the cactus and brush. The single man in charge made the animals all get over to the side of the pathway, took off his *sombrero,* and bowed.

"*Gracias, mi amigo,*" Chet said, and tossed a silver dollar in his *sombrero.*

"Oh, patron, you are too generous. *Gracias.*" His words were in Spanish, and with a big smile across his brown face, he bowed again.

Chet waved at him and then they led the packhorse past the line of already hipshot burros.

Cole shook his head at his generosity. "That was more money than his sticks will bring him."

Chet agreed.

"Tell me about Reg's first wife."

"Juanita came to us to help Susie keep the big house and fix meals. She was a beautiful young woman. I was ready to leave, and an older couple wanted someone to run their ranch, take care of them, and when they died the ranch would be his. Reg married Juanita and they stayed to run that ranch."

"Do you think your enemies killed her?"

"He never mentioned it. I never asked."

"It must have been real tough for him. I can only imagine how hard it would be on me if I lost Valerie. What was the worst part for you back there?"

"The final blow for me was one cold Texas morning when I was checking cattle on the far south end and three of them tried to ambush me. It was in some tall cedars and I did lots of scrambling, but when I left there they were buzzard bait and I was unscathed.

"I see why you left."

"Exactly." The two of them were on the rise by then and fixing to drop off into more desert, but cottonwoods lined the far valley.

"If you don't give them all away, next year, you'll have a Barbarossa colt to ride," said Cole.

"I think Bonnie was well worth two of them. I bet JD thinks so."

"I think from being around him, he appreciates her a whole lot. I wouldn't trade her for my wife, but she's a swell person. You traded some big patron down here in Mexico a Barbarossa for her, didn't you?"

"Hell, we couldn't whip him and I wasn't certain she was even at his ranch. He sent her to us and his men came later and got the horses. It was a good swap."

"Reckon we can do that good down here for this woman?"

"When I left our camp at Tubac two days ago, I had my mind set to bring her home safe and sound."

"Me, too," Cole said, and they went off the hillside trail for the spread-out country below them.

That evening, they found Roamer and Ortega's camp at a small rancher's place. His name was Diego Vargas, and his much younger pregnant wife, Vye, welcomed them with a smile. They put their horses in a pole corral. There was a stack of straw hay that, no doubt, Roamer had purchased to feed the Force's animals when they all got there. Ortega mounted up and left to meet the others and bring them there.

"How have you been?" Roamer asked Chet as they took seats on some crates for chairs under a canvas shade. He was whittling and cutting on some cedar-like wood.

"I've been fine. Who are these bandits?"

"Renaldo Montoya is the leader. He was once a *Federales* officer, who was busted and court-martialed on charges of illegal business. He was sent to prison, escaped, and runs his gang from up here, which is a kind of a no man's land."

"Are these people in any danger for helping us?"

"Some, but they know the risk. Diego wishes him taken down. I told him our job was to recover the woman he kidnapped and get her alive and unharmed. I know that he'd like to have Montoya eliminated — killed off."

"We didn't come here to do that."

"He knows that, but he's hoping Montoya gets caught in some crossfire."

"Where are they holding her?"

"He has a ranch fortress in the hills. From things we learned from snitches, we're sure she's being held there. They have a couple of Gatling guns and a cannon or two. Several of their men were once soldiers and they have a lot of military arms and ammo," said Roamer.

"Single-shot rifles?"

"Yeah, he stole them from the Army."

"A bucket of melted grease and a pail of sand will stop those Gatling guns."

Roamer frowned at him.

"A friend of mine who was in the war served on a gun crew. He said the damn things jammed if you pulled them down dusty roads all day."

In disbelief, Roamer dropped his head and shook it. "I thought they were untouchable."

"I know we haven't got close enough so far to dust them, but we need to think about that. Something they count on for defense of their fort that won't work could deal them a death blow."

Roamer whittled some more. "When this

132

job is over and whenever you go back to ranching, will Marshal Blevins still want this Force of yours down here?"

"I suppose so. Why?"

He threw his stick away, folded his jack-knife, and nodded. "I'd start looking for a place down here. Told my wife that if I could get this job, we'd live down here. It ain't as nice as Preskitt, but she agreed, and I won't ever satisfy Simms. So if you decide to go back to ranching, I'd like your job."

"I'd miss having you help me at home."

"I know, and I'd miss you. But I have four kids, more coming, and I sure need a good job."

"I'll talk to Blevins and I believe he'll want you."

"Chet, you've been a real friend since we fought Ryan off that Verde Ranch."

"It's been a two-way trail. What's the layout for this fort?"

"Head on, impossible. I mentioned the guns, but I think we can slip in the back way and surprise them. Grab her, I hope, and get the hell out before they get organized."

"We need a detailed map and it needs to be accurate."

"There's a man coming tonight that can do that. His name is Fred. I don't know enough Spanish, but Ortega can translate for us. He's worked inside there. I have a map made of the fort and how to get in. But this guy knows the real guts of the place." Roamer pushed his hat back on his head.

Chet thanked him. He was on a good track.

Later, the others arrived. JD came and shook Roamer's and Chet's hands.

"Have a good trip?" Chet asked JD.

"Hot one. No one paid us any attention that I could tell."

"Good, Roamer has a man coming to give us more details on the place where they're holding her. This *generale*'s fort is going to be tough to take. But Ortega heard he likes young *putas* and frequents such places. He thinks we might be able to grab him there and get her back in exchange."

"Not a bad idea," said JD.

Ortega nodded. "There were only two privates guarding his carriage when he went into one of those places. But we were not ready yet to move on him."

"He goes there often?"

"Quite often," Ortega said. "But sometimes he has six guards. We need to catch him with fewer than that."

"Both of you have some great ideas. I

134

think Vye has supper coming. She cooked two goats today, I understand."

"She's good at cooking things," Roamer said.

His crew was all there. They needed a workable plan and to execute it swiftly. He turned his attention to her food. Vye was a great cook and they had plenty to eat. Later, the small man named Fred arrived and he drew plans of the fort for them. He pointed out the barracks where the men lived, their mess hall, the big house that Montoya lived in, the arsenal, and the horse pens. He said some men with *riatas* tossed on the posts could rip them down, drive the horses up the canyon behind and out into the desert, leaving Montoya's army afoot.

"How many men does he have?" Chet asked Ortega, and he translated it as twenty-five, and all trained soldiers.

That was sobering for Chet. "Let's try to catch him at the whorehouse. Then we can go to plan B."

He thanked the man through Ortega and paid him ten *pesos*. The man acted very appreciative for the money.

"Can we check and see if he's there this evening?" Chet asked.

"It's not far. We waited, knowing you were coming. Is that what we should do? Kidnap

135

him?" Roamer looked grim. "They might try to get him back."

Chet shook his head. "They don't want his corpse. They'll know we mean business."

"Saddle up," Roamer said. He shook his head. "I see lots of repercussions. Ain't that the word?"

"It's a good one and we may have them. We aren't the law here, but we have to think like outlaws." Chet clapped him on the shoulder. All he knew was that this plan, if it worked, beat an attack on a military base.

They rode single file and Ortega went ahead when they drew close. He came back in a short while. "He's in there. I counted two guards at the coach. Bronc and I can take them down, then you close in. We don't make a big ruckus, they won't know what's happening. There's a back door."

"JD and Cole, take it. Remember, we need him alive, but bust his head if he gets tough. Alright?"

The men were ready.

"I'll show you the back way," Ortega said as he and his brother prepared to go in and take out the guards.

In the darkness, Chet stood on his toes and tried to see the building that served as a whorehouse. No red lamp anyway. There were lights on inside and he could see the top of the coach parked before it.

"When we get in, there may be some bouncers inside the place." Roamer stood beside him.

"We just need those guards took out, and then take the place," Chet said.

Shawn laughed softly. "Be my first time in a house of ill repute, and for all the wrong reasons."

"You'll get an education on this job," Chet said. "Have eyes in the back of your head. If we get into a fight, cover our backs."

"I can do that, sir."

"Last resort, shoot the sumbitch."

"I will, sir."

"Let's go."

Ortega was coming back. He waved for them. "Bronc is tying and gagging the guards. They were only boys. JD and Cole should be in back. Should we charge the front door and demand to know where he is?"

"Go."

Guns in hand, they crossed the yard and Ortega hurried ahead. Nothing moved. Bronc joined them. They covered the ground to the door; Ortega tried the latch and the door opened, then he was inside. There were some screams of fright, but he told the women to be quiet. When Chet entered the parlor, only some scanty dressed young girls looked bug eyed at them.

"Watch them," Chet said, leaving Shawn in charge. A little red-faced, he made them stand at the wall. The other members headed down the hall, where Ortega had an older woman by the arm talking to her in Spanish, obviously demanding she take him to the room.

With a boot, he smashed the door open, fired a shot, and ordered Montoya not to try for his gun again. The room was full of gun smoke, and Roamer moved to handcuff the buck-naked outlaw. A naked girl stood against the wall, screaming. Bronco silenced her and shoved clothes at her. In Spanish, he told her to get dressed.

Chet told Montoya to sit on the bed. They warned him if he made any move, they'd carry him out feet first.

The grim-faced big man had a killing look on his face. "What do you want?"

"The woman you hold and a pass to get out of Mexico."

"I'll have you all killed on an ant hill."

"You may not live to see sunrise, so quit your threats. We're as tough as you, and sitting here bare-assed, you'll be lucky if we don't castrate you."

"You won't dare."

"Keep talking. These men are cowboys. They can do it faster than you can blink. Now, how do we get word to your people to bring her out to us?"

"She will die in there."

Chet grabbed him by the hair and jerked his face close to his. "You have two minutes to decide. After that, I'm turning a couple of guys loose on you that will make you cry."

"Alright, alright. I can send my *Segundo* a letter."

JD and Cole had joined them, and they dragged Montoya out of the smoky room. The whore and the woman who ran the place brought his clothes and then hurried away to the front. JD and Cole marched him into an office and watched him close as he dressed.

A bull-chested man with a hairy chest, he looked hard at the blank page Chet placed in front of him. They undid his right hand and held a cocked pistol to his head. Chet told him to write for his men to bring the rancher's wife out in exchange for him. To bring her out, and with no strings attached. To have her on a sound horse that did not buck. Not to follow them and that he would be turned loose at the border. Any action to charge them and Montoya would die instantly.

"Tell them at ten o'clock tomorrow she is to ride out and one of our men will meet her. No tricks from there to the border," Chet told him.

He took Ortega aside. "Can you read his message?"

"Oh, *si.*"

"He may write some instructions for them."

"I know. I can read it."

Finally Montoya said, "There it is."

Ortega read each word. When he neared the end of the note, he translated the outlaw's words out loud. "Don't do anything foolish that will upset these *gringos.* I am sure they will kill me."

"We damn sure will." Chet nodded toward Ortega. "How do we deliver it?"

"I will take a white flag and take it to his underman named Valdez."

Chet considered the man's offer. "I don't want you shot."

"Put him on a horse on the hill behind me under a rifle barrel. They won't do anything but obey us."

"Then tell them to bring her out on a good horse. We need to be ready to move right away," Chet said. "Load the packhorses and meet us over there at dawn."

JD spoke up. "Shawn, Cole, and I will get

our things and meet you. Cole knows where it is."

"Good, do that. We won't get much sleep, but we need to be on the move." Chet was anxious, knowing Montoya's bunch might make quick plans to stop them. Lots of loose ends. Was the rancher's wife tough enough to stand the ride? He had no idea.

"You know anything about her?" he asked Roamer who had spoken to her husband.

"Her name is Burnett Higgins, but you already know that. She's twenty-eight. Much younger than her man. She's his second wife. They described her as five-six, medium build, brown hair."

"No picture?" Chet asked.

"Why?"

"What if they send us another woman?"

"Hell, Chet, I never thought of it."

"I hope they don't. Just thought of it."

Roamer shook his head. "Now when she comes out, I am going to be jumpy. I hope it's her."

They rode out under the stars. They had Montoya on Shawn's horse, and he rode back double with the others to get ready to leave when they got her. Chet had given JD money to buy a horse and saddle for Montoya when they came back. Ortega was sure the man would sell them a good mount. The two bound-up guards were made to ride double on a coach horse, so they couldn't go warn the gang.

Chet told them to be careful and join them as quick as they could. When they neared the outlaw's camp, they held back from being observed. The three prisoners seated on the ground were guarded and all in chains, and in leg irons that only let them take small steps, so they couldn't get away.

The two Morales brothers went to sleep, while Roamer and Chet sat guard. The two soldiers slept, but Montoya grumbled the whole time and threatened them.

"How did you *gringos* get down here? You have no authority in Mexico."

"We're bounty hunters," Chet said. "We have no badges."

"Oh, shit, you are a big liar. Everyone in Mexico knows about your Force."

"The only people who know about us are outlaws. The honest people appreciate us. Why kidnap her?"

"Her husband has money."

Chet shook his head. "He's a rancher. They don't have money."

"He found a fortune in gold dust."

"Where?"

"There was a man coming back to Mexico with lots of gold dust. He got snake bit in the desert, on the border we think, and died. His burros wandered around. Her man found them and the gold. He kept it."

"Could anyone prove it?"

Montoya shrugged. "We learned he was selling small amounts of gold he said that he panned."

"He might have panned it."

"No, he had the gold that belonged to that man who died from snake bite."

"How did you find that out?"

"I have my ways."

"How did you know?"

Montoya didn't answer him.

It was getting close to dawn. When he saw Chet was still awake enough to watch them, Roamer fell asleep. When Chet shook him, he jerked awake.

"Wake up the others. It must be the rest of our outfit I hear coming."

"You okay?" Roamer asked.

"Tired, but geared up to get her back."

Roamer nodded, stood up, and stretched. "I guess we are approaching time to give them his note."

"I have food for everyone," Shawn said. He had a cloth sack full of burritos and handed them out to everyone, including the prisoners.

"Thanks," Chet said. "Eat your food and

then we'll start on this exchange."

"I am surprised they have not sent anyone out to look for him," Ortega said between bites.

"Does he usually go home?"

"Yes, we have tracked him going home several nights, usually about midnight."

"They may figure he's a big boy now."

The crew laughed at Chet's comment. Montoya pouted.

Ortega used a small pole for a flagpole with a white sheet tied to it. They put Montoya on his horse chained to the saddle and staked the horse so the bandits could see him. Ortega began his ride downhill holding the flag. The Force members crouched down with their rifles.

Chet noted a buzzard or two circling as if checking out their business there. Good or bad, they were there anyway. He heard someone shout and saw him run for help. Discovery one. That was what he called it. There were soon several bandits out in front of the barricades, pointing and scoping their man on the horse.

Ortega stopped his descent about where Chet felt was far enough. A man on a big dark horse galloped out to meet him.

"If he goes for a gun, shoot him," he told his riflemen down the line.

They knew what to do. The next few minutes could be critical for Ortega's life. But they knew he had their leader and his life was at stake, too. This thing would either blow up or work.

The man took the paper and whirled his horse around, knowing he was under many gun barrels and they could cut him down in an instant. After some time, while Montoya's men probably passed the letter around, the same man returned.

Bronc heard what he said to his brother. "They are going after the woman. It will take time to saddle a horse and send her out."

"Too smooth," JD said, nodding in approval at their reaction.

Chet agreed. "We still have twenty-four hours of hard riding to make the border. They'll follow us, and we can't make one mistake. It could be the longest day of our life. Bar none."

The men on the line agreed as Ortega returned.

"I don't know who was the worst scared," Ortega said, "him or me."

"You did good. I'm going to nap a short time, while they get her. Wake me if anything happens."

"We will."

Chet was asleep for no time when they shook him.

"There is a woman on a horse coming up here."

Chet scrambled up, found his hat, and stretched. She dismounted and he saw she fit the description. He walked out and asked, "Are you Burnett Higgins?"

He thought at first she'd faint. "Thank God. Did my husband send you?"

"Yes, ma'am. He asked for our help."

She almost fell into his arms. "I'm sorry, but it has been a bad few weeks. I didn't think anyone was coming to save me."

He straightened her up. "We have Montoya as an insurance policy to the border. But it will be a hard twenty-four-hour ride. Can you make it?"

"Oh, I'm sorry. I'm going to cry. Hold me, please, until my heart stops fluttering."

He could feel her trembling in his arms. The hot sun on his back, he fetched out a handkerchief for her to use. She thanked him and moved back. A lovely woman who'd no doubt waded through hell for a while.

"Are you strong enough to make this ride?"

"Oh, yes." She looked around for the first time, discovering his team. "God bless you

146

all. I could ride to Hades and back with you and these men."

"I'll introduce you to everyone. That's JD Byrnes, my nephew, and that's Cole Emerson. No matter what happens, they'll get you out of harm's way. Listen to them. Obey them. They are your guards. The rest of us will be ready to fight."

Roamer brought Montoya over, mounted on his horse and his hands chained to the saddle fork.

"Mount up, men. Our flight to the border starts now."

"Hmm," Montoya snorted out his nose. "They'll cut you down before you get there."

"You won't be there to talk about it before that happens," Chet said. "You better hope they don't try us. You'll damn sure die if they do."

They started off for the border. Ortega led the way and Chet rode in the rear. If Montoya's gang pursued them, he'd watch for them with his telescope. Roamer was in charge of Montoya. The rest were bringing the packhorses and ready to fight if they had to. The distance was what worried Chet the most, with him pushing his good roan horse.

JD and Cole rode on each side of Mrs.

147

Higgins, so she was in good hands. Those two would keep her protected. By midday, they were crossing over some small desert mountains. At the top of the pass, he dismounted and used his telescope, thinking he might see dust behind them. No sign of pursuit. That didn't mean they weren't back there. It only meant he saw no sign yet of Montoya's army. He mounted up and rode on.

When someone questioned him, he answered, "Nothing back there."

No need to get too confident. It would be good if they could find a safe place, grab some sleep, and rest their horses. A nonstop trip might ruin their mounts. But where that place could be in this spiny land he had no idea. This part of Mexico was almost all new to him. Much of the desert they crossed through had lots of large cactus that didn't resemble anything in Arizona. The cattle he saw grazing were small, in-bred looking longhorns.

Late that evening, Ortega recalled a man named Don Seville he knew who had a large *hacienda.* It was a short ways off the road and maybe they could sleep a few hours and rest and feed the horses there.

It was close to sundown when the patron came out to see the troop that had arrived in his yard. He smiled at Ortega. "Who is here with you?"

"I want you to meet my *amigo,* Señor Byrnes, patron."

Chet had dismounted and taken off his hat. He gave his reins to Shawn and reached out to shake Señor Don Seville's hand.

"Nice to meet you, señor. We're citizens that have recovered Señora Higgins from a Mexican outlaw, Renaldo Montoya. He's our prisoner and we plan to perhaps release him at the border and go on home.

"We stay outside Tubac at Ortega's ranch. But before you agree to put us up, you need to know that Montoya has an army that might try to rescue him. So, to let us stay could endanger your ranch and people."

"Your name is Byrnes, right? You have a ranch or two up on the Verde in Arizona?"

"I do, señor."

"You are the man who oversees the Border Force."

"Jose!" Seville waved to a nearby *vaquero.* "Put their prisoner in our jail and guard him with your life. He has an army that may come here to get him."

"Patron, his men won't come here. They know the numbers we have here."

Seville nodded.

Roamer handed Jose the keys.

Chet introduced Burnett to their host. She looked real tired, but she smiled and thanked him.

"Go with this girl. She will get you a bath and some clothes to wear. Then we will have food and a bed for you to sleep in."

"Oh, that sounds wonderful. Thank you so much." A girl rushed her off through the front door.

"My men will put up your horses and care for them. I have a shower room and there will be robes for you to wear. There will be food in an hour. I will see you then. Your clothes will be clean and ironed by morning. Roman, show them where to go. And, Señor Byrnes, maybe if you are not too tired, we can talk about ranching in the desert."

"I'd love to. Thank you, sir. I hope we bring you no problems."

He shook his head. "I simply cannot believe you captured Montoya. Why, the *Federales* have ran all over looking for him."

Chet nodded. "They didn't look under the right rock."

Seville laughed. "Maybe they weren't looking at all."

The meal in the house was at a giant table in a two-story-tall room. Giant drapes hung on the walls. A full-size portrait of a distinguished, lovely lady hung on the wall.

"That your wife?" Chet asked.

His host looked a little taken back. "*Si.* She died two years ago. I have been heartbroken ever since."

"I'm so sorry. I wasn't prying. She must have been a lovely woman. I know it's sad for you. I lost a woman in Texas I intended to marry, but she was murdered."

"Cecilia was killed in a stagecoach crash."

"I know how that must hurt."

"You are married now?"

"For over a year, and we just had a son, Adam, born before I came down here."

"How lucky you are."

"I am indeed. I want to repay you for your generosity to us." Chet shook his head to dismiss the man's protest. "If you would like, and have two great open mares you treasure, have a couple of your men bring them to my ranch on the Verde River. I will have them bred to my Barbarossa stallion."

Sounding shocked, he asked, "You have one of those stallions?"

"Yes, he gets great colts, and as far as I know, he's the only one outside their ranch in Mexico."

"He has to be. They control those horses very close and they don't need money."

"Well, I own him and you're welcome to

151

bring the mares. I'd take them now, but with all this business we're involved in, we might lose them."

"Oh, my God. What a generous offer. Of course, we will do that. I am very impressed. That is just wonderful."

"No big deal, but you have been so generous to take us in and all."

"No problem. I am enjoying the company. I heard of a man who had two of your horses. He is very rich."

"I traded him those colts for a young woman whose mother had helped me when I first came to Arizona. Her daughter had been taken into the white slave trade and I didn't have a big enough force then to get her out. She came out very well."

"Well, in time, I will have two colts as well. This is terrific news."

"Yes. Are there artesian wells that water all this crop and orchard land?"

"Yes, but like God gives things away, he also takes them back. Anytime, an earthquake could close them off and this land would be worthless."

"Very sobering thought. I'm looking at a large ranch south of Tucson."

"That is the story of the desert. One shift and it turns the faucet off."

"I'll remember that. I'm almost too sleepy

to talk much more, excuse me?"

"Oh, of course. Antoinette, show him to his room."

"*Si,* patron." The lovely girl in the low-cut dress curtsied and held her hand out to show him the way. "This way, Señor Byrnes."

"Chet."

"Oh, no," she said. "You are the señor." She led him to a great bedroom and opened the thick door with her shoulder.

"You must know that my patron sent me here to serve you in any way." She bowed.

In the candlelight, he smiled. If he was that sort of man, she would be a wonderful prize to have in his bed, but he wasn't even tempted. "Thank you, ma'am, but I have a wife at home every bit as lovely as you, and I don't stray."

She stood on her toes and kissed his cheek. "I imagine she loves you, too. But if you need me for anything, pull that rope beside the bed a few times and I will come join you."

"Thanks." He showed her out and bolted the door. In minutes, he was in the great bed and sound asleep.

His dreams were not particularly comforting. He was in a cave, wrestling with a half-bear man and losing the fight part of the time. Awake, he sat up straight in bed and mopped his face in his hands. He wasn't in a damn cave, nor was there a bear in his room. Whew. He had trouble sleeping, but he managed some light sleeping and then dressed and went into the big room. There was a light on and his host was writing with a straight pen and ink in a great ledger at the end of the table.

A lovely young lady intercepted him. "Sir, would you like some fresh coffee? You may join the Don. He is writing in his journal, but he will be ready to converse with you in a few minutes. Have a seat." Her English was perfect.

With reading glasses on his nose, Seville looked up and smiled. "I want to finish this section, excuse me."

"Certainly."

She returned with his coffee. Then, in a whisper, she offered him breakfast.

"Whatever he's having," Chet whispered back.

After Seville's writing was complete, he set down the pen, blotted the page, and closed the book. "I try to write my adventures down when they happen. They would be of little value to anyone but myself. But I still feel it is important to have them to look back on."

"I understand. Is anyone else up besides the two of us?"

Don Seville shook his head. "Ortega and his brother, Bronc, are already out scouting to see if the army is around. I sent my best men with them to look."

"Thanks. They're good men."

"Yes, they are. Tell me about your life. You mentioned Texas, but you have extensive holdings now in Arizona."

Chet told him about the feud in Texas and leaving there. How he bought a distressed ranch and later turned it around. Then about Heck being killed and his brother, Dale Allen, the boy's father, who was killed in Kansas on a cattle drive by the feuding Reynolds family. Then, his life in Arizona and building the family empire, that he simply called their ranches.

"Why do you lead this Force, getting people like the Higgins woman back?"

"Arizona will never become a state until we end this lawlessness. The separate county sheriff system is not working well enough."

Seville smiled at him. "No offense, but the bad guys in Mexico call you a mean bulldog sumbitch."

"Good."

"Yes, it is. They fear you. Here you are, sixty or more miles from the international line, and you are simply concerned citizens returning a man's wife safely to him."

"With a hostage."

"A man the *Federales* can't find."

Breakfast being served interrupted them. There was food for many, he decided, at first glance. Platters of everything were delivered and held for them to choose, then set on the table.

"We can talk more as we eat."

Chet agreed.

The coffee was cool enough to drink. He sipped on it, then turned back to his full plate. The tall clock chimed four times, early morning yet.

Eggs, flour tortillas, fried ham, refried beans, lots of fruit — peaches, mangoes, grapes, three kinds of bananas, and citrus. Other dishes he was unsure about, but he tried some, imagining they would be fiery hot. But they were only spicy hot, no tears on his part.

"What else do you need?" Don asked.

"Room in my belly."

They laughed.

"If I came to Prescott, could I find a wife up there?"

"Those folks up there call it Preskitt. But I don't know. I haven't been looking for one. My wife, Marge, knows a lot of people, and if there's one available, I bet she'd introduce her to you."

"I may come with the mares and see."

"You can stay at our house. We have lots of room. Of course, the baby may cry."

"You know how lucky you are to have one to cry?"

"Pretty damn lucky for a man who waited thirty-two years to get married. My wife had been widowed twice before I came along, and had never carried a baby full term. Yes, I feel real lucky."

"That will be a pleasant trip. I can see all your operations. If you had time, I'd show you mine. But we may exchange visits after that."

"When we get this big ranch's title straight, I may send my nephew down here to learn the desert farming ways."

"Anytime."

They talked more about ranching practices. Seville shipped a lot of citrus fruit to Mexico City and they sold wine they made as well. His cattle operation was mostly beef for the ranch's consumption.

"Markets are what make cattle work. We have a contract with the Navajo Agency. Until we get a railroad into northern Arizona, we'll all struggle there."

Seville agreed. "And Old Man Clanton

has the south part sewed up."

"He has all those contracts. Several others tried supplying the Navajo, but it's too isolated to get beef there in good enough flesh."

"Can you supply all their needs?"

"No. We have to buy many head from other ranchers, but that helps us all."

"Oh, yes. A market is what makes it work."

"Can you wake up my people? We need to get going."

"Lupe," he said to the girl who served them. "Have them wake up our guests and Señora Higgins."

"*Si*, patron." And she was gone.

Soon his crew filed in and all looked as draggy as he'd felt.

"Good morning," Cole said to both of them. "Where are Ortega and Bronc?"

"They're scouting for Montoya's army."

Cole nodded. "That's good. I was concerned."

JD joined them. "What did you learn?"

"The brothers are out looking for Montoya's army."

"Good." He turned to Seville. "Thanks, sir. We sure needed the rest. Your people have been wonderful."

Their host nodded. "Your uncle says you may come back to see me and look closer at our farming operation."

"Oh, yes, I'd like that. Thanks for that opportunity."

"We will love to show you."

"Is Mrs. Higgins getting up?" JD asked, looking around.

"They are probably fixing her hair," Seville said. "Be seated, more food is coming."

"Good. Do we need to see about our horses?" JD asked Chet.

"No, his men are handling that, too."

"Boy, we need to stay here more often." They all laughed.

Mrs. Higgins soon joined them in a new divided skirt-dress. She spoke to Chet. "His servants found me a new outfit. I am so grateful, not only to you and your men but to Señor Seville for all his generosity. I am about to cry. I never expected to be saved from my hell."

"Chin up, Burnett. In a few days, you'll be home. We all owe our host. For all his generosity, I'm offering him the use of my Barbarossa stallion."

She turned to Seville. "Thank you, sir."

He rose, took her hand, and kissed it. "You are most welcome."

"Yes, but I won't forget you, sir. This past night's peaceful sleep was the only one I've had in two months."

159

Cole moved her chair in behind to seat her. She used a cloth napkin to blot her eyes.

The meal went well. Chet got up and went outside to meet the returning brothers.

"Breakfast is ready inside. What did you find?"

"They must be a half-day behind us, his army and the guns. But I bet he has a smaller band made up to stop us from crossing the border. They might be somewhere ahead, or close to us and not in sight. I think the rest of his army is only a distraction."

Bronc, tight lipped, with a head nod, added, "We couldn't find them in the dark. But I'm like Ortega. I think they are out there."

"Then let's finish up. Grab some food. We'll ride like hell for the border. Our horses will be fresh, so we should be there with no hitches in twenty hours or less."

They both agreed with him.

Some kitchen help brought them tortilla-wrapped meals and everyone mounted up. He shook Seville's hand and told him to write when he could come, that he'd try to be there. As they started out, leaving the *hacienda* in a short lope, the Morales brothers took the lead. JD and Cole followed, accompanied by a refreshed looking Mrs.

Higgins. Then came Montoya, guarded by Shawn and Roamer, and Chet brought up the rear. They soon reached the road. When they swung north, there was no sign of any army or dust, and they were soon well on their way to Nogales.

Chet knew the Morales boys could be right about the bandits attacking them. He made them pull their horses back to a trot. They couldn't afford to wear their mounts completely out short of the border. That would leave them pinned down. The desert country they crossed through was mostly flat and distorted with heat waves on all horizons. Chet felt it would be a hard place to ambush them. But ahead were more small desert mountains for them to cross. That would be the place where the bandits might set up an ambush.

Ortega talked to some people in a small village where they watered their stock and took the opportunity to dismount and stretch. With a toss of his head, a hatless man asked who their prisoner was. No one had recognized him, but when one of the crew told him who Montoya was, they all quickly left their company. That amused Chet. Soon, they were in the saddle and the Force was moving again in a trot.

When he used the scope, there was no visible cloud of dust on their back trail. The skin still crawled on his neck as he watched the back of the outlaw chained in the saddle riding ahead of him. His outfit would risk his life if they tried anything. Mrs. Higgins wasn't worth that to Montoya's gang, but if their leader ever did get back and they hadn't helped him escape, they wouldn't want to face his ire.

They had to try something. But unless they rode all the night before, they couldn't be ahead of them, and if they had, their stock would be done for. The Seville *hacienda* stopover had been a godsend for him and the whole bunch, but until they were in an American settlement with more guns to back them, they could face big problems with his gang.

Chet shifted again in the saddle and glanced back, but the glaring hot sun showed no dust marking the sky. By late afternoon, he saw a sign that said THIRTY KILOS TO NOGALES. Most of those markers were made by estimates and not accurate — but their host had said it was better than thirty miles, and he probably was more accurate having traveled it often.

Ortega dropped back and rode in close. "I think if we keep on we will be in Nogales in a few hours. I read that sign, but I have made this trip many times."

"We came across some hills where I suspected they might be waiting. No sign of them. Maybe we overestimated them, Ortega."

"No, they are military, not dumb outlaws, like we usually chase. I can't believe they don't have a plan to jump us ahead."

"What do you think?"

"We shouldn't ride straight in to Nogales, Sonora. We need to go east and cross like we did coming down, when no one saw us."

"Can our horses stand it?"

"It will take an hour or more, but I feel it will be safer going that way."

Chet gave a head toss for Roamer to come closer, and he rode over beside them.

"Ortega thinks we should skirt around Nogales and come in from the east."

Roamer considered the sun's position. "Be dark soon."

"He's worried they may be set up in town to ambush us."

"He knows this country and the people better than we do. We should do what he says. I'll pass the word along."

"Good." Chet looked down at the shiny wet shoulders of the roan horse under him. *Hang on Red. We've got a few more miles to go.*

CHAPTER 8

The sun had set. Horses grunted, snorted wearily, and saddles creaked. Once in a while, an iron shoe clanged on a rock. Under the starlight, single file, they passed the border post and headed up the dark trail, trusting their mounts to carry them in the near darkness. A few coyotes howled a lullaby on the ridge to the east, and an owl made a silent swoop down the canyon to check out the invaders riding up it.

The skin on the back of his neck stopped itching. They were home. They were U.S. Deputy Marshals again. He recalled his last deal with the Santa Cruz county sheriff.

Never mind this man was going to be a federal prisoner, he'd have to hold him in their jail until Marshal Blevins sent some deputies down to take him to Tucson. Part of his crew could find beds somewhere and sleep the night. They'd take Mrs. Higgins home in the morning and then get back to their base at Tubac.

He still had a lot to do, and no telling what other crimes had been committed while his crew was gone. But getting some sleep would be the thing he would enjoy the most — sleep in the United States. He was ready for it. When they came off the hillside he could see the lights of Nogales, Arizona territory.

"We have him here. What say we charge him with kidnapping?" Chet asked them all.

"Hell, yes," went his gang.

They stopped at the jail. Cole and JD took Mrs. Higgins on to the Rio Hotel with plans to meet them in the morning. The other members unchained and unloaded the grumbling Montoya and shoved him inside where a sleepy official asked who he was.

"He's a federal prisoner. His name is Montoya. He kidnapped an Arizona rancher's wife, Mrs. Higgins."

"I thought they took her to Mexico?"

"They did," Chet said. "She's fine and at the Rio Hotel right now. Lock him up and then chain him. He's pretty jail shy."

The man looked upset and mad. "How did she get back and him get back here?"

"Don't worry about that. Lock and chain him in the cell. He's the most dangerous man you ever have had in this jail. You might

165

call in some extra guards. He has an army out looking for him right now."

When the jailer had Montoya chained to the metal bunk attached to the wall and locked in the cell, they left and walked the block to the Harris Livery. Their weary horses snorted in the dust and stumbled along as they walked and led them. The liveryman said he had some boys to rub them down and feed them — for them not to worry, they'd be well cared for.

Chet thanked him and they went on to the hotel.

"Is she safe enough in her room?" JD asked.

"Are our rooms around her?"

"Yes, all on the same floor upstairs."

"I think so. Is she up there?"

He and Cole both nodded. Chet paid the hotel man for everyone. "Anyone bust in here, you raise hell and we'll be up to help you."

"I understand. Thank you, sir."

Chet nodded to his men it would be okay. "Go sleep."

In bed at last, sleep escaped him. Too many concerns bothered him about his ranches, wife, and the baby — at last he slept, but only for a few hours.

Morning came. Ortega had gone to the

Mexican side to see if there was any threat over there. He returned without much information, but felt they had avoided any interception. Chet trusted his judgment, so he assigned Cole, JD, and Shawn to take Mrs. Higgins home. That way, he had Roamer and the brothers if anything went wrong.

After breakfast and ready to leave, she hugged him. "If my husband and I can ever help you, call on us. I'll never be able to repay you or your men for saving my life. No one else could have done it. And when I get home, I may never, ever, ride another horse again."

They laughed.

Cole, JD, and Shawn rode east to take Mrs. Higgins home, while Chet, Roamer, and the brothers headed north on the King's Highway toward Tubac. When they got there, late in the day, he sent a telegram to Marge telling her he was fine, and another to Blevins informing him that Montoya was in jail in Nogales and to send deputies to get him.

Maria showed him two telegrams. One was from his wife and said Sarge's horse fell on him and broke his leg. He was fine, but Victor had taken over for him and was taking the cattle on to Gallup, and all was under control. She missed him and the baby was cutting teeth.

Victor was a young man who cooked for him and Marge when they went on their honeymoon up on the rim. After that, he went to the Windmill Ranch to be Sarge's cook. The second wire was from Blevins reporting two stage robberies around Tombstone. Not many details, so Chet planned to send Roamer and Ortega over there to see what they could learn.

"Well?" Roamer asked him. "What now?"

"Sarge had a horse wreck and broke his leg and Victor is running things for him. Sounds like he's doing a good job. There's been two stage robberies in the Tombstone area. Perhaps you and Ortega should ride over there tomorrow and check things out. Look up Dodge. Talking to Sheriff Behan is like talking into the wind."

Roamer made a sour face. "Oh, yeah, I recall that scene at the jail. He's a dandy."

Ortega had heard him. "What did they get?"

"Didn't say, but Dodge will know and he'll work with you."

"Do you think we've heard the last of those guys that work for Montoya?" Roamer asked.

"Maybe, but we'll have to stay ready to

meet them head on, just in case."

"The others will be back here tomorrow. Jesus is moving those squatters to Nogales. That settled, I might go into Tucson and see my lawyer about the ranch title. I need that straightened out. JD and Ortega want that ranch working."

"I don't blame them," Roamer said. "Then they can be in the saddle every day looking at cows switching tails, instead of messing with border bandits."

They were all laughing. Plans were laid for Roamer and Ortega to take a few days in Tombstone to learn all they could about the holdups. Chet planned to wait until everyone was back before he left for Tucson.

Jesus came in that evening. "They were all excited in Nogales. Did you bring in that Mexican bandit?"

"Yes. It was a helluva deal. We really rode our asses off coming home."

"They kept saying the Task Force did it. They all wondered how you had the authority to arrest him down there."

"You remember the bunch we got out of that bar in Noco?"

"Oh, yes. That was funny."

"We did him the same way, only it was a hard two-day ride."

Jesus and him laughed. The lost women

169

were off the ranch, settled, and not his problem anymore.

Solving the Diablo Ranch ownership came next . . . always something.

CHAPTER 9

When Chet got off the stage and walked to the Congress Hotel to find a room, Tucson was in a sweltering summer heat. A lot of well-to-do men's wives had summer homes up on Mount Lemon. It probably was over twenty degrees cooler up there in the pines. More like the temperature Marge had up at the Preskitt Valley Ranch. He'd heard that in the old days the Apaches stayed up in the high country in the summertime, on Mt. Graham and the Chiricuhuas.

The lobby was stuffy. The clerk was a sharp boy and remembered his name.

"Mr. Byrnes, I have a corner room on the third floor for you. You should get some air tonight."

"I might, and I appreciate you, Mark." He paid him and went up.

The windows were open and some air was coming across the bed in the center of the room. He undressed and planned to go to sleep. In bed, it didn't come at first, but finally he slept. The morning came early and he was off to get some food from a street vendor, then bought a paper from a boy hawking them. "Former Mexican *Federale* is in the Tucson jail for kidnapping a rancher's wife. Read all about it."

He smiled to himself and gave the boy a nickel and a second one for him to pocket.

"Muchas gracias, señor." The polite youth smiled shy-like and shared a firm nod with him.

A shame Jesus wasn't there, he'd have conversed with the boy. Chet never felt satisfied enough with his own Spanish to talk it. Jesus was busy running down some leads on trouble in the mining camps. Chet felt there was no danger to him in Tucson, so sent Jesus on his way.

He made it to the office of his lawyers, Jensen, Craft, and Rosewood. The secretary, a young man, Neal Lindall, welcomed him. "Mr. Byrnes, how are you today? I will tell Mr. Craft you are here."

"Thanks, Neal." He put his hat on the tree and waited for his return. The offices were very neat, but dusty and hot even by eight o'clock in the morning.

Russell Craft was a short man and wore a white shirt and tie. He shook his hand and invited him down to his office. "I see you haven't been shot again. That was real serious."

He turned back to look for Chet's reaction.

"I'm fine now. Thanks."

He entered the office and Russell told him to take a chair.

"I have really been busy. They usually shut down court business during June, July, and August and wait for cooler weather to do things. This summer, they have been busier than they are in the winter. And the courthouse is really hot."

"It's warmer here than down at Tubac."

"Oh, well, we chose this place. I've spoken with Buster Weeks's lawyer, Jarman Townsend, about the ranch and livestock. They'll be here in an hour to talk about the situation. The judge's opinion on their illegal land holdings settles that. Townsend claims they have five hundred cows, plus calves, down there and wants thirty dollars a head."

"Tell him to get a roundup crew. I wouldn't pay over seven-fifty for them. I can replace them for that. The only way I'll take them is a roundup. His own man told me there were two-fifty. Besides, his ranch foreman, Masters, hired three gunmen to kill me."

"I read that in your letter and mentioned it to Townsend. He said that man is gone."

"Where? To his ranch north of Tucson?"

"He's not supposed to be on the desert ranch down there."

"I'll buy all the cows and bulls he can produce, but using a joint team to count them."

Russell smiled and handed him a sheet from the Pima County Sheriff appraiser's report. Cow count one hundred twenty, bulls ten, horses twelve, and signed by ranch foreman, Larry Masters, as accurate. It was a copy of the original with Larry Masters's name hand-printed on it. The name of the deputy who accepted it was also on it.

Chet chuckled. "I'd accept that as the count."

"I thought so. But I doubt Weeks will. And if we suggest that a deputy will be there at the counting, he might be easier to trade with."

"You earn your money. I never even considered that."

"I knew the deputies went around looking for cattle to count more than they did any law enforcement effort. Obviously, I'd suspect some of them receive under the table money to shorten the count. The sheriff gets ten percent of all taxes collected and uses county-paid deputies for agents."

Chet agreed. "Exactly. I heard that Sheriff Behan received thirty thousand dollars in a past year."

"It's true. He has gold and silver mines down there. But others do much better than ordinary lawmen elsewhere. They have a little known association that provides wine, dinners, and female escorts to all the legislators during the sessions in Preskitt."

"I know about that, too." Chet yawned, then stood up to pace the room. "That's part of the reason why I'm down here. Active law enforcement is lacking, and Arizona will never become a state until we get it done."

"Hey, the real people appreciate that effort. I read the news this morning. There is no explanation for how he ended up on this side of the border."

"Some citizens went down there and brought him back, as well as his kidnap victim."

"I know it wasn't that simple."

"That's the story."

"Excuse me, but Buster Weeks and Jarman Townsend are here," Neal said.

"We're ready for them." Getting up, Russell set up two chairs for them.

Chet stood up, exchanged handshakes,

and they took their places. Russell went back behind the desk.

"My client had no part in any false land records. He purchased that property in good faith and with a search of the records made by the Phillips and Stars firm. We are ready to leave the ranch, though, and get on with our business. Here's Buster's last count of cows in this log by his past foreman, Masters." He handed it to Russell.

"I don't need to see it," Russell said. "I have the certified count of cows on that ranch from the Pima County Sheriff's office's appraiser." He handed the paper to Townsend. "It says you have a hundred cows on that ranch, and it's attested to by a deputy."

Chet saw Buster Weeks flinch at Russell's words. He was still in good control, but he'd bet he was about to explode inside.

"Oh —" Jarman dropped his hand holding the log.

"We moved more cattle down there recently," Buster said.

"No problem," Chet said. "We round them up and count them. I won't pay over seven dollars a head for them. You can take them home, and I'll ask the county sheriff to count them coming off the ranch."

"Excuse us. My client and I need to confer."

Russell stood up. "The office across the hall is open."

The two of them kept a casual look on their faces, but Chet felt they were really upset inside. He waited until the door closed and Russell turned back.

"You ever play chess?" Russell asked him. Chet shook his head.

"It is a game of cat and mouse, and when you have your opponent trapped with no place to go, you say, 'Checkmate.'"

"When the land titles proved false, I think they knew they would lose this fight. But not this severe."

Russell agreed. "I think when they come back we will get a better offer."

Chet agreed, feeling much better about the whole thing, except for Masters's plan to have him killed.

Jarman came back without Weeks and said his client had other pressing business to attend, so had to leave.

He continued, "My client will accept twenty thousand dollars for all his assets down there and give you a title free and clear for them."

"I want a letter from all his bankers that they will accept any such settlement,"

Russell said.

"And my counter offer is sixteen thousand dollars, along with those points he said," Chet interjected.

Jarman shook his head. "That's too low."

"Yours is too high. I buy and sell thousands of cattle a year in my operations. We know his count is way too high. If he will pay half the cost, or provide half the roundup cost, I might pay more. But that's my final offer, and you have thirty days to get them off my land."

Jarman was breathing out of his nose. Chet, standing taller, considered him as the seconds ticked by. He would either explode or accept the offer. The noise and voices of the street traffic outside became audible.

"When will you have the money?" Jarman finally asked.

"Friday. I'll have funds transferred down here by then. What bank shall we meet at?"

"The Arizona First National Bank at ten a.m. I will send the letters of release to Russell. You know you're a hard man to do business with?"

"Do you know his foreman, Masters, hired several men to go up to Preskitt to kill me?"

"I knew nothing about that."

"When I find Masters, you and Weeks better not have had anything to do with it."

178

Chet knew he was glaring at the attorney.

"My client doesn't know anything about it, either."

"If he did, I'll sure find out and I will catch him."

"Good day, Russell, Mr. Byrnes."

Russell nodded. Jarman nodded and left in a huff.

When he was gone, Russell closed the office door and smiled. "I don't want to trade for a horse from you."

"When he agreed, I thought about what you said, 'Checkmate.' "

"Let's go have lunch. There's a fine restaurant atop the Williams building. It's shaded and catches some breezes."

"Sure. I'm busy thinking about all the things that lie ahead for me and my men."

"Well, you know how to handle that. I can't help you." Russell put on his suit coat.

"Do I need to be dressed?"

"No, you aren't a lawyer in this city. Eccentric rich people can do what they want and wear what they want."

"Good. No doubt, my wife would dress me for such an occasion. I love her, but I've spent too much of my life in the saddle to dress up very often."

"And the world is better because you do that."

"Thanks, I feel shrunk by the whole thing."

"No, you will rebound. Have you ever looked into all those *haciendas* in Sonora that have been abandoned because of the Apache?"

"No, I guess I never heard about them."

"When the United States bought the Gadsden Purchase in 1853, we added on land that goes down to Nogales and took in Mesilla over in New Mexico."

By then, they were out in the busy Tucson street full of burro trains bringing water, wood, and even goats for their milk to be sold to housewives. Wagons and trade vehicles all crowded the streets.

Russell continued, "For the most part, those places are still empty. Since the Apache trouble left the northern core of Mexico abandoned, Congress could have bought lots more land south of here."

"My trips down there have all been hurry up to get there and then hurry home."

Russell nodded. "All Congress wanted was a snow-free path for a railroad across the states. They did not want any more brown people or Catholics." He laughed as if amused.

"I bet they regret that someday."

"Of course, they will. Since Jefferson

bought the Louisiana Purchase we have been land hungry."

The restaurant was very high class. A nice-looking dark-complexioned lady took his hat and showed them to a table. There was some air blowing and it didn't feel quite as hot as the furnace blasts in the street.

The waiter brought them sun tea cooled in an *olla*. Lunch was braised steak strips with sweet peppers and onions, served with frijoles and fried bread on the side.

Russell said, "The cook is Hispanic."

"Hey, the food is swell. I'm enjoying it."

"Good. I bet you eat lots worse than this on the trail of outlaws?"

"A pretty steady diet of jerky."

"What are your plans for the new ranch?"

"We have to appraise the water situation. Find the real number of cattle on hand. Build a ranch house for my nephew, JD, and his bride, Bonnie. Another home for his foreman, Ortega, and his family. Things will be busy, and it's a hard place to get supplies and building material to."

"I'm glad all I have to worry about are law cases."

"We both need to go fishing."

"I haven't forgotten your offer. I bet it is cool up there?"

"Yes. Beautiful and cool. But I won't get

181

there soon."

"What's the best place you have for a ranch?"

Chet nodded and grinned. "Where they are."

"You going back to Tubac this afternoon?"

"Yes, after I wire my banker about my money needs. I'll have him send it down here to that bank. Also set up an account there."

"Be careful. I always enjoy working for you."

"Send your bill to Preskitt. Marge will pay you."

"I want to meet her someday and your new son, Adam."

"Yes, he may grow up without me."

"I doubt that."

Chet paid for the expensive lunch. He left a tip as well, and estimated the entire meal cost him nine dollars. Headed for the telegraph wire office, he figured at that price he could have eaten in the street for months. Marge would enjoy the service and food. If she was ever down there, he'd treat her.

After he sent a wire to Tanner at the bank about the money, he wired Bo to complete the purchase, and then another to Marge to tell her he'd closed the deal, plus kiss Adam for him. He walked two more blocks to the bank and met the main man, Ralston Holmes, and set up an account to receive the money.

"You are very wise, Mr. Byrnes, to use this method of payment. So many ranchers insist on packing cash around, not trusting banks, and they get robbed."

"I know all about that. Nice to meet you. We'll be here at ten a.m. on Friday to complete this purchase."

"If we can ever be any service to you, sir, please let us know."

"In the near future, Mr. Holmes, I'll be choosing a bank down here. I'll offer your firm an opportunity to bid on it."

"We would certainly like to discuss your needs at any time."

"Not today." He was anxious to get back south to their camp that evening. There was a late afternoon stage for Nogales, and the driver would let him off at the ranch gate that night, sometime after midnight. After taking a meal with a street vendor for ten cents, he headed for the stage office. The afternoon heat was stifling hot, so he settled on a bench on the porch of the stage office.

The situation with the new ranch occupied his thoughts. When other passengers arrived, he absentmindedly offered his seat to a younger woman and she thanked him.

The coach's arrival with fresh horses jarred him out of his own world. He had to get his senses back. He was too far away from reality to solve any emergency.

Maybe he did need Jesus and Cole with him. He'd remember that. Damn, he missed his wife and baby Adam. Big ranch plans still had him occupied as the stage rocked away, until the female passenger interrupted his thoughts.

"My name is Stephanie Combs."

"Chet Byrnes."

"Oh, aren't you the man from Preskitt who heads the Force?"

"Yes, I am."

"Are you after more criminals tonight?"

"No, just going back to my camp. How do you know me?"

"I've read about you being shot. The article said you owned several ranches in the north and you led the Force that is bringing in all these criminals."

"I didn't read that article."

"No, you were healing, I bet."

"You're going to Nogales?"

"I live there with my parents. My father is superintendent of the U.S. border there. His name is Ralph Combs. I know he would like to meet you some time."

"I'll make it a point to look him up."

"Yes, I am sure you two would have much to talk about."

They discussed various subjects, and he found the single young girl in her twenties to be a smart young woman. But his interest in her was more like what he'd have toward a daughter. When the driver stopped at the ranch gate, he told a sleepy Miss Combs good-bye. Out of the coach and the door closed, he shouted thanks to the driver.

Under the stars and the cooler night air, he walked the distance to their camp.

"You back in one piece, señor?"

"What are you doing up, Jesus?"

"Worrying about you."

"I won't leave without you again, *mi amigo*. You better get some rest. Nothing bad wrong?"

"No. Glad you are alright."

Chet turned in and slept troubled. It being a short night only made it worse.

CHAPTER 10

At Maria's breakfast the next morning, he faced a lot of questions.

"Did you settle with Buster Weeks?" JD asked.

"Did he tell you where that bastard, Masters, could be found?"

"When is it your ranch?"

He held up his hands to stop them.

"Friday, we settle with Weeks. I'm buying his cattle then and the ranch will be ours. JD, you better take Bronc and Cole over there and be sure they don't strip the place when they leave. You can hire any of them you want; the rest I'll give you money to pay them off, if Weeks hasn't done that. Then start making a tally of the cattle. Inventory your immediate needs. Examine the water sources they're using. I better stay here, in case Ortega and Roamer need me. Shawn and Jesus can look after me."

"You men better eat this food. It will be

cold and *no bueno,*" Maria said in a motherly way.

"Maria, we're ready to eat. By the way, I didn't tell you I got word that Adam is cutting his first tooth. These men are going to take their first good look at the family's newest holdings — the ranch in hell."

She shook her head. "And I am going to have to live there."

"Maria, I'm counting on you to help Bonnie some," JD said. "Lands, I told her all about you."

"Just eat, JD. Way I see it, you'll get tired of my face." Then she laughed and shook her head. She said something in Spanish none of them understood and left them to fend for themselves.

"What did she say, Jesus?" JD asked.

"In her words, she say, only the devil could save the whole lot of us. Didn't you hear her laughing, going to her *casa?* She's one of us."

JD nodded. "I savvy." He went to eating his plate of food.

Chet shook his head. The devil might, but they may be too far gone. Her food was good, as usual, and he savored it. It wasn't like Monica's at the home ranch's style, not his wife's way, or his sister Susie's way — it was Maria's way. He knew what his man

187

Ortega saw in her — wisdom much beyond her age. Lots of caring and a big heart, but smart, too.

Roamer came back midmorning. "The stage robbers are hiding out in a canyon over by the Chircuhuas. Dodge and Ortega are making sure they don't come out."

"How many are up there?"

"Maybe six."

"Riding hard, it'll take two days to get over there," Chet said.

"They're waiting till you all can get there. Another Clanton is with them."

"Shawn, saddle us two horses. Jesus, you go with JD, Cole, and Bronc. Shawn, Roamer, and I will go settle with these robbers. Take enough supplies. If I need to make that bank meeting, I can take a stage from Tombstone. Shawn can come along with me to Tucson Thursday night, and I can make the sale closing on Friday."

"We can do that, señor," Jesus said. "But for land's sake, be careful." He was looking real serious at him. "You be very careful."

"I'll watch. I figure you can make more sense out of that ranch than any of them."

Roamer, Shawn, and Chet left within the hour and made Tombstone by sundown. They slept in the hay at the livery for a few hours, found some fresh cinnamon rolls in a hole-in-the-wall café, and then left before sunup. Roamer explained the other factor in this case as they rode — the gang had another family member — Thomas Clanton.

Chet recalled the last newspaper report and shook his head. Lawbreakers were lawbreakers. If he held up stages, he needed to be arrested and tried by the law.

If they pushed hard, they would be at the base of the mountain and the canyon by midday. He and his men trotted their mounts until they could see details on the mountain and the junipers that made the mountain's skirts. Roamer led them up the narrow trail and Ortega stepped out from the dense junipers with his rifle.

"You sure got back here in a big hurry."

"What's the situation up there?"

"One of them stage robbers is Israel's younger brother, Thomas. They've been up there drinking and raising hell for two days. I worried they might want out, but so far they've been content. It's been a long three days, señor."

"It must have been." Chet stepped down and turned to Roamer. "I don't know a thing to do but to take them. If they don't surrender, they'll be shot. Is Dodge here?"

Ortega gave him a frown. "He wasn't

much help. I sent him back to town. I knew you were coming."

Chet shook his head. "Get some rest. In the morning, before daylight, we'll take them. Anyone offers resistance, we shoot them. Don't take a chance."

"Shawn, you take the first watch. Wake us if anyone tries to come out. No fires they can smell."

"I am damn sure glad to see you," Ortega said.

"Yeah, I have to be in Tucson on Friday to sign papers for the ranch."

"But —"

"Don't worry, it only happens when you're a boss. Don't ever take that job."

Ortega yawned. "Sleep, yes."

The crickets kept up a chorus and a few coyotes howled. That left an owl to hoot, then Chet fell asleep. Around two in the morning, Roamer woke him. "We voted to go cover the shack about four o'clock."

"Good time." He took over guard duty in the coolness of the high desert. Be damn cold up there on the mountain's spine. He'd be glad to have this over with. His eyes felt dry as an alkali flat.

When he shook them, the others got up. Shawn rolled up his bedroll. "I don't want to stay in this hotel tonight. Too many rocks."

They all chuckled. They woke their sleeping horses and made sure they were hitched out of sight, so some escaping outlaw couldn't find them. Then, with rifles and ammo, they started up the steep trail in the darkness.

They soon reached their goal, squatted, and looked at the darkened log cabin. The outlaws' horses were in the corral, backed by a tall cliff wall behind it.

"Must have a spring up here," Chet whispered to Roamer.

He nodded. "Have to be a good one to water them and their horses."

"I will cover the back way," Ortega offered. "Give me some time to get around there."

"Good idea. We'll camp here."

Chet, Cole, and Shawn squatted down with their rifles across their laps. He could hear the horses grunting in their sleep. Once in a while, one would stomp his hoof or they'd have a kicking match to settle something private.

When he figured Ortega was in place, they moved in closer. The soft light of sunup was gradually making it plainer to see details. Using a woodpile for cover, he sent Shawn over to take a place by the corral corner. Roamer was to his left.

He fired a pistol shot in the air. "Come out hands high, or die. This is the U.S. Marshal talking. We'll shoot anyone that comes out armed. Gun in your hand means instant death. Now, get out here before I burn that trap down around you."

"We're coming. We're coming."

What happened next was what Chet expected. They came out with six-guns blazing at all or anything. In seconds, the air was full of acrid gun smoke fogging the area. The posse's rifles cut the armed occupants down in the doorway, and a few steps from the entrance, four men sprawled facedown. There was no wind. Not a breath. Only the sounds of the panicked horses in the pens scrambling around and whinnying — heads high over the top bars and trying to escape the hell they were caught in.

"Hold your fire. We can't see anything." Two individuals, coughing their heads off, soon appeared unarmed and in their underwear. Chet, pistol in hand, waved them to comb over the bodies to make sure they were unarmed.

"Any more in there?"

"No. Just us."

"Shawn, watch those horses and try to

settle them down. We've got them."

Roamer and Ortega cautiously dragged each of the dead or wounded off the porch by their arms and out on the bare ground. Shawn calmed the animals in the pen so they didn't break out, then came over to join them.

"What do we do next?" Shawn asked.

"By damn, make us some coffee. My teeth are about to float out. I haven't had any in days," Ortega said.

"What's your name?" Chet asked the youngest prisoner standing barefooted in his long-handle underwear. He had his short pencil and pad in his hand.

"Tom Clanton."

"Age?"

"Sixteen."

"What's your name?" he asked the other one.

"Billy Moore."

"Age?"

"Fifteen."

"You boys got an early start on stage robbing, haven't you?"

"We ain't robbed no stages," Clanton said.

"A judge will decide that. Shut up. Sit on the ground. We'll have some breakfast, then get you dressed. Shawn, cuff them together."

That completed, the young man headed

back to camp to get their horses.

"We will have some food here shortly," Ortega said as they built a fire in the ring.

"Shawn! Bring the packhorse, too," Ortega shouted. "They don't have any good coffee here."

Shawn waved that he heard him and headed into the junipers and live oak for their camp.

Roamer and Chet laughed, then Chet asked Ortega, "Why don't they have any good coffee here?"

"Cheap outlaws, boss man."

"Any of them you drug out going to live?" he asked Roamer.

"Not to get to Tombstone, way I figure."

"Good enough for them. When we get them tied over horses, you two can take your time. Shawn and I are going to head for Tombstone shortly. We'll leave our horses at the O.K. Corral for you two to take back. I'll wire Blevins to send his men to come get these two, and then Shawn and I will catch a stage to Tucson. Tomorrow, I need to buy a ranch for all of us. And we'll take the stage back to Tubac."

"Busy man."

"Roamer, one day I'll sit in a rocker on the porch and count cattle."

"That will only be after you break both

legs falling off a windmill."

They all laughed, except the prisoners.

Shawn soon returned with his saddle horse and the pack animal. Ortega made them coffee and breakfast while the others saddled their horses. They fed the two living outlaws, then loaded the dead or dying belly down over their horses. They found some of the loot. Part of it was gold bars that outlaws hated because they were branded and hard to sell. Most of the money on them and in the dead outlaws' pockets was fresh made.

Chet asked both boys where the rest of the money went.

"Saddles, guns, and the supplies to hole up here until things cooled down."

So, they had all the loot that was left.

When he said good-bye, everyone wished him luck and thanked him. Then he rode double with Shawn to get to his horse. Before the sun had cleared the mountain range, they were long trotting on the dusty road for Tombstone.

Things went fast in the telegraph office. He sent a wire to Marshal Blevins, telling him to send men to take the pair to Tucson for trial. Then he wired Marge that he was leaving Tombstone to go to Tucson to sign the papers. They caught some quick food from a street vendor, then got the back-facing seats on the five p.m. stage and rocked out of town past Boot Hill for Benson and then on to Tucson in the night.

"Did we forget anything, Shawn?"

"No, sir, but when you move you really move."

"I want a bath in Tucson, then a clean white shirt and my pants pressed for tomorrow's signing, and some sleep."

"I hear folks talking about your empire building. I can see, now I've been with you well over six months, that you have some kinda drive in you. You don't hardly sleep and you're up and ready to go. What powers that?"

"Before the War, there was no money in Texas. I mean, pennies were hoarded. Folks were not much richer than their slaves. Slaves were high-priced, but no one could hardly afford to buy them. We never had any slaves, but lots of our neighbors did. They raised their own. Mexican people were even poorer. They came and farmed for us each year. They were good farmers and we had some good land to grow crops. My dad fought in the war to free Texas, and they gave him and my grandfather more land for that. But the war had affected him, and Grandpa was getting on up there, too. One day, when I was fourteen, Gramps told me that I'd soon have to run that ranch and that I better learn all I could, because my dad's mind was slipping away real fast.

"By that time, we'd built a fortress the Comanche couldn't take, and we owned lots of cattle and good horses. But our main income came from the corn the Mexicans raised and we sold. The war ended and we took some cattle to Missouri. Lucky we lived through that drive, but we made real money selling them in Sedalia. The seat of my pants were made of deer hide."

"What happened?"

"Oh, they've got lots of gravel on the way up there called flint rocks. It really crippled the Texas cattle walking on it. Then their cattle caught Tick Fever from ours and died and they blamed us. I rode up and back home with a half dozen boys still wearing Confederate clothes. That might of saved our lives, them being ex-Confederate veterans. I had fifteen thousand Yankee dollars sewed in my saddle blankets and bedroll. When I got home, that money really stunk like a sweaty horse."

Shawn was laughing. "Stinking rich. I love that."

"That was fifteen dollars a head for my cattle. I didn't know the man that bought

197

them probably made three times that when he sold them. I was young and green as grass. But I'd never seen that much money, or even heard of an amount that big being paid for anything. Texas was broke and all the folks in that state were penniless, too.

"I went home feeling like a millionaire. The next year, we took two herds of two thousand head of steers north to the new shipping pens in Abilene. I sent the money home by an outfit named Wells Fargo that said they would get it back to my San Antonio bank. It was over one hundred sixty thousand dollars. My sister, Susie, and I danced in the kitchen when I got home. But we kept it all a secret and paid our debts.

"I was afraid the whole country would collapse. They've had some bad depressions but none like we had in Texas before and after the war. So, when I came out here, I started expanding. No one has any money in Arizona. Ranching won't bloom here until we get a railroad up north."

"How did you see it coming — after the War, I mean?"

"I heard Texas steers were worth ten bucks in Missouri at the railhead in Sedalia. It was hard to get ten cents for them in Texas. What was I doing? Nothing to make money, that was for sure. My brother, Dale Allen, said I was crazy going off up there and I'd get killed."

"What did he say when you got back?"

"That it was a fluke, and I'd never do it again and make any money. So I took two herds north the next year to show him."

"He ever admit you were right?"

Chet shook his head. "He may have seen some light, taking that herd to Kansas, but them Reynolds murdered him."

"I bet that was a blow."

"Big one. Things were crashing down around me. So I went to Arizona and bought the Verde River Ranch."

"Run by outlaws?"

"Oh, yes. It taught me many things."

"Now six, and soon seven, ranches." Shawn shook his head.

"Get some sleep. We'll be busy tomorrow."

"Thanks, I love this job. I'm learning, too. Lots."

Chet went to sleep in his corner of the rocking coach. He slept some between horse change stops. They made Tucson by midnight, where they ate from a street vendor, then bathed at China Joe's who pressed his pants and did their shirts. They slept in two beds in the Congress Hotel, ate a quick breakfast, hired a taxi, and at nine thirty walked in Russell's office.

He introduced his man. "Shawn McElroy, one of my deputies. Yesterday morning, we tried to arrest six outlaws. Four chose to die. Two are in the Tombstone jail, four are at the undertakers. He's here to learn about purchasing property and banking. We're a little road weary."

Russell laughed. "You make my head swim."

"There wasn't that much water. Are we ready to go to the bank?"

"Yes. This outlaw thing came up after you got back?"

"Yes it did. Two of my men located this gang of stage robbers in a canyon east of Tombstone. They needed backup, so they came and got me. We rode over there, surrounded them, and they tried to shoot their way out — that didn't work. There were two teenagers in the gang — one was fifteen, the other, sixteen, was a nephew of Old Man Clanton. They gave up." By then, the three of them were on the busy street walking to the bank.

"Wasn't there a Clanton in the last arrest your men made?" Russell asked, waiting for a freight wagon to pass so they could cross the street.

"Yes, he was older and his name was Israel. He didn't make it and some woman wrote in the newspaper that we'd shot an innocent man. When my men found another Clanton was in this camp, they got me."

"My, my, you do lead a fast life."

Shawn frowned. "Is Tucson always this busy? I mean, all this traffic?"

"Yes," Chet said. "It's a real busy place."

When they entered the bank, Ralston Holmes was there to meet him, and Chet introduced both Russell and Shawn to him.

"Very nice to have you here," Holmes said. "We have a large boardroom in the rear. Neither Mr. Townsend nor Mr. Weeks have arrived. My associate will be looking for them and we may go back and have some coffee."

The boardroom had ceiling fans that stirred the air and it was comfortable. Chet wondered what powered them.

"What powers the fans?" Chet asked.

"A small boiler. A steam engine. I must say, it is the latest invention. It is a rather small one and the firebox needs to be seen about often, because we don't have coal available here. We use split wood, mostly juniper, and the engineer who set it up acted like that was impossible. But it works, and since then he's been busy installing them all over town and telling everyone that juniper wood will work. His biggest buyers are saloons, of course. They make much more money than banks."

Weeks and Townsend arrived and Holmes took charge of the paper signing.

"Mr. Craft, you do have the papers releasing the banks?"

"Yes, they all agreed and I have them on file for my client."

"Then this agreement is acceptable to both parties, or shall I read it aloud?"

"I read the original and told my client to sign it. It contains the transfer of the cattle and horse brand on those my client is buying," Russell said.

"We understand the contents and will accept his money," Townsend said.

"Gentlemen, it requires both of your signatures and for you to sign the check, Mr. Byrnes."

Weeks signed it, looked over at Shawn, and spoke out, "I don't appreciate you bringing an armed guard to this signing."

"My armed guard hasn't hired any men to kill you yet, like your foreman Masters did me."

"Gentlemen." Holmes spoke in a placating voice, but the two men ignored him.

"My man never did that. That's a damn lie."

"Funny thing, Masters has disappeared. If

he was innocent, why did he run?"

"No doubt, he feared you'd frame him, or worse, shoot him like you did that Clanton boy."

"Weeks, some day you and I need to have a fistfight and decide once and for all who is right and who is wrong. But if I ever see Masters, I'm going to do what his hired guns planned to do to me. Send him to hell."

"I'm telling you —"

Shawn blocked Weeks's way when he started for Chet.

"Mr. Weeks, if you don't back down, you're going to find out why I'm here. Now back away." Shawn stood his ground.

Weeks backed up and turned on his heel. "You ain't heard the last of me. You and that punk gun hand of yours."

Chet was about laughing. "Guess you're a gun hand now, Shawn."

"He wasn't going to lay a hand on you or even try to draw."

"I think you are both bullies," Townsend said, and started to leave.

Holmes cleared his throat. "Mr. Townsend. Your client left his check here."

"I'll take it to him." He grabbed it off the table and left.

When they were gone, Holmes spoke

softly. "If this is repeated outside the room I will deny it. That check you signed, Mr. Byrnes, had our name and his on it."

Chet nodded. "I saw that."

"It only covers a portion of what he owes us on financing that operation."

"I hope we do better," Chet said.

"I hope you do. Anything else, gentlemen?"

"I'll be back in a few days to set up an account for that ranch," Chet said.

"I will have the papers ready any time. We look forward to doing business with you, sir."

"Very good."

"What now?" Russell asked when they shook hands.

"Go back to Tubac. Then Shawn and I may look over all this grief I bought for us down there."

Russell smiled. "If I ever needed a guard, I'd hire you, young man. Standing up to Weeks like that took a lot of guts. You did good."

"My job."

"Weeks was impressed, too."

When Russell was gone across the street, Chet said, "From a boy I hired, you made the turn today."

"Thanks to you, sir."

"That stage to Nogales won't leave till five o'clock. I know a real expensive place for us to go eat lunch. Let's try that."

"Do I look good enough to go in there?"

"No, you need a new hat first. That one is kinda old and floppy. There's a wonderful hat maker right down the street."

When they entered the shop, the bell on the door rang. A Mexican man came out and met them.

"What can I do for you, señor?"

"My friend here needs a new hat. Not those," Chet said about a cheaper hat on a lower row. "One of those up there."

"This hat is one of my very best. It costs eighteen dollars. American money."

Chet wondered what other kind of money there might be. Oh, maybe paper *pesos*? "You like that?" he asked Shawn.

"Oh, that is way too high priced for me to wear."

Chet held his finger up. "I'm buying this hat, not you. Do you like it?"

"Well, yes, but —"

"Try it on."

He did so with gentle fingers. The grayish ash-colored felt cowboy hat looked very fitting on Shawn who was as handsome as Reg wearing it.

The hat man made a critical-looking face

at his customer. "Too big. The wind would blow it away. Try this one."

Shawn very carefully exchanged the first one for number two. He nodded when he tried it on.

"Not too tight?" the man asked.

"Maybe a little."

"Give it to me. I can stretch it." He barely wet the leather lining with his fingertips and then put the hat on a screw stretcher and left it there for a few minutes. "It will fit good this time for you."

"Where do you live?" he asked Chet.

"Preskitt, when we're home."

"Oh, I know who you are. You are the man works for the Force, no?"

"Yes. My name is Chet Byrnes. This is one of my men, Shawn McElroy."

"You and your men are doing a great job down here. I wish you luck. Those Mexican bandits all need to be shot."

The hat maker removed the new one from the jig and handed it back. "Ah, *si.* That is a good hat for you. Some *señorita* will see you wearing it and fall in love with you, *hombre.*"

Shawn about blushed. "It's way too good a hat for me to wear."

"No, when people see you wearing it and they like it, you tell them Obregon in

Tucson made it especially for you, *hombre.*"

"I sure will." Then he shook the man's hand.

Chet paid for the hat, and they went to lunch in the Towers. When the fine young lady took Chet's hat, she blinked at Shawn's. "My, what a great hat you have."

"It's brand new, and please don't stack nothing on it, ma'am. It came from Obregon's."

"Oh, he is such a fine hat maker. I will guard it with my life. *Gracias, señor.*"

A waiter took them to their table. Chet was about to laugh. She was pretty and Shawn was awed that his hat impressed her. Damn, he forgot growing up at times. A young woman did that to him one time over at Mason, Texas, about a big stout Comanche-bred paint horse he'd bought. Boy, after that he always rode fancy horses every time he went to town or courting.

The lunch impressed Shawn as much as the hat. And when Chet whispered the cost of their eating, he swallowed twice. Then he whispered, "God almighty, Chet, my hat and our meal cost you a man's monthly wages."

"Worth every dime of it. I should be rid of Weeks any day now and in the ranch business down there."

"We're still early for the stagecoach, aren't we?"

"Yes. I need to find a mercantile in Tucson to supply the ranch. Let's look at some of them."

They spent several hours prowling stores. None of them really stood out, so Chet made no decision about which one to use. Jesus knew lots about Tucson, and his relatives lived there. He could find them a supplier that was a good one.

They climbed on the stage and made the run south to Tubac. Chet wondered about Stephanie Combs, the young lady who'd ridden down with him last trip. If she'd been on this trip, she might have talked to Shawn. She wasn't important to Chet, but she sure might have sparked Shawn's attention.

He had to find a week to go back to Preskitt and check on his wife and Adam. How much longer could he lead this Force? He wanted to resolve a lot of this across-the-border raiding. Until they built a stronger law enforcement structure down there, this job would continue. But it wasn't limited to Mexicans. There were more would-be stage robbers in southern Arizona than any other place he knew. Many of them weren't Mexicans, but Anglo thugs who were forced west by law enforcement in Texas and perhaps in New Mexico.

More commerce in the Arizona section, like the mining industry, made the country more vulnerable than all of southern New Mexico, where nothing but sheep wandered the southern part of that territory. Apaches were still running around. Things weren't too settled in this land, and his Force had a need to fill.

When Chet and Shawn got off the stage at the ranch gate, it was after midnight. He thanked the driver, tipped him, and they hiked up to the camp under a starlit sky. When they arrived, Jesus got up and spoke to them.

"It was pretty quiet, except when I challenged Weeks about his man Masters. But Shawn stepped in and bluffed him away," Chet told him.

"Good for you. He's a big bully."

"You didn't go with them to the ranch?" Chet asked Jesus.

"When Roamer got back, he thought one of us should stay here. So Roamer and Ortega turned around and went to see about some raiders who robbed a store and post office between here and the Fort."

"That's fine. We need continuity," said Chet. "Get some sleep. We'll assess things in the morning."

"Oh, you have a telegram. May and Hampt have a boy, named him Miles. Reg and Lucie have a girl they named Carla."

"Well, our diaper team begins. All we have left is sis to have one."

"You will need more ranches," Jesus teased.

"We have enough of them." Chet went to turn in. Hell, he had plenty of them to look after as it was. He hoped his men held up managing them. With an attempt to put things aside, he went to sleep still thinking about all the things that needed done.

CHAPTER 11

Chet looked for Roamer and Ortega to be back soon. Breakfast for the three went quiet. He planned to write his wife a letter and notes to congratulate the two sets of new parents. Hampt must be busting his buttons over a boy. Reg would be equally glad to have a girl. Hell, his wife was his equal as a ranch hand — her offspring could hardly be less of one.

The day passed and his deputies didn't return. Perhaps he should go see about them. Maria picked on him some about his enlarging family. Her comments were attempts to tease him, but even her tries didn't make him laugh. He went to sleep at dark and woke up in the night.

Cole was back. He went to meet him and lit a lamp. "You're getting around late. Something wrong?"

"We had a few problems, but they're straight now. They're low on supplies. I

211

think it will be a great cattle ranch. I'm impressed with what we've seen. There are about a hundred sixty mother cows in that end of the ranch. So you did good buying them, but no way are there any two hundred or three like we first heard about. But we're out of food. I guess when Masters left, they never got any more supplies."

"I'm going to send Jesus with you to Tucson in the morning. You two can buy a wagon and team and Jesus can find us a good supplier. I'm sure Mr. Holmes at the First Arizona Bank will back my needs with the supplier. Go by and get a letter from Holmes to present to whichever store you two decide to use." Jesus had joined them and nodded that he understood.

"I don't dare leave here until we hear from Roamer and Ortega. In the morning, you two can go handle that. Will that be soon enough?"

"I think so. Those men he hired will damn sure work, but they all have families. They've saved us lots of time counting cows. And we saw lots of places to develop water, where it simply goes in the ground now."

"Sounds good. Does JD like it?"

Cole, weary from his trip, nodded and sat back. "He's really learning a lot. About people and his job as their boss. I think he'll do damn good over there. We're just short on food and a few things. Weeks never overfed them, according to what we've found out."

"I'll write Holmes the letter tonight for you to carry to him. I want you to wire Marge to send his bank five thousand dollars and sign it with my name. I'll write it out. I should have seen to more details. We left Tucson too soon. Jesus, do you know a good supplier in Tucson?"

"My choice would be one run by a Mexican that my family uses. They are fair. Andre Santos Mercantile."

Chet nodded in agreement. "We'll use your selection. Can you find a team and wagon there to use as a chuckwagon later?"

"Since it isn't a buckboard, could we buy mules, if they're available?" Cole asked.

"You two are my purchasers for a team. Just get it done."

"We can handle it," Jesus said. "Let us get some sleep."

"Amen, and thanks," Chet said.

The next morning, he wrote the congratulations letters and worded the telegram to send to Marge. That job done, he ate Maria's breakfast. Jesus and Cole headed out for Tucson to settle the food situation, and things in camp settled down.

Midday, a boy of twelve or so rode in on a drawn small horse.

"Are you Chet Byrnes?"

"I am, sir. What do you need?"

"I'm a messenger for a man calls himself Roamer. He said to give you this letter." He pulled a folded paper from inside his shirt and handed it to Chet.

He unfolded the paper and read:

Chet. We are at a border village south and east of the fort. The bandits operating in this region go back and forth. We think they are at a hideout about ten miles south of the border. I hate to cross that border without enough help to drag him back. We will wait on your word. Roamer and Ortega.

"Where are they?" he asked the boy.

"Canner Creek."

Chet frowned at him. "I never saw it on the map."

The boy shook his head. "It don't got a post office there. I kin show you there."

"I savvy no post office. We'll see."

"He expects us," Shawn put in.

"Yes. You need to load a packhorse. Bedrolls."

"What's your name?" Chet asked the boy.

"Frank Peters."

"Frank, you can lead us over there as soon as we get ready. When did you eat last?"

"Early this morning."

Maria had come on the run to find out about the messenger, and he pointed the boy toward her. "Maria will feed you. Tie your horse, though I doubt he will run away."

"He's a good horse, mister. I rode him from way over there. I started before the sun came up this morning."

"You live over there?"

"Me and my maw do."

Shawn nodded at the boy. "How old are you, Frank?"

"Twelve."

"You're mighty young to be doing this kinda work," Shawn said.

"Mister Roamer didn't think so."

Chet clapped him on the shoulder. "Shawn is just kidding you."

They both laughed.

Maria fed him while they loaded a packhorse and saddled their own horses. Chet had one of his good roans to ride and Shawn picked a big stout bay gelding. With rifles in their scabbards and plenty of ammunition, they loaded Frank on his horse and started east.

Chet told Maria they were going to help Roamer and her husband with some bandits on the border. He figured she knew the bandits must be in Mexico and they wanted him along to apprehend them. Another no badge deal. He hoped this one worked as well as the other two.

The boy on his short-legged horse kept up with them. The next day, they were in a place Chet had never been before in the live oak and juniper country. The road would have been rough on anyone trying to sit on a wagon seat pitching them from side to side. There were some signs of mining dumps and several shacks on the hillsides. Then Frank pointed out a corral with horses. "That's where he's at."

Roamer came to the doorway of a rambling building with his hat cocked on his head. "Where've you guys been?"

"Following Frank," Shawn said. The three shook hands. A tall thin woman in a wash-faded dress in her thirties came in the room and nodded at them.

"Frank's mother runs this boardinghouse. Carol, this is Chet and Shawn," Roamer said.

"Nice to meet'cha guys," she said. "We'll have supper shortly. As soon as the miners that live here come in."

"Thanks, ma'am. We appreciate Frank riding over there and finding us, too."

She smiled and hugged the boy. "He's my man. His paw died in a mine explosion couple of years ago. We had this boardinghouse and the miners asked me to stay. I've got a hundred proposals, but they just never fit, so me and Frank live here and run the boardinghouse for Mill Town. We used to have a post office."

"Well, he's sure a big, grown-up boy. Shawn asked him if he wasn't kinda young to do this job. He told him Mr. Roamer didn't think so."

They all laughed. Roamer nodded his approval. "He's my man. Let's put your horses up."

Chet, Shawn, and Roamer took the horses to the corral while Roamer filled them in.

"Ortega has been watching this bunch. There's a half-dozen of them down there in some *jacales*. I think they're satisfied no one can go down there and get them. They've made several raids over the border. They've been raiding ranches along the border, hitting Mexican families and white folks, too. Really have had a reign of terror, and no one has been able to stop them."

"Who's the leader?"

"They say a guy called Manuel Robles.

He's a tough *hombre.* One Mexican family we talked to said he's a prison escapee. Supposedly murdered a family and was sentenced to life in prison, but he busted out. He raped some women up here, but I doubt any of those women will testify against him. I do have enough men say they will."

"That's what we need, and any evidence of things they stole, if we can find them."

"I bet we can do that down there. They stole several saddles that are marked and can be identified, if they still have them. They also took an old pistol from a man named Decker Coleman. It's one of those first Paterson Colts, and his father's name, also Decker, is engraved on it. He was a Texas Ranger. I have a list of other things, but that revolver would really tie them to the crimes."

"You know, someday, we are going to get caught by the *Federales* down there arresting these outlaws. We've been real lucky so far."

"Want to wait till they make another raid?" Roamer asked.

"No, someone might get hurt. Early tomorrow morning, we ride in and arrest them."

Roamer nodded in agreement.

They left before daybreak. Carol had

made them breakfast. Chet paid and thanked her for keeping his men and for Frank's help.

"Anytime you need something, I'll be here till these mines peter out."

"Thanks, Carol. Good luck to you and that boy."

"You guys are doing lots of hard work. The real people down here appreciate you."

The way into Mexico was by pack train trails. Under the stars, they went through the tough mountain terrain and, at dawn, Ortega met them.

"You ever sleep?" Chet dismounted and shook his hand.

"They are all still here. There are some women and children, so we need to be careful."

The other two agreed.

"The big man lives in the *jacal* on the rise. He has two wives. There are four more men that live in the other *jacales.* Some have women, some don't, but he'll be the toughest one. The others are not that tough."

"You've done a helluva job of scouting them out. Thanks. Roamer, you take the *casa* on the right. Shawn, take the one on the left. Ortega, I'll take the main one. That leaves you the other one."

"Unless you catch him empty-handed,

he's going to fight like a *tigre.*"

"Goes with the job." Chet scoffed it off.

Ortega shook his head. "I don't want anything to happen to you."

"I'll be fine. Let's take them."

The others nodded. Their horses hobbled and six-guns in hand, they started to slip up on the *jacales.* In the dim first light, Chet came in the clearing and headed for the one on the rise. He walked around the corner and heard someone snoring in a hammock. A smile crossed his mouth. The big man was sound asleep not ten feet from him. Ortega must not have been on the south side, and not able to see this hammock. He stepped softly until he was on the far side of the hammock. Then he stepped in and pressed the muzzle of his pistol in the man's face.

"Don't move an inch."

The man's shocked eyes flew open. He realized the pistol was cocked and ready to send him to his reward.

"Who are you, *hombre?*" he demanded.

"I'm a rancher from Arizona. I'm taking you back there for trial for stealing and raiding ranchers."

"You can't do that to me."

Chet jammed the pistol's muzzle in his face harder. "You ready to die? I have no use for you. Roll out on your knees, get flat, and put your hands behind your back. I'm going to handcuff you, but if you make one move, I'll damn sure shoot you."

"Who are you?"

"Chet Byrnes."

"You can't do this in Mexico."

"I might have been told I couldn't, but I am."

No shot so far. He'd listened close. The others had their prisoners cuffed and on the ground outside the buildings.

"Did we get them?" he called out.

"Hell, yes," Roamer said.

"Bunch these prisoners up and go find the evidence we need. Shawn, you guard them."

When Chet went into the big man's house, the dark-eyed women backed away. He looked at the three saddles, no doubt stolen, but Roamer had the list. There on the table was an old pistol. He turned the six-gun to the light. DECKER COLEMAN was engraved in the barrel. He made sure the caps were off the nipples, then jammed it in his waist. That would send Manuel Robles to prison.

He found a large pot on a shelf and looked around. No one was in the room. He took it down and put it on the table. The jug was full of U.S. paper money, and underneath that were some gold rings. Taken from victims, no doubt. Two of the rings had diamonds. He pocketed them carefully and folded up the paper money. Lots of money. He'd count it later.

When he got to the door, Roamer was coming in.

"Three saddles in here. Shawn, you and Ortega better start saddling us horses."

"We're on our way." Both of them were smiling over their surprise attack and how well it worked. Chet felt the same.

"Those three saddles in there were stolen. I have them on my list."

"Good. We're doing great. Let's get them to jail."

"What will we do?" a woman asked in Spanish. "We have no money. No horses."

"I have ten dollars, and I've seen several burros around here. You better use them. These men will be in prison for several years."

Ortega translated his words for the ones who didn't understand English. The older woman took his money and told the other to go catch the burros.

They piled the saddles on some of the stolen horses. In a short while, the grumbling head outlaw was handcuffed to the saddle and on a lead line. Ortega led the chain of horses bearing the prisoners, and they wasted no time getting out of the hills. Chet took them wide of the mining village, so as to avoid any possible confrontations.

Five hours later they crossed San Pedro River Bridge at the stamping mill, and forty-five minutes later they were at the Cochise County Courthouse. Shawn went inside to find the jailer. The mounted prisoners were fast drawing a crowd as Roamer unchained them one at a time and made them get on their knees so he could re-cuff them behind their backs.

The chief jailer came out, a tall man named Yates, and Chet called him over. "That big guy, Manuel Robles, is the leader. He escaped a federal prison in Mexico. I want him chained to his bunk in the cell until the marshals come for him. He broke federal laws by taking stolen goods out of the U.S. They'll be tried in federal court. We have several horses and saddles stolen in this area. We need them as evidence. Some wedding rings, as well. After the trial, they can be claimed at Marshal Blevins's office in Tucson."

Yates told his deputies to take them inside. "Chain the big bastard to his bed. They're federal prisoners."

"I want all this evidence — horses,

saddles, and the rest — guarded. We're going down to Nellie Cashman's and celebrate. Wash up at that pump over there, guys. We'll have a great meal, then come back and round up all this, then put the horses up, sleep here, and ride back to camp tomorrow."

"Boy, I could eat a lot," Ortega said.

"They serve a lot of food," Chet promised them.

Washed up, they strolled downtown. A deputy city marshal who Chet didn't know blocked their path on the boardwalk.

"Check those firearms in this saloon," he said in a belligerent voice, and pointed at the batwing doors to Big Nose Kate's Saloon.

"We're United States Marshals. Stand aside."

"I don't see any badges."

Chet lifted his out of his shirt pocket. "Marshal White knows who we are. Now, get out of the way."

"Next time, wear it where I can see it."

"Next time, know who we are." Chet went right past him, planning to talk to Marshal White about his man.

At supper, he wrote a telegram to send to Blevins.

MARSHAL BLEVINS
MY FORCE ARRESTED MANUEL
ROBLES AND THREE OF HIS RAID-
ERS ON THE BORDER. THEY ARE
IN THE COCHISE COUNTY JAIL.
THERE IS ENOUGH EVIDENCE TO
PUT THEM IN PRISON. SINCE
THEY CAME ACROSS THE BOR-
DER TO COMMIT THESE CRIMES,
I THINK THEY ARE A FEDERAL
CASE.
CHET BYRNES

The large meal didn't disappoint anyone on his crew. Full of great food, he and his weary men walked the three blocks back to the courthouse to secure their animals and gear. Then they walked two more blocks back to the O.K. Corral and Liver. Horses watered and fed, they dropped in the hay and slept. Early morning, before the sun came up, they walked down to a small café and ate a hearty breakfast. Then later, with the sun peeping over the Chiricuhuas, they saddled up and rode for their camp at Tubac.

Chet was on the roan horse in the lead. From time to time, he looked back at his Force. Things were going much better on the border. Time to go over to Rancho

225

Diablo and check out progress. He planned to take Ortega and look at what they had done so far.

Lots of issues in that place needed to be figured out. In the end, it needed to produce marketable beef — three-year-old steers fat enough to eat. Then he'd need to find a market for them.

After dark, they were back at camp, horses unsaddled. Evidence was placed in the big tent. Ortega, arm in arm with Maria, went off to their *casa.* She left them a pot of hot beans on the stove for supper. Everyone was worn down, so they each ate a bowl and turned in.

Maria had breakfast ready before daylight. Shawn had saddled Chet a horse and Ortega brought one of his own with him. Roamer and Shawn were going to hold down the fort, and Shawn wanted to check the horses' shoes. Roamer was cleaning rifles and pistols.

Chet and Ortega rode out in the first sunlight to cross the desert and mountains and head for the ranch headquarters. Once over the steep trail and range of hills, they headed across the desert and by noon were at the ranch headquarters. The adobe hovels and sun-blackened rails in the sprawling corrals were not a bright sight for him. Nice headquarters didn't make money, but they did boost the morale of the workers, *vaqueros,* and even the wives. If nothing else, they needed some palm trees, like the abandoned women's camp and missions had in the area. The Spanish brought them up there centuries ago in their saddlebags and they marked many sites in southern Arizona.

He dismounted and drew dark-eyed stares from several wives who came outside to see who had arrived. Twisted in the saddle, he said to Ortega, "Tell the women to come talk."

"Hey," Ortega waved and, in Spanish, told them the patron was there and for them to come talk to him.

They looked at each other with frowns. Then, one woman waved for the rest to follow her, and they moved to join him at the corral. Many small children hung on their skirt tails and sucked on thumbs. Chet squatted on his boot heels, nodding and smiling at them.

"You translate. My Spanish is too poor."

"No problem. I didn't think they would come at first."

"They need to know us. Tell them I am the boss of all the ranches and I welcome them to our family."

Ortega told them that, plus more that

Chet savvied.

The women still looked stern, with their arms folded.

"Ask them what they need."

After Ortega's question, the older woman spoke seriously and scrambled to her feet to show him two small children that were no doubt half-white.

"She says they need a foreman that does not take advantage of the workers' wives."

"Damn, that is serious. Tell them my men will not do that."

After Ortega's speech, they nodded.

"What else?"

Ortega asked and a few quietly asked for things and others agreed.

"They need cloth for clothes. They want some meat — not all frijoles. They want a garden where they can water and grow their own food."

Chet held up his finger. "Next trip we make, I'll buy several bolts of material, scissors, needles, thread, and buttons, and bring them back on the next shipment from Tucson."

Once translated, smiles crossed the near dozen brown faces and they gave nods of approval.

"Tell them we will get them more beef and hogs."

Ortega told them, and that pleased them more.

"Tell them when we get a windmill, if we have the water underground, they will get a big garden."

A young woman said something to his man in Spanish. Chet knew she had mentioned *agua.*

He turned back to Chet and smiled.

"They said they could water a small patch by hand. But they need seed."

"You will get the seed, too." They knew what he said and clapped their hands.

The older woman, whose name was Angel, told him she would feed him and Ortega lunch. The others agreed and they took him to the row of hovels and sat him and Ortega on a blanket under a canvas shade that flapped in the hot afternoon wind.

Chet turned to Ortega. "I think when we get through, they'll like living on the ranch."

"Oh, yes. Were those children Masters's, do you think?"

"Probably. I think if those women had not been forced, she'd never have mentioned it."

Ortega agreed. "It was a serious thing with them."

"About as serious as Masters hiring killers to come to my house to kill me."

"You still think Masters was the one did that?"

"Yes, Raphael and his men found that out before they hung them. In time, we'll know the truth. Meanwhile, we'll need a couple windmills down here to start with."

Ortega smiled. "I thought the same thing."

"What do you think now?" Chet asked.

"You will win these women. The men will, of course, like that."

"That wasn't much they asked for."

"No. Can you find JD some more tough desert cows in Mexico? The cattle we have on the Verde wouldn't survive down here. But the native cattle in Mexico would think they went to heaven."

"Oh, *si.* I can find them. How many?"

"When we get the water issue settled and figure out what we have, we'll decide. I'm anxious to hear JD's findings."

Waiting for the meal, Ortega hugged his knees and shook his head, smiling. "I can see a great ranch here."

"Me, too. What do you see?" Chet asked him.

"A *hacienda.* Is that enough?"

Chet nodded. That was what he saw.

His thoughts turned toward home. *Marge, I haven't forgotten you and Adam. If things remain quiet enough down here, I'll be home to hold both of you.*

CHAPTER 12

Late afternoon, JD and the crew rode in. Weary and dust-floured, JD had a grim smile on his face when they shook hands.

"How's the rancher?" Chet asked.

"Alright. How are you?"

"Fine. The raider, Robles, and his gang are in jail and will be transported to Tucson."

"Good. We have a rough count of about a hundred seventy-five mother cows. About fifty big steers. Close to a hundred one-year-olds and that many two-year-old steers. There are fifty some heifers that should calf next year and move us over two hundred head. It could vary a few head, but we have put in some hard days."

"Sounds good to me. What about water sources?"

"We need to build some tanks. There are a few springs that need tanks to hold that water. Some natural water, but lots to develop. We're feeding and watering too damn many wild horses. I saw some good ones, but there's a lot of bangtails that aren't worth their eating a blade of grass."

"That's a problem with having lots of land."

"We can clean them up."

"Part of management of a ranch."

"What have you seen that needs done?" JD asked him.

"I guess you need to plant palm trees."

"I probably do." JD laughed.

They discussed his conversation with the women. JD agreed that everything Chet promised them could be accomplished easily. "What about the windmills?"

"They'll take time to arrange, unless we can find a supplier in Tucson and he don't cost us an arm and a leg."

"I'm not giving one of mine," JD said.

Chet chuckled. "That saying comes from artists that painted portraits. A simple painting of you cost so much, but if you added an arm or a leg to the picture, they charged lots more."

"I heard that before and thought it meant amputate them."

Chet shook his head and accepted a plate of food from Angel.

JD told her in Spanish she was going to

spoil Chet bringing him food.

"No, no spoil him." She looked at JD hard. "He will spoil us."

Chet waved thanks to her.

"What does this place need to run? I mean, how many cows?" asked JD.

"Five hundred mother cows. Maybe grow out the steers off the ranch."

JD shook his head as if perplexed. "I am already going to need horse hay to keep them there."

"See what you can line up at Tucson. Jesus has relatives that could help you."

"The supplier Jesus chose are real good people. It's a family-run store, but they are sure helpful. The Valdez family, they brought his first order today, and will be back tomorrow with the rest. Oh, thanks for talking to the wives. I never thought of it. All we had left was frijoles. I guess they never had much to eat."

"Fill them up. You can get more treats and things so they have full bellies. An army fights better like that, they say. Ortega says he sees a *hacienda* here."

"I do, too. But, damn, it is hot and dusty right now."

Chet shook his head.

The next day, while checking on future water developments, a rainstorm swept through the ranch. In their slickers, their horses splashing mud, they headed back for the base camp. Chet, riding beside JD, leaned over. "How do you like mud?"

He shook his head. "I guess you can't please me no way."

"No, in time you'll learn the things you can control and the things you must stand for."

"I promise I'll try to do that." Smiling and laughing, JD pulled his horse down to a walk. "I guess I learned a real boss don't complain about those things. That his job is to keep the spirits of his men up and not weigh them down with his pity complaints."

Chet looked over at his nephew. "That's the way it works."

Two days later, Chet rode into Tucson with Jesus to find a windmill merchant or a mechanic who could build them some. They got there late at night and slept in the livery hay. Next morning, before the sun's rays reached the adobe-walled city, they went to a hole-in-the-wall café. When they returned to the livery, they saddled their horses and rode up near Fort Lowell to see a man who they'd been told made windmills.

The name of the man was August Randall. They found him under some cottonwood trees in a shop full of smoke from his black-smithing. The man's face, blackened by his efforts, looked up and frowned at them.

"What do you need?"

"Two windmill pumps to start."

He pulled off his thick gloves and shook Chet's hand.

"I'm Chet, and this is my man, Jesus."

"Nice to meet you." He made a face about the smoke. "The wind is wrong today. Let's go outside and talk."

"Sure."

Outside, Randall stretched his broad shoulders. "It ain't usually that smoky in there. Where do you need the windmills?"

"I have a new ranch southwest of here. It's big and we'll need at least two to start, plus a water system at our base camp."

"Let me show you something."

"Sure." Chet and Jesus followed him to another swayed-roof shed made of weathered lumber taken from various former buildings. The door dug on the ground when he pulled it back.

"It needs a new hinge. I should get a real blacksmith to make me one."

They laughed.

Chet saw some new lumber boxes and several sections of pipe.

Randall bent over and raised the crate lid.

236

"This is a very well-made windmill. I have two of them. But they cost more than most people want to pay for one. I have been sitting on them. I paid half the cost of them and promised to pay the rest in six months. I thought I could sell them by now. If you take them both, I can set them up with pipe and all for four hundred dollars."

"Overhead water tanks for storage?"

"If you will build the base, I have two used tanks I can let you have for fifty dollars and I'll install them."

Chet looked over at Jesus. "When can we get one built and how long will it take?"

His man nodded. "I can get some adobe men down there in a few days."

"You go find them today. I'll meet you at the stables this afternoon."

"No. Meet me at my relatives' farm tonight."

"I'll be there," Chet agreed. "Randall and I will work out this gold-plated deal."

Jesus gave them a wave and left.

"He's a damn good man." Chet turned back to the blacksmith. "Now, a well driller?"

Randall wet his lips. "There is a man named Crazy Ed. He can pound holes. He's eccentric, but a good driller. I doubt any other drillers would go that far, but you could ask them."

"This Ed is crazy?"

"Aw, he won't eat you, if he killed you."

"Alright, where is he?"

"Probably drunk."

"I need a well driller, not a drunken crazy nut."

"He will drill you wells."

"How do we get him down there?"

"His grandson can do that job. He's solid enough."

"Here I am investing five hundred dollars plus in you, and you're getting me a well driller who will show up and drill, right?"

"Yes, sir. I will need an advance of money to get it hauled down there."

Chet squatted down on his boot heels in the shade of the rustling cottonwoods. "Now let's talk about all this, partner. Those pieces in those boxes are the best windmill made?"

"You ought to see the machine-milled gears, and they run in oil-filled gear boxes, not greased gears outside that gather dust and grind them away. These blades also turn and pump in much less wind."

"What keeps the oil in and them turning?"

"There's packing on the shaft that, in time, you will have to replace, but the gears run in oil and it has better and more bearings that other mills don't have. It's a super product. I thought I could sell hundreds, and if yours work, I will."

"So, my money and your neck are on the line?"

"The system is a solid one. It will work or I'll live down there and make it work."

"I spent five hundred dollars plus a fifty for two tanks. Do I pay the freight bill or does it come off the finished price?"

"It will cost a hundred dollars to freight all this equipment and the pipe you'll need, down there."

"That includes your blacksmith equipment to work on it?"

"Yes, it includes it and me, too. You have a well now?"

"Forty-fifty feet deep. You can't pump it dry with buckets, but it never has had a windmill on it."

"There are shallower wells that water small farms, and some deeper that go dry."

"They do the same in Texas. I savvy all about wells."

"You want me down there in, say, five days?"

"Yes. You have the timber for the mills?"

Randall smiled. "I was so optimistic, I bought them, too. It's in that next shed."

Chet pushed himself to his feet. "What

will Crazy Ed charge?"

"Twenty-five cents a foot and his food."

"Him and his boy?"

"Yes, his grandson."

"My cook may quit. No, we can feed him. Will he be there in five days?"

"Or sooner."

"You go south, take the right-hand fork here off the Nogales road. The ranch is about twenty miles south of there. Don't turn off. Go south on those tracks. It's due west of Tubac, but you can't fly over those mountains."

"I know where that is. You're Chet Byrnes, right?"

"Yes, I work for U.S. Marshal Blevins."

"Oh, yes, you are with the Force?"

Chet nodded. "I head those men. This, however, is my ranch. I have six in northern Arizona. This one makes seven."

"These mills are the latest design. They will pump lots of water for you when the wind blows."

"Before you leave, send me a telegram to Tubac, and one of my men will ride up to lead you in there."

"Thanks. Oh, that used to be Buster Weeks's old ranch? He talked to me about a windmill for down there a few years ago. I

240

gave him a cash price and never saw him again."

"That used to be his place, yes. Here's the freight money. I want a receipt. When we're pumping water, I'll have the money to pay you."

"I trust you do. Of course, the winds got to blow." He made him a receipt on the back of a page.

"Glad to have met you, Randall. I'll see you in hell."

The man laughed. "I didn't buy it."

"It can be a great ranch. I'm a cattleman and I know it can be."

"It simply needs rain."

"That's all hell needs." Chet stepped in the saddle.

"Mr. Byrnes, thanks, you won't regret it." Randall waved at him.

Chet rode for Jesus's relative's place on the river. It would be nice to hear some soft music and the quiet peace of their place. If Jesus had some adobe masons to work, he'd feel better. At last, they were doing things. But much like rebuilding the Verde River place, anything worth having was always a big struggle and cost money.

When he arrived in late afternoon to Jesus's relative's place, his uncle came out to greet him. "Ah, Señor Byrnes. Come, there is much food and music here tonight."

Chet hugged Jesus's uncle and followed him to the sounds of the music. Jesus came to his side. "We are celebrating. I have six men to go build your stand and the houses."

"Mucho gracias." Chet felt better. Things, though expensive, were taking shape.

Guitars played and couples danced under the Chinese lanterns. He had come to a peaceful place. Thank God. Amen.

CHAPTER 13

His mill man, Randall, wired Chet at Tubac that they were leaving for the Diablo Ranch on Wednesday. Chet planned to cross over the mountains that day and then go up to meet them on the road. He figured the freighters could get way down there the first day and the second one get to the ranch. He wanted JD to decide which plan he wanted from the several house plans he'd drawn up. But to have the water system in would mean a lot, and a sure sign of progress to everyone over there.

He wrote Marge all the plans so far and how they were soon going to see some real progress. With no idea about the time involved in windmill construction, or when it would be up, everything moved too slow for him.

He and Shawn left the camp to Roamer, Jesus, and the two younger Morales brothers, Starting up the mountain in the early morning, the air was cool. Hooves clacked on the rocky base. When a rifle shot ricocheted off the hillside in a noisy *karang* sound, Chet quickly dismounted, jerked his rifle out of the scabbard, and tried to spot the source of gun smoke above him on the steep-faced mountain. He slapped his horse on the rump to get him out of the line of fire and ducked low to find protective cover.

Shawn knelt behind a large boulder to his right. Another shot ricocheted off a rock formation to their left.

"How many are up there?" Shawn asked.

"So far, I think, one. Stay down and work to your right when you can. When he stands up to shoot, you may get a better shot at him from out there."

Shawn agreed and crawled on hands and knees for several yards. Then, in place, he nodded at Chet. "I'm going to shoot at him."

"Let me distract him first." Chet rose and fired three shots in rapid succession at the spot in the junipers he thought concealed the shooter. Then he dropped down and a bullet spit off the rock next to him. Shawn took two shots and someone yelled like they had been hit. Shortly after that, another rider left on horseback. His horse scrambling on the loose rock, he headed for the top of the mountain. Despite a charge on foot uphill, Chet couldn't see to shoot at him for all the brush.

"I think you hit one of them," he said to his man.

"I had part of him in my sight. What now?"

"Take our time and go up there. One of them got away. I couldn't ever see enough of him to shoot at him."

"He was out of my sight. I'll get the horses. Mine is downhill and looks fine."

Chet agreed with him. "Mine's up ahead. We're lucky they didn't shoot them."

Shawn nodded. "Hey, it got damn serious."

"Damn serious. I wonder how they knew we were coming up here?"

"I have no idea."

"Maybe they were coming over to get us, heard us coming, and took up to ambush us."

Shawn looked hard at the mountain above them and shook his head. "I'd of liked it better if we'd got that other sumbitch, too."

"We will, in time."

"You're the veteran in getting out of ambushes. I'm still learning."

"You're learning fast." He spoke softly to his horse and about slipped on the cliff side of the horse after shoving the rifle in the scabbard. His hand caught the saddlebags and he stepped around them. Whew, that was close.

"Long ways off that side," Shawn said, eyeing the thousand-foot drop-off.

Chet agreed and pushed his horse uphill until they reached a wide enough shelf to hitch their horses in a juniper. Then with his six-gun in his fist, he went around some more and spotted the bloody man on his back. He was Hispanic and his *sombrero* lay nearby.

Shawn joined him and looked down at the body. "He ain't ambushing anyone again."

Chet nodded and knelt beside the body. The man wore an old ball and powder .44 in his holster. By his clothes, he wasn't prosperous. But he'd never seen him before. He picked up his rifle and hung it by the thong on his saddle horn.

"Let's load him on his horse. Someone at the ranch may know him."

Shawn went for the man's horse and brought him back. "This is a big W branded horse. Isn't that the brand you bought from Weeks?"

"It is. Someone at the ranch may know him then."

"You don't think it was Masters shot at us?"

"It damn sure points to him."

"Whew." Shawn shook his head as they loaded the outlaw's body and tied it down.

"I'll lead him," Shawn said. Chet mounted up and they started up the mountain.

"He might try us again," Shawn said in warning.

"Yes, we better watch for him." He nudged his horse to moving up the mountain trail in his ground-gaining walk. They soon neared the top and a cooler wind swept his sweaty face as he reined up. In the saddle of the pass, he could see there wasn't much place for a shooter to hide on this far slope. Except for a few pancake cactus beds, there was no place to even hide a horse until they reached the desert floor. The shooter must have already reached the floor on that side. He couldn't see him, but he'd had enough time to escape the area. Chet started his own horse off the steep west side. The sure-footed mount slunk down the path like a big cat. Two attempts were too many times to make an effort to kill him. He needed to end that man's career at being an attempted killer.

Chet wondered about his wife and baby. He was already missing some things about

Adam growing up, but he'd catch up in time. If he was at home he'd probably be busy working on the ranch anyway, but being away from them bothered him. They made the last part of the trail and reached the desert floor of tall cactus amid some mesquite thickets. Headed north, they trotted their mounts. He didn't find any tracks to show where the shooter went, so they rode on toward the headquarters.

Midafternoon, they reached Rancho Diablo and several men came running over to them. JD came in fast on a horse and slid to a stop to survey the corpse. "What happened?"

Chet indicated the dead man. "We think it was Masters and this man that shot at us coming over the pass. Masters got away. This guy was riding one of your horses." Chet swung down.

Shawn dismounted and threw the reins at JD, who examined the horse for the brand.

One of the ranch employees took hold of the dead man's hair and lifted his head. "This is Bueller. He used to be Masters's foreman and left when he did."

"I figured it was Masters who shot at us, along with Bueller here. Shame we didn't get him, too."

There was lots of talk going on among the

crew about the man. Ortega joined them and scowled at the dead man. "They hated him. He was a slave driver."

"Good, then he's in hell. Let's get him in a grave. How have you been? Hey, JD, get the others out here. I have some news for the ranch. But first I want to talk to Jesus and his men."

While Ortega gathered the crew, Chet went to find Jesus. He found him overseeing the brick makers. Six men could make a lot of adobe bricks in a few days. The ranch wives were hand-cutting straw to make the bricks stronger, and already there were many rows of bricks drying in the sun. Two men stomped the reddish clay and straw until it was mixed. Then with trowels, they filled the wooden forms that held six bricks. When the bricks dried they shrunk from the wood; then the workers slid them out of the molds, careful not to break even one. The bricks then were set up slanted on each other to further dry. Already several rows of them wound like a serpent along the ground.

"This is going great. Come over for my speech."

Jesus followed him, and Chet began to speak to the ranchmen. "I've hired a man named Randall to set up a windmill. He'll set up a water holding tank and make a faucet to get water from it."

He let Ortega translate before he started again, "Jesus, you know, has six men making adobe bricks. They'll build a stand for that tank next. There'll be ditches to dig to bury the pipe he's bringing. There's a well driller coming to drill more wells. There is also a second windmill for the second well."

The men nodded in approval to each other.

"We have two houses to build, and then we'll build you and your family bigger quarters. When you are out on the ranch, bring in any young palm trees you find and replant them here. When the water system is complete, and if we have enough water, we will buy seeds for the women to plant and raise food. I want this to be a great *hacienda* for you and me and everyone."

One man stood up and held up his hand. "If — we have — enough *agua,* can we grow grapes for wine?"

Chet shouted, *"Si."*

They all cheered.

"They are as excited as I am," JD said. "What else?"

Randall had telegraphed Chet that he'd started for the ranch. "Tomorrow, you need to send a man up there to meet him and his freight haulers bringing the mills and pipe."

"No problem. Chet, years ago, when we were in Texas and I was a kid, I realized you were a doer, but you've really became one out here. These guys will dig ditches, or do anything, to make this dream come true. Ortega and I have found them to be loyal and anxious to make it work. It ain't a job with them — it's their way of life."

Chet agreed and wanted to laugh. His nephew had talked more in the last few minutes than he ever had before in his life. He was learning fast what made a ranch tick — the people who worked it.

The midday heat was still sweltering. He and JD sat in the shade of a tarp. They got plenty of hot wind and some grit from an occasional dust devil that came twisting across the desert country that stretched for miles to the south.

"I'm sure we can keep this place going, if you'd like to take a quick trip to Preskitt," Chet said.

JD shook his head. "I can go later. She understands I have work to do down here. I need to learn all I can about both the well driller and the pump man. How much were the windmills?"

"The two cost, with pipe and tanks, over five hundred dollars. Be close to seven

251

hundred, I figure. John is building some windmills at the Verde Ranch, but he can't make enough for all our operations. This man, Randall, I think, can get us more of them, if we can find enough water."

"I understand. I'm learning so much I didn't know before. But, hey, you want something changed, all you need to do is say so."

"Thanks. We need to do things different down here than we do up at the north ranches. We may have to use crossbred bulls, instead of purebred bulls. We're considering it. Learning to live and ranch with this dry country will be trying, but there's a way."

"I think so, too. What else?"

"Select a new man to head the adobe crew. I need Jesus."

"I can do that. I know he's part of the team, and with two of us over here that cuts you shorthanded. Where do you think Masters went to after shooting at you?"

"He knows this country like the back of his hand. He can be anywhere. We'll just have to keep an eye out for him."

"Are you going to get some others to look for Masters?"

"I'll get the other marshals to see what they can learn about his whereabouts. You make sure that your men go out in pairs and have rifles."

"I never thought about him doing anything to them. But you're right, he might take it out on them. Shawn and I think they might have been headed for our place at Tubac and met us on the way."

JD nodded. "That could be the case. I better go figure out who can lead the adobe brick maker. I'll talk to Jesus."

"You have time. And we need to select a house plan, too."

"Bonnie and I talked about it when I was up there. You'll be here. Let me go see about the adobe business first?"

"Fine."

They'd get it all resolved. JD was thinking like a ranch manager. He planned to stay over to see how Randall and his deal worked out, plus meet the well driller. Then he'd gather his three men and get back to work. He really needed to set up a team and get excused to go back to ranching.

Things were simmering down on the border. Fewer reports were coming in about raiders and crimes caused by border crossers — maybe they were finally getting a handle on it. He hoped so, anyway. Annette, the wife of one of the ranch hands and a young mother, brought him some fresh coffee. She and two other wives did the cooking for the men. They were sweet workers and he knew they worried a lot about the patron being there.

Chet and his men continued to catch up on things. Ortega told him there were some real wild maverick cattle on the place that would pose a challenge to capture. He wanted to hire some *vaqueros* and round up the broom-tailed mustangs and drive them to Mexico.

"They eat the grass our cows and horses could eat."

Chet agreed but wondered if the cost was worth it.

"I think I can get some Mexican traders to buy them down there," Ortega said.

"How many are there?"

"Maybe two hundred or more."

"How many men would we need?"

"A dozen men on horseback."

"How long will it take?"

"Maybe three weeks. Maybe less."

"Can we be sure they'll stay down there and not get away and come back?" Chet was concerned the Mexican buyers could only handle so many horses at one time, and the rest would hightail it back to the ranch.

"I see what you mean," Ortega said. "It would be foolish to round them up and have them come running back."

"We might hire hunters to shoot them?"

"They could make food that poor people could afford, if we could sell them to butchers."

"A dozen *vaqueros* and their food, plus support, would cost several hundred dollars. If you can insure those bangtails won't come back to the ranch, I'll spend the money. Otherwise, find me some horse hunters to shoot them."

Ortega nodded.

"I know you want to feed the poor down there, but if we get rid of those horses, I want to be sure I'm rid of them."

Ortega smiled. "I understand. We plan a roundup to get the best older horse colts rounded up for our own remuda."

"You'll need them."

Ortega smiled. "There is a blue roan horse down there among the bachelors. He is three or four. I think you would want him."

"You kind of teasing me about a great roan horse?"

"No. I will catch him and show you a great horse."

"Ortega, I believe what you tell me."

"What if I hire less to take them off the ranch and down into Mexico."

"You think it will work?"

"I will see and get back to you."

"Good, I trust you. You and JD have that to solve. But I sure want to see that good roan horse."

Ortega laughed. "You will really like him."

He was looking for Randall and the windmill. They should be there in another day. Earlier, he'd met the well drillers, Crazy Ed and his grandson Mike, who were setting up their small derrick to drill on a rise west of the headquarters. The old man was what he called a geezer, but they both worked hard and sure acted grateful for the workers JD sent to help them set up. When Chet went to bed on the ground that night, he wondered if there were any more problems hatching.

One of the riders sent to meet Randall came in at dawn. Chet and JD got up from their breakfast to greet him.

"The freighter had some wagon spoke problems," the man said, and shook his head. "We bound them with rawhide, but if they get it here today, I will be surprised."

"Thanks, Chavez," JD said. "We figured you had problems and were going up to see about you today."

"That equipment they bring is real heavy.

And those wagons are — what you say — old?"

"Well, why don't we get what we can down here and then go back to get the rest with their good wagons?" Chet asked.

JD agreed. "I can ride up there and do that. Chavez, get all the men ready. They'll need help to unload them here when they arrive, so we can go back and bring in the rest."

"*Si,* I can do that."

"Since I hired them, I'll go along," Chet said, and they soon rode up the dim wagon trail that led north.

They met Randall in a light wagon well ahead of the train.

He introduced JD and they discussed the new plan.

"That would work," Randall agreed. "I'll tell my contractor the plan and with your men's help we can move the rest on the good wagons to the ranch."

"You look tired," Chet said to the man.

Randall shook his head wearily. "It has been a helluva trip down here so far."

"Well, we'll help get this done. What's the freighter's name?" Chet looked at the dust they raised on the northern horizon.

"John Acorn. He's tired, too."

"We'll get this worked out."

"Thanks, Chet."

"Nice to meet you," JD said, and they rode on to meet the rest.

Acorn was a tall man in overalls, riding a stout bay horse with sweaty shoulders. He shook their hands. "Been a helluva trip. Never realized I'd have this much trouble."

"Park the wagons you have problems with. We'll go on to the ranch, unload, and come back, and transfer the load to the good ones. We have help and JD has some good blacksmiths who can repair those wheels and get them all rolling for you to go back."

"My God, man, that takes a big load off my shoulders. Let's do that then."

They soon had the train stopped. The drivers of the two most rickety wagon wheels unhitched their teams to ride and lead them on to the ranch. Everyone on the wagons looked dirty faced and worn out. They headed for the ranch, arriving in late afternoon.

The women had cooked a big meal in preparation for their arrival. The visitors took baths and were in good spirits when someone struck a guitar up and they had a *fiesta.*

Randall sat on a bench with Chet. "You really think this will make a ranch?"

"Yes. All we need is water development."

The man laughed. "That's all they need in hell — water."

"There, too, maybe. We're getting set to make it one anyhow."

"Tomorrow, I'll start making the pipe for the windmill pump. It must be a strong well."

"You know as much as I do. It's watered stock and these people here over the last five years."

"Oh, I imagine it's a good one. We should be pumping water in a few days. Will they have the water stand built?"

"I plan to get them on it tomorrow."

"Good. I brought more steel stock tanks. I figured we'd need them once we got things going. I also have two sheepherder shower fixtures we can install."

"I may have to send for lumber. JD told me he has hay coming for the stock. But we might need to thin those numbers of horses we feed down some. We'll need to feed his horses, after we get Acorn unloaded."

Randall agreed. "Oh, I'm sure Acorn needs to get back."

"Good. Hay is not cheap hauled down here."

"I bet that's right. Maybe you'll get an artesian well and can irrigate some of this land."

"We'd love that."

"You met the driller and his grandson?" Randall asked.

"Yes. They are going to start a well tomorrow west of here on a high point, in case they get a gusher."

"It pays to plan. Great food and music here tonight."

"Mexican people love both. They'll be glad when you have the windmill going."

"Take me a few days. But they are good windmills and, if maintained, will serve you for a long time."

"They'll be maintained."

JD joined them. "We should have those other two wagonloads back down here and unloaded tomorrow. I spoke to Acorn about bringing the wheels down here and us fixing them. But he's going to try to pull them back to Tucson with no load and may skid the axle. He just wants to get home."

"I'll pay him his hauling bill," Randall said.

"Fine. I can't understand why he won't let us fix them, but that's his decision."

"Hell, I think he just wants to get out of here," JD said, and laughed. "There are other haulers, if we need more pipe."

Chet nodded in agreement. "I'm going back over to Tubac if all this is settled in the

260

morning. JD, you can figure out the rest." He turned to Randall. "I appreciate your coming and installing the windmills. Hope the driller finds water and we have two up and running. We'll consider buying more from you when we need them."

"Thanks, sorry we had so much trouble."

"No problem, Randall, it goes with the business. Good night."

In the morning, he took Jesus, Cole, and Shawn back with him to Tubac. On the way, he went by to check on the well driller and his teenage grandson. The old man, Crazy Ed, was odd sounding, but the boy showed lots of get-up-and-go. Their little steam engine was thumping the cable drilling rig. Wood to fire his boiler might be another problem, but the men had so far snaked a lot of deadwood in for them. He left them working.

He planned to wind up the Force business and then go home for a spell. The ranch was JD's to make it work. Plus, he had Ortega to help him. He had water development and the buildings soon going up. They would see about the rest in the future.

The next day, when Chet and Shawn arrived, Roamer had a few things for them to check on. He left that for Chet to decide after he read them.

"Number one, they stole six horses from a rancher up north of Tucson. He thinks they're going to try to sell them in Tombstone. The market for horses there is sky high and no one asks questions. The horses all wear the rancher's brand, the HKY. They're well-broke ranch horses. I have their ages and colors. Let's see, his name is Ace Stroud. Florence, Arizona Territory."

Chet nodded, sipping on the steaming Arbuckle's coffee Marie poured for him in a tin cup. "Those rustlers may already be over there."

"May be," Roamer said. "Business number two, this says Bill Hunter and Slim Blandon cheated a rancher named Harley Wiles on a gold flimflam scheme. The two men brought him some gold-flecked specimens to his ranch and offered him half interest in their claim for five hundred dollars. He bought it and they left. He later went to their socalled mine and found nothing but caliche. I have a description of the two. They're supposed to be in the Tombstone District. Lord knows where."

Roamer continued. "Third, a man named Trent Marks shot his brother, Abraham Marks, and killed him. They were both drunk, supposedly arguing over a woman, name unknown, over on Whiskey Creek, and got into a gunfight. Abraham's body was found at their homestead and no one has seen his brother since then."

"What the hell do Behan's deputies do over there?" Cole asked in disgust.

"Sit on their thumbs and count cattle for tax purposes," Roamer said.

"That's probably right. Roamer, you and Cole see about the rustlers. They may be holding those horses outside of town until they find a buyer.

"Jesus, you and Bronc see if you can locate those phony mine sellers in the Tombstone area. Then Shawn and I will ride up on Whiskey Creek and try to find out where that shooter went. No border crossers doing mischief up here?"

Roamer shook his head. "Nothing like we've had in the past. But that don't mean they ain't around."

"Four days from now, we'll meet that evening at the O.K. Corral Livery. We'll have a good supper at Nellie Cashman's place. If you're still out chasing, you can just wire me there. I'll check at the telegraph office for any telegrams."

After a predawn breakfast, they left out, separated enough to not be recognized as a

263

group. He told Marie his plans, then he and Shawn headed east. Whiskey Creek was north of the mining district. He had little hope of solving much, since the crime had happened a week before and the tracks were probably gone. Maybe someone knew something — that would be his only hope to solve a crime like this.

They had a packhorse and bedrolls. The high temperatures had slipped a little lower as they moved into fall. It was already September and the year had progressed so fast. But he was about ready for a change. His job had shrunk to almost the duties of an ordinary deputy sheriff. Marshal Blevins could hire some good men to do this kind of housekeeping, if local sheriffs wouldn't do their jobs. Arizona needed Rangers, but they were politically a disaster in the legislature. After passing the legislation for them, they had conveniently dropped any funding for the new arm of the law.

This killer needed to be removed from society. But running him down should be under the sheriff's authority and he should handle it. But even in his own county, it wasn't being done. Why should he expect Behan to do it? The constant newspaper stories of rope justice being done by citizens told him people didn't trust the law to curb the criminal element. Riding through the chaparral, cactus, yucca, and century plants with Shawn that morning, and listening to the sharp cries of the California quails, he wondered if all his team's efforts were really curbing the lawlessness in the territory. The two of them and the mourning doves had the grassland to themselves.

They avoided going into Tombstone and camped north of the town. The next morning, at a small store, they spoke to the keeper about the murder.

"My name is Chet Byrnes. I'm a U.S. Marshal, Mr. Cline."

"Call me Mel. How can I help you?"

"Trent Marks supposedly shot his brother, Abraham."

Mel nodded. "Yeah, they found his brother's body up there two weeks ago."

"Did he do it?"

"If he didn't, no one else had a reason that I know about."

"I understand this incident was over a female."

"Oh, you mean Carol Scott."

"Who's she?"

"Well, I think she has a place next to them, and I understand she" — he dropped his voice to a whisper — "entertains men."

"Busy lady. Where is she?"

"About four miles north of here, at her ranch, the Y-Y-T-Four."

"Thanks. I'll check back. You learn anything else, I'll be back."

"Sure, Marshal. Nice to meet you, and your deputy, too."

"Thanks."

They rode up the wagon tracks that went north through the brown grass and century plants to finally rein up at the hand painted sign. SCOTT RANCH.

Turning up the lane, they rode up to the house. A woman in her forties came out on the porch in a new-looking dress. Tall and straight backed, she looked on the tough side when she pushed the graying waves of hair back from her face and gave them a pinned-on smile.

"Carol Scott?" Chet asked, leaning a little on the saddle horn.

"Yes. What'cha boys need?" Kind of like she'd perked up, expecting some business from two strange waddies at her door.

"A little information."

"Oh."

"They say Trent Marks shot his brother."

"How would I know?"

"I understood you were friendly with them."

"Friendly? What does that mean?"

266

"That you were having relationships with them."

"What if I was? I never shot him."

"Ma'am, I'm trying to find out who shot the man. I could haul you to Tombstone and have you talk to a judge about this case."

"No, thanks. What do you need to know?"

"A brother named Abraham was shot?"

She nodded her head. "They found him."

"Who was that?"

"Rick Harmon, Clyde Bloomer, they found him. Said he was shot and they took his body to Tombstone."

"No one has seen Trent since then, have they?"

"I haven't seen him."

"Do you think he shot his brother?"

"How would I know that?"

"People tell me you were close with both of them."

Her brows knit close; she glared at him. "You're saying I'm a whore?"

Chet shook his head. "I don't give a damn whether you are or are not. There was a man killed. If his brother did it, I want him brought in to face charges."

She turned up her palms. "I have no idea where you would find him."

"I may be back. Where can I find the two

men who found his body?"

She snorted. "Those dumb dinks don't know anything about it."

"I have to talk to them."

"The second place north of my gate goes to their place. I can warn you, they're too dumb to think. Good day." She turned on her heels and closed the door.

Shawn looked at him with a grin. "I guess she settled with us, Marshal Byrnes."

Chet reined his horse around. "I guess she did. Was that a brand-new dress she had on?"

"I reckon so." Shawn snuck a peek back at the closed door. "Why do you ask?"

"Details. It may not amount to a hill of beans. But I'd say that was an expensive new dress to wear around the house doing housework."

Shawn nodded. "Thanks, I'd never have noticed that. But I seen when she figured we wasn't looking for her company, she was sure wanting rid of us."

With a nod, he booted his horse for the road. "She knows a lot more than she told us."

"Could be," Shawn agreed. "A woman like her would have buffaloed me ten times more than she did you. I guess my mother taught me to respect all ladies."

"Not a bad idea. We touched on a sore point. I'm not so sure she told us all she knew about the killing."

"Well, I bet you're going to have to pull her teeth out, one at a time, to learn more."

Chet laughed and they rode on up the dusty wagon tracks.

They passed the low-walled cabin set back off the road under some drab cottonwood trees.

"That must be the brothers' place. We can check it later."

Up the road, they found a white-whiskered man soaking a buckboard wheel in a tank of water to swell the spokes.

Chet introduced themselves as U.S. Marshal Chet Byrnes and Shawn.

"Clyde Bloomer." He dried off his hands to shake with them. "Well, Marshal, what brings you up here?"

"The Trent murder. Can you tell me anything about what you found?"

Clyde squeezed his beard and then tilted his old weather-aged hat back, exposing the untanned part of his forehead. "He was sure enough dead. Been so for a couple of days. We hadn't seen them boys in near a week, so went to check on them. Boy, it wasn't a good thing to find, either. Hot weather and all. No sign of his brother around there anywhere."

"Was there a horse gone?"

Clyde spit to the side and wiped his mouth on his age-spotted hand. "Funny thing you asked, he must not took a horse, 'cause they were all turned out. I seen them a few days ago out west. A couple of bay geldings."

"How would a man skip out of here, if not on a horse?"

"Ain't no telling. He's simply gone. I figured they was arguing over her and had a shoot-out. They did that a lot. Even had a few good fistfights. But I never figured he'd kill him over her."

"You are talking about Carol?"

Clyde gave a high-pitched laugh. "Hee, hee. Them two was paying her well for the privilege, mind you."

"You mean for having sex?"

He spit. "Durn tooting. Trent got drunk one night and told me and my partner she was better than any cathouse girl he ever used."

Chet nodded. "Them boys have much money?"

"Strange you should ask. They got some money a while back. Their uncle left them a farm in Illinois and a lawyer sold it and sent them the proceeds in a check. Them boys both went right to Tombstone and cashed it. Neither one of them trusted a bank and told us that on several occasions. I guess the money is still down there somewheres."

"A large sum?"

"I'd have to ask Rick, my pard, but I think around eight thousand dollars. It was more money than they ever had in their life that I knew about, but they were kinda stingy. I bet they never spent more than a hundred dollars of it, unless her prices went up." He chuckled about that.

"You guys ever use her services?" Chet asked.

"Naw, she was too damn high priced. There's a *chiquita* named Rosita down at Gleason will do it for fifty cents, and she ain't bad, if you're interested."

"Not today. What did Carol want?"

"Two dollars a round, she told my pard, was her lowest price. That wasn't all night, either. Them boys used her. Not me or Rick. We liked that Messican sandwich better at her prices." Then he slapped the knee of his wash-worn pants and the dust flew.

"Wonder what happened to the money they had?"

"I figured Trent took it with him when he hightailed it out of here."

"But he didn't ride a horse away?"

"Hell, he could have waved down the buckboard mail carrier that goes through here and went over to catch the Overland Stage at Bowie."

By then, the three were squatted on their boot heels in the shade, discussing the disappearance of the second brother. Shawn was taking it all in, listening, and Chet figured from his solemn facial expression that he was making a case out of it all.

"I sure thank you. Who owns that place now they're gone or dead?"

"I don't have any idea. They've got a good well and it ain't a bad place. It's been proved on as a deeded homestead. If they had more water, some of it could be farmed. Three hundred twenty acres is the desert homestead size."

"I know, thanks. Well, Shawn and I need to go look at the place before it gets dark. I appreciate your help. We may turn up something yet."

"I hope you do. A shame he's dead and his brother lit a shuck. They were two good neighbors."

"I bet they were."

They rode back to the homestead and hitched their horses. Shawn had asked Chet a few small questions on the ride back. One was, did he think the money was still there?

"I have every reason to believe that the second brother took the money, if he left here."

"If. That's a big question. He'd never have left on foot, right?" Shawn asked.

"He didn't take a horse. They were out on the range."

"The mailman could solve that for us. Where will we find him?"

"We can ride over and check at Bowie. The answer may be closer than we think." He forced the door open with his shoulder. The copper smell of death struck his nose.

"Whew, it's going to be bad in here. Go get some candles from my saddlebags. We'll need some light in here. A few rows of bottle glass windows don't let in much light."

He used a couple of unwashed tin plates from the dry sink to put the candles on. Each man had a light. Chet found the dark spot on the wood floor where the deceased must have laid and bled to death. Shawn counted two saddles and bridles in the room.

There was a large flour canister out and flour spilled around it.

"They must have been making biscuits," Shawn said.

"Or someone withdrawed the money that was in it."

"There you go, outthinking me again."

"All we've got right now is I supposes."

"I agree. But it's the way a lawman has to think."

"Yes. Now all we need is the other brother's body."

"Oh, hell. You think he's dead?" Shawn asked.

Chet nodded. "We have one prime suspect."

"Her, huh?"

"Those two up north could have done it as well. But I'm thinking we didn't make the one that was home upset when we asked him questions about the murder. I think he was very open with us. The lady, she acted put out and not wanting us to know anything — makes her the prime suspect at the moment."

"But where is Trent Marks?"

Chet put down the candle plate on the table, folded his hands together, and poked his finger atop his lip in deep thought. He finally moved his hands apart and spoke. "Let's search her place tomorrow. We might get lucky and find some evidence there."

"Let's get out of this stinking house, too. I seen some split firewood, so we can cook something we brought. I'm starved, even with breathing in this foul-smelling air in here."

"I can put up the horses while you start that," Chet said. "It's a good idea."

"Coming up here, I really never thought we'd ever find a dang thing but the place where they found him."

"There's always answers to a crime. They aren't always easy to find. You simply have to search for them and then get lucky. Today, we might have got lucky. Word we had was that he fled. But how did he do that without taking a horse? Two saddles in that cabin means to me he didn't ride out of here. The fact his horse is still here is number two. Next question is, where is he?"

"Now you're thinking he's dead and the finger's been pointed at him for running away?"

Chet agreed. "It did, until two hours ago."

They ate the beans and bacon supper Shawn fixed, drank some good coffee, and rolled out their bedrolls. Chet thought a lot about his new baby and wife up north until he fell asleep. Good chance they might solve this murder — maybe?

Chapter 14

Dawn had a chill to it that Chet's long-sleeved cotton shirt couldn't quite cover. A greasewood and juniper smell filled the air, mixed with live oak wood smoke. In the early morning air that spoke of a push toward fall, his senses sharpened to a keen edge.

"Shawn, you may make a cook yet. These sourdough biscuits are almost real good."

The young man laughed. "I bet Jesus was a real cook."

"That, or he'd find a good Mexican woman vendor. He's a real good man, but so are the rest of you. I got shot at by an Apache while we were taking cattle east once. His arrow struck in my saddle swell and I ran him down. Cole shot another one on horseback and came down there. I told him to tie him up and bring him along. Pretty soon he came back by himself. I asked where the Indian was. He said he drew a knife on him and he shot him. Poor boy killed two Indians in ten minutes. That was his first two."

"I heard he was tough. I've been in some of those shooting scrapes right beside him and he's really a scout to have along. I hope I can do the same someday."

"That, and your cooking, and you'll do fine." They both laughed.

Leaving the packhorse there, they saddled up and rode over to Carol Scott's place. They'd return to spend the night before leaving the country.

They rode up in the yard and saw Carol Scott in her garden. Chet dismounted and walked over to the fence while Shawn hitched the horses.

"I guess you found the place," she said rather curtly.

"We did, ma'am. Shawn and I want to look around your place."

She leaned on the long hoe handle. "What for?"

"Did you know that Trent never rode off on a horse after the shooting?"

"No. I supposed that he had."

"No. His horse is out on the range and his saddle is still in the house."

Back at her hoeing, she said, "I guess he left on foot then."

"Not too likely, is it? I'm going to search your place."

"You don't have my permission."

"I can search it anyway."

"I'll file a protest in the Cochise County Court against you."

"Go right ahead. You must have something to hide."

At that point, she threw down her hoe. "Search all you want. You won't find a damn thing here." She went to the gate, closed it, and stalked off to the back door, which she slammed.

"She upset?" Shawn asked.

"Yes, I'd say very upset."

They searched the cow shed area and then the chicken house. Behind it, he scraped aside some loose hay with his boot and decided the new turned dirt there just might be a grave.

"Is he under there?" Shawn asked.

Looking hard at the closed back door of the white clapboard house, Chet said, "I think we'll find him under here. I'm going up there and ask her if he's here."

Shawn made a disapproving face. "She may shoot you. Be damn careful."

"I will."

"Do we need to dig him up?"

"Wait till I ask her." He set out for the

house. His guts were crawling. She might shoot at him. If she'd shot two men, he might be the third one.

On the back steps, he knocked and called for her. No answer. He did it again. Nothing.

He turned the knob and the door opened. He saw the spilled-over ladder-back chair first, and then the hem of her dress and button-up shoes above the floor. She'd hung herself.

There was no note. He went to the back door and yelled at Shawn, "You need to ride to Tombstone, get a justice of the peace, the coroner, and some men, to exhume his body. She's hung herself."

Shawn made a sour face after he saw her. "We need to get her down?"

"No, the coroner can do that. I'm going to look for the money while you're gone."

"Hell, she couldn't stand it, could she? Us finding the body. Man, oh man, I am sure glad you are getting some men to dig up his body. I was about sick, thinking about us doing it. I'll be back when I can. May take me the rest of the day."

"No rush now. I'll be here waiting."

Shawn soon rode off for Tombstone. In a few hours, two men came by. Seeing his horse grazing there, they stopped. Clyde

279

introduced his partner, Rick, to Chet.

"What's happening? Where's she at?"

"She's in the kitchen. She hung herself a while ago. I think we've found the other brother's grave."

"Well, damn almighty," Rick said. "I was about to offer her two bucks for a toss in the hay."

"She mighta wanted more money with her two customers gone," his partner teased.

"Where you figure he's at?" Clyde asked with a frown.

"I believe he's in a grave behind the chicken house. That's why she hung herself."

"She tell you that?"

Chet shook his head. "She didn't have to."

Late afternoon, Shawn showed up in a cloud of dust with the coroner, a funeral home wagon, and four Mexican workers to exhume the body. A justice of the peace also came. In his prowling, Chet found over six thousand dollars in cash. Also a recent receipt where she'd paid off a fifteen-hundred-dollar loan on her place at the Tombstone Bank. It was dated after the brothers' deaths.

Before sundown, the digging crew found a corpse in the shallow grave. Clyde and Rick identified him as the other brother.

They told the JP that he had a nephew in Silver City, New Mexico, named Rory Marks who could be the heir. The justice took all that down and gave Chet a receipt for the money.

"This crime would have gone untouched save for your efforts," JP Crowley said, and shook both their hands.

They went back to their packhorse, slept a few hours on the ground, and then headed for Tombstone to a reunion that evening with his crews. Chet felt much better. He wired Marge to say things were going better in the southland and he might take a break and come home for a short while. His left shoulder only hurt at times and that was when he overused it.

His four deputies were all waiting at the livery in Tombstone. They met him with smiles, telling him that word was out already that they'd solved a double murder. A stable boy took his horse and another got Shawn's and the pack animal.

"Sounds like you had good luck," Roamer said.

"Long story; we can tell it later. That case is solved."

"Cole and I got three horses back of the four stolen. But the rustlers got off to New Mexico. The owner from up in Florence is coming after the horses we recovered. We considered going after the rustlers, but they had a two-day lead."

Jesus smiled. "Hunter and Blandon are in the Cochise County Jail and the prosecutor says he will have a good case against them."

"Any news from Maria at the telegraph office?"

"Nothing is there for you," Jesus said.

"Roamer, you're in charge. Cole, you're the other married man. You want to go home with me for two weeks?" Chet asked.

"I'd sure like to go home."

"You go," Roamer said. "You two can catch the late stage for Tucson tonight."

"Fine. The rest of you are okay?" he asked.

Head bobs and smiles went around the circle.

"Let's go eat Nellie Cashman's good food. Cole, you run up and get us two stagecoach passes for Tucson, and verify the time we leave. Here's the money. We don't want to miss it."

They all walked to the restaurant through the crowd of mine-floured men and flirty whores on the boardwalks. It was a nice evening, cooling down after the sun set. The food and talk were congenial. The meal, as always, proved good and they had an easy relaxed evening.

Walking back to the livery, Chet took Roamer aside. "You okay staying down here for two more weeks? Then you can take a break and go home."

"I'm fine. She writes me every week and I try to answer her. No problem. You know, with the rewards and all, we've been banking our money. I never did that before in my life. No, I have no problem staying here. I'm grateful for the opportunity."

Chet clapped him on the shoulder. "It really has worked with all of us pulling so hard. I'll check on everything up there and be back."

"Don't rush. I know your ranch interests are important."

Before midnight, they caught the stage to Benson and connected with the Overland one to Tucson. Saddles and gear in the back, they found the coach empty and slept during the trip north. Before sunup, at Benson, they caught the more crowded westbound stage and headed for Tucson. Cole sat on top with the driver. Chet wedged in beside a large banker, and they reached Tucson by lunchtime. Chet recalled the Mexican restaurant Jesus took them to, so they had lunch there. He went by to see his lawyer, but Craft was in court. U.S. Marshal Blevins was also out of pocket. The stage didn't leave until nine that night, so they had a street vendor meal and hung out at the stage office.

"You met your wife on this stage ride, didn't you?" Cole asked.

"We had a long ride together. Interesting woman. I never imagined we'd someday be married and have a son. It was never in my plans or thoughts. I wanted a ranch my family could live on and be at peace from that feud in Texas."

"And now you have a good ranch or two, well, seven of them." Cole ticked them off on his fingers. "The Verde River Ranch; you and Marge's place — the Prescott Valley one; Lucie and Reg's up on the Mogollon Rim; the Windmill Ranch that Sarge and Susie run; Hampt and May's place at the East Verde Ranch; the Oak Creek Orchards; and now the Rancho Diablo that JD has."

"We've got lots of them."

"Sure do."

Chet shook his head, considering the situation up there. "I wired Marge earlier, so she knows we're coming."

They made it to Hayden's Ferry the next day and then took the Black Canyon Stage on to Preskitt. He'd had all the rocking around in a coach he needed when they climbed down. Marge ran to hug him.

Valerie kissed her husband, and then came over and kissed Chet on the cheek. "Thanks, I needed him."

"Hey, he said you did."

They laughed and he helped his wife in the buckboard.

"If you need me," Cole said, "send word."

"I won't go anywhere without someone with me. Raphael has some good men, and I can use one of them. But if I need you, I'll holler. Have a good time together."

Valerie waved. "We will. Thanks, again."

Chet drove the team for the ranch. He told Marge about their last case, and how well it went.

She hugged his arm. "I am simply glad to have you home. Oh, Reg and Lucie's girl, Carla, is doing fine."

"Great. May?"

"Their boy Miles is good, too."

"Everything going okay, you think?"

"Oh, I think May will be fine. She's the veteran at this baby business."

"Well, JD said we'd have diaper country. Our boy alright?"

"Perfect baby. He's growing in leaps and bounds. And I'm back to riding my horses."

"Good. I know you're happy to be doing that again."

"I enjoy it. But I am very proud of Adam.

He is a miracle in my life. I never imagined I'd have a child of my own, and having him with you makes it even greater."

"Marge, I know it's hard for us to be apart so much, but we're making Arizona a better place. If I didn't think it was worth it, I'd quit and come home."

She clamped a hand on his leg. "I understand you, Chet Byrnes, and it's the flame in your heart. How is JD?"

"Busy getting a couple of windmills set. The adobe brick crew that Jesus set up is working full steam ahead. They'll soon begin building houses for JD and Ortega. Those people down there are like your *vaqueros* up here. Loyal and hardworking. They're excited about the improvements. We'll expand their houses as soon as the main houses are finished."

"The government has paid us for more past cattle sales. Tanner sent me notice that several were paid."

"We're fortunate to have that market."

"Yes, it gives us lots of flexibility. Susie is staying at the Verde Ranch. She had a scare and thought she might lose the baby, so Sarge moved her back there. So far, she's staying down a lot. Monica found her a housekeeper. She's an older widow woman and a good one. We think and pray that

286

Susie will be alright."

"It's good to know about those things. And it's good to be home for two weeks and be sure we are doing what we need to be doing."

She hugged his shoulder. "It's always good to have you home."

"I made that ride again that we shared back when we first met. Made me remember."

"You may not recall, but I grew more interested in this tall Texan as we rolled north. It was the quickest trip I ever made from down there. Now, how was I ever going to show him how much I wanted to turn his head?"

"Marge, I don't regret a thing you did. I think about you all the time I'm away, and when I'm here."

"Good."

After she showed him his sleeping son in his crib, they went to bed. They fell asleep quickly in each other's arms.

CHAPTER 15

Tom, foreman from the Verde River Ranch, was there early to talk to him at the kitchen table.

"We're starting a nursery," Chet said. "Must be something in the water."

"Could be. Hampt is coming over in an hour or so. He wants to be sure everything is alright."

"He didn't need to come over. I'll be here for a while."

"You know Hampt."

"He's a good man."

"Oh, yes. He would be hard to replace, and to get as much done as he does."

"Well, how are things on the Verde River?"

"Good. We'll have enough large cattle to make some of those shipments to the Navajos this coming fall."

"Great. How's that operation going?"

"This year's calf crop will climb up in the eighty percent range. We aren't feeding a lot of dry cows anymore. Still have more to cull, but we're finding them."

"Good. We'll need those cattle in the future."

"I've had to replace three teams up at the mill. They broke down. Robert explained the work in the timber was hard on all of them. Those horses had some age on them, too. But that business is still making us good returns. We hear all the time the lumber market is going down and yet their sales go up."

"Good. That timber operation alone has paid most all of our ranch expenses. And it's been a good deal while we've been rebuilding the East Verde Ranch, too."

"Yes, it's a real moneymaker and Robert makes it run smooth. Reg will have a few cattle shipments next year. That's working good up there. He and I put our heads together with Hampt and Sarge a few weeks ago. I think we'll have a good number of cattle to fill the market needs. We don't have many unbranded cattle left on the East Verde. Hampt has several of the Ralston Estate cattle, and he keeps riders working that line."

"Maybe we can settle that one day. JD is long on bangtail mustangs. To clean them up would make room for lots of cows down there. If we had a market for them in Mexico I'd round them up, or we may simply have to shoot them."

"What are you doing about it?" Tom asked.

"Ortega is looking for some dealers below the border to buy them, if we round them up."

"JD likes it down there?" Tom glanced over at him.

"Yes, he's very involved in the operation. They're making adobe bricks for the houses and well drilling, plus windmills."

"Ever find that guy wanted you shot?"

Chet shook his head. "No. He tried to ambush Shawn and me when we were in the hills going over to the Diablo Ranch. We took out one of his helpers, an ex-ranch employee."

"Reckon he'll try again?"

"Who knows? I should have just gone after him and captured or shot him, but I didn't want to look like it was just my getting even. We have a good capable law force, and we get enough bad publicity out of some people in our normal operations."

"I read that woman's letter to the paper. That was stupid. But you're right."

"Good morning," Marge said, still looking sleepy and packing Adam into the room.

She handed him to Chet and nodded at Tom.

"I was busy feeding Mr. Byrnes Two." She laughed. "May's doing good with her new son. Tom, your wife, Millie, helped the midwives. May is such a capable woman for all of us. I hated I wasn't there helping her."

Chet recalled how he always thought his brother, after being widowed, married May to raise his kids. But Chet really loved her for all her efforts for the family over the years. She and Hampt must be very happy. Why, that cowboy probably was higher than a star with his own son to raise, along with her kids.

"Bet Hampt's busting his buttons," Marge said. She inclined her head toward Tom. "Hey, if Tom is tired from getting up all so early to come up here, we have a bed."

"No, thanks. I need to get back to the ranch. Things just go better. I have a good crew, but things happen it seems when I'm gone for very long."

Chet smiled and nodded, rocking his son in his arms. "That's why I have you. We can talk more later."

"That boy's really growing, Marge," Tom said, excusing himself.

She agreed, balancing a cup of coffee on a saucer from Monica. "He'll be roping chickens any day."

They both laughed.

"What are your plans?" Tom asked Chet.

"Spend a few days around here and then go see Reg. How's Sarge's leg doing?"

"Healing. Victor is doing a great job. Sarge may let him take some other drives up there."

"The cattle drives are one of our most important operations. Assembling them and then driving them up there takes a lot of skills. I'm glad Victor studied it while being cook and took it over when Sarge got laid up. Marge and I are that boy's fans. He was our cook and guide on our honeymoon."

Marge met Chet's gaze and smiled, then took back the boy when he began to fuss.

"We can talk later." Tom put on his hat. "Oh, Susie is alright. She came back to the Verde River Ranch for a while, but, according to Millie, she must have overcome her problems and went back home to Sarge at the Windmill."

"We hope she's alright."

Marge nodded while bouncing Adam in her arms.

Tom left and Chet went to talk to Raphael. He found his foreman busy braiding a *reata*.

"Oh, how are you, señor?"

"Chet. I'm fine. Don't get up. How are things here?"

"No problems. I want to cull some cows. We have enough hay. Tom has me five new Durham bulls, and we are going to start stacking firewood."

"You like the shorthorns?"

"Oh, *si*. Those calves are lots better than the longhorns. He said the white face ones are too hard to find, but he will get me some next year from the herd you have down there."

"We will have a bigger crop of bulls next year. I thought we'd solve the bull shortage buying those cows, but we need so many. Those shorthorns will work good."

"Tom told me all about it. He is a good man and works real hard for all of us, too."

"Good. If you need something, tell me."

He set down his braiding and wiped his sheep-greasy hands on a rag to shake Chet's.

"You be careful, *mi amigo*. There are bad *hombres* out there that would kill you."

"I know. Raphael, I'm proud of you and your care of this ranch."

"*Vaya con Dios, mi amigo*. Oh, do you need a horse saddled? Jimenez is busy saddling Mrs. Byrnes's horse, so she can ride him this morning."

"I can saddle my own."

293

"No. No. Which one you want saddled?"

"Pick one. I'll go back and tell them where I'm going."

"He will be saddled."

"Thanks." No sense arguing with him about it. He walked briskly to the back porch and Marge opened the door.

"I'm sorry. Is something wrong?"

"No, I'm going to town and see Bo, Jenn, and Tanner at the bank."

"I can cancel riding my horse."

"No, I'm just checking on things, and I know how important getting back to jumping is to you. Who has Adam?"

"Oh, you have not met Rhea. She's his nanny."

"Oh, that's fine. Have fun and be careful. I can meet her later." He kissed her. "We can have some private time in the next two weeks."

"I am counting on it. Tell everyone in town hi."

"I will."

He strapped on his gun and holster, then reset his hat and went to mount the horse Raphael saddled for him. Jimenez had Marge's horse ready and was down by the course with him.

He swung up, thanked his man, and rode into town. He went by Bo's office first and found his land man busy with a desk full of papers.

"Hello, stranger. I read about you in the Tucson paper. Rancho Diablo is all yours. And I've bought a dozen homesteads in northern Arizona adjacent to your other property. I'll send both Reg and Sarge all the information about them."

"The Ralston property?"

"They're still asking too much for it."

"What do they want for it?"

"Fifty thousand. I offered them thirty-five."

"I'd give forty to get it straight. Hampt is tired of range riding to keep their cattle off his range."

"I'll try then."

"Oh, did you know he and May have a new boy?"

"Good for them. I'm courting a nice lady. It may be too soon, but she is a nice young lady and we get along."

"It isn't too soon. I'll be pleased to meet her."

"Thanks. I will arrange it when you get some time."

"Thanks. I better get around."

"See you. I have plenty of work to do."

"That's good." He left and went by to see Ben at the store.

Ben was out, but his pregnant wife, Kathrin, met him. "He's gone to Mayer to collect an overdue invoice."

"Part of the business. Tell him I was by and needed nothing."

"How is your new son?"

"Growing. His name is Adam."

She nodded. "I know. I was there when he was born. Always good to see you. Tell your deputies, Cole and Jesus, I still appreciate my rescue from Utah."

"No problem. I'll tell them."

He left the store and went to the bank. Tanner must have seen him come inside the lobby and came out of his office to greet him. The tall banker shook his hand.

"How is that new boy?"

"Fine."

"We keep redeeming those warrants from the treasury. You're piling up a lot of money."

"We closed the Rancho Diablo purchase and it will require some improvements, but we're moving forward. Our ranch programs will start showing up next year. We've been lucky the timber business has worked so well."

"Yes, that business is so speculative. I don't finance much of it, but they sell a lot of lumber and timbers up there."

"We're staying busy hauling logs for them."

"Oh, your man at Oak Creek brought me two bushels of apples. He and his wife are so happy to have that garden operation up there. I had meant to tell you. He's been generous with me. I love his strawberries."

"They provide lots of produce to my ranches. I knew he was the man I needed up there. It's a Garden of Eden."

"I don't know anything else, unless you have something?"

"No, simply came by to check with you."

"I've read a lot about your law efforts in the southern part of the state. I think you are winning that war."

"Win some and lose some. We'll have to see."

Tanner shook his head. "How you manage all that is beyond me."

"I have good help."

He left the bank and rode over to Jenn's Café. Her daughter, Bonnie, greeted him. "I heard about May's boy already. How are you?"

"Fine, and your husband is busy putting up windmills, water systems, and making adobe bricks for your house."

"He wrote he was busy. That sounds good."

"Hey." Jenn arrived and hugged him.

"Hampt has a boy of his own."

"I got the news, too. It traveled fast. How is your wife?"

"Back to riding again. So that tells you how well she's doing."

"Her jumper, huh?"

"Yes, she's done that for years. When she was pregnant, though, she feared losing the baby and quit, but she's back in the saddle."

"I know she talked a lot about it when we were together. I'm glad she's back riding again."

"So am I."

"Bonnie is getting you a plate lunch. I'll get you some coffee. Have a seat. Cole and his wife went to Oak Creek for a few days, if you need him. They have two cabins ready up there."

"Good. That'll give them some time to be together."

He slid into the booth and she seated herself opposite him.

"Everything alright here?" he asked, considering his hot coffee.

"I know you're busy as hell, but I have a situation. You don't know them, but Martin McCully's daughter, Petal, rode off with some no-account guy. Martin's on crutches, lives here in town, and mends saddles and harness. He wondered if you had time to find her."

"How old is she?"

"Underage. McCully's wife died a few years ago and he's had a tough time. We all try to help him. He's tried to raise her but, well, you know the story. I tried to raise Bonnie and tried to stop her, too."

"Where did they go?"

"He's not sure and has no transportation. But I figured you might have someone could find her and maybe bring her back home."

"Where does he live?"

"A small house down there on Bayard Lane. I know how busy you are and all."

"I can look into it. What's her name, again?"

"Petal McCully."

"If Cole was back, I could use him to find her. But I'll go by and talk to him. If he's good, I might find him more work."

"He does real good work. Folks say he made the best saddles, but I think that's too hard for him now. He can't do much getting around."

"I understand. I'll go by and check."

He left the café and rode over to the man's shack. The front door was open and he stuck his head inside. He saw the bent-backed man raise up from his stool where he had a harness spread over a frame.

"Stay there, McCully. I'm Chet Byrnes and came by to see you. Jenn down at the café said you had a problem."

"Oh, I'm so glad to meet you, sir."

"Stay seated. I'm just another rancher. I guess I never heard about your services, either."

"Oh, I get by. I can't do much in a day. But my daughter left me and I don't blame her. We live kinda poor. But she's just a girl, and I'm worried the man she left with will abandon her when he's through with her. You know what I mean?"

"Yes. Do you know where they are?"

"Down by Crown King, I understand. I just learned that."

"What was his name?"

"Ralph — let's see. Ralph Thornton."

"How old is he?"

"In his thirties."

"She's in her teens?"

"Yes, sir."

"I think I can find you a better place to live and do your work. This place must leak when it rains." He looked it over, seeing a lot wrong.

"Oh, I don't need charity."

"I ain't offering charity. I'm making you a business offer. You and I would be partners.

I'm sure there are sons of some of my *vaqueros* that need to learn a trade, and could do all the moving around you need done, if you'd teach them this trade. They could cook some, too, and work for you and me. I have lots of saddles and harness that needs repaired. You would charge me a fair price, like you charge anyone else. Until you get going, I'd pay the boys' wages and the food bill."

The man looked about to cry.

"Now, me or one of my men will go see how well she's doing down there. She may not want to come home. But if she does, we'll return her. Don't cry. I know you're a proud man, but you need help and I can give it. I'm going to find you that place to move to, and I'll send someone to learn about her wishes, or go down there myself."

The old man's shoulders shook as he shed tears of relief. Chet patted him on one shoulder. "You take care of yourself. I'll be back."

He dropped by Jenn's and told her to send McCully a plate of food. "He's not eating right. I'll pay for it. I'm going to find him a better location, and find him some boys to help him do the lifting and the rest. Plus, they can learn the business."

Jenn kissed him on the cheek. "My hero

rides in and does the right thing. What about her?"

"I'm going to handle that, too."

"I'll be sure he gets food every day."

"Thanks." He waved good-bye to Bonnie and headed for Bo's.

His land man had three houses listed and they walked over to the best one a few blocks away. A small, tight, two-bedroom house with a good well. It also had a tight barn that could be McCully's shop and heated in winter. It needed a little work to close in the back porch to make a good bedroom for the boys he intended to find to help him. Bo knew the contractors to fix it and to make him some frames to hold harness, as well as shelves to store whole hides in the barn. He'd also have them install a wood stove for heat in the winter and an entrance door with a small office.

"He's on crutches and has no transportation. I intend to find him a buggy and a horse that one of the boys can drive him around in."

Bo agreed. "The corrals and small pasture will work."

"Since we don't want straw in that barn with a wood heater in it, build him a shed for the horse and a place to store hay."

"I can get that done." Bo shook his head

at the plans.

"What does the place cost?"

"Seven hundred."

"Get the rest done for three, and have him a sign painted that says McCully's Saddle and Tack."

"You amaze me at times, Chet Byrnes. You dried me out and made me build a land office business that really is busy. If not for you, I'd still be a drunk down at the Palace Saloon. I can walk by that place now and never turn my head."

"Good. You made a good partner — sober." Chet laughed and shook his head. "My wife will want the house all painted."

"Want me to get that done?"

"No, our ranch hands can do it under her guidance. Since I'm going to ask for some of their boys to learn this trade, I want them to have a part in it. I think he can train some of the best saddle makers in the country here."

"Chet Byrnes, you can make the world turn. I don't doubt a thing you tell me."

He shook Bo's hand, then rode back and told McCully he had a place and to sit tight. They would move all he needed, and set up the rest. He urged him to eat hearty and be ready to go over to the new location as quick as he could get it done.

In two hours, he was back at the ranch. When he gave the boy his horse, he told him he needed to talk to Raphael when he had time.

Marge and the baby came to meet him. He washed his hands and took Adam. They sat down at the kitchen table to talk.

"Well, what happened in town?"

He told her about his plans, and how she and the ranch crew would paint the house.

"And this girl?"

"When I get it all done, or close, I'll ride down to Crown King and see what her wishes are."

"This man is crippled?"

"Yes, and he has no transportation."

"You said Jenn would feed him?"

"I'm afraid he was so upset by his girl's leaving, he hasn't been eating. But he'll have food now."

"Chet," Raphael called from the porch.

"Come in here, *hombre,* we've made some big plans."

"I've been working cattle and am all dirty."

"Come on in, we live here. Taking care of our cattle is our business. I have more work for you."

The clunk of his heavy spurs preceded him into the kitchen, and, bareheaded, he bowed at Marge and Monica.

Chet made him sit in a chair, then told him his plans. Raphael agreed there were several boys who needed to learn a trade. There was a small buggy hid in one of the barns he could fix for Mr. McCully to use, and he had the right horse to pull it.

Marge spoke up. "Chet wants all of us to go paint the house inside and out. The men, women, and children can all have a big celebration up there."

Raphael smiled. "We can do that and have much fun. I will talk to my people about the boys to work and learn that business. It is a good opportunity."

"I will pay them, too."

"Oh. They could not go wrong."

Everyone laughed.

"How long will it be before we do this?"

"Marge can go look tomorrow and order the paint and brushes. Your women can make her a list of things they would need to cook. We'll all be there, and invite some of the town folks. I figure Tom and his crew would come, and so would Hampt and his bunch, and some town folks."

"Oh, we're going to have lots of folks there," Marge said.

"It's a ranch function," Chet said.

"Raphael, butcher a big steer," Marge said.

"Oh, *si,* and a pig, too?"

She smiled. "A pig, too."

"This is Monday. Let's plan to do it on Saturday."

"I'll send word to Hampt," his wife said.

"Tom, too, so he's ready. I think I'll go down to Crown King tomorrow and see if I can find Mr. McCully's daughter."

"You heard him, Raphael. Send a man with him," Marge said, cutting a disapproving glance at him.

"Oh, *si.* I know Jesus is away and he needs a good Messican with him."

Chet shook his head and spoke to the baby. "Adam, they think I'm your age."

The baby never answered him.

Plans were rolling, and as well as they all liked a *fandango,* they would have a real store opening for McCully in Preskitt. It would take him some time to get his supplies and be ready for business, but he'd be open and folks would find him.

Word was out fast and Hampt sent a note back that he'd be there at dawn to ride with Chet down to Crown King.

"The boy who took the notice of the party must have told him," his wife said.

"I don't mind. Hampt and I haven't had a day to ourselves in a long time. It will be a swell one, I'm sure. I'll go tell Raphael about a change in plans."

"Supper will be ready when you get back," Monica told him going out the door.

"I won't be long."

"I'm telling you, because I know you so well."

Their cook and housekeeper was a mess, but he loved her. Things were halfway fun for him now, to be home scheming and planning the Saturday event. He hoped his ride to Crown King turned out well. He had no idea about the outcome — but he would sure learn the McCully girl's wishes anyway, if he could find her.

Morning came early. Hampt came stomping in the kitchen and right off hugged Monica. Chet thought he about embarrassed her. Then he did the same to Marge and oohed at the baby she held in her arms.

"I'd have brought mine, too, but May thought he was a little young to ride along. Your nephews, they were kinda sour faced that I left them, too, but I said we had some real work to do and they could come along another time." He sent out a paw for Chet to shake and they lightly hugged each other.

"Good to see you," Chet said, and showed him a chair.

Hampt sat down, dropped his hat on the

floor, and smiled at them. "Boy, Adam looks good. Our boy's growing and he has his mother's lungs."

They all laughed.

"What'cha got into now, boss man?"

"Oh, there's a man in Preskitt named Mc-Cully has a saddle repair shop. But it's in a poor location off the street and falling in, and he's crippled. So, him and I made a partnership. I found him a house and a barn for a leather shop. Everyone is going to paint it Saturday. He's going to use some of the young boys from the ranch and teach them the leather making business. They can do his work, like moving the heavy stuff around, and learn the trade. The poor man is on crutches. He's in a mess and we're fixing him up."

"That sounds like fun. Now, why are you going to Crown King?"

"McCully has a daughter in her teens and she ran off with an older guy. No way he could stop her or go check on her. They're supposed to be at Crown King. I want to find her and find out if she's happy. She can decide what she wants to do."

Hampt nodded like he understood and began building his plate off the dishes Monica handed him. Scrambled eggs and cheese, bacon, hash browns, biscuits and gravy, and butter and strawberry jam.

"One of them Chet Byrnes rescues. Saving the poor and downtrodden — like he saved me, and forced his sister-in-law to marry me." Hampt laughed loud. "And don't you know that man he saved up there in Oak Creek has made us all strawberry jam addicts? Now ain't that a sight?"

"Hampt, you are a prince," Marge said, trying to stop laughing.

"Whew, May and I have eaten more good things this summer and canned two wagon-loads of things for winter, and all of it from him. Oh, we had some from our garden, but that Leroy is a real hand at producing things. How he has time to bring it all around, I don't know. You done good hiring him, boss man."

Before he left, he asked Marge to stop by and tell Jenn to warn McCully they were having a party for him on Saturday night and not to worry about it.

After breakfast, they left for Crown King and reached there in the afternoon. When they arrived in the mining area, Chet reined up his horse and stopped a worker walking beside the road.

"Hey, we're looking for a guy named Ralph Thornton."

The man made a pained expression from behind his whiskers. "Only Ralph I know lives in the gulley behind the Five Star Saloon."

"Thanks." He looked over at Hampt.

"I know where that saloon is, but the gulley, I can't answer you about."

Chet nudged his horse on. "They may know about him in the saloon."

Hampt agreed and they rode on. They dismounted in front of the tall steps that went up the hillside to reach the batwing doors. Chet shook his head. "Bet a lot of drunks fall down those steps."

"It could be a real problem," Hampt agreed, sounding like a veteran of them.

When Chet and Hampt entered the big room that reeked of tobacco and sour whiskey, there were cardplayers on one side of the room. At the bar, they both ordered a beer and Chet paid for it.

"We're looking for a Ralph Thornton, you know him?"

"He lives in the canyon just past here."

"What's his place look like?"

"Third one on the right. It ain't much, but houses are hard to find up here."

"With all these miners, I bet so," Chet said.

The man delivered the beers. "They could

310

use a lot more."

"There you go. Build some houses up here and rent them out," Hampt teased him.

"If I did that, you'd have to be the land-lord."

"No way, I'm proud of my ranch job."

"We won't do it then. You have any food?" Chet asked the barkeep.

"I can bring you some hot roast beef and fresh bread."

"Bring it then. We missed lunch."

"Good idea," Hampt added.

"We might finish this business today and sleep in the hotel tonight."

"I wouldn't disagree with that. Sounds like you and the crew have been doing big things in the south. You've got some good men."

"They've gotten better. Tougher, too. Like I told you, we arrested some, recovered three horses, and solved a murder."

"If you two hadn't gone down there, she'd have got by with it being blamed on the other brother who was already in the ground."

"You never know about criminals."

The meal was good, the bread fresh, and they ate it at a side table. Chet thanked the bartender and paid him, then they went out to their horses. Mounted up, they rode up the narrow road to the third house and stepped down from their saddles.

When a girl came to the door, Chet removed his hat. Her dress was patched and wash-faded. "My man ain't here, if you're looking for Ralph."

He removed his hat for her. "You must be Petal?"

"I am, but I don't know you."

"Your father asked me to come up here and ask you if you wanted to come home."

She blinked her eyes. "It ain't no business of his."

"No, Petal, but it's your business whether you want to stay or go home with us."

She shook her head. "I ain't going back."

"We didn't come here to make you go back. But many girls leave home and then they find their new life is not roses and want to go back. Your father will soon have a new house to live in and a shop, plus two boys to help him do his work. He'll have a buggy and a horse to pull it, so he can get around."

"How did he get all that? Rob a bank?"

"No. A man went partners with him. We're painting the house and shop this Saturday and moving him in. A kinda grand opening."

"I already done this business of taking up with him." She dropped her chin.

"Is he going to marry you?"

"He never said so."

"Well, maybe he won't, or maybe he will."

"You shouldn't have come. You're going to make me cry."

"Your daddy cried when he talked about you to me."

A man rode up on a poor horse, jumped down, and rushed in the yard. "Who in the hell are you two, messing around with my woman?"

Hampt caught him by the shoulder and pressed a thumb into him. "It ain't who we are. We're making certain this fine young lady is where she wants to be."

"Ralph, I never called for them. My daddy sent them to ask me if I was happy here." She began to bawl.

Her man shouted, "Tell them you are. Tell them we're getting married soon as I can get ten bucks."

Hampt eased up on his grip. "I've got ten bucks. Where's the preacher?"

She looked bewildered. "Ralph, you never mentioned that before. You never did."

"Petal, I love you. You're my woman. You know I love you."

"Petal, go back to your father's house. Help him. If Ralph really loves you, he'll come along, find a job, propose, and marry you. It will be winter soon, and if he has no work, you'll freeze or starve to death up here."

"You ain't got no business messing with a man's woman —"

"You didn't mention marriage to her, because you ain't divorced from the last one." Chet tried a ploy on him.

His face melted at the accusation. "How did you know that?"

"You just told me."

"I asked you three times if'n you was married. You said no and never. Ralph Thornton, you lied to me," cried the girl.

"I can't help what I done before. I love you."

"When you get your divorce papers, she'll be in Preskitt," Chet said.

Petal nodded. "I'll go back with you two."

"Get your things." Chet sent her inside.

"Damn it. Who in the hell are you anyway?" Thornton demanded.

"He's Chet Byrnes, owns Quarter Circle Z on the Verde, and I'm one of his foremen, Hampt Tate."

"I'll be gawdamned. You're the guys got all those outlaw gangs?"

Hampt nodded. "You're lucky, too. We usually shoot first and ask questions later."

"I don't even wear a gun."

"That might be why we didn't shoot you."

Chet gave Hampt her blanket-wrapped things. He lowered his left arm and brought her up behind him in the saddle.

"Let's ride."

Hampt was on his horse. "You ate anything today?"

"No."

"My wife, May, sent along some fried pies that ought to fit us all."

"Bless May's heart. She just had a baby a few days ago," Chet said over his shoulder to her.

"She must be a mighty fine wife," Petal said.

"Petal, if I started now and talked all the way to Preskitt, I couldn't tell you all the good things she is and does for me in my life," said Hampt.

"Believe me, he has that many stories to tell."

Busy eating her fried pie, she asked him, "Would she show me how to make these?"

"You'll meet her Saturday night. You just ask her."

"Mr. Byrnes?"

"Yes, Petal."

"I sure hope I'm doing the right thing. I'm convinced, but I don't ever want anyone to see me again."

"Petal, you hold your head up. You're a lovely girl with a lifetime to give to a man who has a job and a place for you to live. Don't ever let me catch you with your head down. God forgives us for our sins and he will forgive yours."

"I'll try to remember that, sir."

"I'm just Chet."

"May God bless you for me."

He knew she was crying, sitting back there behind the cantle. But as the evening sun settled west of the Bradshaws they were on top of, he knew she'd find her a real life. When Marge learned about the problem, she'd buy the girl a new dress to wear for Saturday night. He could always count on her to do the good things he couldn't handle. Damn, he was lucky to have her.

CHAPTER 16

Chet, Hampt, and their ward rode all night to reach Preskitt after sunup. When they stopped at Jenn's Café, Petal didn't want to go in. Chet took her arm and guided her inside. Bonnie found them a table in the back.

"You're up early," Bonnie said.

"We ain't went to bed," Hampt whispered.

"Oh, yes, you are McCully's daughter, Petal. They went and brought you back?"

Petal dropped her head and never said a word.

"You are so lucky. I'm so lucky, too. They brought me back from Mexico where I was a slave. Don't act so upset. You're free now and no one can ever take that from you. Hold your head up." Bonnie took a napkin and carefully wiped away the tears from Petal's face. "They did that for me. You were lucky, too."

"Yes. I never knew that."

317

"Now you do. Don't be sad. Live your days like every one of them is precious."

Jenn brought them coffee and smiled. "Fast trip."

She patted Petal on the shoulder. "Nice to have you back, dear."

"Thanks, Jenn."

After breakfast, they took her home. Once off the horse, he pressed ten dollars in her palm. "My wife's name is Marge. She'll be here to get you some new dresses. One to wear Saturday night."

"Yes, sir."

McCully came out of the door, shaky and too fast on his crutches. She caught him around the waist and saved him from a fall.

"Oh, thank God, my girl is back home!" he exclaimed as they hugged each other.

Chet and Hampt rode off for the top ranch where they fell across their beds and slept for several hours.

Around six p.m., Marge woke them up, gave them clothes, towels, and soap so they could go clean up. "Monica has lots of food fixed. I hope you two are hungry."

"Only thing we had to eat was some of May's fried pies," Chet teased.

"Well, you two didn't have Jesus along to cook for you."

"We're fine. It turned out good; I promised you would help her find some new dresses to wear, and especially one for our *fandango.*"

"I better do that tomorrow."

"I'm sorry, but she's in rags."

"I can handle that. I'll get Jenn to help me."

Chet and Hampt showered and dressed before going back to the house.

"When we were fighting for the Verde River Ranch, we'd sure have gave a lot of money for a shower and a cooked meal," said Hampt.

"Hampt, I wondered how crazy I was to have come out here to buy a ranch and run into a deal like we had down there. Starving Indians to feed. I wasn't sure at all I had the patience to do all we did."

"I'm just damn glad you picked me to help. I was a saddle bum. Out of work, except some day jobs, and I figured I'd never get to cowboy again."

"You, Tom, and Sarge are the greatest men I ever knew."

"Hey, I go along. But you find good men. We just needed a man to figure things out, so we could carry out his plans. I bet that little man on crutches builds some helluva good saddles."

"If we can find him some good leather

stock, I bet he can."

"I better eat and ride home."

"You can spend the night."

"I can be home in a few hours. I enjoyed you taking me along, but this old married man misses his wife and the kids. Those two big boys and the girl are mine now, too. I won't forget them, but Miles is a treasure."

"Let's eat. I'll have them saddle a horse for you." They went by the barn and he told Jimenez to find Hampt a good horse and put his gear on him.

Monica had supper on the table. With large cuts of beef on their plates, they passed bowls of potatoes, gravy, green beans, and fresh baked sourdough bread. They worked hard at eating, bragged on her cooking, and laughed a lot.

"What convinced his daughter to come home?" Marge asked.

"When your husband asked him if he was divorced yet. Petal said he'd denied ever being married. I guess she figured out then that he'd lied to her," said Hampt.

"Poor girl."

"She's had a rough life," said Chet. "Lost her mother. But her father's on the mend in his life. Maybe not from his handicaps, but they will live better in the future."

"How did she get hooked up with that man?"

"There are buzzards like him floating around all the time, looking for poor girls."

"Well, I am lucky none found me," Marge teased.

"No, I'm glad none got you, too."

After the meal, he sent Hampt back to his wife on a good fresh horse that he could run home on.

With Marge under his arm, they headed for the bedroom where they fed the baby and went to bed. He found sleep fast and woke before dawn. Monica was downstairs in the kitchen with coffee made and he sipped on a hot fresh cup.

"Where are you going?"

"I need to go up on the Rim to see Reg and Lucie, and their new baby, but I can't leave until Sunday. I never realized all the things I'd need to do here."

She shook her head. "You'll still be helping people when the Good Lord comes for you, and he'll have to wait."

"Oh, Monica. I'm just one man who likes to ranch and wants this territory to become a state."

"I better get Marge up, so she can help that girl find some dresses. You taking her to town?"

"No, I may go look at the East Verde Ranch, and come back tonight."

"You tell her. I don't want to be the mail service here."

He looked at Monica's back and shook his head, but she never saw him do it.

She delivered his fried eggs, pushed the bowl of German-fried potatoes at him, along with the bacon. Then she went for coffee and poured it in his cup.

"Something wrong?"

"Why?" She whirled around and frowned at him.

He held up his hands. "You sound awful sharp this morning."

She pointed her finger and shook it in his face. "If you tell her I told you, I will never tell you another thing."

"What is it?"

She leaned over and whispered in his ear. "She fell off that jumping horse yesterday. I've tried to get her to quit but, of course, she made me promise to not tell anyone, especially you. She could have been hurt. But don't you say one word about it."

Her words sobered him up sharp-like. How in the hell did he handle that? Her number one thing in this world was jumping her horses. And the baby was here, so she had nothing holding her back. Maybe

322

he better take her to town and see if she would tell him anything about her fall. Damn, sometimes things in life made a big mess that was harder to handle than a ranch or law problem.

Not much in their lives they hadn't worked out, but her jumping was something he knew she wanted to do so bad. The whole notion hurt him, but he damn sure didn't want to lose her.

"Eat your breakfast," Monica said. "It won't be good cold."

"Yes, ma'am."

She shook her head in defeat. "You ain't no tougher than I am about this matter. I can see that now."

"I may shoot the damn horse."

"Oh, no. You wouldn't do that. Ain't his fault anyway."

"No, but I'm tempted."

He found Jimenez and had him hitch the team. Maybe he could convince her to jump lower ones. No need to bring her groom in on it. All the poor boy did was what she told him to do. After that, Chet went down and checked the course. On the third jump there was a new bar in the top notch. She probably broke it in her fall.

He shook his head and went back to the house.

"Going to the Verde? Monica said you didn't tell her where you were going today."

Liar. "No I'm going to drive you to town to get Petal a dress or two. I can go by to see Bo and check on the contractor he hired to fix the place." He kissed her. Then he sat down. "Jimenez is hooking the buckboard for us."

"It will take me a little longer to be ready. I thought you might go to the Verde today?"

"I can go Friday, or next week, when I go to see Robert, as well as Reg and Lucie."

"Oh, hey, I'm grateful you're taking me to town."

"Good." He clamped his hand on top of hers.

She winced at his touch.

"You hurt?"

"No, I just jammed it a little, that's all."

"Is it broke?"

"No, silly. I'm fine."

"I hope so."

"I better go see how Adam and his nanny are doing. Then I'll be ready to go to town."

"No rush. The horses are ready." He noticed her slight limp on the right side. As she went to check on the baby, she was doing her best to hide it. Damn.

"She's pretty sore," he whispered to Monica.

She shook her head. "I know. I know. You can't tell her a thing about that jumping."

"Thanks. I owe you one."

Marge came out wearing a canvas duster coat. The morning was cooler than usual. He helped her on the seat and she sat down gingerly.

"It's so nice to have you home. I almost feel like a wife again."

"Good to be here. What else did you hurt when you hurt your wrist?"

"Oh, nothing. My hip is a little sore."

"You don't need the doctor to check you?"

"Of course not. I just tripped and fell. Clumsy me."

"Alright. I'm just concerned."

"Alright. Alright, my horse took a fall. I know you worry about me jumping, but I've only had some minor spills. The dirt in the pen is sandy and not caliche hard. I won't jump him that high again, unless I'm certain he can clear it. Oh, Chet, I didn't want you to worry about me. I'm sorry."

He hugged her. "You and Adam are all I have close to me. Make those lower jumps, please?"

"I will. Now did that ruin your day, finding out about me being clumsy?"

"No, but I worry about your safety, for both our sakes."

"Well, you go and get shot."

"Someone has to bring justice to this territory. I don't take many chances."

She squeezed his leg. "Let's have fun today. Tell me about this poor girl."

"She's young. But all girls have become young to me. Her and her father live in a trap. And I don't think they always have food. He's a craftsman, but I can see he has no leather to make things. Have you gone by their new house?" he asked.

"Oh, yes, that's a nice place, and with paint it will be great for them."

"I thought so, too. Poor girl is in rags. Lost, and she agreed to come back on her own free will. I think she saw the mistake she'd made."

"Should I have a doctor check her? She may have been exposed to some disease."

"Yes, but make it her wish."

"I understand."

"You take the world on your shoulders. Are we going by Jenn's first?"

"If she can get off, I'm sure she'd like to go. Cole and Valerie are up at Oak Creek honeymooning. Jenn may not have enough help."

"We'll see. I enjoy her company and she can help me boost this girl's morale."

"She needs a ton of that."

They went by for Jenn who had enough help and, with him standing in the back of the spring seat, they drove to Bo's office and let him off.

"I can make it from here. When you get done this afternoon, I'll be at Jenn's place. Take Petal to lunch. You need any money?"

"No, we're fine," Marge said after he kissed her.

"You two are a great couple," Jenn said, and they drove off.

He and Bo walked over to the house.

"You can meet my new lady," Bo said. "Marge invited me to the party."

"Hell, you knew you were invited."

"It was still nice to be asked. You will meet her anyway."

"I'll look forward to meeting the lady."

"Rhineheart, the contractor, says we're lucky they have the matching wood siding on the house here in stock. So he can make a pretty good match on that enclosure on the back. The shed is going up and the barn renovation is going good, too. He went by and looked at Beam's saddle shop and got ideas how to make him racks and shelves. Good enough?"

"That should work."

"He's making a place in the barn to park the buggy inside, as well as harness racks on the wall. There's way more room in that barn than he'll ever need for his shop. So, they're making a heated area that can be opened up in summer weather. Making a stall in the back of the barn for the horse to get out of the weather, and a hay shed at a distance so the shop won't catch on fire, or the barn, either."

"You sound like you're getting it done."

"I guess Marge's got enough paint and brushes. She said your foreman had enough ladders and they're bringing them."

"I guess so."

"How did your trip to Crown King go?" Bo asked.

"She agreed to come home with us. Hampt went with me."

"Yeah, if I got in a fight, I'd want him to back me — or stand in front of me, would be even better."

Chet shook his head. "Hampt is a prize. He married my sister-in-law, May, and he's got her singing and playing the piano. As long as she was around all of us, we never knew she could do that."

"Now isn't that something."

"They have a new boy named Miles."

"I knew that. You and Reg each have a new one. Who's next?"

"Susie, my sister."

"You will soon have a tribe."

"I do now. JD says we will be diaper-ville."

"I'm scaring up a few more places that are for sale around that Windmill ranch."

"Good. I figure, in time, we'll need them."

"They're cheap enough."

"If you can stand the temptation, let's go down to the Palace Saloon and have lunch."

"No problem. What will you do next?"

Chet shook his head. "Maybe finish up down there at Tubac, come home, and put my boots up and relax."

"What are you going to do the other twenty-three hours of that day?"

"Hunt and fish."

The two were still laughing when Chet held the batwing door back for him to enter the Palace Saloon ahead of him.

They found a table and ordered the chicken-fried steak and frijoles with sourdough bread to go along. The girl went off to turn in the order and bring their coffee.

Chet wondered how his Force was getting along in the south. Were JD and his bunch getting the windmill setup in place? He would have this business about setting up McCully at the house and shop done by the weekend.

One of the boys would need to bring in that horse and buggy for Petal to drive her father to the party on Saturday. When he met Marge later, they could figure it out. That whole day Saturday might wear that poor man to death. No, McCully'd make it — he was tough and had his daughter back to support him. Marge's horse wreck worried Chet, too — if anything happened to his wife, he didn't know what he'd do.

After their lunch, he parted with Bo Evans and went back over to Jenn's. They were seated in back in a booth, talking.

"You need lunch?" Jenn asked.

"No, I ate at the competition. You get her dressed?"

"Oh, she cried," Marge said. "But we have her fixed for the occasion, and after that, I think she is relieved to be back home. I had the store send him some new clothes, too. Your friend, Kathrin, said they would handle it. I was so busy having that baby when Kathrin came to help me that I didn't realize it, but she's going to have one, too."

"I told you that."

"I must have forgotten. She and her husband are coming Saturday. They knew what I bought the paint and brushes for. I invited them."

"We'll have a crowd. Bo and his lady friend are coming."

"Who is that?"

He shook his head. "Jenn may know. I don't."

"I'm not sure who she is, either. He's a nice guy. He'd be a good catch since you dried him out," said Jenn.

They laughed.

"My man does it all," Marge said, smiled, and patted his arm friendly-like.

"Let's go home. I need them to bring him the horse and buggy in Friday so she can bring him to the party."

"Oh, yes, we can do that. The ranch hands scrubbed it clean. It was under a foot or so of dust and cobwebs."

After helping Marge climb aboard, he clucked to the team and turned them around in the street. "Thanks for taking care of those two so well. Did Petal talk to you and Jenn?"

"Yes. She is glad you came for her. I think she was desperate was why she went off with him."

"I figured that."

"You look tired," Marge said.

"I'm fine. We'll have lots to do in town to get set up for Saturday. Tomorrow, I'll help Raphael get everything in there that we can move."

"I bet he'd enjoy having you. He is a great admirer of you."

"I admire him and his men."

"Oh, Chet we are so lucky. You have all these ranches going so well. We have a son that I thought I'd never have after my past experience. And you are generous to all of us. That little man needed this break and he told us he was so pleased. I know he will do well."

"I think he'll make good saddle makers out of some of the ranch boys."

"You're going north to see Robert and Reg next week?"

"I need to do that. Robert's efforts are paying our ranch payrolls. I don't think we appreciate him enough. I don't want him to have the big head, but he is really doing a great job."

"I know. I do that payroll. We have to use some money from our bank account for large expenses. But Robert is doing his share of earning this ranch's expenses."

"Sarge's cattle sale operation is still the best moneymaker. And he's doing it right."

"Were you surprised about Victor taking his place?"

"No, we are bringing on good men. Victor is one of them."

"What will you do?"

"Find them a good cook and make Victor Sarge's right hand."

"Good. What about Robert?"

"I want him to pick a foreman and make him a supervisor."

"Why do that?"

"Cowboys don't like to drag out timber. The men he needs are more farmer types who enjoy driving horses."

"I am learning. What about Reg?"

"Those two have built a ranch out of that place with mavericks. Like the old days, when my grandfather and my dad caught wild mavericks and built the first Byrnes herd in Texas. I'm glad Reg got to become experienced at doing that."

"Did that amaze you, that they could do that?"

"Not only me, but Lucie, who was raised on a ranch west of there, was also surprised that there were that many mavericks roaming our new ranch."

"It's a large place."

"Yes."

"I'll be glad when I can go see it again. They have a big house and all."

"Yes. Maybe next summer that boy will be big enough to take along." He turned the team in the driveway.

"I bet he will be. He's really growing."

"He sure is. Raphael must be waiting for

me to get back. I see him coming to meet us."

"I bet it's all about the party."

"We can handle it."

He helped her down and told her he'd be in shortly.

"Chet," Raphael said, "with the two wagons I am sending, we have lots of oak and mesquite to cook those two carcasses. There is enough. I have a cooking crew picked. They know what to do and are excited. They'll all go in and get set up. They brought up the spit from the Verde that John built. He also made one for the hog we butchered. It is real nice. John is such a great blacksmith. We plan to take four wagons to town in the morning early and get busy cooking. We have two large pots to cook the beans the women have cleaned. We have some ovens to bake bread. Monica gave us the sourdough starter. Mexican women can make delicious sourdough bread."

"I've had some they made. When you get an empty wagon, send someone to go get the beer I ordered at the Palace. He's expecting someone to pick it up."

"*Si*. We are taking bedrolls. A big number of us will sleep there tomorrow and Saturday night. I have three good men to stay here on the ranch to be sure no one raids this place."

"Good idea. Is there music?"

"Oh, *si,* we always have music. Will Señora May be there?"

"I'm sure she will be."

"She can sing. Oh, she is very good."

"She'll be proud to sing."

"There's lots of open land and trees up there where the house is to park rigs. Scotch the wagon wheels. It's on that hill."

"Oh, *si.* We will have a good time."

Chet made it to the house in time to wash up and eat the supper Monica was putting on the table.

"How's Adam?" he asked his wife.

"Fine, Rhea's putting him to sleep."

"Good. I'm taking a shower and will probably go to bed early. There's lots going on tomorrow."

"You want breakfast before dawn?" Monica asked in her motherly manner.

"I hate to bother you."

"Just tell me and I will have it ready."

"Yes."

"Good. Now eat supper. The rest can wait."

He had a hard time holding down his laughter at her reaction. Bless her, she was the boss of the house. His wife might think she was the boss, but the fortyish Hispanic woman had command over the house and kitchen. He knew she always burned candles in the Catholic church for his safe return. Some time back, a widowed rancher had courted her, but his daughters made him break it off out of prejudice, he was sure, against a brown-skinned woman marrying their father.

That man missed a lot. Monica was a treasure.

He and Marge went to bed early. The baby's nanny said she'd take him to her room and Marge could sleep for a full night.

He went to bed holding Marge and, despite his concerns about things needed done the next day, he fell asleep.

Before dawn he woke, dressed, and went downstairs. The aroma of Monica's coffee in the air led him to the kitchen. She smiled at him.

"Good morning."

"Yes, it is. I hope you can come in and enjoy the festivities tomorrow night."

"I will see."

"We would like you to join us. This man and his daughter have lived in a shack and had little business. When I saw his work, I knew he needed a shop and some help. His daughter is a treasure."

"He is on crutches?"

"Yes. My agreement with him is for him to teach some ranch boys how to make saddles. They would be his apprentices and do the work he can't handle."

Monica smiled. "I know your plans. Everyone on the ranch crew is excited."

"It will take time. But it can be a good thing, and everyone from close by is coming in for the party."

"If I can find a way —"

"We have buckboards. A boy will be assigned to take you in and back."

"I would be a bother then."

"No, you wouldn't. You're part of this outfit."

"I will go in for it then."

"Good."

She smiled and then shook her head. "What would this empire do without you?"

"Get bigger. Get better at making money."

He leaned back and sipped her coffee until she slid his platter of breakfast in front of him. With a nod of approval, he caught her wrist. "What would this house do without you?"

"Hire a real cook."

"I need to find someone good to take Victor's place. He's going to be Sarge's *Se-*

337

gundo."

"He's such a fine young man. They will miss his cooking."

"There's a cook somewhere. But he needs to be tough, too. They make a cattle drive every month in heat and snow up there."

"You will find someone."

"Glad you have such trust in me."

"Your sister is up there at the Windmill, she won't be able to come down here."

"They say Susie has had some scares."

"I know; we correspond. We have been blessed with so many babies and no real problems this far."

"I better eat. They'll leave without me."

She laughed. "They are all like kids. Excited to be included in this *fandango."*

"I'll speak to Raphael about your transportation."

He finished his food and soon joined the ones leaving. Jimenez brought him a saddled horse and smiled.

"Good morning. Lots of things are happening."

"Oh, *si, señor.* They are really excited."

"Good."

He mounted, checked the horse they called Sam Brown, and started for the gate. Sam walked on eggs for a hundred feet, like he wanted an excuse to buck in the cooler morning. His mind-set at last changed, and he single-footed to keep up with the loaded wagons. Some were packed with excited women who waved, laughed, and talked nonstop to each other.

He caught Raphael on his good horse in a few miles and they rode side by side. He told him about Monica wanting to go, and his man said it would be no problem. That cared for, they rode on making small talk and his foreman told him his plans. They didn't need his directions to paint and get ready, so he stopped by Jenn's and had coffee. The early morning café crowd was gone to work, so she slid in the booth.

"How are things going?"

"We'll have a big time tomorrow."

"It's a shame Cole and his wife are up at Oak Creek."

"They needed the time together."

"I agree. But they may come back for it."

"They may. Marge sent word up there to Robert as well, I'm sure."

"I better get to work. I am so glad you are doing this for those two. A lifesaver, that's what you are."

"I better get up there. They may need a flunky."

She laughed. "Don't work too hard. Your shoulder may go to hurting again."

He nodded and went outside, swung in the saddle, and rode over to the busy yard and house.

Carpenters had the new room walled in and the siding was up and ready to paint. The two new windows were being installed. The contractor had found newspaper to roll up and put in between the two-by-four studs. It made good insulation, and then he planned to lath and plaster over it.

"I may be next week getting it plastered."

"If that's all you lack, don't worry."

"Thanks, we've worked hard to get all the surfaces ready for your wife to paint tomorrow."

"That's what counts."

"I want to tell you, I heard the story — why you are doing this, and I'm impressed with your generosity."

"No, I'm fortunate to be able to help him. I have several young men at the ranch that will learn the saddle making business under his tutelage. That will help them and help me."

Rhineheart shook his hand. "I also know what else you've done to hold down crime. If I can ever help, you call on me."

"Thanks. I will." He slipped out of the house to give the workers better access.

Raphael met him outside. "We are cooking. That John, the spit he made us for the pig is great. The steer will be good, but that pig he will be *mucho bueno.*"

"I bet you're right. Have fun doing this."

"Oh, we will all have fun."

He agreed. Things under good control, he rode back to the ranch.

"Everything alright?" Monica asked.

"You got a good Mexican in charge, *no hay problema,* huh?"

"Yes, you crazy man. No problem." She went off laughing.

"What has her laughing?" Marge asked, getting up from the couch, holding the baby.

"Not much, I'm picking on her."

"You two are a mess, but the laughter always sounds good."

"Hello, little man." He peeked at Adam, enveloped in the folds of the blanket. "Great work we did, making him."

"It dang sure was fun, too."

He put his arm around her and kissed her cheek. "I need to catch up my reading in the older Miner newspapers."

"Fine, he's getting sleepy for his nap."

"You over being sore?"

"Pretty well. I'll be fine. I've been spilled before."

"But you didn't have a baby then, or me to worry about you."

"I know. I'll be back to normal soon. You leaving for the north Sunday?"

"Yes."

"I better not leave Adam. Maybe next spring I can go up there. I love Lucie and Reg."

"Don't we all."

He began reading the newspapers. Sam Kincaid was suing William Kimes for alienation of affection with his wife, Connie Mae Kincaid. He was asking for a thousand dollars and her wedding ring back. Poor Sam must not want his wife back. John Chrisman was suing Able Carter for letting his hogs loose in Chrisman's potato patch and ruining a crop valued at a thousand dollars. That would be a whole lot of spuds.

Rufus Campbell wanted a lying horse thief named Carlos McClure to bring back his driving mare he swindled him out of. He offered a ten-dollar reward for McClure's whereabouts.

The sheriff's office had arrested several men for public intoxication. One Lighty Mae was arrested for indecent exposure of her body to a policeman. She had been arrested and fined two dollars and was told by municipal judge Simmons to not come back in his court again. He fined her a dollar more for contempt after her yelling at him, "You dumbbell, he brought me here. I'd never come here on my own, stupid."

Chet, amused by the whole thing, decided his problems were small compared to dealing with others.

Saturday morning started with the sunrise. He was already up checking on things. Jimenez was preparing to drive Monica to the *fandango* after lunch and bring her back home. Raphael's guards loafed at the barn and welcomed him.

"It's a shame someone has to stay at home," he said to them.

"No, señor. This place is all of our jobs. No one needs to damage it. We are pleased to sit around today and keep an eye on things."

The others nodded their agreement.

Raphael had really explained the problem to them. "I thank you, and I will dance some for you."

"Oh, good, señor."

"I guess I'll need a team and buckboard in a few hours."

"We will have it ready."

"Gracias." He went back to the kitchen.

"This place is nearly abandoned," Monica said.

"Most of the crew is in town cooking,

painting, and getting ready."

"I know that. They were excited about their chance to show off to you and also have a good time."

"That was my plan. Have some fun, and show folks in town we're part of the community."

"Good idea. I know the ranch people are proud."

Monica had his breakfast ready and Marge joined him.

"Nice to have you here," Marge said.

"Nice to be here." He laid his palm on top of her hand. "They'll have a buckboard ready when you are."

"I won't be long."

"No rush. Things are in good hands in town."

It was midafternoon when they drove into town. The paint Marge had picked out had already been applied, and she looked in wonder at it. One of the ranch hands took their buckboard and parked it. He and Marge strolled the very busy grounds. Sawhorse-supported board tables were set up. Smoke from the cooking fires swept his nose, and he winked at Marge who shook her head. "He has it all painted," she said.

"That's his way. Things are moving along.

They've got water barrels set up to get a drink."

Raphael joined them, taking his *sombrero* off for her. "The beer is cold. We ended up with kegs. The man at the Palace said it would cheaper and we have a pump and it is covered in ice. When we run out, they can drink coffee or water. We have lots of frijoles cooked, the women will make tortillas and biscuits in the Dutch ovens. So many are coming, I hope that some will bring their own plates. We have a lot of them, but otherwise we will wash them to feed someone else, huh?"

"That's all we can do. You have it planned well."

"Thank you. When we get started eating, we will make peach pie in the Dutch ovens. The women have the peaches ready. Leroy sent us plenty."

"That sounds good."

"Next year, we could grow about ten acres of frijoles at our ranch. There is enough water in that one windmill to water it. And have them for all the ranches, huh?"

"You're in charge, amigo."

"*Gracias.* Some of the men and women thought about that. Leroy is growing lots of our food. We can do that for the rest of the outfits."

When they were alone, Marge said, "He's a real foreman."

"A real good one. Nothing those men of his can't do and do it right."

Lupe, one of the men's wives, brought some roasted beef over for them to taste. Chet took a piece off the plate with his fingers. In his mouth, the saliva flowed. He nodded and chewed. "Wonderful."

"They said you needed the first bite."

"You tell them I hated it."

"I should do that?"

"Then tell them I said it was so good I wanted it all for myself."

She left them the plate and, skirt in hand and laughing, she went back.

"We are going to have lots of company tonight," Marge said. "They look prepared for all of it."

"No problem."

"Raphael has a shade up and chairs for the ladies. If you, or anyone else, gets tired, go over there."

"I may do that until folks arrive," she said.

"Good."

Hampt, May, and the new baby, Miles, arrived with the three bigger kids on their horses. The boys gathered their smaller sister and came on the run.

"Uncle Chet, we sure appreciate today."

"What for?" he asked the youngest one.

"So we can get to make some new friends."

"That's a powerful idea. How are things at the ranch?"

"Going good," the oldest spoke up, and about then Hampt showed up.

"Marge took May and the baby over in the shade. You can see him later. Where's McCully?" Hampt asked.

"I think Petal will bring him. Raphael has him fixed up with a tame horse and buggy."

"Good. My cowboys are coming. We left Troy to watch the place. Damn shame you have to leave anyone out, but times have sure changed. Used to be no one bothered a thing wasn't theirs. Today, they'd rob you blind."

Chet shrugged. "Different times and different folks. Lots of desperate people are out prowling for something to rob."

"A good sheriff would have them kind moved on."

Chet nodded.

"My Bailey mare had a colt out of your yellar stud this week. Boy, he is a proud looking devil."

"What color?"

"I think he'll be a buckskin."

"Good luck. We'll have some more on the

Verde after the first of the year."

"I'll take her down there on the tenth day and see if I can get her bred back."

"It works a lot of the time."

"Man, he sure gets powerful colts."

About then, Chet got busy meeting others arriving and the party getting under way. Tom, Millie, and their kids arrived. Chet sent her to the tent shade, and Tom joined him and Hampt. Then Roamer's wife and kids came.

Hampt shook his head. "Things are really going on here, Chet Byrnes style. Raphael has handled things well. He's a good man and sincere about everything."

"Yes, I know. When he turns his men loose on raiders, you can bet they won't come back."

"He's a damn good man to have on our side," Hampt said, then wandered off.

Bo Evans drove up in a buggy with a handsome woman seated beside him. Chet didn't know her, but supposed it was the lady friend Bo had mentioned. Bo reined up.

"Shelly Newcum, I want you to meet the man that put me to work."

Chet shed his hat. "Shelly, nice to meet you."

"I've heard so much about you. I'm so

348

glad you are having this party."

"This is Tom, my ranch foreman. My wife, Marge, is over under that shade. I'm certain she would like to meet you, too."

"Nice to meet you, sir. I'll find her."

"Have a good time, both of you."

"We will," Bo said, and they drove on.

He turned to Tom. "You know her?"

"No, but she's sure a looker."

"Leave it to Bo to find her. Maybe someone knows something. I bet Marge finds out."

Tom shook his head. "I believe she must have recently moved here, or else I'd have noticed her before today."

"I agree. He could meet anyone, out looking for property. I want to talk to the crew here and thank them. They've been working hard since yesterday."

"I'll go find Hampt and see what he's up to."

"See you later."

He hugged a few ranch women, all busy working. Several he knew by their name and they laughed at his attention.

"You all making it okay?"

"Si, señor," Lupe said. "It is a wonderful thing. We are having fun." Then she used her apron to dry her wet face. She came out of it smiling. "We love it."

He patted her on the shoulder. "Oh, Lupe, maybe you lie a little."

"No. No," she protested. "This is not work. We are proud to work for you and have fun, too."

The banker and his wife arrived. Several of the ranch cowboys rode in. Ben from the mercantile and his wife, Kathrin, came. The liveryman, Frey, and his wife Gloria, and several town folks. A couple of drunk cowboys showed up, and some of Hampt's hands showed them where to leave and not come back. The Quarter Circle Verde bunch backed them. There was music all the time and the food was eaten as soon as it was ready. About the time the McCullys arrived, Chinese lanterns were lit.

Chet introduced them and everyone gave them a round of applause. Tears streamed down the old man's face as he stood on his crutches and shook his head.

"Petal and I came up here yesterday and I saw this house. Now you have it all painted. In a week, I'll be set up to fix and make harnesses and then build saddles. Me and Petal thank Chet and Marge Byrnes for all they have done for both of us. Have fun tonight, and God bless you all."

Chet showed him to a bench at a table and sent Petal to get him some food. He clapped him on the back and told him, "It's all going to be okay."

"I know it will now. Thanks to you."

Chet got a plate and took it to stand by Marge's chair. He refused a chair offer and asked if she'd eaten.

"I have, with May. Bo brought by his lady friend, Shelly Newcum. She's new here. Very nice lady. A widow woman."

"Tom and I met her earlier."

"She must have money."

"Must." He was busy eating beans with a flour tortilla for a scoop and using his jack-knife to stab the beef and eating off it. "You worn out?"

"It has been a busy day. Our help sure painted all of the house, inside and out. I saw McCully made it and his daughter brought him."

"That dress you bought her looked very nice."

"I hope she's not carrying that man's child."

"That would be a concern. I hope not, too." He ate some more of his meat.

"If you're going north tomorrow, do you have a partner to ride with you?"

"No. I'll ask Raphael to appoint one."

"Kinda late, isn't it?"

"No, he'll have someone." He finished his

food and went to drop his plate in the washtub set up where they could be washed and reused to feed others.

He caught his foreman eating. "I'm going to ride up north tomorrow; I'll need a pack horse, supplies, a bedroll. One or two men to ride with me. Be gone about five days."

"I will have you covered. Go have fun."

"I may take Marge home. She's tired."

"No problem. It is a great party."

He told the others he was leaving, then hugged May and her baby. Shook some more hands, and Hampt had his buckboard waiting.

"When you see Reg, tell him hi. You two don't wreck going home. It'll be dark shortly," said Hampt.

"You do the same. See you when I get back." Chet helped Marge in the seat and drove the team around rigs until they were going downhill for the city.

"Raphael has a man?" she asked.

"He said two men will be ready at sunup and loaded."

"You have wonderful help."

"I really do." He couldn't say enough nice things about his employees.

At home, a few hours later, they turned in. Adam and his nanny, Rhea, were already asleep. They climbed in bed and after some moments that brought back memories of their honeymoon, they went to sleep. Even as he drifted off to sleep, though, his mind was busy with thoughts about the high country and the trip ahead.

CHAPTER 17

When Chet came downstairs the next morning, Monica had his breakfast and coffee ready. She told him what a nice time she had at the party the night before. Marge came down to kiss him good-bye before he left.

In the cool predawn, two of his *vaqueros* rode with him out the gate. Waco, the older of the two, was perhaps thirty and the other rider was Phillipe, who called himself Phil. Both men were armed with cap and ball forty-fives and carried 44/40 Winchesters under their stirrups. Waco was married and his wife, Nona, was still in Preskitt working with the cleanup crew that morning. Probably busy packing up the picnic things.

When they headed out the gate, he was glad for the warm jumper he wore. His winter coat was on board one of the packhorses and he knew early snows were part of the high country. They went off the mountain, crossed Verde River on a wooden bridge, and headed skyward for the north rim. They'd be at Robert's house and camp on the rim by midafternoon.

Robert's tall wife, Betty Lou, met them, blond braids shining. Her face beamed and she was excited to hear about the big party in Preskitt the night before. Chet filled her in on the details and asked how she liked living up there.

"Wonderful. I'm getting used to the altitude. I had some headaches at first, but not anymore. Next year, I'll have a garden and can grow a lot of our food. That wonderful man in Oak Creek sent up lots of produce and vegetables that I canned. He'd catch a freighter and have him bring it up here to me. It worked wonderful, and we got peaches and apples. We were so blessed. And I like my house."

"Good. Where's he?"

"Oh, he'll be here about five. I can make some coffee. I make it for him. He drinks it, but I doubt he would tell me if it was bad."

"You're a Mormon?"

"Yes, and he's not, but we get along fine. Some of my girlfriends told me not to ever marry a gentile. They said I would never be happy. But I'm very happy, and he's a thoughtful, great husband."

355

"I'm certain Waco and Phil would drink some, too." Standing by, hatless, they nodded they would.

"I'll make a big pot of it then. I want to feed you three. His men eat over at the cookhouse, but I can cook. He eats it, anyway."

"I'm sure if we don't have to cook it, that we'd eat it, too."

His men laughed.

They took seats at her table. And after more conversation, they raised their cups to thank her and ate some of her rich oatmeal raisin cookies.

Robert arrived and shook their hands. He looked like he was frosted in sawdust and stepped back outside to remove his outside shirt, and she swept off his pants with a corn broom.

"Sorry, I made a mess, hon. It's just great the boss came by to see us."

"Yes, we've had a nice visit. I can sweep it up. It isn't like it's cow manure."

They all laughed. Robert told them where to unload their horses and to put anything a bear could eat in the shed and bolt it shut good. The two agreed and he sat down with Chet at the table and had some of Betty Lou's coffee.

"What do you want to know?" He spread

his calloused hands out on the table.

"I've looked over the books for your operation. Marge sends you the reports. What you're doing here is keeping us open. I want you to hire a *Segundo,* as the Mexicans call them. A man who can run this place when you're gone or want to take a few days off. We can pay him ten more a month. But when we have meetings over at Preskitt Valley, your wife needs to come over and shop."

"That sounds good, doesn't it, hon?"

"Wonderful. Mr. Byrnes, I mean, Chet, Robert works seven days a week. But you know that."

"I know. Him skidding logs is a great way to make money, if you have a good man in charge. I never imagined it could be so profitable. We set it up to keep the mill running."

"Thanks for trusting me. I was pretty young to have that much responsibility," Robert said. "But I have some good men, too. They don't shirk any work that I ask them to do. Today, we had some tough places to get the logs out, but we're right on schedule. I was down there making sure they were able to get them out."

"How is the mill doing?"

"They have lulls that worry me. Then they

get mine orders or house orders and away they go. They don't want the log-hauling part back, either. They thank me all the time for our on-time deliveries. I keep an eye on their log supplies and make sure they don't run out."

"You're doing it well. And even got this Mormon gal brewing good coffee."

Robert smiled and hugged Betty Lou, who stood beside his chair, around the waist. "I promised her she wouldn't go to hell for doing it."

They both laughed.

"Keep up the good work, you two."

"How is your baby?" Robert asked.

"I thought you'd never ask. Adam's doing fine. May has a boy named Miles, and Susie is waiting for hers. She came over to the Verde place a little scared she might be going to lose it. But she got better and went back home to the Windmill Ranch. Sarge, you know, had a horse wreck and broke his leg. Victor is herding the cattle to the Navajos now."

Robert shook his head. "Man, there's lots happening."

"An outfit like this, there's something all the time."

"Reg's baby doing good?"

"Last I heard, she was fine."

Then he told them about JD and the new Rancho Diablo. After a nice supper and a big breakfast the next morning, him and his two supporters rode north for the big San Francisco Peaks, which the Navajos considered sacred.

Midmorning, he found several freighters and rigs stopped in the road. He rode up where they were gathered and looked over the situation.

"Something wrong here?" he asked a man standing nearby.

"They found a feller that's been shot. Says he's been robbed by two men."

Chet tossed his reins to Phil and dismounted. "I'll go see what I can do."

They had the man lying on an old military blanket beside the road. He looked badly shot up.

"What's his name?"

A heavyset man pushed off his knee to stand and talk to him. "Says he's Talburt Eden and he comes from Goldfield. Said he had lots of gold on him and his horses, and that they took it after shooting him."

"Does he know the ones that shot him?"

"He said Don Sheets and Kelly Monroe."

"He knew them?"

"Yeah, they all mined together down there. Got in an argument last night and they shot him and took all the gold."

"What brand was on the horses they took?"

"He never said."

"Ask him. That will make finding them easier."

The big man knelt down again. "What brand was on your horses?"

"A JT on a bay and the sorrel horse had an Eight-H on his shoulder," the wounded man gasped out.

The man rose and Chet told him, "We got that. There isn't a doctor short of Camp Verde. I don't know of any up here."

"Hey, you guys, headed south," said the man. "Take this man to the sawbones at Camp Verde."

"Reckon he'll live that long?" Chet asked.

"Yeah, he's lived so far. He's worth trying to get him there. You the law?"

"I'm an excuse for one," Chet said to the big man in the flannel shirt, who was busy spitting tobacco aside.

He wiped his lips with a bear paw of a hand. "What's your name?"

"Chet Byrnes."

"Why, you're a U.S. Marshal. Okay. We'll try to get him to a doctor. Boys, easy like, load him in the back of the first wagon."

"Can you report the crime to the authorities?" Chet asked them.

"We'll do that." He looked around for support and many of the others nodded.

"Good. Then we'll try to find his attackers." Chet took the reins from Phil and gave them a head toss and the three of them rode north.

Waco did a lot of leaning out of the saddle for a ways to look at the tracks in the dirt road. When he straightened up, he nodded. "I can track their horses. They're fresh shod and make good prints."

"I guess that will be the next thing, to find them. Thanks. Show Phil what we're following."

"See that print there? That horse steps hard on his right front shoe. He may be a little lame. But he puts it down harder."

Phil looked to where he pointed. "I think I see it. I see their tracks that the wagon didn't press out. But I never saw that in the prints."

Waco laughed. "The more you track him, you'll figure out a lot about the horse you follow. Look at how different horses step, then check their hoofprints."

"Where are they going?" Phil asked Chet. "We've never been this far north."

"There's a road ahead runs east and west that folks call the Marcy Road. A Captain

Marcy came out of Fort Smith and went to California. He mapped it, reported the water sources and the mileage. We used his maps coming out here from Texas. There's another road goes north and skirts the Grand Canyon. Going to Utah. We went up there and rescued some people held by kidnappers up there."

"Jesus told us about that trip. He said it was cold and tough."

"It wasn't for the faint of heart," Chet said, amused. "It was hell, but cold. We need to get these two before the snow falls up there."

"They can't be far, and they don't know a lawman is after them already."

"Three lawmen. You're my deputies."

Phil looked over at Waco and pointed a finger at him. "Señor Thomas, you are a U.S. Deputy Marshal."

"Ah, Señor Milgram, you are one, too."

Chet shook his head, laughing. "Deputies, we need to move faster. It'll be dark soon, and I'd like to find them before sundown."

They trotted their mounts and crossed a great wide-open meadow surrounded by the ponderosa pine that covered the country. The sun would soon set, and he hoped to reach Reasor's Ranch on the far side of the great meadow before complete darkness.

Reasor's, a saloon, café, and store served as a resting spot for travelers.

"What if they are there?" Phil asked him as they trotted their horses.

"They won't know us, any more than we'll know them. When we find those two branded horses, we'll know they're there. Then, we'll see what happens."

The sun was down and the long twilight of the western country had set in. Even in the hill country of Texas it never stayed light so long as it did in Arizona. There were five still sweaty horses at the hitch rail at Reasor's. When they dismounted behind the spent-looking hipshot animals, the lights went on inside the log building that served as saloon, café, and store. Waco quickly looked at the red horse's left shoulder and stepped out nodding.

Chet, in a stage whisper, told Phil, "Go around back. Don't shoot unless they come out armed. Order them to drop their guns. Then you be ready."

"I savvy." He left on the run.

Waco, face grim in the gathering darkness, nodded he was ready. Chet went up the three steps and onto the porch. There were no batwing doors, and he could see the store portion. The café and saloon were to the right. When he came into the light and

363

his eyes focused better, he saw two trail-dust-floured men at the bar turn and blink at him.

"Which one of you is Sheets?" Chet asked.

"Who's asking?" the mustached one asked.

"A U.S. Marshal."

"Go to hell."

"Get your hand away from that gun unless you really want to die."

"Alright. Alright."

"Disarm them, Waco. You two are under arrest for the attempted murder of your partner and robbing him."

"You can't prove that."

"Oh, I can. I have a dozen witnesses to testify they heard him say you two shot and robbed him."

Chet removed the mustached one's gun and then the other man's weapon. Phil was there with handcuffs and leg irons.

Chet also put their knives on the counter, then his men handcuffed them.

A small crowd of tough-looking men circled the situation, and one of them spoke up. "Why waste time on a trial? We've got some rope."

A chorus behind him said, "Yeah."

"Gentlemen, I agree with your intentions. But wild as we are, Arizona needs to show we are not the wild west. No, the trial and the verdict of the law is better."

"How far back did they do it?"

"This side of the sawmill. Maybe half a day's ride."

"Where's the law at?"

"Preskitt. Let's all have a drink. I'll buy the first round and toast a better territory."

A big man wiped his mouth on the back of his hand. "You must be the big rancher that wears that badge?"

"My name is Chet Byrnes."

"Riley Cobble. You ain't an ordinary guy."

"Yes, I am. But I believe this lawlessness has to stop. I want my family to grow up in a peaceful place."

"Amen," the crowd said, moving in to get their free drink.

His men took the two over and sat them in chairs. The owner came over wearing a stained white apron. "I have a log shed we can lock them up in."

"Good. We better feed my men first. Thanks."

"Reagan Reasor. Nice to meet you. My wife can fix you and your men up with supper."

"We need to feed them, too."

"Oh, I knew that. She'll feed them. I better get back to work."

"Thanks."

Chet paid his bar bill for the gang in the saloon portion.

"It's three dollars and seventy cents," the man behind the bar said.

Chet paid him and thanked him.

"She'll have your food ready shortly."

"Fine, we can wait."

"Boys, boys," the bartender said, "let's toast our new friend and his crew, Marshal Byrnes. May the law straighten out Arizona."

"Yeah," went the cheer.

He ordered a beer apiece for his men and then sat back in the captain's chair.

"You don't drink beer?" Phil asked.

"I've lost my taste for it."

"What next?" Waco asked.

"We go back to Preskitt to deliver the pair of them to the sheriff. Stop at home and start back north again." He lowered his voice. "There's no one here I could trust to take back all that gold they're supposed to have on them and their horses."

"I think you're right. No one else should do it." Waco made a tight-lipped nod.

"I have never arrested anyone," Phil said. "But they didn't fight you?"

"They're lucky. They didn't neither one look like gunfighters to me, and they would have died standing at the bar."

"Or coming out the back door."

Chet chuckled. "Yes, you were out back there."

"I was ready, but when I heard you order them to give up, I said to myself that they'd better do that, and they did."

Waco was ready to sip more of his beer. "I was glad, too."

Chet agreed — it went smoothly.

After their meal and with the prisoners fed, they borrowed two candle lamps from Reasor and put the prisoners in their irons behind the locked shed door with a blanket apiece.

Earlier, they'd searched the pair and found each wore a gold-dust-filled money belt around their waists.

They were heavy, too. And there were more pouches in their saddlebags. Chet knew there was a lot of gold, but had no idea about the total worth. He felt certain the amount would be several thousand dollars. Not enough to murder a man over — if the man died. Greed ruined many people's lives.

"Looked like they had enough for all," Phil said.

"Damn shame," Chet said.

"Who will get all this gold?" Waco asked.

"The heirs, I guess."

"Can we get in the will?" Phil asked.

The other two laughed at his plan. They took turns guarding the gold and the prisoners. Chet took the last duty and dawn found them loaded. Reasor's wife, Nettie, fed them breakfast and they headed south. They didn't stop until they reached the Verde River Ranch that evening.

Tom met them and arranged guards for the prisoners and gold. Chet was still several hours away from his wife and their house. At his request, they saddled a fresh horse for him. Tom promised to bring the prisoners in a buckboard with their gold and gear the next day.

Chet swung in the saddle and headed for home under the stars. His arrival awoke the house, and his wife met him at the back door.

"What's wrong?"

"We arrested two men for robbing their partner and Tom is bringing them up tomorrow. Let's go to bed. I'm bone tired."

"Glad you're alright," Monica said, standing nearby in her robe. "Good night."

"Good night."

Arm in arm, they went upstairs as he gave

Marge a sketchy report on things that happened.

He undressed, fell in bed, and slept hard.
He awoke groggy and smiled at his wife.
"Good to be here with you."

She kissed and hugged him. "Always."

He had a lot to do to get back to his trip
to see Reg and Lucie on the Mogollon Rim
Ranch.

CHAPTER 18

The next morning, the men reached the ranch with the buckboard and prisoners. Chet shook both men's hands, thanked them, and sent his two off to get some rest. Tom and his three cowboys could handle whatever was needed to deliver the prisoners. Chet took a new horse in the cool morning air and smiled at Jimenez.

"Sure he won't buck?"

"No, señor. But, sometimes the calm ones buck."

"I know. Thanks."

He checked the gelding and he side-stepped, making like he was tiptoeing on eggs. With his head held high by the bit, Chet booted him forward to join the buckboard and riders preparing to leave.

"I sure thought he'd buck," Tom teased.

Chet shook his head like it was nothing, and they left the ranch.

■ ■ ■ ■

Once in town, they drove to the courthouse in the square. Chet and Tom went inside and told the deskman they had the two men outside that robbed and shot Talburt Eden.

The man nodded his head. "Eden is still at the doctor's house and he's not sure the man will live."

"Their names are Don Sheets and Kelly Monroe. There is considerable gold dust, some that they stole from Eden. I have no idea how much. And there's their horses, as well as his."

"The sheriff's at Crown King this morning, investigating another murder-robbery. We've interviewed Eden and have all that information. I'm shorthanded. Could you board the horses at the livery?"

"Sure, we can do that. Thanks for your cooperation."

"No problem, Marshal Byrnes."

They brought in the prisoners, removed the handcuffs and leg irons, and they were marched off to a cell. Chet and his outfit took their horses to Frey's Livery and then went by Jenn's for lunch.

Cole was there. "Hey, I thought you were on the Rim with two *vaqueros*?"

371

"Oh, we ran into a robbery and shooting and then captured the pair that did it."

"Hey, I'd sure have rode with you up there."

"Those two with me did a great job, but I'll accept your offer for the next one. I plan to start out again in the morning." He nodded to Cole's wife, Valerie, who was approving the change.

"I'll be there."

"Thanks."

Bonnie stopped by then and handed him a letter. "It's from JD. He's excited. Your windmill is working."

Chet stopped and read it. JD said the blades were whirling and water coming out of the pipe, and it was gorgeous to see. The rest of the letter was that of a man in love with his wife.

"Thanks, Bonnie." He handed it back. "Sounds like something good is happening down there."

"Tell us about the arrests you made," Cole said.

He told them the story as the girls brought plates of food out to the crew. He sat down and Jenn patted his shoulder. "We heard about the wounded man they brought back from up there, but there was no mention about you."

"Those *vaqueros* and I went after the robbers, and I sent him back with some freighters for medical attention. They obviously got him back in time to maybe save his life."

Everyone agreed.

"Well, I've lost a few days, so Cole and I will head north again in the morning."

"Be careful."

Back home, Chet took a bath, shaved, and put on clean clothes, then he told Raphael how much he appreciated his two hands' help, but Cole would be going back with him. He told his man that if he ever needed men to ride with him again, he'd use them.

In the predawn, Chet and Cole rode north. They were camped near the crossroads under the San Francisco range on the second morning, and the next day they rode all day for the North Rim Ranch, arriving late in the evening. Some barking stock dogs greeted them, and the lights came on in the house. Two sleepy cowboys got up and hollered at them before Reg busted out shouting, "Is that you?"

"Me and Cole."

"Get their horses, guys. How have the two of you been?" Reg asked.

"A little cold riding over, but I've been trying to get here for a week."

Lucie handed her husband the baby and bear-hugged Chet. "You rascal. It's so good to see you. I thought you'd never make it up here. You guys come on in. I bet he's got stories to tell us we ain't never heard."

"This the new boss?" He took the baby wrapped in a small blanket.

"That's Carla."

"Well, she's a big handful."

"My sister is helping me. It's been a long time since any of us has been around a baby. She's a tiger."

Chet nodded at her sister, Fern, who had joined them. "Nice to see you again. You all know Cole. He and I and the rest have been down south chasing bandits. Me and two of the crew had to catch some robbers who shot a man on the road north of the sawmill. Took them back to Preskitt, then I changed guards and Cole came up here with me."

"Good to have you with us. You ate supper?" Lucie asked.

"We're fine."

"Hey, sis and I can whip up pancakes. Everyone sit at the table and we'll go to work. Reg, you can hold the baby."

Chet handed the now squirming bundle to her father. "Well, Reg, how are things up here?"

"Good. We made a lot of hay with our own

equipment. I hired some local boys to work in it, and they got lots done. We may have a two-year supply, but we can always use it. We've built some elk-proof stack holders. How is the windmill going down at Rancho Diablo?"

"The letter JD sent to his Bonnie says the first one is pumping away. Our main manufacturer, John, says we can make them at our shop. So we're working on it."

"Those homesteads that Bo Evans bought for us have wells that'll work with windmills," said Reg.

"Good, we can't have too much water in this country. Over the winter we'll expand the mill building."

"Good. Tom, I know, is looking for more bulls. But we have fewer British bulls than the rest of the ranches," said Reg.

"They aren't easy to find," Chet said. "We aren't orphaning you. We're looking at some half-bloods to use, until we can get enough bought or raised."

"Just so you're thinking about us."

"We are. Maybe we don't look like it, but we really are."

"I guess Lucie and I are impatient. But we've caught a herd up here."

"I know, and you two and these two cowboys are doing wonders. But even if we could find them, it's near impossible to get them up here without a railroad close by."

Reg turned his palms up, then shifted his daughter and patted her on the back. "Treated like stepchildren."

"Not on purpose."

"Don't be so hard on him, he's being the law and trying to run a widespread empire, all at the same time," Lucie said from the stove, flipping flapjacks.

"If I was home, I doubt you'd get much better service."

"Ah, hell, Lucie, he knows me. I'm antsy as all get out to get this ranch up to Tom's standards."

"I know, but I bet you'd have to go clear to Kansas or Nebraska to find enough British bulls."

"Hey, coming from Texas to here by myself was enough trailing for me for a lifetime. I never knew Arizona was so damn far out here."

"There you go. Are you having any trouble up here?"

Reg nodded. "We get a little. I think most of it is jealousy."

"They're just jealous that we're growing and getting all this done," Lucie said from behind her spatula, working at the stove. "Taking care of our business and doing it right. If we ever have a real hard winter up here, and with no more hay than these ranchers have put up, lots of them will lose their entire herd."

"She knows this country and the weather. She's been here the better part of her life," Reg said.

Chet agreed, leaning back as the recipient of her first pile of flapjacks. "Thanks, ma'am."

"We aren't unhappy here, Chet."

"I know that, and if I can find a dozen British bulls I'll drive them up here by myself."

They all laughed. Chet poured syrup on the stack. "I'm eating now. Thanks, Lucie."

"You're welcome. Cole, yours are coming."

"No hurry. I'm enjoying your fine house."

"Hey, we're pretty proud of it, too. Sis, here, and my other sister call it a mansion, and considering the closest town is Hackberry, it might be at that." Lucie laughed, took Cole's pancakes out of the skillet, and put them on a plate. "Anyone else want some?"

The other three shook their heads.

Her sister took over to wash the pan, and Lucie picked up the baby. "Any word on Susie and her baby?"

"Still coming along good when we left. In her last letter to Marge, she sounded like she was doing fine now and had gone back to Windmill."

"Tell us more about JD and his place," Reg said.

"It's a huge desert operation. We have around two hundred cows I bought from Buster when we ran him off. With some water development and getting rid of the mustangs, the place could easily run twice the number."

"You have any trouble, besides the attempted raid on your ranch at Preskitt?"

"Oh, when we were winding up the sale, Buster got his back up and Shawn McElroy was with me. When he took a step toward me, Shawn got in his face. Some of you don't know him, but he's a real hand on the Force. I don't think he's twenty years old, but he backed that windbag down. I about laughed."

"Sounds like a guy you need," Reg teased.

"Cole, or Jesus, or any of my help, takes care of me. There was a guy ran off with a man's daughter and Hampt went along with me to ask her to come home. Her father is crippled, by the way. He's going to train some of the boys from the ranch how to make saddles and harness. He's repairing our things at the ranch now."

"We got that letter about him," Lucie said, "and the party that we couldn't make."

"Good. Anyhow, we found her down at Crown King and were talking to her about going home. This jerk she ran off with came blustering up about us messing with her. Hampt got him by the shoulder and I guess put a thumb in him, and he got plumb friendly."

"Lord," Reg said, "he'd scare anyone looking a little mad."

"She came back with us, and now she and her father have a new house and business." Then he went on and told them about solving the murder and the other Force activities.

The next morning, they rode out to a nearby homestead that Bo had bought. It had ten acres of alfalfa the crew had cut and stacked behind elk-proof board fencing. The low-walled log cabin was tight and would do for a line rider shelter.

While they examined the corrals and sheds, Reg said, "Late-born calves need to be watched and pampered that first winter more than the others. I want to install a well pump and put a hand up here this winter to water and feed them. We're going to have about forty or so, and the hay we have here should get them through in good shape. Oh, some wind shelters might be needed. But we can get them put up before it gets bad."

"I'd say it's fine. Pipe and a pump, plus a bigger tank should do it. You'll have to wrap it good to keep it from freezing."

"Yeah, we aren't in Texas anymore." Reg laughed. "If Hampt would show me how, I could plant more alfalfa up here and expand this operation," Reg said.

"I'm certain he would show you."

"Tom says he's the man. Can I put in a rail fence and use around thirty more acres and do that?"

"Go ahead, and we can schedule this place for a windmill in the next year. John is getting lots of barbwire made down there. You might put in for a wagonload of it."

"I can't wait to tell Lucie. She'll be tickled pink."

"Good. You aren't having rustling or any other problems up here?"

"No, we're isolated enough it's pretty quiet. I ran off all the squatters on these places, and don't let any others start to move in."

"Good. Now, if you had twelve bulls, you'd be set."

"I don't lack much. You hear anything about a railroad coming?" Reg asked.

"That would solve a lot of all our problems, but best I can tell, it's still in Kansas and not coming fast enough. At the current rate, it'll be ten years getting here."

"My daughter will be riding by then." Reg laughed.

"It could be that long."

"Chet, I know you have lots of things on your mind and places to manage. Those bulls would help and I may sound sour, but I'm the luckiest guy in the world to have Lucie, the baby, a new house, and a ranch to expand. It ain't Texas up here, but it ain't crowded, and we're blessed you found all this when you came out here. It's almost like them damn Reynolds did us a favor, driving us out of Texas. You'd never have found a woman you fit better with than you do with Marge."

Looking back, Chet had to agree. But it was the experience he gained in Texas that set him up for Arizona. "I know you had some big losses, and setbacks in your life, but I'm glad you found Lucie and we have these ranches."

"Chet, I never think about that anymore. I'm looking at all I have now and what Lucie and I'll have in the future. How is Marge doing?"

"Oh, fine. She's back to riding her jumping horses, and that boy is growing a lot."

"You've done well out here, too. I can recall riding after them horse thieves with you and JD like it was yesterday. Sounds like JD's settling down?"

"He really is."

"Good."

Chet, Cole, and Reg rode on to the next place. The homesteader had about twenty acres under fence he must have tilled for a few years.

"Will it grow alfalfa?"

"I have no idea. Tom or Hampt better come up here and tell you. It's fenced and not so far away you couldn't come over and cut it. I think, though, as many deer and elk as there are up here, you may need to keep someone with a dog up here."

"I never thought about that. The sagebrush is gone and that's tough stuff to dig up so you can plow."

Chet agreed and was amused. "They can tell you. I'm not the farm man."

They went back to the ranch house where Lucie had fresh coffee made. While they drank the hot brew, Chet told them about Robert's Mormon wife making him coffee.

Reg chuckled. "Lucie and I like her. She's not stuck up, and she's willing to make things work."

"He's got a real practical gal," Lucie added.

After supper, they went over their plans for the next day. Reg wanted Chet to see some of the cattle in the morning. Then the day after that, he and Cole would start back home. Chet had a list of the things they needed, but the operation was taking shape.

While they were preparing for bed, the dogs began barking. Reg answered the door and shouted to someone outside.

Lucie was behind him. "It's Arthur Taylor from Hackberry. I recognize his voice."

"Arthur, come in. What's wrong?" He let the gray-headed man with his hat in hand in the house.

"I'm sorry, Reg and Lucie, but them Berkley brothers got drunk in the saloon tonight and they shot and killed Marshal Crown. They held up the bartender and then robbed Roe over at the store. Folks are forming a posse to go after them in the morning. They sent me out here to ask you to join us."

"Art, this is my uncle, Chet Byrnes, and this is Cole Emerson from Preskitt. They're U.S. Marshals."

"Well, I never expected to find you up here. Last time I saw you a few years ago, sir, you had arrested some outlaws in Hackberry."

Chet nodded his head. "What got into them doing that?"

Lucie spoke up. "Those boys are grown. They've been troublemakers all their life. Crown had arrested them several times and the JP fined them. They had a bad problem with him, especially when they got roaring drunk."

Reg agreed. "I don't know if he has time, but Chet is the man we need to go find and stop them."

"We can find time," he said quietly.

Cole agreed. "Will there be a real tracker?"

"They're supposed to get one tonight."

"They must have a good head start. A posse made up of family men and people that aren't use to this kind of hard riding are better left at home. A smaller unit can move fast, and with their lead it will take lots of tracking to find them."

"You're right. They won't be held back like those guys that stole our remuda when we were still in Texas," Reg said.

"Right. Any idea where the Berkley brothers went?" Chet asked Taylor.

"No, they rode off, is all I know."

"Reg, as much as I'd like you along, you have a wife, a baby, and a ranch to run. And winter's coming on. You better stay here. Cole and I can find them, unless they dig a hole we can't locate."

Reg looked hard at him. "I sure will be antsy, sitting here and worrying about you two."

"We can handle this place," Lucie said. "Our two hands, my sister, and I can run this ranch. Take him along. Why, he'd be so hard to live with, knowing you two were out there alone trying to arrest those three crazy troublemakers."

Chet looked at Cole, then shook his head. "Our boss has spoken. Mr. Taylor, we're going to find you a bed. Cole will put up your horse, and we'll get up early, pack our pack animals, and go over to Hackberry and start there." He hugged Lucie and laughed.

She shook her head. "I know him way too well for you to leave him behind, Chet."

Both the ranch hands were at the house by then and got filled in on the situation. They took Taylor with them to get some sleep, and then they planned to be up early and head for Hackberry. The two hands were concerned and wanted to join them, but understood they had to stay and help Lucie run the ranch.

Long before dawn, everyone was up and

busy using lamps to saddle and load the packhorses. The women were making breakfast and food for them to take along to eat on the trail. While they drew up their cinches, the fragrant smoke from Lucie's cookstove carried to them on the cool morning air, and she called them to come get it.

They washed up on the porch and went inside to eat. The smell of food filled the dining room as the two women rushed platters of pancakes, fried bacon, and oatmeal to the table. Without many words, they set in to eat their meal. Chet knew they realized this was the last good meal they'd have for some time. He'd better enjoy it, too.

Chet kissed Lucie's forehead, hugged her sister, and thanked them both for all their hard work. Outside, he stepped in the stirrup and swung in the saddle, and they headed out under the stars. He wanted to be in Hackberry before it was too late in the morning to help form the posse. In the confusion, his horse forgot to buck and that fact pleased him. They were all trotting their horses, and the surrounding dark bunches of small pines looked foreboding. But there was nothing out there that would halt or veer them off their course.

Three hours later, with the sun rising, the

cluster of Hackberry's buildings came in sight. When they rode up the main street, a black funeral wagon sat parked before the church. No doubt, for the marshal's internment.

Reg had already described the three brothers to them. Tee Berkley was in his twenties, Norm Berkley was probably twenty, and Hayes about seventeen. Their father had been killed a few years before in a gunfight with some area ranchers, started by him being caught with some stolen horses. After his death, his three sons became the town bullies. According to the stories Reg heard, they'd had many run-ins with Marshal Dave Crown.

"Folks were sick and tired of those three running over people. There was a secret meeting a week ago to send them packing. I think they learned about it and had nothing to lose, so they shot Crown and robbed the saloon and the store, because those were the only places in town had any money."

"Is the post office in that store?" asked Chet.

"Sure, why?"

"Then I have the authority to go after them. I'd go after them anyway, but this robbery makes it a federal posse and I can hire deputies that will be paid."

"What does that pay?" Reg asked.

"Dollar a day and an allowance for expenses incurred."

"They pay that like they do those cattle you sell the Navajo Agency? In script?" Reg acted amused when they dismounted before the saloon to hitch their horses.

"Same way, but you can discount it and let someone else wait for it to be paid."

Several men came out to welcome them. The Justice of the Peace, who called himself Judge Webb, was a portly man who shook their hands.

"That Indian tracker we sent for will be here soon," he hurried to inform them.

Chet spoke up. "Good. Cole and I are U.S. Marshals. Since this involved a post office, I'm forming a federal posse."

"Very good," Judge Webb said. "We're lucky to have you here. I have read about your hard work down south."

"Thanks. Does anyone here know which way they went after the crime?"

"Back to their ranch," a tall man holding open the batwing doors spoke up.

"They still there?" Chet asked.

He shook his head. "I doubt it."

"How far is their place from here?" he asked Reg.

"A couple of hours' ride."

"I've waited for Indians before. Let's get everyone out here on the porch so they can all hear me." The men all came outside and Chet told them what he wanted.

"I only want men in this posse who can safely leave and not leave a wife and children in harm's way. I want men who are tough and can ride hard fourteen hours or more a day. They must have stout enough horses or mules that can do that. This chase may take up to several weeks. The rest of you need to comfort the folks here, help put this brave lawman in his grave, and leave the law enforcement to the professionals.

"This is Cole Emerson, one of my men. That is my nephew, Reg Byrnes, who ranches up here, and I'm Chet Byrnes. And now, you that meet the requirements should get your horse, bedroll, slicker, and get out here with us. Someone can bring that Indian tracker on to catch us."

He noticed a younger boy leading his mustang out with the handful of volunteers.

"How old are you, son?"

"Sixteen, sir."

"You better stay at home with your family."

"I ain't got none of them. Apaches killed them all five years ago. It's just me and Crowbait. I need to go along. Marshal

Crown looked after me. They killed him. I can shoot good as any man. I can ride that horse of mine farther than any man here can ride his."

"What's your name?"

"Spud. Spud Carnes."

"Alright, but no wild shooting at them when we surround them and they agree to surrender."

Spud made a face like Chet didn't know anything. "You know them boys killed him?"

"No. Do you?" Chet said.

"Yeah. They'll die fighting, to stop you bringing them back."

"Why?"

" 'Cause they know that judge down there in Preskitt will hang them till they're dead fur what they done to Dave, and then I'll feel justice was served, sir."

"Yes, I imagine you will. You're in the posse, Spud."

"That make me a deputy U.S. marshal, sir?"

"Yes, it will."

"Good, I'm proud to ride with you and the rest." They shook hands.

Chet spoke to the next man who joined them. "I'm Chet."

"Dirk Mayes. No family. I do day work on ranches."

"Welcome to my posse."

The next one spoke up. "Benny Drews. I don't have a wife and I want to go with you. I've been riding horses and cowboying all my life on my father's ranch. I'm tough enough to stay hooked."

"I can vouch for him. He courts Lucie's sister, Fern," Reg said. "And that next guy coming rode in the Army with General Custer in Kansas. He's Connors."

"You know my rules?" Chet shook his hand and the older man nodded. "Glad to have you along, Connors."

The last man was black. He wore overalls and carried an older model Spencer repeater in his hand.

"That's Deacon Moore. He's the black-smith here."

"Mister Byrnes, they can get along here without me for a while. Dave Crown helped me get started here in my business. He staked me to enough money to stay here till folks trusted me to fix their broken things and shoe their horses. I won't hold you up none."

"Deacon, you can ride with us."

After he shook the man's tough calloused hand, he turned to the judge.

"Have a good man follow us with that Indian to their place. He don't catch us by then, we'll go on without a tracker."

"He should be here by now."

"I know. But Indians live in a different world than we do. They can't help it. We'll figure it out. Thanks, nice meeting all of you. Been better under other circumstances. I know you've lost a good man here. We'll try to catch his killers."

CHAPTER 19

His posse was ready to ride out. There were nodding heads in the crowd of men, and women standing on the porch murmured soft blessings for him and his men's success. Chet mounted up and they left town.

He and Cole rode behind Reg and Bennie Crews who would show them the way to the Berkley ranch. Pushing their horses in a trot, Chet felt satisfied he had a working posse.

They moved through the vast rolling country west of Hackberry on the tabletop of the rim, with scattered pines, junipers, and bunch grass. A great cow country by his consideration, but the lack of an easy market without long drives would keep the country from prospering until the iron rails came. Only the good Lord knew when that would become a reality, but his outfits would be ready when it arrived.

Bennie rose in his stirrups and looked

back at Chet. "The Berkley ranch is at the base of that mountain range." He pointed ahead of them.

"Thanks." He turned and the rest of his posse nodded that they'd heard and understood.

If they weren't at their ranch, where would they go? A good question. Chet doubted the Indian tracker would ever catch up with the posse. Somehow they'd manage, though a tracker would be helpful. They had a vast country to search, and those three probably knew every nook and corner of it, if they hadn't quit the entire area.

The posse rode up the two tracks with Chet in the lead. Bennie knew their mother, and told him it was her standing on the porch and the younger woman beside her was Tee's wife, Abbie.

"Good morning. We're here to arrest your sons for murder."

"You sonsabitches get off my land. My sons didn't kill anyone that didn't need to be. That old bastard's been picking on them forever. Get the hell off my land," she shouted. Gray-streaked hair hung in her eyes and she wore a hard look on her sun-wrinkled face.

"Search the place," he said to his posse. "The house, too. Reg, you and Bennie can do that."

"I'll kill you —"

The two tall men set her aside and went in the front door with hardly a word except a low, "Excuse us."

The others went to check out the rest of the place. He dismounted, keeping an eye on the two females in case they got out of control. Tee's wife looked pie faced about it all. Either in shock or some mental state. When the two came out shaking their heads about the search, he wasn't surprised. He'd felt sure they weren't in there.

Spud rode up. In a low voice, he said, "I found their tracks. They rode north."

"How many horses?"

"Three. One mule."

"Good job." Chet looked north. He hadn't expected them to go that direction. The great barrier of the Grand Canyon lay that way and he hadn't heard of a way to cross it anywhere up there. No telling.

"We have their tracks, men," he said. "Saddle up."

He ignored their mother's threats and swearing to see them in hell. With a nod to Spud, he said, "You show us where they went."

"Yes, sir."

Those mule prints meant they had a pack

animal with them and maybe supplies to carry them a great distance. No telling, these were tough, horse-savvy people and they'd ride hard to avoid their capture.

Spud and his mustang had already set out to follow them. Cole came back with the others, swung up on his horse, and rode him over to Chet. "I figure they have a day on us."

"No doubt."

Reg caught him when they rode out, not listening to their mother screaming about her innocent sons. Shaking his head, he said, "That was the messiest, filthiest house I have ever been in."

"You're plumb spoiled." Chet chuckled, imagining the scene in there. He'd been in those "pig pens" before, too.

"Your boy find their tracks?"

Chet nodded. "Spud's on the ball. Says they have a mule, which means they have supplies."

"Don't you think it strange they went north?"

"Yes, but they have plans to run for it, I think."

Reg nodded. "Lucie tells me there's some rough country west of here, but I've never seen it."

"It is tough country, but it don't look like

they wanted to go there," Bennie put in as they spread out in a line to trade notes.

Deacon rode over and Chet turned to him. "What did you find?"

"One of those horses has a bad shoe on his right front foot."

"Thanks. We can wish them all the troubles they can have, huh, Deacon?"

The black man agreed with a grim smile and reined his horse behind them.

The day progressed. To tide them over until evening, Chet's bunch shared some of Lucie's biscuits and bacon with the rest, washed down with tinny-tasting canteen water. Midafternoon, they took a break to stop and stretch. Connors rolled a quirly and puffed on it, looking pleased with the break. He shared his makings with Dirk, who did the same. Chet walked around, flexed his stiff shoulders, and wondered about Marge and his son. How were they were managing, and how long would it take for Lucie's letter to get there to inform Marge of his latest chase?

"There's a ranch ahead to the right," Dirk said. "Couple of brothers live there. They've got water and they'd let us camp there tonight. Mathews, Nick and Murray."

"Thanks, we can head there," he said after hearing the cowboy's longest spiel since morning.

He loped his horse up to his scout's position. "We're thinking we should go over south to a ranch that has water and a place to spend the night. Can we pick their trail up tomorrow?"

"Oh, sure."

"Good. Let's cut off here and go get some food and rest. They won't outrun us."

"Strange they avoided this place we're headed, ain't it?" Spud asked.

"They must know this country."

"Yeah, but the water ahead is gyp. I'd of stopped here."

Chet had no answer for him.

In a short while, he met the two bearded old men who batched alone out there. Their water was sweet. They acted open to the posse, and the older one said, "I wouldn't let them three bastards on this place. They came here a couple of times and tried to bulldoze over me and Nick. We sent them packing with our guns. No way they'd stop here."

Chet and Spud shared a nod. They had their answer.

They borrowed firewood from the Mathews to build a cooking fire in the yard. Cole helped Deacon and Reg get things going and Deacon made Dutch oven biscuits.

Frijoles were put on to boil. The others checked over the horses and gear to be ready to ride at daylight and unrolled bedrolls. Things set up, they lounged around as the sun set, waiting for the meal to cook.

The first batch of biscuits took the edge off their appetites and they bragged on Deacon's cooking as he put in another batch to go with the beans. The meal finished, Reg banked the fire so the beans would be easy to heat for their breakfast.

Chet got in his bedroll, wishing he was at home and in his own bed after taking a warm shower. He rolled over on his side and went to sleep still wondering where the brothers were headed.

The next two days they followed the brothers' tracks. It had become a monotonous business, and they swung around the backside of the sacred mountain headed perhaps for Horse Head crossing at the Little Colorado. Chet knew this was an outlaw hangout and many were thought to be in the area. He'd led a raid in that area six months before to arrest a large gang of robbers. They rode in that direction with no idea what these killers would do, but he had faith in Spud's tracking them. So far, that had been no problem.

"There's a hangout east of here," Dirk

mentioned. "They might be there."

"We better send in a small group to scout it."

"Be good."

"You and Connors might not spook them?"

Dirk agreed. "They'd sure know if Reg or Bennie showed up."

"We can wait and see what you two can find out. Don't take any chances. You spot them, come get us."

They shut down and had a parley. Everyone else rested while the two went on to the outpost to check on the fugitives.

"I forgot how long these chases were," Reg said. "But we damn near rode clear to the Indian Nation to get our horses back that time."

Chet smiled at the memory. This chase wasn't bad yet, but he hoped they'd have some luck at this place. So far, they'd made a wide near circle to get there. His posse rested in a draw while the two went to see if the Berkleys were around there. Time ticked slowly.

Dirk finally returned. They all rose, brushed off their butts, and moved in to hear his report.

"We saw Hayes sneaking around. Connors is watching him. The others must be hiding somewhere nearby. He has the mule, so I think he's getting supplies."

"What do you say we should do?" Chet asked the cowboy.

"Grab him and squeeze out of him where they are."

"Good, mount up. Spud, you bring the packhorse and stay back some."

"I got him, sir."

"Good, let's go. We're about to run out of daylight."

The small huddle of shacks and a store or two were in a pocket surrounded by grassy hills. When they rode up, the mule and horse stood hipshot out back. He sent Reg and Cole around front, and he and the others rode up to the animals, where they dismounted. About then, someone with an armload of goods started out the door and looked in shock at them, dropped his load, and went for his gun.

It was a bad mistake. Shot twice, he collapsed in the doorway. Chet, smoking gun in hand, rushed over to the downed outlaw to see if there were any more inside.

A frightened man in the store, wearing an apron and with his hands held high, screamed, "I'm unarmed. I'm unarmed."

"Anyone else in here?"

"No. No. Who're you?"

"U.S. Marshal Chet Byrnes. Where are his brothers?"

Cole and Reg rushed in the front door. "You alright?" Reg asked.

Chet waved off their concern and holstered his six-gun. "I'm fine. He looks to be alone."

"He won't be alive long," Dirk said, and knelt down by the body at the back door.

"Ask him where the others are."

The wounded outlaw gasped, "Clover . . . Springs. . . ."

"Where the hell is that?" Dirk asked him, but he'd died.

"That's about four miles east of here on this main road," the clerk said.

"Dirk, you and Deacon borrow a shovel and bury him. Then bring his two animals and catch up with us. Those other boys will be antsy and may head out if he's not back. We have some twilight left. Rest of you, let's ride east. Sorry for any damages."

"I-I didn't know him. I didn't know he was an outlaw."

"Not your fault. Mount up, men. Time's short."

They hurried to get in their saddles and left out fast. With the wind in his face, and leading the posse on what he hoped was the end of the chase for the two remaining killers, lots of things floated through Chet's mind. Hooves thundering on the ground, they made lots of dust, but that couldn't be helped. The slowly dimming daylight was a big factor in being able to see them.

One down, and two to go. Hayes Berkley was dead back there through his own fault, reaching for a gun in the face of the posse. Two more survived. They approached a camp of brush-framed, canvas-covered hogans, with many sheep and goats that scattered at their approach. On the run, he sent two men around to the left and two others to the south side. He and Spud rode into the camp, not seeing any horses except some painted Indian ponies.

He slid the big horse to a halt.

An Indian woman came out wrapped in a green blanket. "What do you need?" she demanded.

He removed his hat and nodded. "U.S. Marshal Byrnes. Sorry, we came here for two killers named Berkley."

In the dimming light, she nodded. "They left an hour ago."

"Any reason why? We thought they were waiting here for their brother."

"They abused a girl. Some of us have guns, and we made them leave."

"I don't blame you. You're lucky. Those

men are killers."

She straightened some more. "So are we."

"I understand. We won't bother you anymore. May we water our horses and camp on the far side? We won't cause you any trouble."

"Yes, you may."

"Boys, she says we can water our horses and camp over there. Thank the lady and her family, then let's get them watered."

"Thanks," the chorus went up, and they rode or led their animals to the large spring tank.

"Who is she?" Reg asked.

"The chief here, I guess," Chet said, looking back. "I don't know. But she made it plain that Navajos kill, too, didn't she?"

"Bet they get lots of trash like them two coming through here on the run," Cole added.

"Yeah, and I bet she knows Sarge from the cattle drives we make up here every month."

"Reckon they circled back to see about their brother?" Reg asked.

"There'll be tracks come daylight. They won't get far."

They finished watering their animals, then went and made camp with a supper of jerky and coffee that Spud fixed.

"Wasn't for your coffee, I'd of thought I was a stepchild, Spud," Bennie said.

"I agree we needed the coffee." He laughed.

"I figured you'd take it good or I'd never've jabbed you."

"I will miss the marshal. But I sure appreciate all of you treating me so good, even you, Bennie. I don't rightly know what I'll do, now that he's gone."

"Talk to Chet," Reg said. "He can find you a place."

Chet bent over and poured himself a second cup. "Yes. The Quarter Circle Z has a place for you."

"Wow, thanks, sir. You've really made my day."

"No problem. Our grave detail is coming in. Someone show them over here."

At last, everyone was settled in camp for the night; Chet told them they'd find the killers' tracks at first light and ride a ways until they found some wood or a food supplier, if the chase didn't look pressing. According to the grave detail, the other two had not gone back to find out about their dead brother.

CHAPTER 20

"How far can they get without supplies?" Reg asked.

"No telling. Excuse me, someone is headed toward us from her camp." Chet walked out to meet the figure coming from the Navajo camp.

"Marshal?" she asked when she was a few feet away.

"Yes, ma'am."

"Do you have a ranch and supply my people with beef?"

"Yes, we bring beef up here every month."

"I thought that was the name I heard. But you don't bring the beef, do you?"

"No, my sister's husband, Sarge Polanski, brings them up here."

"Then you are the man who gave Blue Bell a horse, too?"

Hat in his hand, the cooler night wind swept his whisker-stubbled face. "That was the trip when I brought my entire family to

Arizona."

"She is my cousin. I remember she called you her friend."

"She needed a horse for her buggy and we had one."

"My name is Bright Star, and I am glad to meet you at last."

"It's my pleasure."

"I would have been more hospitable, but I was still upset by those men and what they did earlier."

"No problem. We caught the youngest one at the store back west a few hours ago. He went for his gun and my men buried him. We'd hoped to find the other two here."

She nodded, standing tall, wrapped in a blanket against the night. "Can I do anything?"

"No, we're fine. We'll ride on at first light and find those two."

Her head inclined. "It was my pleasure to meet the man behind the name. Good night, sir."

"Good night, and tell my friend hello." He watched her walk away in the starlight.

What was her story? The second tall woman from her tribe he'd met. Obviously, they were cousins. They even shared many of the same facial features. No telling. He would never know their stories.

Walking back, he thought about another tall woman in his life, who was at home riding her jumpers and fussing over their son. She would be glad when she heard from him. He would be even more pleased to be back with her.

Come morning, they found the pair of tracks, and the posse went on, taking with them an empty saddled horse and a pack mule that brayed a lot. When they reached the next settlement, he'd have to replenish their own packhorse. One thing he'd observed — there were three bedrolls on the mule. That meant the other two outlaws had no bedding. And the nights grew colder as they advanced into fall.

In two days, they were in Gallup. He sent wires to Marge, Cole's wife Valerie, Roamer at Tubac, and Marshal Blevins in Tucson, to tell them the outlaws rode east only a day before they'd arrived.

Reassembled at the livery, he asked if anyone needed to go back home. There were some powerful headshakes from his men.

"We come to get them three, and we only have two more left," Bennie said. "They may not be any farther than the Divide up east of here."

The rest of the men nodded in agreement.

"Alright. We'll go on in the morning. I'm

buying supper tonight. They say there's a cantina down the street that serves great food. Let's go celebrate for getting this far."

The meal was good as promised, and they slept that night in the livery. At the crack of dawn, a vendor woman fed them and they rode on.

Their first day's ride was uneventful and the second day they reached the Continental Divide that determined east from west water flow. The place consisted of a few adobe cantinas, a store building, and a Catholic church, with *jacales* on the hillsides that housed residents. When there were no Berkley-branded horses at the livery, they spread out looking for them.

Spud came riding back hard to point Chet at the north side. "They're at the *casa* on the hill, in a corral."

The men formed a line, and with rifles ready, they spread out, going around houses, wagons, carts, and small garden fences. The sight of the line of armed men sent mothers to gathering scattered brown children into the safety of their houses.

A hatless man came out of the surrounded *jacal,* saw the line of armed men, and shouted back at the house, "Them bastards are coming, Tee."

Another man, without a shirt and pulling

up his galluses, looked out the door and ducked back inside. The line of riders with Chet kept coming.

"Three on the right, go around," Chet ordered.

They spurred their horses up the steep hillside until Chet stopped the line to give time for the others to take a position. He cupped his hands to his mouth. "Come out hands high, or die."

"Go to hell!"

His crew dismounted and took positions, rifles ready. A few shots came from the *casa* and then silence.

"We're coming out! Unarmed!"

"Watch them. It may be a trick," Chet shouted.

Both of them burst out the door with six-guns blazing. They didn't get ten steps before the posse's rifles cut them down. Then the wind blew away the gun smoke and both of them lay on the ground in the last throes of death. The last of the Berkley brothers were on their way to hell.

Good riddance, but they cost him time away from his family and the Force. Near two weeks had been stolen from his life. As he stood over the silent killers, he hoped all was well with his family.

"Reg, you and Bennie go find an undertaker."

"Thank God," Dirk said. "You and me don't have to bury them, Deacon."

"Yeah, thanks. I be right proud them's gone, but I be also proud me and Dirk don't have got to bury 'em."

Everyone laughed. Chet told Spud to find them a place to eat. He added, "Maybe a bath and shave, too."

"Yes, sir. Dirk, you can bring the pack animals."

"Get out of one job and get another." He went off laughing and grumbling.

The curious villagers had begun to come out cautiously to see about the gunfight. Chet spoke to them in his halting Spanish. "They were . . . killers of a marshal over in Arizona."

One man asked, "You are a lawman?"

"*Si,* I'm a U.S. marshal. These men are my deputies."

He nodded. "I wondered. You have come a long ways."

They shook hands.

Spud returned. "The undertaker is coming. I talked to a lady who has a café. She can have us food ready shortly. There's no bathhouse, and the barber is sick."

"Guess we can eat her food dirty."

411

"I'm sure. She's excited for our business."

"You did good, scout. Let's go eat."

The next morning they headed west. The trip took four days to reach Reg's ranch. Lucie came out to welcome them back. Reg hugged her and swung her around. Bennie kissed Fern, and the rest left to put up their horses.

The ranch hands built a fire under some big iron kettles to heat water, and the women served them hot coffee. Two bathtubs were set up in the heated bunkhouse. Towels and soap made ready, they all bathed, besides eating some hot fresh donuts and washing them down with good coffee. Razors were sharpened. Lucie had some shears and offered to clip anyone who wanted it after bathing.

Chet offered them twenty dollars in script from the Marshal's fund, or he'd pay them that amount out of his ranch account.

Dirk spoke up. "I hate to charge you for this, but if you can afford it, I'll take your offer, 'cause I'd never get that script cashed up here."

Others nodded.

"Lucie will pay you. I appreciate your help and caring. If we, Reg or I, can ever do anything for any of you, come and ask us. Spud, you can ride back with Cole and me."

"Mr. Byrnes?" Bennie asked. "Do you have a place for me, too?"

"It's a long way to come back and court someone."

"She said she'd wait for me, if I found a job on one of your places."

"We head back tomorrow. You're welcome to join us, Bennie. What about the rest of you?"

"I got me a blacksmith business. I'm proud of it, and I'll be going back to it."

"Good, those people need you, and I know you only came because they shot your best friend." He shook Deacon's hard hand. "You ever think about making barbed wire?"

"No, sah."

"Our blacksmith over on the Verde Ranch makes it. I can finance you making it and Reg will need a lot."

"I can get over there and look at how they do it. They can make it, so can I."

"See my foreman, Tom Flowers, at the Verde Ranch. I'll tell him you're coming."

He turned to the other two. "You two got any plans?"

"Me and Connors are going to join Reg here. He says he can use us. We're right proud to be a part of your outfit, too."

"Yeah," Connors said. "We was kind of second-class citizens. We'll damn sure ride for the brand and for you and him."

"Good, we better add on to the bunk-house," Chet said.

"You can send us two hundred more cows," Lucie said.

"And more British bulls," Reg added.

Feeling much better after his bath and shave, he nodded. "I get the message. We're a large sprawling outfit, but I know we all work together."

"Chet, when you came out here from Texas, did you ever expect it to become this big?"

"I had no idea. I bought a big ranch run by a crook who wouldn't let me have it. But I never imagined we'd be setting on this large an operation."

"We love you, for all you do. We just all want to be the biggest and the best ranch you own," Lucie said, then hugged him and kissed his cheek.

"I understand."

In a few days, he'd be home. He had two more hands to find work for. Spud and Bennie. Maybe they'd fit the Force for the present time. He'd decide in time.

"I'll look at those cattle in another trip. Cole and me, plus those two, are going home tomorrow. We'll be a few days getting there, but I have some other responsibilities, which include my wife and son. Cole's wife will be glad to have him back, too. I truly appreciate everyone who has worked so hard on this task.

"Aside from my men in southern Arizona, you are the least complaining bunch of men I ever rode with. Thanks."

They laughed, and Lucie announced supper was ready.

"You see now why he chose you all," Cole said. "He hates town folks in a posse, 'cause they gripe all day long."

"Amen," Chet said.

They left at daybreak. The mule in the horse corral brayed until they were out of hearing. Privately, Chet had told Spud they didn't need the animal and to leave him for Reg to use. Crossing the rim country, they laughed at not having him along to honk at them all day.

The second day, they reached Robert's outfit. Things were going smooth and Robert introduced his headman, Fred Roach. The new man, Robert, and Chet talked some about the operation and things they needed. They especially needed harness repair, so they planned to send it to McCully in Preskitt. They also ordered new ones and gave him the collar sizes needed.

Chet was impressed with Roach and decided Robert had made a good choice.

Their stopover in late afternoon at the Verde Ranch was a short talk with Tom and then they went on to the Preskitt Valley place, arriving there late at night. Marge and Monica were soon up and making food for them. Both Bennie and Spud were awed by the house. Cole kissed Marge on the cheek and then he rode on to his wife and their small house in town.

"Well," Marge said when they sat down to the breakfast on the table. "You all made it to New Mexico and back unscathed."

"None the worse for wear."

"Your sister had a boy. They named him Erwin. He was somewhat premature, but doing well. She's fine. I guess Tom had no time to tell you."

"We were in a hurry to get up here."

"I'm tickled pink about that."

"So are we, to be back."

"Mostly, ma'am, 'cause we don't have that braying pack mule anymore. We left him at Reg's," Spud said.

They all got a big laugh out of that.

Later, they all turned in. Home in his own bed at last, Chet felt totally at ease. With his wife in his arms, he had not one big problem going to sleep. Roamer had sent a telegram that all was quiet down around Tubac. JD sent one saying the second windmill was watering a small garden, and both house walls were going up. The lumberman had the material coming for the houses and they were all fine. More wells were being drilled, and they planned to install four more windmills. No artesian wells, so far.

He finally dropped off to sleep and didn't wake up until midmorning.

"You let me sleep all day."

"Oh, you needed it." Marge opened the drapes and let the light in. "I have water heating. It's hot now. Spud and Bennie rode off with Raphael to see the ranch. We'll have a get-together tonight. I sent word to Bo Evans and for him to bring his lady friend, Shelly. Mr. Trent at the bank. Ben and Kathrin, Hampt and May, Tom and Millie, and Jenn and the girls — they'll all be here. Monica is cooking a great roast, of course, and we should have a nice reunion."

"You sound like you have it in hand."

"Come, we have some Danish for you to eat. Then you can bathe. It's all going fine, other than we have no requests for your services today, so far."

Dressed, he kissed her hard. "How is my son?"

"Doing fine. Growing and kicking —

outside me — thank the Lord." She laughed and shook her head at him.

His arm over her shoulder, they went downstairs. "It's just good to be back here with you."

"Always, always. Tell me about those two you brought in."

"Spud is an orphan. Apaches killed his parents. The marshal the Berkley brothers killed was his caretaker. He's ages beyond his real age. He can ride with the Force. Bennie Crews is a ranch-raised young man who's courting Lucie's sister, Fern. He and Reg are good friends and he needed work. He'll make a good man. I'm putting him on the Force, too."

"He serious about Fern?"

"Serious enough he asked her about going to work for me."

"That sounds serious. But he'll be miles away from her."

"There isn't much to do up in the rim country. His father's place is probably small, and he's anxious to prove himself."

"And my husband needs good men."

"You're right. Monica, how are you?" he asked, entering the kitchen, heavy with the smell of rich food.

"Oh, busy, like usual. I'm getting to where you can stay gone longer. So these reunions aren't so close."

Laughing about it, he caught her and hugged her. "You're spoofing me."

She straightened and shook her head. "You know we love to have you here, and I like reunions, or else I'd get me a new job. Those Danish are on a plate and I have made fresh coffee especially for you. Now sit down. I have work to do."

"Yes, Mother."

"I am not your mother, either."

"Yes, ma'am." He winked at Marge behind her back.

"Where you running off to next?" Monica asked.

"South, I guess, and help the Force."

"You ever figure they could run that and you could stay up here and look after all you've got going on up here?"

"How would you ever have reunions, without me coming home?"

She dried her face on her apron and looked up at him. "I bet I could get by without them fine."

Then they all three laughed.

That afternoon, he went over the books with Marge and bounced Adam on his knees.

"The bank account keeps growing as we settle with the Army for the delivered cattle.

We are, of course, paying for the cattle we buy to make the sales to the Navajo, but each drive still makes good money. Besides, Robert's operation is the one that does so well," Marge reported.

"He has a man to help him now, named Fred Roach. He'll be his foreman. Robert needs more harness that McCully can fix or build at his new shop. I imagine he'll need more teams by springtime. They work them hard up there, but they really care for those horses, and that helps."

With his first bite of the Danish, his mouth filled with saliva and the rich strawberry filling in the sweet crust, and he felt himself relax. A man could do a lot worse than this.

CHAPTER 21

Folks began to arrive early. Hampt and May in a buckboard with their new baby, and their three older kids rode in on their horses. The youngest girl, Donna, about five, rode like some Apache child, and the two boys would close in any time she looked in trouble on her paint pony.

Ty, the oldest, rode up and reined his horse up short. "Uncle Chet, Hampt says I can drag calves to the branding fire next spring."

"I'd be proud to see you there, Ty."

He nodded. "I'll be there. Ray, get sister off that bronc," he said to his younger brother who dismounted and helped her down.

"Good to see you all here," Chet said, and moved on to shake Hampt's hand and hug May, whom he'd taken off the buckboard with her baby in her arms.

"Those two." May meant the older boys.

"Now they're full cowhands."

"I noticed how good they take care of Donna."

"Oh, they do that well. They'd fight a grizzly to save her. But they want to grow up way too fast."

"They mean well, is all I can say."

"You been alright? Chasing down more killers?"

"Yes, we got them in New Mexico. They won't kill any more town marshals."

"You are a wonder. Glad you're fine."

"Glad to have you here — always."

"Thanks, you know I never thought I'd ever have a real life after Dale was killed, but I don't know now what I'd do if I lost Hampt. He treats those other three so good — like they're his and, of course, this one, too. Chet, I'm the luckiest woman in the world, and to think I dreaded coming to Arizona. That's a joke now."

He hugged her and kissed her cheek. "We've crossed a lot of rivers together and it's always been better on the other side."

"Amen. Come see us, always love to see you."

Hampt had put up the buckboard and came back when May went in the house.

"I've been thinking about the Ralston place some more."

"Are they willing to sell it at a reasonable price?" Hampt asked.

"I think they will. But it's overgrazed and needs some relief. How many cows they have over there?"

"Maybe four hundred?" Hampt guessed.

"We cut that in half, take two hundred up to Reg, and you could get by a lot easier with the rest?"

"Right. But we'd need to move them sometime this fall. You can't move them when they go to calving next spring."

"You're right, Hampt. Bo will be here today. I'll see what he has going on about that buyout."

"Whenever you get ready. I think sending half those cows to Reg would be good and let that ranch rest some."

"Thanks. He has two more hands to help them feed this winter. They're both real hands. They rode with me after those killers. And they needed the work. I better go greet guests."

"Go on. We can talk later."

Chet welcomed arriving parties. As host, he wore a white shirt and a suit coat against the cooler fall air. The ranch hands took the guests' rigs and horses to park them. Everyone was dressed up.

His banker, Andrew Tanner, arrived. One

of the boys took his team and buckboard, and Chet sent him in the house for a drink at the bar. Marge had someone working as bartender, so they'd be taken care of. Bo arrived with his lady, and he asked him about the Ralston place.

"I sent them a contract for thirty thousand," Bo said. "They agreed to it, because I told them there was no hay on their ranch and if we had a tough winter they'd be out a lot of money to keep those thin cows alive."

"When will we get hold of the ranch? I want to move half those cows up to Reg. He has the feed and the grass. We'd have to rebrand them and move them before the snow comes."

"I will wire them tomorrow. They've accepted that price, so there should be no problem. But I'll get off a wire first thing. We should know by sundown tomorrow."

"Do you want to do something?" His lady friend, Shelly, stood aside.

Chet removed his hat and spoke to her. "I'm sorry, you two get inside. It's warm in there."

She shook her head. "No problem. I hope you two can close the deal."

"Thanks. We'll get it done."

Bo took her to the house.

He talked to others arriving in the sun-down, and collected kisses on the cheek from Jenn's daughter, Bonnie, and Valerie. Cole had driven them and Jenn out there and came up to shake his hand. "You get any rest?"

"I'm fine. I think Bo has the Ralston place bought worth the money. We'll know tomorrow if we can move part of the cattle up to Reg. He has the feed for them and it will help rest that overgrazed place."

"Good. Will it be a big job to move them up there?"

"Big enough. Sarge and his crew can't help us. They have a drive of their own each month. But we can round up enough help. It'll take two weeks to get them up there and it needs done before it snows. Hampt reminded me we can't wait till spring, because they'll be calving."

"Right. I'll herd them inside," Hampt said, amused, "and we can talk more later."

He gestured at the women standing around. "Ladies, time to go inside. They have the fireplaces going. I can smell the smoke."

Chet smiled. Then he went to greet Ben and Kathrin who'd just driven up. Things were fine with them, so he went on to welcome Tom and Millie from the Verde Ranch.

He gave Millie a hug. "Go on inside, Millie. I need to talk to Tom."

"I'm not standing out here waiting on you two to finish. I know where the party is. Good to see you as always."

Tom joined him. "Anything wrong?"

"Bo is closing the Ralston. Hampt says they have four hundred cows. We need to send half of them up to Reg. He has the feed and wants them."

"That'll rest that ranch some. Good idea. Hampt thinks they really hurt it with all those cattle. We need to do it."

"We'll need to brand those cows — all of them."

Tom looked serious about it, with them standing in the dimming light. "It will take time to get them up there, too."

"About two weeks, if we don't hit lots of snow. Bo is going to get us a go-ahead to get to work on the cattle and handle the papers later. I'm sure they don't want them. He dropped the purchase price to thirty thousand and they accepted it."

"You going to use their men?"

Chet shook his head. "They aren't very industrious ranch hands."

"That's my opinion of them. But they

might not have had any leadership over there."

"I guess the three of us can look at them. Well, you be thinking on it. You'll have to send help and probably be involved."

When they came in the kitchen, where the ranch wives and daughters were helping Monica, Hampt met them and they went out on the back porch.

"Bo said we could get the Ralston Ranch cattle to work tomorrow," Hampt said under his breath.

Chet nodded. "We'll meet tomorrow and make plans."

"Whew. That will be a challenge. Huh, Tom?"

"Yes, a big one. But we've been in wild deals before."

"Damn right. I'll be quiet, but you don't know what a relief this will be for me. I have two cowboys turning back their cattle every day. I have the feed to get the rest to spring, and they'll need it."

"If we get going, how long will it take to get those cattle up and branded?"

"Man." Hampt clamped his lips tight. "Two weeks."

Tom shook his head. "There's hundreds of yearlings and two-year-olds all over the place. If there are four hundred mother cows, and we're sure there are, we'll need to cut out two hundred, brand them, and take them to Reg. After we get them up there, we have all winter to get the rest worked."

Chet agreed. "That's how we do it. Cut that many good cows out and send them before it gets too late."

"That's what we need to do. Time is our biggest enemy," Hampt said.

"We better get inside or we'll all three catch hell," Chet said, and herded them inside.

They joined the seated crowd at the three tables in the dining-living room.

"Excuse us, folks, we've been doing some ranch business," Chet said.

"You are excused," his wife said. "Now, you are giving us the prayer."

"Oh, yes. Let us pray. Our Father in heaven, we are fixing to share a meal with our friends, family, and others. We thank you for the blessings you have bestowed upon all of us. We ask you to keep everyone in the palm of your hand. Bless the food we are about to eat, and Lord, be in our hearts when we leave here. In Jesus's name, we pray. Amen."

"Thanks, everyone, for coming. Monica has made lots of great food. Give her some applause. Thanks. Let's eat."

He took his seat.

Marge passed him a platter of sliced beef. "What is happening?"

"The Ralston place is going to be ours — Hampt's, anyway."

"Isn't that ranch a big mess?"

"Yes."

She looked to the ceiling for help.

He elbowed her and laughed. "We about have it figured out."

At dawn, Chet led his three foremen on hand over to Hampt's place. Raphael from the home ranch — Prescott Valley, Hampt from East Verde, and Tom from the Verde River Ranch. A cold morning for men or beasts, all were breathing out fog. Hampt's roan gave him a high-flying ride until he finally drew his horse's head up and settled him down. Everyone applauded his ability to remain in his saddle, and they all laughed.

Chet rode in among them. "Now that Hampt has his horse in hand, let's use all our skills today to figure out how to cut two hundred cows, with no calves, out of the Ralston herd, cross out their brand, and put the Quarter Circle Z on them. Then drive them up to Reg's ranch on the rim."

"You know, we could take them out through Chino Valley, then across country, then up on the rim out west," Hampt said.

"There's a way through there?" Chet asked.

Tom nodded. "It's more a stock trail than a road, but I bet it would cut several days off trailing them up by the military road to the San Francisco Peaks."

"Can we get a chuckwagon up there on the rim using that trail?"

"Hell, we can get a chuckwagon about anywhere we want to put it," Hampt said.

"Tom, when we get back home, you go look it over. Take someone with you; that's tough country. I crossed it once when I was chasing down Ryan and his crooks."

"No problem."

Hampt nodded. "I bet that would cut fifty miles off the other way."

"That could cut three or four days that we need to save off our drive." Chet was pleased as his men began to come up with solutions.

He turned his attention to Raphael. "How many of your men can you send us to help cut out and brand these cows?"

"Four men. Count me as one of them. That would leave two to be certain the stock are fattening and the horses are fed and all goes well, huh?"

"That's great. Hampt, who else?"

"I have four hands and me. Kenny, who's kinda busted up from a horse wreck, and your nephews can do all there is at the ranch and handle it with May's directions."

"Thanks. Tom, how many can you send?"

"Is five enough?"

"I hope so. A dozen boys and I handled two thousand steers on my first drive north."

"Cole's been up that trail, too."

"I'm counting him, and maybe use Jesus as the cook. Once we get on the trail, we won't need but a handful. These cows aren't the crazy Texas brush busters we drove to Kansas."

Hampt nodded. "Hell, boys, those cows've been worked. They won't run off if we handle them right."

"Let's draw a map, send Spud with it back up to Reg's, and have him show it to Reg, then he can meet us. He and the boy can scout that end of the trail and meet us when we start into that country."

Tom agreed, and so did his other two bosses.

"Let's look at some of the cattle on their range, now that they're ours."

"Who's going to inform that crew they don't work here anymore?" Tom asked.

"We may have to," Chet said.

431

"You expecting any trouble?"

"I guess I was born in trouble, Tom. If you three don't want those men to work on your ranches, I'll have to settle with them and pay them their wages owed."

"Don't go over there by yourself," Tom said.

"Hell, no. I damn sure want to back you," Hampt said. "I have a few bones to pick. They've dogged my turn-back boys, who've tried to keep their cattle over where they belonged."

"I'll take you along, Hampt."

"Better bring three hands along to stay and guard the place, too," Hampt said. "Or they'll be back and rob us."

"Oh, I hope not, but I better get Jesus to set up to start cooking for a crew over there. Have your men bring their bedrolls, warm coats, gloves, and scarfs. It may be a cold trip."

The band of grazing cows moved away at their approach, but not in panic. Typical longhorn cows without calves, they moved away, looking back to check occasionally to see if they might be threatened. A dark brown cow bossed them, and she hooked a few stragglers with her longhorns to herd them together and away from these men on horseback.

Chet had known lots like her. A bossy ruler in a small group, banded together for their own security against grizzlies and wolves. Coyotes in bands were dangerous threats to newborn calves left unprotected, but no match against such a band of cows. In cases of extreme hunger, wolves could pull one of them down by cutting apart the tendons in their back legs, but not without tasting some sharp horns. And many times the combined force of the herd won those tussles with the killers, throwing wolves in the air and piercing them with their horns. Chet knew about the full-blood longhorns, which came originally from Africa to Spain by the Moors who for a few centuries ruled Spain. These cattle survived a long boat ride from Spain to Mexico to eventually migrate up from Mexico and establish themselves in the Texas brush like deer and multiply.

Sitting on his horse, with the men he most trusted and liked, he wondered if they would eventually see, through their cross-breeding to the British cattle, those breeds as the adapted one in the future. He had his doubts about the Diablo Ranch down south, but in the mountains he felt sure Herefords and Shorthorns would be the answer.

"Our first plan is to gather and brand two

hundred cows for Reg. Then get them up there. Leave the ones we think are culls here. Reg don't need them to drive back to Windmill or here."

"We don't have a hand that don't know the real culls," Tom said.

Raphael agreed.

So did Hampt. "We won't send that boy one cull. We're all one on this outfit. Right, Raphael?"

"Ah, *si*. We are family, no?"

"Damn right. But we better run them hands off this place tomorrow," Hampt said.

Chet quickly agreed. "I'll be at your place early, Hampt, with Cole and Jesus. After we send the crew packing, I'll leave Jesus and Cole in charge of it and we can start. Tom, you can send Spud and the boys you chose to help us."

"No problem. You just be careful running them off."

"I'll be ready to ride over there in the morning." Hampt shook his hand. "I can't say fixing that place up will be easy, but if it will rain a little, you won't know it in a few years."

"Hey, we're counting on that — and you."

That settled, they rode back to the Preskitt Valley outfit and lunch — Hampt went back to his own house on the nearby place. Tom rode back to the Verde Ranch.

By noontime, he had Jesus and Cole ready to go into Preskitt and get enough supplies to feed the crew going to work at the new ranch. Chet told them to figure on feeding at least fifteen men. "We're going over tomorrow morning and fire his crew. So get all the cooking things you'll need. I have no idea what's over there. Put the tarp on the wagon bows. We plan to haul it up there, going the back way up through Chino Valley and across to Reg's. You two can join us and help."

"Sure thing. How many will there be?" Jesus asked.

"As many as fifteen. We need to work the cattle and move them up there before it snows."

Cole smiled. "That could be any day."

"That's why I'm putting so much emphasis on getting it done. Oh, get some tents, too. We may need them."

"I had that in mind," Jesus said with a grin.

"Anything else?"

"We'll make a list, get everything today, and be ready in the morning to drive over there." Jesus glanced at Cole.

"Right, boss man. We should be there in time to cook lunch," said Cole.

435

Cole and Jesus soon left for town and Chet watched Marge making some jumps on her big bay. Then, seeing how happy she was riding again, he went on to make a list of things he'd need to do. Get the state brand inspector over there while they branded, or get his approval. Learn what they must do for holding corrals, and the buildings' condition.

How many cattle needed to be culled? He knew they had some crossbred bulls. Tight as the purebreds were to get, he'd maybe have to put up with them for one more breeding season.

Roamer must have things well in hand down south. No wires, but they might come anytime in the law business. In the house, he took off the heavy coat he'd worn and went to his desk in the office to work.

Monica offered him some fresh coffee that he readily agreed to, and the young nanny, Rhea, brought baby Adam by for him to hold and rock.

"He is such a good baby, señor."

"Thanks, you do a good job with him. Rhea, you talk it over with Marge, but I want him to be bilingual when he grows up."

"Oh, yes, I will. And, thank you, I love this job and working here so much."

"We love having you. Here's the boss man.

Thanks for coming by."

"*Gracias.*" She curtsied and took Adam back, talking softly to the smiling boy in the blankets.

He went back to dipping his straight pen in the ink and writing out things to be done. Back home in Texas, before he moved them all out there to Arizona, he'd never thought about eventually having so many irons in the fire. But they all worked smoothly. And he'd damn near never thought he'd eventually have a son and heir to run the place when he couldn't.

He wrote a letter to Marshal Blevins and told him Roamer could handle the Force down there and he'd join him when he could, but he had cattle to disburse. Then he wrote Roamer to tell him that it would be several weeks before he could return and relieve him. Next, he penned a letter to Reg and Lucie to be carried by Spud, telling Reg about the plans and about the cows that were coming to him.

"How is it going?" Marge asked from the office door, pulling off her riding gloves and coming over to kiss his cheek.

"Fine. It's getting lined up." The swivel chair creaked when he spun around. "Jumping going well?"

"Oh, yes, we're doing fine."

"You know, I learned something back years ago taking cattle to Missouri. Those folks used wooden rail fences to keep the free-range livestock out of their crops. But only the rebel forces and Quantrill's Raiders could jump those fences. The Union Army had to take them down to get through, so for the southern efforts, it was easy to escape."

"I knew that. My first husband cussed that fact. He could ride a jumper, but they had none trained to do that."

He hugged her around the waist. "I can't tell you much you don't already know, can I?"

"Chet Byrnes, I never meant it that way."

"I didn't take it that way. I'm glad you know so much, so I don't have to explain."

"Good. Wash up. Monica has your fresh coffee and our lunch."

"Alright, jumping Yankee." They both laughed.

He left before daylight with three *vaqueros* and Raphael for Hampt's place, where he and two of his men joined them, and they rode straight for the Ralston place. Hampt told him a new foreman had been recently hired at Ralston's. When they arrived, the new foreman, Cy Mullins, came out of the lighted cook shack into the frosty morning with a steaming cup of coffee.

"What brings you and your posse out here so gawdamn early. We ain't done nothing wrong."

"Tell all the men to come out here. This won't take long."

"What for?"

"Just tell them to come out here. I have a message for all of you."

"What the hell for?"

"I said —"

"Hey, guys come out, the big man is here. He says he needs to talk to all of us."

"Thanks."

"No problem. You know I run this place?"

"Yes, I know that."

"So why talk to them?"

"It concerns all of them."

The crew came wandering outside, half asleep.

"They all here?"

"Yeah, 'cept the cook. Norris, get the hell out here. He wants all of us to hear his speech, I guess."

The string bean in a stained apron took his place in the rosy cold morning light.

"They're all here."

"Thanks. My name is Chet Byrnes. This ranch will today become a part of the

Quarter Circle Z. I'm sorry, but I have no jobs for you or your men. You'll be paid off as directed by the estate, and you must leave this ranch today."

"Ah, shit. We were promised a year's wages if they sold out," one of the men grumbled.

Chet shook his head. "I will pay what they say they owed you, is all I can do. You can hire a lawyer and sue them for any breach of contract. But they're a big law firm over in California, if you need their address."

The grumbling and complaining grew throughout the ranks of the group.

Hampt cleared his throat and dismounted. "Anyone wants to buck this deal, come see me."

They all shook their heads.

"Go eat, or finish. I'll be back to pay you. Gather your things up after that. Some of you have horses here of your own. Those who don't have animals, I can loan one to ride into town on, and you can leave them at Frey's Livery."

One man spat tobacco aside. "That's damn neighborly of you, mister."

Then they filed back inside.

"We almost have that settled," Hampt said.

Chet chuckled. "Hell, you knew none of

them wanted to fight with you."

"By damn, I gave them a chance."

"You sure did. Raphael, would you check the corrals and look over their horses for me? I'm going to get set up inside to pay them."

Under his breath, Hampt said, "That's a good job for him. He's a stickler for having things right."

Raphael and his men rode off to see to the horses.

Chet brought in his heavy saddlebags and set them on an empty table in the cook shack. It was a dusty, cobwebbed hideout and he knew Jesus would have to clean it before he served food in it. His foremen's evaluation of this bunch was right — they were not ranch employees like they hired.

He called them in one at a time. He asked if they had their own horse — though the information was on the estate lawyer's telegram. Everyone was honest and promised to leave the borrowed horse at Frey's Livery. He owed most of them fifty dollars for two month's pay. When he got down to the foreman, Mullins, the paper said to pay him for two months plus six, as they promised.

Mullins stood there and scratched his ear with his index finger. "My agreement is payment of my wages for one year, plus two months at fifty bucks. I knew they'd sell out one day, and I wasn't taking this job unless I got that guarantee."

"My page says pay you for two months, plus six months, as per contract. Now, if they wire me that was wrong, I'll pay you the rest of the money. But that's not what the telegraph said I should pay you."

"They got it down wrong."

"Here, read the telegram."

He took the page from Chet and used his ear-scratching finger to go down the list to his name. "Gawdamn it, that ain't right."

Hampt stepped in behind him. "What Mister Byrnes is telling you is right. You want to start a fight over it, we can go outside. Now, you telegraph that lawyer and complain to him when you get to Preskitt. I've done heard all the BS I want coming out of your mouth."

Mullins whirled on his boot heels to face Hampt. "Well, I aim to fight them in court over this."

"I don't give a damn what you do besides get the hell off this ranch, or go feet first."

"They owe me two horses to ride off here. That was part of the deal, too."

"They've got a short memory. It says nothing in there about two horses," Chet said, then folded his arms and sat back in the ladder-back chair.

"The no-good bastards —"

"Take the money and leave right now. Chet offered you a horse to ride to town. You can pack one, too, but leave them at Frey's or face horse theft charges. And, I can tell you, we will run your ass down. Them *vaqueros* Raphael has won't bring you back to court, either."

Mullins's face paled. "Alright, I'll take the money and see them in court."

Hampt nodded, still grim-faced, and waited for him to leave. He nodded when Mullins went out the door. "Life's getting slow. No one wants to fight me anymore."

Chet laughed and paid the string bean cook his eighty dollars. He went out the door muttering under his breath. That settled, Chet knew Raphael had the description and brand on every horse and who took it in his logbook.

The shorter Mexican man came inside and wrinkled his nose. "This place is a pigpen."

"Have one of your men ride back to the ranch and hire some of the *vaqueros'* wives to come over here and clean up this mess. Have them bring the paint left over from the McCully house and fix this up. I'll pay

443

them and when the cow deal is over, we'll have a *fiesta* to celebrate."

"I will do that now." Raphael went outside and sent a man back to the ranch for help.

"I thought for a while, Hampt, he was going to fight one of us."

"Hell, he ain't no big problem to whup."

"Let's see about the corrals and what we have to work with."

Most of the hands had ridden off by then. Raphael showed Chet and Hampt the bad gates that needed to be repaired. The squeeze chute also needed some fixing. They planned to haul a wagonload of live oak wood over from the ranch to use for the branding iron fire, plus several irons. There was little firewood around the buildings. No pens were large enough. They'd have to hold that many head of cattle outside in a herd. There was only so much horse hay — they'd need more than that. The graze around the home place had been eaten to the ground. And the ranch horses, on the whole, weren't worth much, either — he'd sell them for whatever he could get. They'd also have to feed the cows. This was going to be expensive before he got it handled.

"I can bring some hay over. That's not any trouble, but we better send my boys over and bring it back today," Hampt said.

"Do that," Chet agreed.

Cole and Jesus arrived with the chuck-wagon to be.

"Raphael is sending a man back to get some women to clean and paint the quarters and cookhouse. Until they get that done, use a tent. It's a pigpen," Chet told them.

"You have any troubles with them?" Jesus asked, climbing down off the seat.

"No, Hampt was my man to complain to."

"They cussed us out on the road."

Chet shook his head. "Even Mullins didn't want to fight him."

Hampt sent a man to get a wagonload of hay from his place, and Raphael sent a man to get the women.

Chet went to check the house. He and his crew found it draped in more cobwebs and dust. At one time, the clapboard house had been a nice dwelling. The leather furniture was cracked and pack rats had opened more of its stuffing. Even the books on the shelves were buried in dust.

"My bunch will have this nice in two days," said Raphael.

Chet agreed with him. "Hampt has his house like he wants it. I'll need to find someone in the bunch to live here. An empty house falls down quickly."

They went to help set up tents and unload.

When things were set up, he and Cole rode back to the ranch for the night. Chet told him to come eat breakfast early at the house and they'd go back and start the roundup.

Marge had to know about it all. When he finished telling her, he considered his first day as well spent.

"Who will live in the house?"

"I may talk to Cole, and see if Valerie would like to live out there rather than in town. There was once a garden and there's water. Save him rent, and she'd have a house of her own. I'll ask him."

"Good."

"Will you go into Preskitt this week?"

"Sure. What do you need me to do?"

"Tell Frey to sell the horses those cowboys left with him. We don't need them, and they're junk to me."

"I can do that."

"Good. That will handle that for me."

"Let's go to bed, big man. Your plans are to get up early."

He put his arm over her shoulder. "I agree."

Before the sun even colored the eastern rim of the horizon, the two men were headed east on the frosty wagon tracks. Cool enough to enjoy his wool-lined coat, Chet listened to the night birds and waking quail from out in the pancake cactus beds and the sage with juniper bushes. He'd come to enjoy the smell of sage mixed with the strong aroma of ponderosa pines on the hillsides. It meant he was home.

"Those ranch women are all excited about cleaning up your new ranch. They'll descend on it today, so don't get in their way." Cole chuckled.

"They're a nice bunch of women. I don't want you to decide today, but Marge and I talked about whether you and Valerie would like to live out there."

"I'll ask her."

"I just thought after the house is cleaned up, it'll be nice and spacious, and I believe someone needs to live in a house or it will fall down."

Cole nodded in the growing daylight. "Thanks. I appreciate being considered, even if we don't move out here. I really feel a part of your ranch, and it's nice of you to think of me and her."

"She may hate ranch living out here."

"No, but we never talked about it. She's a real sensitive woman and concerned. She never nags me, but she does lots of thinking. I'm proud of her."

"She puts up with you being gone, too."

"She knows we're building for our future.

I'm proud of the savings we've made from the rewards on my job."

Chet agreed and told him not to worry about it. She could decide and there was no rush.

The men were saddling horses. Jesus's cooking fire smoke filled his nose. He came with two cups of coffee for them when they dismounted.

Raphael was taking three hands with him and going south to find cows. Hampt and his men were going east, and Cole rode off with them. Though he was anxious to get in the saddle and round up cattle himself, Chet decided to stay to meet the cleaning women.

"How's it going?" he asked Jesus, squatted on his boot heels and sipping his second cup of coffee.

"Good, kind a fun not to have to worry about outlaws and only have to hear complaints about my cooking."

"Can we make this a ranch?"

"Oh, *si*. It is a good ranch that had been overgrazed. But it can recover. With Hampt in charge, he'll make it better or bust."

They both laughed.

"He's determined, isn't he?"

"Oh, yes."

"You've not found a woman?" Chet knew

the loss of the woman Jesus loved had ridden his helper hard.

"No." Jesus laughed. "I have been busy."

"Tending to my business."

"Oh, I enjoy every day."

"I'm glad you're one of my two right arms."

The women arrived in a wagon. They set in to first clean and paint the cook shack, then the bunkhouse. Things were taking shape. Those women were really making things go.

Carlotta, one of the *vaqueros'* wives, teased him. "We should make a company to clean up these places. That house will take us much longer. Have you seen it?"

"Oh, yes."

In midafternoon, Raphael and his crew drove in a herd of about three dozen cows and corralled them. One of his *vaqueros* lost his horse in an owl hole and had to be destroyed. A man went back to bring ten fresh horses from the ranch herd for them to use.

Chet rode around in the corral with Raphael to cut out six older cows that they considered too old for the drive.

"No way to separate them on the range," he said to his man. They'd done well and he knew Hampt would try to bring the most in.

November days were short, and the sun was about to set when they arrived with around forty cows. They drove them in the other pens for separation in the morning.

The cook shack had been cleaned from top to bottom and painted white. Coal oil lamps lit the interior and guitar music filled the air as they served Jesus's food. The men dove into the fire-roasted beef, Dutch oven biscuits, frijoles, and an apple cobbler. The crew and the house cleaners were starved, and they put a lot of it away.

"Thanks to the ladies who cleaned this place today and the bunkhouse," Chet said, and everyone applauded them.

"Thanks to Jesus and his helpers for the meal. We're working short days, so we'll wake you up early, and you can start out in the dark. If you need a fresh horse, they brought a dozen from the Preskitt ranch today. We turned out their horses; they were all too sorry to gather cattle on. Hampt and I will sort out any culls from your bunch and then he can rejoin you. At this rate, we should be on the road in a few days."

The nods around the room convinced him they were all eager to start. Tom's men should be there by the next day, then they could wind it up fast. He went to bed thinking about his wife and son, and with his nose full of the smell of fresh paint. Things were going great here, and he hoped so elsewhere.

CHAPTER 22

Both crews were gone in the predawn. Cole had taken Hampt's men. Chet and Hampt saddled horses to ride out of the pen at first daylight. When they were in the pen, Hampt noticed an older cow with giant horns. "Granny needs culled." He pointed her out to Chet.

Chet moved his horse through some others and nodded he saw her. She spun and clacked horns with another. That angered her and she put down her wide rack, charged, and lifted up the cow she disliked. Then she tossed her over on her side and spun like a fighting bull to crash into Chet's horse's side. Her attack hit his leg and foot in the stirrup. He felt the horse going down and then heard a shot.

The wide-eyed old cow charging was three feet from him when she stumbled and went nose down. Hampt had shot her again. Chet was on his feet by then and headed for the corral wall in a sea of panicked angry cows. One of them was down on her knees from a collision, and he jumped over her. After a scramble up the side, he was soon belly down on top of the corral. He looked back. Hampt was all right. Pale faced as ivory, but he had his smoking gun in his hand.

"Get the hell out of there," Chet shouted.

"I'm coming. Open the damn gate."

Women working at the house had heard the shot and were coming on the run.

Every step hurt Chet's foot, but he didn't care. He wanted Hampt out of the bawling, disturbed herd that charged around in the rising dust, upset by the smell of fresh blood and gun smoke.

Carlotta was at his side, helping him jerk the dragging tall gate aside enough for Hampt on his horse to charge out past them. Then they slammed it right in the face of two cows intent on escaping, and she secured it with a hemp rope while he braced it closed with his butt.

Then he slid down the gate behind him to the ground. "Get my right boot off, before we have to cut it off."

Hampt was off his horse and helped her extract it. Chet clenched his teeth and nodded grim-like, looking at the already swollen limb.

"Oh, my God, how did you run around to here?" she asked.

He put his arm up for Hampt to help him up on his good foot. "Some things you just got to do."

She shook her head.

Hampt under one arm, and her beneath the other, they hobbled him to the house and soon laid him on a mattress in the newly painted bedroom.

"My horse?" Chet asked through his teeth.

"He was on his feet. I'm sure he'll be sore, but we'll get him out of that pen later when the boys come in."

"Five Verde cowboys have arrived with extra horses," a woman announced.

"After they put up their extra horses, tell them where to find those cows. We'll leave the sorting till later."

"We're taking you home and letting the doc look at your foot," Hampt announced.

Chet shook his head. "I don't have time for that."

"Time or not, we're hitching a team and taking you home. I don't want three women chewing on my ass. May, Susie, and Marge. Doc can decide what's wrong. Put some hot cloths on it to reduce the swelling," he told the women. Then he went out to meet the men.

Chet decided he must have passed out for a short while. The cowboys, all looking concerned, carried him out and placed him onto the mattress in the soon-to-be chuckwagon and they were ready to take him home. Hampt was in charge.

"These woman can feed you. I'll take him home," Jesus said.

Hampt agreed. "Will you need our help over at the ranch?"

"No." He scrambled on the seat and unwrapped the reins.

They left in a lurch and he hollered back, "I am sorry, Chet. Hold on."

Chet looked back at the tailgate. It was in, so he shouldn't slide out the back. No telling about them rolling over. He shook his head to himself. Jesus was shook and going to deliver him back to his wife no matter what risks it took.

Near dark, they came up the lane and Jesus shouted, "Ring the bell. The boss has been hurt."

Monica and Marge rushed out of the house. Men and women came from everywhere. Two brought lanterns and lit them.

"Hey, I'm fine," Chet said, sitting up in the wagon bed.

Standing in the bed with his hat tipped back on his head, Jesus said, "Yes. It is his foot that got smashed."

Two of the *vaqueros* took out the tailgate and pulled the mattress with him seated on it to the back of the wagon bed. Then they each took one of his legs and under Marge's direction carried him in the house and into the living room. She told them there was a fold-up bed in the closet — the one she used to give birth to her son.

It was soon unfolded and made up by all the people helping, and the boss was set on it. The room silenced and Chet said, "I'll be fine. Thank you."

"Has someone gone for the doctor?"

"Jesus went himself," one of the *vaqueros* said.

Chet shook his head. "That boy worries about me a lot. I'll be fine. It's too far from my heart to kill me, folks. Go get some sleep and check on me in the morning. I'm sure I'll be alright."

They all nodded and left him to Marge and Monica.

Once the room was silent and empty, except for those two, he smiled at them. "A cow ran into it. She was mad, but I think you could pour me some of that good whiskey your father left here and I won't care."

"You — you want a jigger of it?"

"Darling, we don't need to save it. I want a glass of it."

Monica laughed. "I know he seldom drinks, but he needs a good painkiller tonight, my dear."

Marge brought him the glass and poured it three-fourths full of the liquor.

"Can you tell us how it happened?" Marge asked, taking a seat beside him.

"We had real good luck. Got sixty or seventy head in the first day. Hampt and I were going to separate some old cows out to send to market. One got mad and rammed my horse. My foot was in the stirrup, which protected it some. I managed to get my other foot out when the horse fell over. She came back for more of me and Hampt shot her. By then I'd ran for the corral side wall and made it over. But Hampt was still in the pen, so I ran around that way to the gate. Carlotta and I let him out safely and kept the wild cows in the pen. Then they pulled my right boot off and it puffed up fast."

He drank some of the whiskey, then nodded in agreement with himself. That was damn smooth bourbon.

"And Jesus brought you back in that wagon?"

"And he wasted no time, either." He took

457

another swallow, then handed her the empty glass. "I'll be fine until Doc gets here."

Despite the earlier pain, he fell right asleep and didn't wake up until Dr. Norman arrived. Must have been hours later. The doc twisting the foot around didn't help him one bit.

"That cow may have broken some bones inside your foot. Your foot has the most bones of the body — twenty-seven. But I think two months' bed rest and you will be fine." The man frowned. "Why are you all laughing at me?"

"Doc, there isn't a straitjacket could hold him down for that long." Marge said.

"Doctor, what other advice do you have for him?" Jesus asked.

"Damn sure don't walk on it. Use crutches, and don't let another cow butt it."

Chet smiled, despite the pain. "Thanks. The women will make you breakfast or you can sleep in one of our bedrooms a few hours and then eat."

"I will accept the meal. But I better go back to town after that."

"I'll get our stable boy to take you back," Marge said.

She turned to Jesus. "You want to eat?"

"No, I am going to sleep out in the bunk-house. Don't let him leave without me." He pointed at Chet, who laughed.

"We have any crutches?" Chet asked. "I hate them, but I'll need them. I broke my leg once, and tore up my ankle another time in Texas. Crutches are not funny."

"Want some more whiskey or laudanum?" Marge asked, as if she didn't care if he had crutches or not.

"Whiskey. Doc, you want some good Kentucky bottle and bond?"

"Thank you. I'd take a shot."

"Bring me a glass," he said after Marge who'd gone for it. "He ain't hurting as bad as I am."

His foot, ankle, and calf really swelled from the bruising. When he woke up the next morning, Jesus had crutches ready for him. By then, besides being swollen, his foot was turning purple and yellow. Throw in the pain up to his hip, and he felt like a sore-toed bear. They fixed him up with a metal bathtub beside his bed, but he couldn't bend his right knee enough to get it in the water. So he bathed, and then sat on the bed to wash it.

Marge shaved him and, finally dressed, he went on crutches to the kitchen to eat breakfast. The entire situation and sharp pain kept him on edge most of the day. Hampt came over the second afternoon.

459

"We've got two hundred head and have them culled," he told Chet as he sat in a chair and turned his hat over and over in his hand. "We'll brand them tomorrow. I fixed that squeeze chute. That means I plan to leave there the next day. Tom was by yesterday and went back to the Verde. He's sending Spud up to tell Reg our plans. Then he aims to come by and see you."

"You better take Jesus here with you."

"No, we've got a cook. One of the Verde boys can cook for us. He ain't Jesus, but we all want him to stay here with you. I know I'm taking too much help along with me, but if we get along good I'll send them home. I'm not your brother-in-law, Sarge, who herds cattle every month, nor are my hands."

"Not worried about that. You're right on schedule. Don't get anyone else hurt."

Hampt crossed his fingers. "I've been praying about that."

"Jesus, you figure they have enough supplies unloaded over there to feed them?" Chet asked.

"Plenty."

"You taking the chuckwagon back?" he asked Hampt.

"Yeah. One day of branding and we'll start northwest the next. Weather is holding, so

460

we'll be off for the Rim Ranch. Me and the boys figure it'll take us ten days one way to get up there, three to get back. I'm taking Cole because he's had more cattle-driving experience and he can keep us lined out. Two of the Verde Ranch boys say they know the way. Like I said, if I don't need that many men, I'll send them home."

"That's the least of my worries. Tell them all to ride safely and God be with you."

Hampt drew in a deep breath. "I think I've got it all. That leg still hurts, don't it?"

Chet lifted it and reset it. "It ain't bad."

Hampt chuckled and shook his head. "You'd be dying and you'd say that."

"I'm damn sure not dying. Have a good trip. Wish I could go along."

"Hampt," Marge, standing beside her husband, said, "we appreciate all you and the crew do for us. Hug May for me, will you?"

"I've never been away from her much since I married her. It'll be different. I lean on her a lot."

"You two have a wonderful marriage and deserve each other."

"Yes, ma'am. We surely do. Jesus, you got any advice?"

"No. Good luck. I will be sure he does not get in any trouble while you are gone."

"Fair enough. I better get that wagon hooked up."

Jesus shook his head. "The boys have it ready for you to go."

Hampt chuckled. "Things get done fast around here, mighty fast. See you in a couple of weeks."

"Vaya con Dios," Chet said, after shaking his big calloused hand.

They'd go to the Rim Ranch without him. Damn, that leg hurt.

CHAPTER 23

The day they were to leave on the drive, wispy clouds began covering the sky. On the porch in his jumper, crutches under each arm, Chet wondered about the approaching weather while the cool south wind swept his face. His wife was riding her jumping horses, and he figured the arena was too far away for him to hobble clear down there that morning. In time, though, he would. Besides, his leg was still throbbing a lot. He wheeled around and Monica opened the front door for him.

"Why, you're as handy as a pocket on a shirt," he said.

"Don't expect it every time. Is she doing alright?"

"Yes, if she sticks to those lower bars, she'll be fine."

"Okay. I have things to do." Their cook went back to the kitchen. He knew that she shared his concern about Marge's jumping.

Hell, she'd done it all her life, and it was her main interest outside of being a mother. What could he do as the late arriving husband to this household? Let her jump.

He read the latest *Miner* newspaper. One story was about a recent stage robbery east of Tucson on a stagecoach headed for Benson. One of the robbers listed as shot and killed by the guard during the crime was Larry Masters. That was good riddance, if it was really him. The Pima County Sheriff was seeking two others involved in the robbery. Anyone with information should contact him or Wells Fargo. That firm was offering a reward for their arrest.

Damn! One good thing happened while he was laid up. His archenemy had been shot and killed. When Roamer found that out, he'd wire him the good news. They could all celebrate. In the morning, he'd go to town with Jesus who was busy shoeing ranch horses that day. If there were no troubles on the drive, Raphael was coming back when they crossed halfway up there. May and the kids were all coming over the next day to visit. She'd sent word to Marge. His wife had also written everyone — north and south — about his wreck, plus the progress on his foot.

JD, to his surprise, had written him a

lengthy letter about his progress on the Diablo Ranch. He'd bought two more windmills for newly drilled promising wells. Two were set up and pumping, and the women had started the garden. He couldn't count the number of palm trees they'd planted. The houses were framed and the shake roof was nearing completion on his house.

They'd trapped thirty wild horses and sold them for three dollars apiece. The brothers had several other mustangers working the ranch, and the wild horses would soon not be eating their grass. He also planned to trap the maverick cattle on the place and brand them. They discovered several head of them while on the horse-hunting trips. They had his blue roan horse captured and it was being gentled down.

His final note — "we are working our hind ends off down here. JD."

Roamer had Shawn write him a letter on the Force's operation. Ten border bandits were arrested on various charges and turned over to local law or the federal court. Most were for hold-ups. Nothing in major crimes had been happening down there.

May and her baby Miles arrived with the rest of her tribe. Her oldest stepson, Ty, drove the buckboard over and the other two kids rode horses. Sarge and Susie drove in later with their baby Erwin. They hadn't heard about his wreck until the night before and set out early to make the trip to check on him.

Chet was standing in the back doorway. When Sarge went around and swung Susie and baby off the rig, he still had a bad limp from his accident.

"You alright?" Sarge hollered.

"I'm taking food and nourishment," Chet said, amused.

"Good," Susie said, coming up the stairs with a smirk on her face. "They shoot good horses with tore-up legs. You both are lucky."

They laughed and he ushered them into the kitchen. There'd be no getting ahead of his sister's sharp tongue.

"That baby doing fine?"

"Yeah," Sarge said. "They're lots of work. I never realized they were that much. How are you?"

"I'm fine. We have the diaper crew here today."

"Chet, sit in a chair," Marge said, "and tell them about your wreck."

"We were sorting cows from the Ralston place we'd just bought to take up to Reg's. There were supposed to be four hundred cows over there. We don't know the full count yet, but before it snowed, we wanted to send them up to him. That will sure rest that range, which has been overgrazed. We also didn't want to take any culls up there. So, Hampt and I were sorting them and some old gray-muzzled sister got mad and charged my horse broadside. No way he could turn, and she struck my foot in the stirrup. Then she wanted more of me, and my horse was on his side, so Hampt shot the cow. I scrambled over the corral and, aided by one of the ranch women, we got Hampt out of the pen.

"That was about all. Jesus brought me back here at breakneck speed in an old wagon, and Doc came out and looked at it. He said I should lay in bed for two months and those three — Marge, Monica, and Jesus — laughed about that."

"I bet they did," Susie said. "Have they gone with the cattle?"

"Yes, Hampt took half the men and they've been on the road a few days. He was concerned because he never made a drive this large and he didn't have Sarge's experience. Why? Do you think it will snow?"

"It might. There are some fuller clouds coming off the rim this morning."

467

"They have supplies. We'll have to wait and see, because they wouldn't let me go along."

Everyone laughed and Monica served them coffee and some fresh sliced bread, butter, and strawberry jelly.

He and Sarge retired to the living room. Glad to be off his crutches at last, they talked about the cattle deal with the Navajos.

"Victor is taking the drive over again this time. I'll be good enough to go back to riding next month. He's pretty sharp at that business, and may be better than I am at it. I hate this happened."

"No, this stuff happens. Look at me. You still favor that leg."

"I know. That's why I sent him again."

"Hey, I don't question your judgment or why. You're the boss over there. And you have a good man who we need to pay more for what he does. In the end, you have to make it work like Robert up at the sawmill. I had him find a number two man. I think he was doing too much work himself to keep things going. Not a crime, but we all need a man under us who can do the job — if we aren't there."

"Thanks. I've been some worried about the accident."

"Well, stop worrying. Actually, the log hauling and the cattle sales to the Navajo Agency are the profit makers in this enterprise."

"Good. We'll do all we can. I looked at our new places Bo bought. There are some wells that with a windmill we could get water up for the cattle and spread out the grazing. There's lots of graze on those places, but water development would allow us to spread out."

"Okay. You need how many windmills and tanks?"

"I could handle two or three. Two we could make earthen ones, but the other one would need to be masonry."

"Can we get some shelf rock close by?"

Sarge shook his head. "I don't think so."

"Let's get the earthen tanks built and a windmill on each of them first. Maybe we can solve the last one with pipe and metal ones, but they cost more. So we'll do that last. Can you hire a couple of men and teams up there to dig it?"

"Yeah, there are several homesteaders can use the work."

"When you go back, get them started."

"Oh, that'll be great."

Susie came in with their baby, Erwin. "What's great?"

"We're hiring some local men to dig two tanks on those homesteads Bo bought."

"Sounds like we're going to be busy. Do you think your foot will heal?"

"It'd better is all I can say." He looked the child over. A lot smaller than Adam, and several months younger.

"How is JD?"

"Working his backside off down there. Read the letter over on the desk."

"So, he sent you a letter. I never get one from him."

She handed the baby to Sarge. "I want to read it. Lucie sends me letters. Marge, and May, too. Is his wife down there yet?"

"No, she's still in Preskitt. They're building her a house down there."

"Oh, I know all about that building a house." She read the letter and nodded. "That's a long letter from him. Sarge, you need to read it, too. He's been busy."

"I will," he said, and she handed it to him.

"So far, he's really involved in it," Chet said.

"Oh, I can see that. Sounds great."

Monica served lunch and the talk continued nonstop.

After lunch, May told him to behave, then left for home with her stepson driving, sitting tall on the spring seat beside her. Susie and Sarge spent the night, then left early the next morning. Concerned about the trail drive, everyone was eyeing the thick clouds rolling in.

Chet had halfway expected Raphael to be back. Maybe they had trouble. He could sure kick that damned old cow for butting him. Dang her hide.

After lunch, it started to snow in the form of small flakes swirling on the wind. But by the hour chime on the grandfather clock, the snowfall increased until, by dark, there were several inches of wet accumulation on the ground. Marge worried about him going out on the porch every hour to check on it.

"You'll fall down if you hit a slick spot. I'll go measure it if you want me to."

He shook his head and smiled. "I'm just plain worried."

"You can be worried here, or up there. You still couldn't truly have done anything if you were with them. Those men can think it out. You have the best men money can buy. Don't fret so."

"I can't help it."

"I can. There's plenty of whiskey left. Have a drink and simply relax."

He shook his head. "I'll drink some and try to simmer down."

471

"Good." She went for the liquor.

"I hope those two stayed down at the Verde when it started snowing."

She poured him half a glass. "They're not children. Sarge fought with the Army in the snow in Montana. He's not stupid."

He raised the glass. "Here's to all the smart people I have working for me."

They both laughed.

Chapter 24

The next morning, Jesus came into the kitchen.

Chet looked up from his food and saw his serious face. "Ain't one damn thing we can do for them. How deep is the snow?"

"Five inches. But it is melting underneath."

"Not fast enough."

"Sit down at the table," Monica said. "I'll get you some coffee. This is going to be a long talk about what two men can't do about the snow, and what they want to do with it."

Marge laughed. "You know you're right, too."

"The snow may melt, a lot of it," Jesus said, taking a seat.

"Ah, we knew we had a chance of it. We better enjoy the moisture and runoff."

"We sure can't help them." Jesus shook his head and laughed. "Where do you think they are by now?"

"I hope on the rim."

"They might be. But I bet Reg is hauling them hay anyway."

Jesus agreed.

"Everything alright here?"

"Yes, I helped them load one rack of hay already this morning for the cows on this ranch. The cows are coming in this morning. They know where the food is."

"You don't need to go pitch hay, either," Marge said.

Chet looked at the ceiling for help. Inside his body, he had more unrest than six people. Clear enough there was not one thing he could do for Hampt and crew or the ones on the ranch there, either. It would probably be 80 degrees today down at JD's ranch.

When Jesus left him, in order to escape all of his pressing concerns, he took a nap.

Marge woke him for supper. Their baby, Adam, was acting upset, but he had no fever. He knew that a child's survival rate to reach age six these days was fifty-fifty. That made another concern for him to worry about. He really wanted to escape all those thoughts, but with his aching foot and ankle to pester him, it would be hard.

In a few days, the snow was gone, except in the shade. There'd been no word from the cattle drive, and there was no way for any news to get there except by the mail. He got along better on the crutches and he guessed his foot was healing, but too slow for him. It still was sore enough to wake him when he tried to roll over in his sleep. Also, he protected it from anxious horses and crowds stomping on it. Jesus took him to town in the buckboard, and when he hobbled into Jenn's Café, the girls jumped him.

"Any word from my husband?" Valerie asked.

"No, ma'am, or I'd have it here with me today. There's no telegraph up there and they are out in the wilds."

"I get letters, anyway," Bonnie said, and kissed his cheek.

He shook his head. "There are enough men with them to get through. They should be there in another few days and started home. I am as concerned as you are."

"Sounds to me like JD is getting lots done down at Diablo, on the water supply and your house."

"Yes, he is."

"Hey, let him sit down girls," Jenn said. "He's on crutches."

"I'm fine. They're just concerned."

"Don't get in a booth. I have chairs for you two at a table back here. How is Marge? With the snow, I missed talking to her this week."

"Doing fine."

"Good. Since we went to Tombstone together, we've become very close."

"She sent her best to you." Chet stood his crutches against the wall.

"You doing alright, Jesus?"

"Yes, fine. Thank you."

"Big job, taking care of him, isn't it?"

"No. But I like my job."

Jenn laughed, then shook her head. "You men stick together."

"We have to," Chet said.

"Your lunches are coming," she said, and moved off to take some customers' money at the cash register.

"Maybe you are the smart one. You don't have a wife," Chet said to Jesus. "I love her and Monica, but they sure can get feisty."

"I know she means well."

Valerie brought their plates of food and set them down.

"I'll get your coffees. Sorry, guess we're busy."

"We'll be fine," Chet assured her.

"Those girls are good workers and they try hard. This is some busy business."

Chet agreed. "And when she doesn't have them anymore, she'll be in a tizzy for help."

Jesus agreed and began to eat. Their coffee arrived and Chet thanked her.

At the end of their meal, Jenn refilled their cups. "Tell Marge hi for me. You two get enough to eat?"

"Plenty," Chet assured her. "And we'll tell her."

"Where you going next?"

"To see my banker, Tanner."

"He's a pretty straight guy. We get along. I borrow some money from him from time to time."

"You never asked me?"

"After you ransomed my daughter with horses worth thousands of dollars, I'd be too embarrassed to ask you for any money."

"Don't be. That's water passed under the bridge. I ended up with her as JD's wife, anyway."

She agreed and looked close to crying. In a rush, she hurried away to the kitchen.

"I recall that trip down in Mexico."

"Jesus, you can't not consider a person's

worth. Horses are nothing."

"Even Barbarossa ones." Jesus knew how he felt about the trade.

They drove to the bank and Jesus gave him a hand getting down. They went inside and a clerk waved him over. "Mr. Tanner is sick today. He plans to be back to work tomorrow."

"Serious?" Chet asked in a soft voice.

"He doesn't think so."

"Thanks. I just came by to check with him."

"Mr. Marsh has access to your accounts. Could he help you?"

"Nothing I need. Tell him to get well. Thanks." They left the bank for Bo's office.

Bo was deep in papers on his desk and looked up at him with a blank expression. "Oh, Chet, what do you need?"

"To get the hell out of here. You look buried in papers today."

"Yes, I mean I am covered. No, Chet, did you need anything?"

"No, I wanted to be sure you were alive and taking food."

"I am fine. Sober as a judge."

"Good. Stay that way. I'll be back."

"I heard about your wreck. Damn glad you survived. See you next time. I'll take time for you then."

"No problem. We'll be back."

"Tell Marge hi from me."

"We will." He closed the door and buttoned his coat. There was a cold wind coming. Someone turned the heat off on them, he decided. They drove home in the dropping temperature.

On the twelfth day, several bundled-up men on horseback rode up the driveway and someone rang the yard bell. Chet grabbed his crutches and hurried through the kitchen and outside.

Raphael drew up his reins. "Good afternoon. We are back."

He dismounted and Chet, crutches and all, hugged him. "Is everyone alright?"

"A little cold. A lot tired, but we are all back here. We never lost a cow. Cole went on to see his wife. Hampt and his boys should be home now, too."

"After you see about your wife and family, and the men, come to the house. I want to hear it all. Bring everyone, for we all want to hear about it."

"I am awfully dirty. So are the men."

"Come to the house. A little dirt doesn't matter. You've been doing my job. We all want to hear how it went."

In Spanish, Raphael gave the men orders to get their families, children and all, and come right back to the house. Then he nodded at Chet. "They will all be there shortly."

Chet turned to his two women on the porch, both wrapped in long tailcoats. "Make some coffee. Everyone is coming to the living room and tell the story of the drive."

Marge still stood out there to wait for him. "Everyone is alright?"

"Yes, he said everyone was alright."

When he hobbled in after his wife, Monica was already working at the large range. "Are the ranch women coming?"

"Yes, everyone."

"That's good. They can help me make bear tracks for everyone. It will be a treat for the children, too."

"Save me some." And he went on in the living room.

"Rhea and I can fold up your bed and store it, so we have enough room," Marge said. "You go sit in your big leather chair and play host."

"Yes, ma'am."

"Did he give you any clues?"

"Yes, the best one. Everyone is alright and all the cows are up at Reg's."

"Cole, too?"

"Yes, he went on to his wife in town."

"I bet May's happy to have Hampt back."

Rhea excused herself to go check on the baby, while Marge went to answer the back door. People were already arriving.

They began to file in — sleepy children with their mothers, *vaqueros* with beards, and single men nodding to everyone, with their *sombreros* in their hands. Monica drafted Raphael's wife and another woman to help her make bear tracks, and Jesus joined them to oversee the cooking.

When everyone was there, Chet told Raphael to start his story.

"The drive went well. We crossed Chino Valley and started north in the snowstorm. Cole told me we better keep going and not stop. So we drove them all night. He had a compass and kept us going north. When we stopped the next day, the cattle were tired enough they stayed in place.

"We had some firewood in the chuckwagon and Haze cooked a meal. That evening, Reg and one of his men brought us hay wagons. That settled the cows and we backtracked to his place. But the hero was Spud. He knew that country and led Reg to us.

"Everyone was so exhausted, we stayed there two days and let the snow melt."

"Fine, you all did wonderful. Did you bring the wagon back?" Chet asked.

"Yes. We left it at Tom's. We came back by the roadway, in case it snowed some more. There's no one out there on that route we took." Raphael shook his head.

"Was Reg happy with his cows?"

"Oh, *si*. Very happy, and his wife, too. He has a nice ranch up there."

"Lucie is a great gal. Eat the bear tracks and enjoy yourself. This was a good page in the ranch history. Thanks to all of you."

Everyone, the men and their wives and the children, were all smiles and headed to the kitchen for Monica's bear claws.

For the first time in months, he slept through the night.

The next morning, he walked in his felt slippers to breakfast without his crutches. Monica frowned at him. "I bet that hurts."

"Not bad. I need to get used to it. These damn crutches need to be retired." He eased himself onto a kitchen chair. "I damn sure won't run any foot races."

"I bet Hampt wants to rebrand all those new cattle as soon as possible."

"Oh, yes. I figure he'll have it all planned out. He's a good man to have on that job." Chet blew on his hot coffee. "Oh, yes. Everyone is growing up. I think JD has really made a great turn."

"Yes. It sounds that way."

"Between great men like Hampt, Raphael, Tom, Robert, and the rest, I'm very fortunate. And JD has really made a great turn for the better."

"That's great." Monica wiped a dish and spread the towel across the counter.

"Yes, and not just JD. Everyone is growing up, marrying, having children. The next few years will be great, watching the young ones grow and become part of our family."

"You are lucky to have so many good men. Your ranches are spread too far apart to not have reliable men like them. What comes next?" Monica put his breakfast on a plate before him, pancakes, fried eggs, and bacon.

"Hampt's branding project. Counting all the yearlings, and two-year-olds on that place, I'll bet we have five hundred head to work."

"Good thing you took those cows to Reg."

"We had to. Come spring, we'll send most of those big steers to Windmill. He'll have lots of graze up there and they'll need to be fattened. That will help all that range over there."

"Why didn't their man sell the big ones off?"

Chet shrugged. "They were never fat, and until we get a railroad up here there's little market."

She took a seat across from him with a cup of coffee. "I can say this, I know you get concerned when you have to stay here, but both Marge and I like it."

"I really like it, too. Both of you, and the boy, are my family."

Clean-shaven, Hampt was there the next day and laid out his plans to borrow two of Raphael's single men and two of Tom's men to get on with re-branding the Ralston cattle. They could use the cleaned-up house on the new place, and if Jesus could cook for them — he'd be set up to do it.

"Come spring, I want all those steers moved to Windmill. Sarge has the grass up there. So they can get fat and be moved out on our contract."

Hampt looked relieved. "Boy, that will give that range a real chance to recover."

Chet nodded. "You're on the right track. When do we start branding?"

"Get set up Sunday and start Monday. Weather holds, we should get it wound up in a week."

"I'll talk to Jesus about being your cook."

"Good. That boy from the Verde was alright, but Jesus is better."

Things moved fast. Jesus agreed to be the cook, and they took cots over for the men to sleep on.

Hampt and his men worked over the corral some more. Chet and Jesus made a trip to town for food and supplies, including a large roll of hemp rope to make lariats. The trip took all day and they spent the night at the Preskitt Valley Ranch. On Saturday, they took the supply wagon to the Ralston headquarters. Cole joined them and rode a quiet horse to accompany them over there.

After unloading things at the house, Cole gave the place a thorough going over.

"Did you ask her about this place?" Chet asked.

"We talked a lot about it. Since the ranch women cleaned the house, it looks pretty damn nice. But I worry because we are gone so much. Oh, she says she's not afraid, but there ain't anyone close to here."

"Hey, it isn't necessary. I just thought I'd offer."

"Thanks, Chet. I'll tell her to stay in town."

"That's fine. I hope this easy weather holds until we get the branding completed."

"You and me both."

His men helped set up his kitchen and get ready to cook. Jesus took a bedroom for himself and got the large potbellied stove ready to fire up for that night. Chet planned to stay and get ready for the next day when the crew would be coming.

Hampt's cowboys drove a herd of using horses over and corralled them. There was hay already set up there for them and water in the pens. They paused to talk and drink some of Jesus's coffee. Chet felt proud looking over things from the front porch. This place would be a good addition to the family empire.

Cole took him home in the wagon and said he'd be back for him Monday morning early.

"I'll ride a horse over there then."

"You better get that horse handler to ride him some tomorrow. You aren't ready for a bucking session."

On Sunday, he went to church with his wife. The sky was clear and by midday the temperature rose into the sixties.

Marge beamed at having him along as they drove home after services. "It's great to have you to show off."

"You don't have much." He chuckled.

"Oh, yes, I do. People all over Arizona look up to you, for all your hard work to make this a better place to live."

"We try."

"A lot more than that."

"I'm proud of our marriage and you. The

boy is an extra gift. If my foot keeps healing, after this branding, I need to go down south to help JD and Roamer."

"I know there are things you have to manage."

He checked the team some going downhill. "Things in the future look to be in good shape to make money with our ranches. We've been real lucky to be here."

She hugged his arm. "We're lucky to have each other."

"Amen to that." He leaned over and kissed her cheek.

He met Cole at dawn the next morning. He'd told Marge he was taking his bedroll and staying over there for a few nights. They kissed and he climbed in the saddle on one of his roan horses. He never even switched his tail, and Chet saluted Jimenez. "Thanks."

The young man smiled and told him to have a good day.

According to Jesus, Hampt's teams had left by the time they arrived. Cole went on to find one of the crews to help them round up cattle. Chet remained at the headquarters and helped Jesus get ready for the evening meal.

By noon, one outfit drove in a large herd of mixed cattle and calves. There was lots of bawling and dust boiling up in the corrals when they swung the gate shut.

Cole came in with them and swung down. "It's going to be a long winter. Hampt's going to have to start feeding them or many of them won't make spring."

"Looks like they aren't fattening well on the dust," Chet said.

Cole nodded in agreement.

They had a lot of cattle in the pens by midafternoon. Hampt sent two men to go get loads of hay. When they finished branding them, he planned to start haying them, to keep them separate from the range cattle.

Branding started the next morning, and the hay arrived. The plan was to not turn the cattle out until all were branded, and then move them to a tank with lots of water and feed them. That way, they'd stay away from the pens and not get mixed with the unbranded ones.

"We can't keep them all apart," Hampt said. "But we'll be able to do that by next year."

Chet nodded. His foot ached some from being on it so much, but things went well this first day. He was in the kitchen helping Jesus do the final things before serving supper.

"Hey," a ranch hand said. "Someone is

488

driving a buckboard out here like he's on fire."

Chet frowned and Jesus dried his hands to join him to see who was coming.

He recognized Raphael driving as he swung the buckboard around. He halted the lathered team and jumped down. Chet knew from the look on his face that he brought bad news.

"I am so sorry, señor . . ." He huffed for his breath. "I am a bearer of such bad news."

"What has happened?"

"Your wife . . . she is dead. She had wreck jumping her horse, and she is gone. Nothing we could do."

Chet felt like he'd been kicked in the stomach by a mule. Marge, gone? It couldn't be. He felt frozen, unable to move or think. Then he looked at Raphael.

Tears poured down his foreman's face, and he looked so sad, Chet reached out and hugged him. "I know you did all you could for her, my friend."

"Oh, we tried everything."

"How is Monica?"

"You know how she loved your wife. She went to her room and closed the door. My wife wanted to be with her, but she refused her help. They went for the *padre.* My whole family — the whole ranch, is in tears."

"Come inside and sit down."

"What can we do?" Cole asked him.

"Cool out that team he drove in."

"I'll tend to that."

"Good." He patted the pain-faced Hampt on the shoulder. "Then you better go tell May."

"Oh, hell, Chet. I hate this for you."

"She was . . . doing what she loved."

"Where is Art?" he asked, recalling one of the young men's name.

"Here, boss man."

"We need to send word to Tom, Robert, Susie and Sarge, and Reg and Lucie, I guess."

"I can handle that. Tom will know what to do."

"Good. Get to riding, but be careful. You hear me?" The cowboy stopped and told him he would. Then he went on.

The room was full of grieving faces. He went out and made the sobbing Raphael come in and sit on a chair.

Jesus shook his head as if unable to talk. "We better eat."

Chet agreed. "Everyone get a plate. I know how hard this is on us, but she would want you to eat."

Cole was back to report on the team. "Those horses are run in the ground. You want to ride back?"

"Yes." He shook Raphael's shoulder. "Eat something. We'll get you a horse to ride back with us."

"*Si.*"

He drew a deep breath, and at that moment, the emotional shock really struck him. He was alone in the world. The greatest treasure in his life wouldn't be there when he arrived home. Had he put the ranch ahead of her? No, she knew why he went to the branding camp. Damn, should he have sold those jumpers? No way she would have let him do that. What would he do without her? Lose his mind.

CHAPTER 25

He'd heard the phrase many times. *The long ride home.* With a bloody, sinking sundown facing them, Cole, Jesus, and Raphael accompanied him on the ride back to the ranch. The situation reminded him of bringing his nephew Heck's body back to the Black Canyon road. Marge came like an angel that night with her carriage and saved his sanity. Sure, he knew she wanted him, but it wasn't a selfish thing for her to do. She really cared and did all she could for him, with no guarantee that on his return from Texas he wouldn't bring a bride back.

Memories flooded his mind — Susie saying Marge wouldn't go camping with him because she was educated and had been to finishing school — their camping honeymoon up on the rim — her shining face when she handed him their son.

Damn. He swallowed hard. This would be a damn long, sad time to get through. And poor Adam would never know his mother and all her plans for him — even college. *Marge, I'm going to have a tough time facing life without you.*

He realized the enormity of the entire ranch's loss when he saw it written on the ranch crew's faces. He had to hug several wives, and even men, when he dismounted. Despite the falling temperatures, they were around bonfires. The priest was there and came forward to meet him.

"My son, this is a very bad time for us to meet."

"No, Father. I'm so pleased to meet you. We need your strength to help my people get through this hard time."

The priest crossed himself. "You are most generous. I see the strength in you that my people have told me about. May God be with you, my son."

"I'm sure he will have to be. I must go now and check on my son and my people in the house. If I can ever repay you, come see me."

"Yes." He made the blessing sign at him and then nodded.

He entered the house. Too quiet. "Monica?"

No answer.

"She is in her room," Rhea said, rocking his son in her arms and coming from the living room.

"He doing alright?"

"He is much better."

"Thanks, I will count on you a lot in the days ahead."

"I understand. Your wife was a wonderful woman."

"Yes, the most." He looked at his son wrapped in the blankets. "I'll tell you all about her someday, son."

Then he looked up at the nanny. "Did they take her away?"

"Yes, the funeral man did that."

"Thank God. There'll be lots of sadness in the next few days. Let's try to keep it as usual for the baby."

"Oh, I will try hard to do this."

"I trust you, Rhea. You need any help, just let me know."

"I will, señor."

"Good. I need to comfort Monica now."

Rhea nodded quickly. "It has hurt her bad."

"I can imagine."

He rapped on her door and Monica opened it with a tear-streaked face. With a loud, "Oh," she fell into his arms. "What will we do without her, Chet?"

"I don't know, Monica. But we must be strong. This can't scar our lives. She wouldn't want us to do that or let it happen. In memory of her, we have to show strong faces."

She nodded. Then she dried her eyes on a cloth. "You are right, but, oh, I will miss her."

"We all will. Someone is at the back door. I'll go see about them."

"You have supper?"

"Yes, Jesus fed me over there. Excuse me."

He'd wanted some time to grieve in private, but Jenn, Bonnie, and Valerie were all at his back door. Wet faced, they all hugged him and murmured condolences. Cole stood on the porch behind them and held up his hands as if in surrender.

Tom and Millie arrived shortly after.

"I sent word to Reg and Lucie, as well as Susie and Sarge. My rider is going north and will tell Robert and his wife," Cole said. "Word will also be taken to Oak Creek, too."

Chet thanked him and led them into the living room.

Monica had dried her tears and was making coffee and treats. Best thing for her — keep busy.

"Did anyone wire the Force?" asked Tom.

Cole said, "I wired Tubac and JD."

"Thanks."

"How did she fall?" Bonnie asked.

"Raphael told us he thought maybe the horse broke a bone in his back leg when attempting the jump and fell over on her. It was obvious to poor Jimenez that she was dead when he reached her."

"Oh, my God," Bonnie cried out. "She was such a great lady." Then she went into tears, comforted by the others.

They made beds eventually for everyone and Chet slept on the couch downstairs. He woke early and went in the kitchen after stoking the big fireplace.

"Do you have enough food for all these folks?"

A much improved Monica nodded and said she did.

"That's good. You are going to be busy."

"Yes. She would have expected me to do it, too."

He hugged her. "Yes, she'd want us to be brave. Even if we don't feel like that inside."

"She was a very intelligent lady."

"I forgot. I need to wire her father down in Phoenix. Damn, I knew I'd forgotten someone."

"He will be upset, too."

Chet closed his eyes. "He may be, but he knew how much she loved jumpers and he couldn't have stopped her from doing it. She gave it up to have my son, but she wouldn't quit for anything else."

"Write the wire," Monica said. "I will have a boy take it to the telegraph office."

"Boy, we survivors have lots to think about."

"Yes. I have coffee. You can pour some."

"I imagine my sister will be here next." He filled a cup of the fragrant-smelling brew.

"She won't take it any better than the rest of us."

"I suppose I better make some arrangements today. If I can wait until Thursday, maybe Reg and Lucie will be here."

"That's quite a wait."

"I know, but things like distance make it necessary."

Jenn came in the kitchen. "What can we do?"

He smiled. "Ask Monica."

Rhea arrived behind the girls, handed Bonnie the boy, and went to fix his bottle.

"Could I stay and be your assistant?" Bonnie asked her, swinging him around.

"Ask Chet. He's my boss."

Everyone laughed and it was good to hear them. Monica fixed his plate. Jenn served him and patted his back. "Thanks. You are a real rock for all of us."

He turned his hands up. "What did I do?"

"Eat, you will need your strength," Jenn said, motherly like.

He busied himself eating the food set before him, swallowing around the lump in his throat as best he could, and then excused himself to write the wire for her father. Damn, this part would be real hard.

He finished it and Monica went to the back door and called to a youth. She gave him orders in Spanish and then took money from her pocket for him to pay for it.

"Hey, I can do that."

"No. This is mine."

No argument with her. Cole came downstairs.

"Eat. We have to go to town," Chet said to him.

"I can —"

"I'll get the horses saddled. You eat."

"Yes, sir." Cole smiled and took a seat.

Chet went to the horse corral and met with Jimenez. "Saddle us two horses. One for me, and one for Cole. We must go to town."

"*Si, señor.*"

"I can help."

"No. I will have them ready shortly, huh?"

"Shortly is fine."

498

"Señor? You know if I could have caught and saved her, I would have been there."

He swallowed and nodded. "I know that, and I don't blame you. I know she was your friend and companion. You did so much for her." When he couldn't find any more words, he hugged the lanky youth. "Jimenez, God must have needed her. She's with him. I'm so proud of you, and how hard you work for us. Don't blame yourself. It just happened, an accident, and remember how much she enjoyed those horses."

"I know this is hard on you, señor. But, thank you. I was worried people would think I should have done more."

Chet shook his head. So far he had not cried — so far. "We will get through this — somehow."

Cole came out of the house. Buttoning his coat and heading for their horses, he waved at Jimenez and thanked him for saddling them. Chet nodded and mounted his own horse.

"What do we have to do?" Cole asked.

"I guess plan the funeral. I only did this once before with Heck, when the stagecoach robbers murdered him, and Marge helped me then. She helped me through all this."

"You decided where you will bury her?"

"No."

Cole reached over and squeezed his arm. "I didn't ask that to make you feel bad."

Chet's eyes focused on the blue skies way over Preskitt, and nodded. "I know where you come from, Cole. For the last almost two years, I had a perfect woman to handle things like this. To point me where to go. Back in Texas, Susie did that for me. I worried about business and handled that part. Then I had Marge to handle other things, while I took care of the ranches. I can't expect anyone else to do what has to be done today. This is my problem. If I fall out today, though, you'll need to take the lead. I fear I may fail at this task."

"No problem. We should have brought my mother-in-law — she'd have got this done."

"She would be a lifesaver, but this is really my burden."

"I can back you."

"Good."

"After you make the decisions, then we need to start informing folks when we plan to hold it. They will want to know, so they can make plans. The first choice you must make is where to bury her — on the ranch, or in her church's cemetery?" Cole said.

"You buried Heck down on the Verde Ranch. But I think you need to bury her on the ranch up here or at the church."

"I don't want to separate her from the ranch, but in time, her being in the church cemetery for eternity might be best. She loved the church. I agree. Good thinking. Eternity is a long time."

"That funeral director is going to walk you through it. I went back to Texas when my mother died and helped Dad. I rode two horses to death to get there. But I helped him."

"I want May to sing a hymn and then have a short service and thank everyone."

"You can get that done your way. Marge have a special dress?"

"I'll let the women choose it."

"Good idea. A coffin will be hard."

"I figure so."

They met Lamont Cannon in his office at the funeral home. A young man in his thirties, who acted very subdued during their meeting about the funeral plans. He showed them coffins, and Chet chose one to keep from looking at any more. That completed, he asked Cannon about waiting a few days. "I have people coming from a distance. Can we hold off until Thursday afternoon?"

"The weather is cold, and there's always the icehouse. But I will need her dress today."

"We'll get it to you this afternoon."

501

"Good. Thursday afternoon for the services?"

"Yes. I will have the minister informed and my sister-in-law will sing a hymn."

Cannon looked concerned. "I doubt the church will hold them all. We can have visitation here on Wednesday night."

"Thanks. We'll have another of her fine dresses to drape over the casket. We can have the funeral services outside, and make the service at the cemetery short. Cole and I must get back home for the dresses."

"Thank you."

They shook the man's hand, then the two rode hard for the ranch. When they reined up in the yard, Jimenez ran outside to meet them.

"Saddle Cole a good horse. He needs to take a package back to town in a hurry."

"What is wrong?" Jenn shouted from the porch.

"I need her best dress and the second best one wrapped. Mark them. Cole has to take them back to town."

Jenn turned to face all the women and they went inside in a rush.

"Why two dresses?" Monica asked as she caught his arm going through.

"One to wear. One for draping the casket."

"Oh. You still alright?"

"Do I look crazy?"

She smiled. "No, you look like you do when you're mad enough to fire everyone."

"I never get that mad at my people."

"Sit down. You can't help this dress selection business. There are enough of them to do it right." She brought a coffeepot. "That boy coming in?"

"He's taking them back tonight. Too much to explain."

"I wondered if I should feed him."

"Is May here?"

"Yes. Why?"

"I want May to sing 'Nearer My God to Thee.' "

"I already asked her for you. She agreed. Was that all right?"

"Very good. I love that girl, but it saved me another crying session."

"I have the horse saddled," Cole said, coming in the back door.

"Sit down," Chet said. "They're choosing the dresses. They'll select the right ones and wrap them. That isn't a man's way of sweep them up and go."

Cole agreed.

"I have some fried ham and I can make some German potatoes," Monica said to Cole.

"That will be fine. Don't go to any trouble,

503

Monica."

"You stay and eat. Those dresses won't melt. They can be a little late."

Chet chuckled. Monica was in charge again.

She poked him going by. "You stop laughing."

"Yes, ma'am." He straightened up to listen to her.

"What if it snows?"

"The service at the Methodist cemetery will be short."

"Very well."

He got up. "I'm going to see about my son and Rhea."

"That girl works hard. That boy is her life and she dotes on him."

"I know, and Marge knew how good she was with him."

He heard a dog bark and knew they had more people coming. Who now?

"It's Susie and her man," Monica announced.

Susie. He had dreaded that face-to-face meeting more than any other. With heavy heart, he turned and went to greet her.

She had her baby boy, Erwin, in her arms, and she about fell in his. Tears streamed down her face. "Oh, dear God. How are you? I can't believe this happened to her."

He took the boy and handed him to Monica. "Susie, it really happened. God needed her. We know she's in a better place." Then he rocked her shaking body in his arms and all those emotions he'd held down began to rise inside him. He could feel her sobs and wanted to stop them.

"We all have lost someone close. Why did we lose them? There's no answer here on earth for the ones left behind. We can all savor the good days we had and face the future. May, Lucie, you, and I have babies to carry on our legacies. Some day they can worry about cattle sales, droughts, challenges, and planting us. I'm going to bury her in the Methodist cemetery. She loved that church, and this ranch may not be here someday. The cemetery will always be there."

"Good. Chet, I'm going to move back to the Verde River Ranch. I can keep the ranch books. Sarge and I talked, and he and Victor can share the drives to New Mexico. Millie's been helping Marge do the bookkeeping, but she's unsure she could do it all. When we have time to think on it . . ." She broke off with a gut-wrenching sob, but stopped herself to continue. "Then, we can make other decisions." She rested her forehead on his chest and used his kerchief to dry her face.

"That will work."

"Good. I knew you could see it. What about Adam?"

"Rhea and him have a good connection. Between her and Monica they can manage him. If I see anything different, I'll reconsider it."

"When is the funeral?"

"Thursday afternoon."

"Will Reg and JD be here?"

"We sent them word."

"Oh, I understand. They are a long ways away."

"Have you two eaten?" Monica asked.

Susie shook her head.

"Here, hold him, and I'll fix some food." She handed the boy back to his mother.

"Thanks. Who else is here?"

"Jenn and her girls."

"You have it planned?"

"Yes. May has agreed to sing 'Nearer My God to Thee.' The service will be short. The family and close friends will gather here that night. Several of the ranch women will help Monica cook and serve that meal and breakfast."

"You have it all planned."

"Yes. Go in the living room and rest.

Thanks for your concern."

Thursday afternoon, all the family from the far corners were there. Jesus drove him and Monica to the cemetery, along with Sarge and Susie and their baby. Cole and Valerie, JD and Bonnie, and Jenn came in a coach. Reg and JD's mother, Louise Byrnes, with Harold Parker, came dressed warm enough in a two-seat buggy. May and Hampt and the kids, and Reg and Lucie and their baby were there. Marge's father and his wife also attended. All their friends, the other ranch people, business associates, rancher families — best he could calculate, everyone was there.

The preacher said a prayer in the cold air. May sang the hymn, and it stabbed Chet's heart. But he knew Marge had loved it. The sermon was short and they asked him to say some words, if he could.

He held his hat in front of him, head bowed, and thought for a moment. Then he began, "Marge Byrnes was a generous woman, a loving mother and wife, and a great partner to me. This afternoon, she is in a better place. Her son, Adam, and I will use the strength she gave us to continue on with our lives. Marge, we will miss you, but we will try to have the conviction you had to lead our lives. God bless you. Lord, keep her in your hands. Amen."

He shook hands and accepted their kind words. Under his heavy coat, he hardly felt the chilly temperature. Jesus had taken Monica back to get ready for the crowd that would gather to mourn Marge, but also to celebrate her life.

Hampt had brought along one of his good roan horses for him to ride back. There were so many well-wishers, he thought they would never end. But he knew they only came to help him overcome his loss, and each one meant well.

The last were a ranch couple he'd spent the night with once. He'd only met them that one time, but they'd traveled a long distance to be there for him during the loss of his dear wife. Though swamped in grief, he couldn't help thinking of all the people whose lives had been touched by both he and Marge.

Hampt rode up leading the roan and handed him the reins. "Time to go home."

And he did.

A NOTE FROM DUSTY FOR HIS FRIENDS AND FANS

With this book, we close another chapter in Chet Byrnes's life. Nothing ever comes easy, and life is left for the living to carry on.

In my computer is book number seven, and Chet Byrnes has a lot of things to face in his future — but this may be the greatest challenge of his life. An old friend who helped him get into the cattle-driving business years before, a banker in San Antonio, Texas, desperately needs his help. The past spring he financed a large herd of cattle headed from south Texas for Ogallala, Nebraska. Thirty-five hundred head of steers.

His man, a black drover, Bo Decker, and thirty some ex-slave boys are driving these cattle north with a greasy sack outfit. Only thing is, no one has heard from them in months. The banker makes Chet an offer to go find them and save the loan. I call it "The Lost Herd" Book.

Thanks to your continuing support, the Byrnes family series rides on, and within its pages, so does the West. I appreciate all of you who make that happen. Like the Lone Ranger on radio so many years ago always said — *Hi, Ho, Silver.* Thanks to you all.

— Dusty Richards
dustyrichards@cox.net
dustyrichards.com

ABOUT THE AUTHOR

Author of over 85 novels, **Dusty Richards** is the only author to win two Spur awards in one year (2007), one for his novel *The Horse Creek Incident* and another for his short story "Comanche Moon." He is a member of the Professional Rodeo Cowboys Association and the International Professional Rodeo Association, and serves on the local PRCA rodeo board. Dusty is also an inductee in the Arkansas Writers Hall of Fame. He currently resides in northwest Arkansas. He was the winner of the 2010 Will Rogers Medallion Award for Western Fiction for his novel *Texas Blood Feud* and honored by the National Cowboy Hall of Fame in 2009.

The employees of Thorndike Press hope you have enjoyed this Large Print book. All our Thorndike, Wheeler, and Kennebec Large Print titles are designed for easy reading, and all our books are made to last. Other Thorndike Press Large Print books are available at your library, through selected bookstores, or directly from us.

For information about titles, please call:
  (800) 223-1244

or visit our Web site at:
  http://gale.cengage.com/thorndike

To share your comments, please write:
  Publisher
  Thorndike Press
  10 Water St., Suite 310
  Waterville, ME 04901